THE
SISTERS GRIMM

THE FAIRY-TALE DETECTIVES
& THE UNUSUAL SUSPECTS

MICHAEL BUCKLEY

PICTURES BY PETER FERGUSON

AMULET BOOKS
New York

ABRAMS
THE ART OF BOOKS SINCE 1949

115 West 18th Street
New York, NY 10011
www.abramsbooks.com

ISBN: 978-1-4351-4487-3

Printed and bound in China
Manufactured August 2012

Lot 1   3   5   7   9   10   8   6   4   2

THE SISTERS GRIMM

THE FAIRY-TALE DETECTIVES

· BOOK ONE ·

In memory of my grandparents,
Basil and Relda Gandee

THE SISTERS GRIMM

THE FAIRY-TALE DETECTIVES

THE DENSE FOREST BRANCHES *scratched at their faces and arms, but Sabrina and Daphne couldn't stop running, though they had long since passed the point of exhaustion. Fear was fueling each step now.*

Another thunderous bellow rang in the distance, followed by the terrible sound of falling trees and shrieking animals.

"We have to find a way to stop it," Daphne cried between gasps.

Sabrina knew her little sister was right. But how? They were two children versus a vicious monster.

"I'll think of something," Sabrina said, dragging her sister behind an enormous oak tree for a much-needed rest. Sabrina squeezed her sister's hand to reassure her, while she forced oxygen into her own burning lungs. Her words were empty. She didn't have a plan. The only thing going on in her head was the thumping of blood roaring through her eardrums. But it made no difference. It had found them. Splintering wood and damp soil rained from the sky as the tree they stood next to was violently uprooted.

The two girls looked up into the horrible face above them and felt hot breath blow through their hair.

What's happened to our lives? *Sabrina wondered. When had their world become unrecognizable? And what had happened to her, the eleven-year-old girl who only two days ago had been just an orphan on a train?*

1
TWO DAYS AGO

 'm going to die of boredom here, Sabrina Grimm thought as she looked out the train window at Ferryport Landing, New York.

The little town in the distance seemed to be mostly hills and trees next to the cold, gray Hudson River. A few two- and three-story brownstone buildings huddled around what appeared to be the town's only street. Beyond it were endless acres of evergreen forest. Sabrina could see no movie theaters, malls, or museums, and felt using the word *town* to describe Ferryport Landing was a bit of a stretch.

Worse than the town was the weather. It was raining, and rain always made Sabrina melancholy. She tucked her long blond hair behind her ear and turned her head away from the window, promising herself that she would be strong and not let her sister see her cry. She had to be the strong one; after all, she was almost twelve years old.

Not that Daphne would have noticed her tears. Sabrina's seven-year-old sister had had her face pressed against the window throughout the two-hour trip. Daphne had marveled at each ugly little spot on the map they rolled through, taking a break from the view only to ask the occasional question about their destination.

"Do they have bagels in Ferryport Landing, Ms. Smirt?" Daphne now asked the woman sitting across from them. Ms. Minerva Smirt was the girls' caseworker. She was a pinch-lipped, humorless woman in her late fifties. She had had her hooked nose buried in a book for the entire train ride. Sabrina knew she was reading only so she wouldn't have to talk to them. Ms. Smirt looked up at Daphne with an annoyed scowl and sighed as if the question was more than she could bear.

"Of course they have bagels. They have bagels everywhere," Ms. Smirt snapped.

"Not on the moon," Daphne replied matter-of-factly as she returned her gaze to the window.

Ms. Smirt snarled, which caused Sabrina to snicker. Watching Daphne drive Ms. Smirt crazy was one of Sabrina's favorite pastimes. Smirt had made a mistake when she chose a career working with children, Sabrina thought, especially since she didn't seem to like them. Ms. Smirt complained whenever she had to touch their sticky hands or wipe their runny noses, and reading bedtime stories was completely out of the question. She seemed to especially dislike the Grimm sisters and had labeled them rude, uncooperative, and a couple of know-it-alls. So, Sabrina was sure it was Ms. Smirt's personal mission to get the girls out of the orphanage and into a foster home. So far she had failed miserably. She'd sent them to live with people who were usually mean and occasionally crazy, and who had used them as maids, house sitters, or just plain ignored them. But this time she had gone too far. This time Ms. Smirt was sending them to live with a dead woman.

"I hope you don't bother your grandmother with all these ridiculous questions!" Ms. Smirt said curtly, which was how she said most things to Sabrina and Daphne. "She is old and cannot handle a lot of trouble."

"She's dead! I've already told you a million times, our grandmother is dead!" said Sabrina.

"We did a background check, Sally," Ms. Smirt replied. "She is who she says she is."

"My name is Sabrina." Sabrina sighed.

"Whatever. The orphanage would not release you into just anyone's custody," said Ms. Smirt.

"Oh really? How about Ms. Longdon, who swore her toilet was haunted?" said Sabrina.

"Everyone has their quirks."

"Or Mr. Dennison, who made us sleep in his truck?" Daphne chimed in.

"Some people love the great outdoors."

"Mr. and Mrs. Johnson handcuffed us to a radiator!" Sabrina cried.

"Dwell on the negative if you choose," said Ms. Smirt. "But you should be grateful. There is not much of a demand for rude little girls. Imagine how embarrassed I was when I heard what you said to the Keatons!"

"They locked us in their house for two weeks so they could go on a cruise to Bora-Bora," Sabrina said.

"I think it was the Bahamas," Daphne said.

"It was Bermuda, and at least they brought you back some nice T-shirts from their trip," said Ms. Smirt. "Anyway, it is all water under the bridge now. We found a *real* relative who is actually eager to take you into her home. But to be honest, girls, even if she was an imposter I would hand you over to her. We have run out of families who want you." With that, Ms. Smirt put her nose back into her book. Sabrina looked up at the title. It was called *How to Get the Love You Want*.

"What's an imposter?" Daphne asked, not bothering to turn her head away from the view through the window.

"It means someone who is pretending to be someone she's not," Sabrina said as she watched the rain outside. It had been raining the day her parents disappeared. That was over a year and a half ago, but it still made her heart ache. She remembered rushing home that afternoon with a report card safely tucked inside her raincoat. Excited about her As in math and English and her B in Science (and a little disappointed by her C-minus in gym), she had proudly taped it to the refrigerator for everyone to see. It had seemed odd that her parents weren't home from work, but Sabrina didn't worry until Daphne's kindergarten teacher called to find out why no one had picked up the little girl. That night the girls slept in their parents' bed, waiting for them to come home as thunder and lighting crashed in the sky around their apartment. When the social worker came three days later to take them away, it was still raining, and Sabrina's report card was still hanging on the refrigerator awaiting its praise. For all Sabrina knew, it was still there.

The police had started an investigation. They searched the family's New York City apartment for clues. They interviewed neighbors and coworkers. They dusted for fingerprints and filed reports, but they found nothing. Henry and Veronica

Grimm had simply vanished into thin air. Months later the police found their abandoned car. The only clue was a blood-red handprint on the dashboard. The police assured the girls that the print was not blood, only paint, but they still had no leads. Their investigation had come to a dead end. Meanwhile, the orphanage where the girls had been taken began an investigation of its own, searching for next-of-kin, but came up as empty as the police. No aunts, uncles, grandparents, brothers, sisters, or even distant twice-removed cousins existed. The girls' parents had always told them that they were all the family they would ever need. So naturally, the girls were shocked when a woman claiming to be "Grandma Grimm" applied for custody.

Now the train pulled into the station and Daphne turned away from the window, cupped her hand over Sabrina's ear, and whispered, "Do you think that she could really be our grandmother? Dad said she died before we were born."

"Not a chance," Sabrina said as the train came to a stop. "Don't worry, we'll be gone before the crazy old bat knows what happened."

Passengers got up from their seats and took their bags down from the luggage racks above. They tossed half-read newspapers onto the coffee-stained floor and headed for the doors. A conductor announced that Ferryport Landing was the last stop.

"Ladies, let's go!" Ms. Smirt ordered, causing Sabrina's stomach to flip-flop. She didn't want to meet the imposter posing as her grandmother, but Ms. Smirt wasn't one to argue with. The old crone had a reputation as a pincher and she had left more than a few nasty purple bruises on back-talking orphans. Sabrina stood up on her seat, dragged their two tiny suitcases down from the storage racks above, and followed Ms. Smirt and Daphne off the train.

The late November rain was bitingly cold. Daphne began to shiver, so Sabrina wrapped her arm around her sister's shoulders and held her tightly as they stood with Ms. Smirt on the crowded platform.

"When you meet her you had better be polite or there is going to be trouble," Ms. Smirt said. "No sass, no back talk, stand up straight, and act like young ladies for once, or so help me I'll—"

"Ms. Smirt?" A voice interrupted the caseworker's threat. The girls looked up to find a chubby old woman standing in front of them. She was dressed in an ankle-length, navy blue dress with a white knitted shawl around her shoulders. Her long, gray hair was streaked with red, hinting at its original color, and she wore it tightly tucked under a matching navy blue hat with an appliqué of a big fuzzy sunflower in the middle. Her face was a collection of wrinkles and sagging skin. Nevertheless, there was something youthful about it. Perhaps it was the old woman's red cheeks and clear, green eyes.

Next to her stood the skinniest man Sabrina had ever seen. He had a full head of untamed platinum hair and enormous, watery eyes buried beneath eyebrows that were in desperate need of a trim. He wore a dark pinstriped suit that was several sizes too big and held a wide umbrella in one hand and his hat in the other.

Ms. Smirt gave the girls a hard pinch on the shoulder, which acted as a warning to behave, and, Sabrina suspected, a last opportunity to inflict some pain.

"Yes, Mrs. Grimm. It's us," Ms. Smirt said, forcing her usual frown into a smile.

"Sabrina? Daphne?" the woman cried with a hint of a German accent. "Oh, you are both so beautiful. What little darlings! I'm your Grandmother Grimm." She wrapped her chubby arms around the girls and hugged them tightly. The girls squirmed to escape. But the old woman was like an over-affectionate octopus hugging them and kissing them on their heads and shoulders.

"Mrs. Grimm, it's so nice to meet you," Ms. Smirt interrupted. Mrs. Grimm raised herself up to her full height, which wasn't very high, and cocked her eyebrow at the caseworker. Sabrina could have sworn she saw the old woman smirk.

"It's nice to meet you, too," said Mrs. Grimm.

"I am just so thrilled to have helped you and the girls reunite."

"Oh, I'm sure you are," said the old woman, turning her back on the caseworker and giving the girls a wink. She placed a hand on each girl's shoulder and turned them toward her companion.

"Girls, this is Mr. Canis. He helps me take care of our house and other matters. He lives with us, too, and he'll be helping me look after you," she said.

Daphne and Sabrina stared up into the old man's gaunt face. He was so skinny and frail-looking that it seemed as though the umbrella he was holding would collapse on him at any moment. He nodded at the girls then handed Mrs. Grimm the umbrella, picked up the suitcases, and walked down the platform toward the parking lot.

"Well, girls, this is good-bye," said Ms. Smirt as her eyes darted to the open train door.

She stepped forward and limply hugged Daphne, whispering something in her ear that made the little girl cringe. Then she hooked Sabrina in her uncomfortable embrace.

"Let's make this the last time we see each other," the caseworker snarled into Sabrina's ear.

"Good luck, Mrs. Grimm," Ms. Smirt said as she released Sabrina and reached out to shake the hand of the old woman, who looked as if the caseworker were trying to give her something smelly and dead. Ms. Smirt, sensing disapproval, hemmed and hawed for a moment and quickly reboarded the train without looking back. The doors shut and the train pulled away, back to New York City. As happy as Sabrina was to be rid of Ms. Smirt, she realized that their caseworker had left them in the care of a complete stranger.

Mrs. Grimm's barrage of kisses continued all the way down the platform to the parking lot where Mr. Canis was waiting for them beside the oldest car Sabrina had ever seen. Dingy and covered in rust, it squealed and protested when Mr. Canis opened the back door and the girls crawled inside.

"Is this safe?" Sabrina asked as Mr. Canis and the old woman settled into their seats.

"It got us here." The old woman laughed. "I suppose it will get us back."

The car sputtered, backfired, and then roared to life, belching a black fog out of its tailpipe. The engine was an orchestra of gears grinding so loudly that Sabrina thought she might go deaf. Daphne had already plugged her fingers into her ears.

Mrs. Grimm turned to the girls and shouted, "Put on your seat belts!"

"What?" Sabrina shouted back.

"What?!" the old woman asked.

"I can't hear you!" Sabrina yelled.

"More than six!" the old woman replied.

"Six what?" Sabrina screamed.

"Probably!" The old woman laughed, turning back around.

Sabrina sighed. Daphne took her fingers out of her ears just long enough to hold up the torn straps of her seat belt. Sabrina rolled her eyes and then looked for hers. She reached down into the ripped-up seats and pulled out a filthy old rope.

"I told you to put on your seat belt!" Mrs. Grimm said.

"This?!" Sabrina shouted, holding up the rope.

"Yes, yes! Here!" The old woman leaned into the backseat and tied the torn straps of Daphne's seat belt to Sabrina's filthy rope so tightly the girls could barely breathe.

"There, snug as a bug in a rug!" the old woman hollered.

"I love dolphins, too!" Daphne exclaimed.

"Not since I hurt my toes!" Mrs. Grimm shouted.

Sabrina put her face in her hands and groaned.

They drove through the little town, which consisted of a two-lane road bordered by a couple of antiques stores, a bicycle shop, a police station, the Ferryport Landing Post Office, a restaurant named Old King Cole's, a toy store, and a beauty parlor. Mr. Canis made a left turn at the town's one and only stoplight and within seconds they were cruising out of the town proper and into what Mrs. Grimm called Ferryport Landing's "farm country." As far as Sabrina could tell, the only crop this town grew was mud.

Mrs. Grimm's house sat far up on a tree-speckled hill fifteen minutes away from the closest neighbor. It was short and squat, much like its owner, and had two stories, a wraparound porch, and small windows with bright blue shutters. Fat green shrubs lined the cobblestone path that led to the front door. It all would have looked cozy, but just behind the house loomed the forest—its branches hanging over the little roof as if the trees were preparing to swallow the house whole.

"You live in a dollhouse," Daphne declared, and Mrs. Grimm smiled.

But Sabrina wasn't amused. The place was creepy and she felt as if she was being watched. She squinted to see into the dense trees, but if anyone was spying they were well hidden.

"Why do you live all the way out here?" she asked. New York City was a place where everyone lived on top of each other, and that was exactly how Sabrina liked it. Living out in the middle of nowhere was dangerous and suspicious.

"Oh, I like the quiet," said Mrs. Grimm. "It's nice not to hear the honking of horns."

And there's no one to hear the screaming of children up here, Sabrina thought to herself.

Mr. Canis unlocked the car's huge musty trunk, pulled out the two tiny suitcases, and led everyone to the front door. The old woman followed closely behind, fumbling with her handbag until she fished out what looked like the largest key ring in the world. Hundreds of keys were attached to it, each different from the others: skeleton keys made from what looked like crystal, ancient brass keys, bright new silver ones in many sizes, and several that didn't look like keys at all.

"Wow! That's a lot of keys," Daphne said.

"That's a lot of locks," Sabrina added as she eyed the front door. It must have had a dozen bolts of all shapes and sizes.

Mrs. Grimm ignored the comment and flipped through the key ring, inserting one key after another into the locks until she had unlocked them all. Then she rapped her knuckles on the door three times and said, "We're home."

Daphne looked up at her sister for an explanation but Sabrina had none. Instead, she twirled her finger around her ear and mouthed the word *crazy*. The little girl giggled.

"Let me take your coats, *lieblings*," Mrs. Grimm said as they entered the house and she closed the door behind them, turning the locks one after another.

"*Liebling*?" Daphne asked.

"It means *sweetheart* in German," the old woman said. She

opened the coat closet door and several books tumbled to her feet. Mr. Canis quickly restacked them for her.

"Girls, I must warn you. I'm not much of a housekeeper," Mrs. Grimm said. "We'll have dinner in about an hour," she said to Mr. Canis, who picked up the girls' suitcases and headed for the stairs.

"Ladies, let me give you the grand tour." She led them into the living room. It was enormous, a much larger room than seemed possible in a cottage so small. Each wall was lined with bookshelves, stuffed with more books than Sabrina had ever seen. Stacks of them also sat on the floor, the tables, and every other surface. A teapot perched precariously on a stack that looked as if it would fall over at any moment. Books were under the couch cushions, under the carpet. Several giant stacks stood in front of an old television, blocking any chance that someone could watch cartoons. On the spines Sabrina read the strangest titles: *Birds of Oz*, *The Autobiography of an Evil Queen*, and *Shoes, Toys, and Cookies: The Elvish Handcraft Tradition*.

Mrs. Grimm led them through another door where a dining room table sat littered with books, open and waiting to be read. Sabrina picked one up and rolled her eyes when she read the title: *365 Ways to Cook Dragon*.

The old woman led them from room to room, showing them where she kept the snacks in the white-tiled kitchen and how to get the rickety bathroom door to close. Sabrina pretended to be interested but in reality she secretly "cased the joint." It was a technique she had picked up after spending a year in the foster care system. In each room she noted where the windows and doors were, eyed locks, and paid close attention to creaky floorboards. But it wasn't easy. She kept getting distracted by the odd books and the dozens of old black-and-white photographs that decorated the walls. Most of them were of a much younger Mrs. Grimm and a stocky, bearded man with a wide smile. There were pictures of them hiking in the jungle, standing on an icy glacier, scaling a mountain, and even riding camels in the desert. In some pictures, Mrs. Grimm was carrying a small child in a papoose, while the bearded man stood next to her, proudly beaming at the camera.

Daphne was just as distracted, and when they arrived back in the living room, she walked over to a picture and looked at it closely.

"That was your *opa*, Basil," Mrs. Grimm said wistfully.

"*Opa*?" Daphne asked.

"Grandfather, *liebling*. He passed on about eleven years ago," she said.

"Is that your baby?" Daphne said.

The old lady smiled and studied the picture as if she weren't sure. "That's your papa," she said with a smile. The little girl eyed the photo closely, but Sabrina turned away. Babies all looked the same. An old photo couldn't prove anything.

"Oh, my, I've forgotten the cookies," the old woman said as she dashed to the kitchen. In no time she returned with a plate of warm chocolate-chip cookies. Daphne, of course, happily grabbed one and took a bite.

"These taste just like my mommy's," she exclaimed.

"Where do you think she got the recipe, angel?" Mrs. Grimm said.

Sabrina refused to take a cookie, giving Mrs. Grimm an "I know what you're up to" look. She wasn't going to be bribed with sweets.

Just then, Mr. Canis walked into the room.

"I was about to introduce the girls to Elvis," Mrs. Grimm said to him.

Mr. Canis gave a slight smile, nodded, and walked past them toward the kitchen.

That's a weird man, Sabrina thought as she noted two loud creaks in the middle of the living room floor.

"Is he your boyfriend?" Daphne asked the old woman, who was trying to balance the plate of cookies on top of two uneven stacks of books.

Mrs. Grimm blushed and giggled. "Oh, dear, no. Mr. Canis and I are not courting. We are just good friends," she said.

"What does *courting* mean?" Daphne asked her sister.

"It's an old-fashioned word for dating," Sabrina replied.

Suddenly, there was a great rumbling in the house. Books fell from their shelves, windows shook in their frames, and the tray of cookies slid to the floor before the old woman could catch it. And then something enormous came charging through the room and right at them.

It moved so quickly Sabrina couldn't tell what it was. It pushed over lamps and chairs, leaped over an ottoman, and knocked the terrified girls to the ground. Sabrina screamed, sure they were about to be eaten when, much to her surprise, a gooey tongue licked her cheek. She opened her eyes and looked up at the friendly face of a giant dog.

"Elvis, please, get off of them," Mrs. Grimm said, half commanding and half laughing at the Great Dane. "He gets very excited around new people." The enormous dog gave one last lick to Sabrina's face, leaving a long trail of drool, before sitting down next to the old woman, panting and wagging his immense tail.

"This is Elvis. He's a member of our little family and completely harmless if he likes you," said Mrs. Grimm, scratching the beast on his immense head. The dog licked the old woman on the cheek.

"And if he doesn't?" Sabrina asked as she climbed to her feet. The old woman ignored her question.

Daphne, on the other hand, jumped up and threw her arms around the dog. "Oh, I love him! He's so cute!" She laughed as she covered the dog with her own kisses.

"This is the only boyfriend I have." Mrs. Grimm smiled. "And probably the smartest one I've ever had, too. Watch!"

Daphne stepped back and she and Sabrina watched as Mrs. Grimm put her hand out to Elvis. "Elvis, shake," she said, and the dog reached out a huge forepaw and placed it in her hand.

Daphne giggled.

"Play dead," Daphne said hopefully, and the dog fell stiffly over onto his side. The impact dislodged several books from a nearby shelf.

Mrs. Grimm laughed. "You two must be starving after your trip. I suppose I better get started with dinner. I hope spaghetti and meatballs is OK."

"I love spaghetti and meatballs!" Daphne cried as Elvis gave her a fresh lick.

"I know you do," Mrs. Grimm said with a wink. She disappeared into the kitchen, where she began rattling pots and pans.

"I don't like this at all, Daphne," Sabrina said as she wiped off the last of the dog's goo. "Don't get used to this place. We're not going to be here long."

"Stop being a snot," Daphne said as she laid a huge smooch on Elvis. *Snot* was her favorite word lately. "She wouldn't hurt us. She's nice."

"That's why crazy people are so dangerous. You think they're *nice* until they're chaining you up in the garage," Sabrina replied. "And I am not being a snot."

"Yes, you are."

"No, I'm not."

"Yes, you are," Daphne insisted. "Anything is better than living at the orphanage, right?"

Daphne had a point. Sabrina walked over and examined the photograph the old woman claimed was of the girls' father. The rosy-cheeked baby in the photo seemed to stare back at her.

• • •

Mr. Canis had cleared the big oak dining room table of enough books for everyone to eat comfortably. He had left an exceptionally thick volume entitled *Architecture for Pigs* on Daphne's chair so the little girl could reach her dinner. As they waited patiently for Mrs. Grimm, who was still making a thunderous racket in the kitchen, Mr. Canis closed his eyes and sat silently. Soon, his stillness began to unnerve Sabrina. Was he a mute? Was there something wrong with him? In New York City, everyone talked, or rather, everyone yelled at everyone, all the time. They never sat quietly with their eyes closed when people were around. It was rude.

"I think he's dead," Daphne whispered after staring at him for some time.

Suddenly, Mrs. Grimm came through the door with a big copper pot and placed it on the table. She rushed back into the kitchen and returned with a plate of salad and set it in front of Mr. Canis. As soon as the plate hit the table the old man opened his eyes and began to eat.

"How did you know I like spaghetti? It's my favorite!" Daphne said happily.

"I know lots of things about you, *liebling*. I am your *oma*," Mrs. Grimm replied.

"*Oma*?" Sabrina asked. "What's this weird language you keep speaking?"

"It means *grandmother* in German. That's where our family is from," Mrs. Grimm answered.

"My family is from New York City," Sabrina said stiffly.

The old woman smiled a sad smile. "Your mama sent me letters from time to time. I know a great deal about you both. In fact, when I stopped getting them I knew that . . ." She sighed.

"That they'd abandoned us?" Sabrina snapped. Suddenly, Sabrina felt as if she might burst into tears. She ducked her head, fighting their escape down her cheeks.

"Child, your mother and father didn't abandon you," Mrs. Grimm cried.

"Mrs. Grimm, I —" Daphne began.

"*Liebling*, I'm not Mrs. Grimm. I'm your grandmother," the old woman said. "You can call me *Grandma* or *Oma*, but never *Mrs. Grimm*, please."

"Can we call you *Granny*? I always wanted a granny," said Daphne. Sabrina kicked her sharply under the table and the little girl winced.

"Of course, I'll be your Granny Relda," the old woman said with a smile, as she took the top off the pot.

Sabrina stared inside. She had never seen spaghetti like this. The noodles were black and the sauce was a bright orange color. It smelled both sweet and spicy at the same time, and the meatballs, which were emerald green, were surely not made from any kind of meat Sabrina had ever had.

"It's a special recipe," Mrs. Grimm said, as she dished some out for Daphne. "The sauce has a little curry in it and the noodles are made with squid ink."

Sabrina was disgusted. There was no way she was going to eat the old woman's weird food. This sicko had lied about being someone's dead grandmother. Who knew what she had yanked from under the kitchen sink and added to the recipe: arsenic, rat poison, clog remover? No, Sabrina wasn't going to eat a noodle. Of course, Daphne dug in with gusto and had already swallowed a third of her plate before Sabrina could warn her.

"So, Mr. Canis says your suitcases felt almost empty. Don't you have any clothes?" Mrs. Grimm asked.

"The police kept them," Daphne said, shoveling a huge forkful of noodles into her mouth. "They said they were evidence."

"Kept them? That's crazy! What will they do with them?" She looked at each of them and finally at Mr. Canis, who shrugged.

"Well, we'll have to go into town and pick you out new wardrobes. We can't have you running around naked all the time, can we? I mean, people will think we're nudists."

Daphne laughed to the point of snorting, but when she saw Sabrina's disapproving face she stopped and stuck her tongue out at her sister.

"I was thinking that we—" Mrs. Grimm started, but Sabrina interrupted.

"Who are you? And don't say you're our grandmother because our grandmother is dead!"

Mrs. Grimm shifted in her seat. Mr. Canis, obviously seeing

the question as his cue to retire, got up, took his empty plate, and exited the room.

"But I am your grandmother, *liebling*," the old woman replied.

"I said our grandmother is dead. Our father told us she died before we were born."

"Girls, I assure you that I am who I say I am."

"Well, then why did he tell us you died if you didn't?"

"I'm not sure it is time to discuss your father's decisions. We are all just getting settled in and we can talk about it later," Mrs. Grimm said. Her eyes dropped to her lap.

"Well if you really were our grandmother, I would think you'd be happy to discuss it," Sabrina snapped.

"Now is not the time," Mrs. Grimm said softly.

Sabrina leaped up from her seat, sending her fork clanging to the floor. "Fine! I'm tired and want to go to bed."

Mrs. Grimm frowned. "Of course, *liebling*. Your room is upstairs. I will show you—"

"WE'LL FIND IT OURSELVES!"

Sabrina walked around the table, grabbed Daphne's hand, and dragged her from her chair.

"But I'm not done eating!" said Daphne.

"You're never done eating. Let's go!" Sabrina commanded.

She marched through the house and up the stairs with her sister in tow. At the top of the stairs they found a long hallway with five closed doors, two on each side and one at the end of the hallway. Sabrina yanked on the closest one, but it was locked tight. She turned and tried the door behind her. It opened to a bedroom decorated with dozens of wooden tribal masks, wild-eyed and smiling hideously. Two ancient swords were mounted on the wall alongside the masks, and there were pictures of Mrs. Grimm and her husband, Basil, everywhere. Like the ones downstairs, each photo was of a different part of the world. In one picture, Basil was standing at the top of an ancient stone temple; in another, the couple were guiding a gondola through what Sabrina guessed were Venetian canals. She closed the door, realizing that this had to be the old woman's room. She tried the next door.

Inside, Mr. Canis sat cross-legged on the floor, his hands resting on his knees. Several candles lit the nearly empty room, illuminating its sparse furnishings and a small woven mat on the floor. There were no pictures or decorations at all. Mr. Canis opened his eyes and turned to look at the girls, his eyebrows arched.

Sabrina slammed the door without apologizing. "What a nutcase," she muttered. The next door opened to a queen-sized, four-poster bed with their suitcases resting on top. Sabrina pulled Daphne inside and slammed the door.

"That woman is hiding something!" she said.

"You think everyone's hiding something."

"And you would hug the devil if he gave you cookies."

"Well, I like her!" said Daphne. She sat down on the bed and let out a *Harrumph!*

Sabrina looked around the room. It was painted in soft yellow and had a slanted ceiling and a fireplace. A red ten-speed bicycle sat in the corner, an old baseball mitt rested on a desk, and several model airplanes hung from the ceiling. A nightstand sat next to the bed with an alarm clock perched on top. And on every wall were dozens of old photographs. A particularly large one showed two young boys staring out over the Hudson River.

Sabrina went to the window and looked out at the porch roof below. She could probably jump off it and then to the ground, but Daphne might hurt herself.

"Let's give her a chance," Daphne begged.

"A chance to what? Kill us in our sleep? Feed us to that monster dog of hers? No way!" Sabrina said. "While you were shoveling in those meatballs did you ever think that they might be made from the last couple of kids she claimed she was related to?"

Daphne rolled her eyes. "You're gross!"

Suddenly Sabrina heard a faint whistling sound, almost like a flute, coming from outside the window. She peered into the dark forest behind the house. At first she thought she had seen something or someone sitting in a tree, but when she rubbed her eyes for a clearer look there was nothing there. Still, the music continued.

"Where is that coming from?" she said.

And like an answer to her question, a little light flickered outside the window. Sabrina thought it was a lightning bug. It flew up to the window as if it was trying to get a better view of her. It was joined by another light and the two danced around each other, zipping excitedly back and forth in the air.

"Amazing," she said.

Daphne rushed to the window. "They're so pretty," she whispered as dozens more lights joined the original two. Within seconds there were almost a hundred little lights blinking and flashing outside.

Without thinking, Sabrina reached up and unlocked the window. She just wanted to get a closer look, maybe grab a couple to keep in a jar in the room, but as she undid the window's latch, the bedroom door blew open with a crash. Startled, the sisters spun around and found Mr. Canis looming in the doorway.

"Girls, you'll leave that window closed if you know what's good for you!" he growled.

2

Mr. Canis stomped across the room, pushed the girls aside, and locked the window. The little lights outside flew around, bounced off the glass several times, and buzzed as if in protest. A moment later they were gone, and the whistling sound faded away. Mr. Canis turned and stood over Sabrina.

"You are never to let anyone or anything inside this house," he said in a voice as low and scratchy as an angry dog's.

"It was just some lightning bugs," said Sabrina. Her face was hot and red with shock. Who was this man to think he could tell her what to do?

"No one comes into this house. Do you understand what I have just asked of you?" Mr. Canis said.

The girls nodded.

"Very well. Good night." He stalked out of the room, closing the door behind him. Sabrina stood dumbfounded, trying to comprehend what had just happened.

"What was that all about?" Daphne whispered, but Sabrina said nothing. She didn't want her sister to hear the fear in her voice. Since her parents had run off, Sabrina had had to be the tough one. Her little sister needed to know there was someone strong by her side, even if it meant Sabrina had to pretend sometimes.

There was a knock on the door and Mrs. Grimm entered the room. "It's been a long day, hasn't it?"

"Mr. Canis yelled at us," Daphne cried.

"I heard," the old woman said as she sat down on the bed. "Please don't be too upset by Mr. Canis. He can be a little grouchy from time to time but he has your best interests at heart. Believe me, *lieblings*, we are both very happy to have you here, but there are a few rules you have to follow . . ." she said, pausing as she looked into Sabrina's face, ". . . and I know that what I tell you might not make a lot of sense but the rules are in place for a reason.

"First, never let anyone or anything into this house without asking Mr. Canis or me if it is OK," she said. Her tone was stern and serious and no longer that of the sweet, loving old lady with the funky spaghetti.

Mrs. Grimm took the girls' hands in her own. "Second, there is a room down the hall that is locked. It's locked for a reason and I ask that you stay away from it for the time being. You might hear some unusual noises coming from inside, but just ignore them. Do you understand?" she asked.

The girls nodded.

"As for the rest of the house, feel free to explore. You'll notice there are plenty of books to keep you occupied."

"Really? Books? I didn't notice," Sabrina said sarcastically.

"If worse comes to worst we can always dig out that old TV," Mrs. Grimm continued, as if Sabrina hadn't spoken. She got up from the bed and crossed to the door. She turned to smile at them one last time. "Who wants pancakes in the morning?"

Daphne's face lit up. "I do!"

"Are you warm enough? Do you need anything to sleep in?"

The little girl opened one of the suitcases and pulled out two extra large T-shirts that read "Bermuda Is for Lovers."

"No, we have these," she said.

"Very good," Mrs. Grimm said. "Good night, don't let the bedbugs bite."

"She's nice," said Daphne when the old lady was gone.

Sabrina clenched her fists. "It's all an act. That woman is hiding something and we aren't sticking around to find out what it is. Get some sleep. We're running away—tonight."

• • •

Sabrina lay in bed staring at the ceiling, listening to her hungry belly grumble, and planning their getaway. With a little luck she and Daphne could hide in a neighbor's garage for a couple of days and then hitchhike back to New York City. After that, she didn't know. In the past they had just gone back to the orphanage, but this time Ms. Smirt might act on her threat to skin them alive. The next place she sent them would be a million times worse. The girls were on their own now.

"We have to go," Sabrina whispered to her sister when she was sure the rest of the house was asleep.

Daphne sat up and rubbed her eyes but said nothing. Her heartbroken face said it all. *Why is she acting like such a baby?* Sabrina wondered. Running away wasn't exactly a new experience for the two of them. The sisters Grimm had pulled off several daring escapes from foster parents in the last year and a half. They had tied bedsheets together and climbed out of the Mercers' window one night, feeding their pit bull, Diablo, meatballs stuffed with cayenne pepper to keep him busy. And after the Johnsons had ordered pizza, the girls had slipped into the backseat of the delivery boy's car and were miles away before he even noticed them. Mrs. Grimm was no different than any of the other lunatics they had run away from. Eventually, Daphne would understand.

When they were dressed and packed, Sabrina slowly opened the door and looked out into the hallway. It was empty—and as the two girls crept out with their tiny suitcases, she used her skills to the fullest. They tiptoed down the stairs, being careful to step close to the wall to avoid making them creak. At the bottom, Sabrina slowly opened the closet door so the latch wouldn't click and the stack of books inside wouldn't fall over and wake the house. She snatched their coats and the girls put them on, then walked to the front door. Sabrina was just thinking that this was the easiest escape they had ever made when she tried to turn the knob. The door was locked. When she looked closely she noticed something unusual that she had not noticed before.

"There's a keyhole on this side, too," she said. They were locked in. "We have to find another way out."

The girls crept through the house, doing their best to avoid knocking over any books. They tried all the windows only to discover each had been nailed shut. They found a back door off the kitchen but it, too, had a lock on the inside.

"Let's go back to bed," said Daphne.

"We have to get her keys," said Sabrina.

The little girl cocked an eyebrow. "How are we going to do that? She has them."

"You'll see," Sabrina whispered.

The sisters found their way back up the stairs to Mrs. Grimm's room. The door was shut tight, but Sabrina was happy to find there were no locks on it. She slowly turned the knob and it swung open.

The old woman's room was scary at night. The tribal masks they had seen after dinner were even creepier in the dark, and the swords mounted on the wall flashed a ghostly light around the room. Mrs. Grimm was asleep in her bed, unaware of their presence, and snoring loudly. Daphne had the same annoying habit.

"Where are they?" Daphne said, only to have Sabrina's hand clamp over her mouth.

"Keep quiet," Sabrina whispered. The old woman turned in bed but stayed asleep.

Sabrina scanned the room and spied the keys glinting in the moonlight, on a table on the far side of the bed. She looked at Daphne, pointed to herself with her free hand, and then pointed to the keys. Daphne nodded and Sabrina let go of her mouth.

Sabrina took a small step forward to test for creaky floor-boards. *This is going to be easy,* she thought, but as her confidence was building, she noticed that Daphne had taken an interest in one of the masks on the wall. The little girl took it off its nail and held it against her face.

"Don't do that!" Sabrina whispered.

"Why not?"

"Put it back. Now!"

The little girl frowned and placed it back on its nail. "There! Are you happy?" she whispered. A split second later the mask fell off the wall, landed with a loud clunk, and rolled toward the bed. Both girls dove to the floor as Mrs. Grimm sat up.

"Who's there?" she asked. "Oh, it's you. What are you doing down there?"

Sabrina was sure they had been caught, but the old woman leaned over, picked up the mask, and set it on the nightstand. "I'll have Mr. Canis give you a new nail tomorrow."

Then she fell back onto her pillow and within minutes was snoring as loudly as ever.

"You did that on purpose," Sabrina seethed.

"Whatever," Daphne whispered, and rolled her eyes.

Sabrina scowled. Was her little sister trying to sabotage their escape?

Sabrina crept around the bed to the table, picked up the keys, and then tiptoed back across the room and into the hallway with her sister behind her. Downstairs, she quietly went to work on the front door lock. There were so many keys, it took a long time to find the right one, but eventually she heard a loud thunk. The girls waited for several moments, sure that someone had heard, but when no sound came from upstairs, they scurried outside.

"Good-bye, dollhouse," Daphne said sadly as she ran her hand lovingly across the door.

"We'll go through the woods. We don't want anyone to see us on the road and call the police," Sabrina said, grabbing her sister's hand and leading her around to the back of the house.

The girls looked into the dark forest in front of them. Crooked limbs twisted and turned in painful directions. Sabrina had the sense that the trees were horrible, mutated guardians, threatening anyone who stepped onto their land. A cold wind whipped through the branches, bending some of the smaller trees over and making a breathy moan. Sabrina knew it was just her overactive imagination, but the woods seemed to be alive and reaching out for them.

Behind them, the girls heard a surprised yelp and Elvis suddenly appeared. He trotted over and planted himself between them and the trees. His happy face was now serious.

"Go away, Elvis," Sabrina commanded, but the dog refused.

"See, he doesn't think we should go, either," said Daphne as she wrapped her arms around the big dog and kissed him on the mouth. But Sabrina had made up her mind. She pulled her sister away and into the forest, with Elvis trotting after them.

Inside the trees, everything was deadly still. There were no scurrying animals, rustling branches, or snapping twigs. Even the whistling breeze had faded away. It was if someone had turned the volume down on the world.

Suddenly, a high-pitched note filled the air. It seemed to come from deep inside the woods.

"What was that?" Daphne said.

Sabrina shrugged. "Probably the wind."

Elvis whined loudly. Then he rushed to Sabrina and clamped his jaw onto her coat sleeve, trying to yank her back toward the house. She pulled away. The girls hurried on with the dog close behind, barking warnings.

Just ignore him. He'll go back when he gets bored, Sabrina said to herself as something zipped past her eye. She turned to get a better look and saw it was a firefly, just like the ones that had been outside their window earlier that night.

"Look, Daphne. Here's the big menacing invader Mr. Skin-and-Bones was afraid would get into the house." Sabrina laughed. The little bug fluttered around her head and then circled her body.

"Pretty," Daphne said, only to find that she had her own little bug floating nearby. "I've got one, too!"

Elvis let out a very low growl.

"What's the matter, buddy?" Daphne said as she scratched the dog's ears. This did nothing to sooth Elvis. The Great Dane howled menacingly and lunged at the lights with snapping teeth.

"Hush up!" Sabrina ordered, but the dog wouldn't stop. He was going to wake Mrs. Grimm and Mr. Canis if he didn't calm down.

"Sabrina," Daphne said. The nervousness in the little girl's voice pulled Sabrina's attention away from the dog. Daphne had her hand over her nose, but what startled Sabrina was the fear in the little girl's eyes. She had seen the same look the morning after their parents disappeared, when they had woken up in their parents' bed, alone.

"What's wrong?" Sabrina asked.

"It just bit me," Daphne said as she removed her hand from her nose. It was covered in blood. Sabrina was shocked. Lightning bugs didn't bite. At least no lightning bugs she had ever heard about. And at that moment, she felt a sting that brought blood to the top of her hand. "Ouch!"

Daphne cried out. "I got bit again!" Blood trickled down her earlobe. Sabrina rushed over and wiped her sister's ear with her sleeve. The two bugs became ten and then a hundred and then a swarm that circled the girls—thousands of angry little lights, zipping back and forth, diving at their heads and arms and lighting up the ugly trees around them. Elvis growled at the bugs, but there was little he could do.

"Cover your face with your hands and run!" Sabrina shouted. The two girls ran as fast as they could, with Elvis at their heels. Sabrina looked back, hoping the bugs weren't following, only to see the swarm close behind and gaining.

In seconds they were stinging the girls again. Daphne cried out and tripped over a tree root. She curled into a ball and tried to hide any exposed skin. Elvis leaped on top of the little girl, doing his best to cover her as the bugs dived, stinging her uncovered hands and legs.

Sabrina had to do something. Elvis couldn't protect Daphne. She waved her hands and screamed at the bugs and they instantly darted in her direction. She turned to run, but before she could take even a step she slammed into something and fell to the ground. It was Mrs. Grimm.

"It's OK, *liebling*," she said.

"We have to run, Mrs. Grimm," Sabrina cried, but the old woman stood calmly, as if she was daring the bugs to come closer. When the swarm was nearly on top of them, the old woman raised her hand to her mouth and blew a soft blue dust into the air. Many of the bugs froze in midflight, falling to the ground like snowflakes. The blue mist took out half of their numbers. The rest regrouped and began to circle the old woman again.

"I have a whole house full of this," Mrs. Grimm shouted. Incredibly, the bugs seemed to weigh their options, and in one mass they darted deep into the woods and disappeared.

"That wasn't very nice!" Mrs. Grimm shouted into the forest. She turned back to Sabrina and extended her hand. "I'll need your help getting Daphne into the house."

• • •

Sabrina was sure the old woman would be furious with them. There was no telling if her craziness could extend to violence. Who could tell what a woman who had swords hanging over her bed was capable of? But Mrs. Grimm didn't seem angry at all. In fact, she looked genuinely concerned.

She asked Sabrina to undress her sister while the old woman rushed into the bathroom and returned with a bottle of calamine lotion and some cotton balls. She applied the lotion to Daphne's stings and tucked the little girl into bed.

"She'll be fine in the morning, maybe itchy, but fine," Mrs.

Grimm said as she handed the calamine lotion to Sabrina. "Pixies are harmless unless you are overwhelmed by them."

"Did you just say *pixies*?" Sabrina asked, unsure if the old woman was joking.

Mrs. Grimm wrapped her arms around her and gave her a big hug. "*Liebling*, it's OK now. You can stop crying."

Sabrina wiped her face and felt the tears on her hand. She hadn't known she was crying.

● ● ●

In the morning, Sabrina was as hungry as she had ever been. But she was still not going to eat. She'd already looked like a crybaby in front of the old lady. She wasn't about to give up any more ground. By the time the girls heard Mrs. Grimm calling them for breakfast, Sabrina had spent twenty minutes trying to explain her philosophy to her sister.

"You can stay up here if you want, but I'm starving," said Daphne. The idea of skipping a meal was beyond the little girl's imagination.

"We're not eating that woman's food," Sabrina said, her stomach growling. "We can't let her think she's breaking us down. We have to stay strong."

"I have an idea," Daphne said. "Why don't we have breakfast, eat her cookies, play with Elvis, and enjoy the bed. She'll think she's won us over and then one day, when she least expects it, we'll be gone."

Sabrina thought about her sister's plan. She had to admit it was pretty good. She just wished Daphne hadn't sounded so sarcastic when she said it.

The girls got dressed and walked tentatively into the hallway. As they approached the stairs, Sabrina heard something coming from the locked room across from Mrs. Grimm's. It sounded like a voice, but she couldn't be sure. She put her head to the door and the noise stopped.

"Did you hear someone talking in there?" Sabrina asked her sister.

"It was my belly. It's screaming for breakfast." Daphne grabbed Sabrina's hand and dragged her downstairs to the dining room. Much to Sabrina's relief, creepy Mr. Canis was nowhere to be seen. After several moments, Mrs. Grimm came out of the kitchen with a big plate of pancakes.

"I hope everyone likes flapjacks," she sang.

"Yum!" Daphne cheered as the old woman stacked three on her plate, along with a couple of sausage links, then turned to serve Sabrina, whose mouth was watering. Sabrina hadn't had pancakes since her parents disappeared. Her empty belly was telling her to seriously consider Daphne's plan.

"Hold on, *lieblings*. I forgot the syrup," Mrs. Grimm said, rushing back into the kitchen. As soon as she was gone, Daphne looked underneath her pancakes as if she were expecting a buried surprise.

"They're just pancakes," she said.

"You sound disappointed," Mrs. Grimm said, laughing, as she returned with a large gravy boat.

"Well, after last night's spaghetti I thought maybe you cooked like that all the time," Daphne said wistfully.

"Oh, *liebling*, I do." The old woman tilted the gravy boat over Daphne's pancakes and a sticky, bright pink liquid bubbled out. To Sabrina it looked like gelatin that hadn't had time to set. When Daphne saw it her eyes grew as wide as the pancakes on her plate.

"What's that?" she cried.

"Try it," Mrs. Grimm said with a grin.

Naturally, Daphne dug in, greedily wolfing down bite after bite. "It's delicious!" she exclaimed with a mouth full of food.

"It's a special recipe. It has marigolds in it." Mrs. Grimm, proudly poured it onto Sabrina's pancakes before the girl had a chance to refuse. Sabrina looked down at the funky, fizzing sauce. It smelled faintly of peanut butter and mothballs and

Sabrina's stomach did a flip-flop in protest. She dropped her fork and pushed her plate away.

Suddenly, there was a pounding from upstairs.

"So, perhaps we should discuss last night's excitement," said Mrs. Grimm as she sat down at the table and tucked a napkin into the front of her bright green dress. She gazed across at Sabrina and arched a questioning eyebrow.

"It wasn't my idea," Daphne said. Sabrina scowled at this betrayal.

"Well, no harm done. No broken bones or anything," the old woman said.

"Granny, you have some mean bugs in your yard," Daphne said as she poured more of the syrup on her breakfast.

"I know, *liebling*. They sure are mean."

"What is that hammering?" asked Sabrina.

"Mr. Canis is nailing your windows shut," Mrs. Grimm said as she took a bite of her breakfast.

"What?!" the girls said in shocked unison.

"I can't take any chances that something could get into the house or someone might try to get out," the old woman replied over the loud banging.

"So, we're your prisoners?" Sabrina cried.

"Oh, you're just like your *opa*." Mrs. Grimm laughed. "What a flare for the dramatic. Let's put it behind us. Today is a new day with a new adventure. This morning I received a call. There's been an incident that requires our attention. How exciting! You two haven't even been here a full day yet and already we're in the thick of it."

"In the thick of what?" Daphne asked as she placed a fat pat of green butter on her second stack of pancakes.

"You'll see." The old woman got up from her chair, went into the living room, and came back with several shopping bags. She placed them next to the table.

"Mr. Canis went to the store to buy you some clothing, just a couple of things to tide you over until we can go shopping."

Sabrina looked in the bag. Inside were some of the strangest clothes she had ever seen. There were two pairs of bright blue pants that had little hearts and balloons sewn onto them. There were two identical sweatshirts that were as awful as the pants— bright orange with a monkey in a tree on the front. Underneath the monkey were printed the words "Hang in there!"

"You expect us to wear these?" Sabrina moaned.

"Oh, I love them!" Daphne said, pulling the orange monkey sweatshirt out and hugging it like a new doll.

After breakfast, the girls got dressed and looked at their new outfits in the bedroom mirror. Daphne, of course, thought her crazy outfit was the best she had ever had and strutted around like a giddy fashion model. Sabrina, on the other hand, was sure Mr. Canis was trying to punish them for attempting to run away.

"Hurry, girls, we have to get going," Granny called.

"I feel like a movie star," Daphne said as the girls hurried downstairs.

"You look like a mental patient," Sabrina remarked.

• • •

The sisters stood by the door, waiting for the old woman to collect her things. Mrs. Grimm rushed around the house, grabbing books off of shelves and from underneath the couch, creating a tornado of dust that followed her from room to room. When she had collected as many as she could carry, she handed them to Sabrina.

"Almost ready," she sang as she rushed up the stairs.

Sabrina looked down at the top book. It was entitled *Fables and Folklore: The Complete Handbook*. Before she could question the book's purpose, she heard the old woman pull out her keys and unlock the mysterious door upstairs.

"She's going into her secret room," Sabrina whispered to her sister. Daphne's eyes widened and she bit the palm of her hand. For some reason Daphne did this whenever she was overly excited, and though it embarrassed Sabrina, she let it pass. If she tried to curb all of Daphne's odd little quirks, she would never get any sleep.

"I wonder what's in there," Daphne whispered back.

"That's probably where she keeps the bodies of all the other kids she's stolen from the orphanage."

Daphne stuck out her tongue and gave her sister a raspberry.

Sabrina had to admit she was curious about the room. Whenever she was told she couldn't do something, Sabrina found it was all she could think about doing. But the great thing about rules was that you could break them and drive adults crazy.

"Do you hear that?" Daphne asked.

"Yeah, she's talking to someone," Sabrina replied. "Probably Mr. Canis."

Sabrina strained to hear the conversation, but before she could make out anything, she heard Mrs. Grimm leave the room, lock the door, and head back down the stairs.

"Ladies, we're off," she said as she ushered them outside and went to work locking the front door. Then she knocked on the door three times, as she had the day before, but this time she said, "We'll be back."

"Who are you talking to?" Sabrina asked.

"The house," Mrs. Grimm replied, as if this were a perfectly natural thing to do.

Daphne knocked on the door as well. "Good-bye, doll-house," she said, causing her sister to sigh and roll her eyes.

As they turned to go to the car, Sabrina looked up and nearly stumbled. Mr. Canis wasn't upstairs! He was standing on the path with Elvis at his side. He returned her stare with a look of slight contempt. His gaze unnerved the girl, but no more than the realization that Mrs. Grimm had been talking to herself in her secret room.

"We're ready, Mr. Canis," Mrs. Grimm said, and he nodded. They all climbed into the squeaky car, including Elvis, who laid his huge body across the girls' laps.

"Did you have a chat with our neighbor?" Mrs. Grimm asked Mr. Canis as they all buckled or tied themselves in.

"We began a conversation," the old man grumbled. "But he can be stubborn."

"Well, he'll get used to it eventually, I suppose," Mrs. Grimm replied.

"He doesn't have a history of getting used to things," Mr. Canis said.

Mrs. Grimm sighed and nodded.

"Who are you talking about?" Daphne asked.

"Oh, just a neighbor. Nothing to worry about. You'll meet him soon enough."

Sabrina looked around. She was sure they were miles from the nearest neighbor.

Mr. Canis fired up the engine and the car rocked back and forth violently like a bucking bronco trying to get rid of a cowboy, calming down as they drove out the driveway and through desolate back roads. Sabrina reexamined Ferryport Landing, the world's most boring town. There was little obvious life, except an old dairy cow standing on the side of the road. Mrs. Grimm leaned over and honked, then waved wildly at the cow as they passed. When Daphne giggled about it, the old woman smiled and told her how important it was to be friendly. Meanwhile, Sabrina made the best of the trip by memorizing street names and calculating how long it would take to walk to the train station.

They came to a mailbox with the name *Applebee* marked on it and Mr. Canis turned the car down a long, leaf-covered driveway lined with ancient cedars, pines, and oaks. The car passed a tractor sitting alone on a little hill and pulled over into a clearing where a massive pile of wood and pipes and glass sat surrounded by yellow emergency tape. Mrs. Grimm looked at Mr. Canis and smiled.

"Well, we haven't had to deal with something like this in a while, have we, Mr. Canis?" she asked.

The old man shook his head and helped her out of the car. Once she got on her feet, Mrs. Grimm opened the back door, reached in, and scratched Elvis behind the ears.

"Girls, do you mind if I borrow my boyfriend for a moment?" she asked as she winked at Daphne.

The Great Dane crawled clumsily out of the car, stretched a little, and looked up at the old woman for instructions. She fumbled in her purse and took out a small piece of fabric that she held under the dog's nose. He sniffed it deeply, then rushed over to the huge pile of debris and began hunting through the rubble.

"What are we doing here?" Sabrina asked.

"We're investigating a crime, naturally," Mrs. Grimm said.

"Are you a police officer or something?" asked Daphne.

"Or something," the old woman said with a grin. "Why don't you get out and take a look around?" She walked away, apparently to snoop through the rubble.

Having a two-hundred-pound dog lie on her lap had given Sabrina a charley horse, so she and Daphne decided to get out and stretch their legs.

"She talks to the house, and cows, and has all these crazy rules. Now she thinks she's Sherlock Holmes," Sabrina muttered.

"Maybe it's a game," Daphne said. "I'm going to be a detective, too! I'm going to be Scooby Doo!"

Despite all of Sabrina's warnings, Daphne seemed to be having fun, something she hadn't had in nearly a year and a half. It was nice to see a smile on her sister's face and that old light in her eyes. It was the same look she used to have when their father would read them the Sunday comics or when their mother would let them invade her closet to play dress-up. Sabrina smiled and put her arm around the little girl's shoulders. She'd let her have her fun. Who knew how long it would last?

Just then, a long white limousine pulled into the clearing. It was bright and shiny with whitewall tires and a silver horse for a hood ornament. It parked next to Mrs. Grimm's car and a little man got out of the driver's side. He couldn't have been more than three feet high. In fact, he was no taller than Daphne. He had a big bulbous nose and a potbelly that the buttons of his black suit struggled to contain. But the most unusual thing about the man wasn't his size or his clothing. It was the pointy paper hat he wore on his head that read, I AM AN IDIOT. He rushed as quickly as he could to the other side of the car, opened the back passenger door, and was met with a barrage of insults from a man inside.

"Mr. Seven, sometime today!" the man bellowed in an English accent. "Do you think I want to sit in this muggy car all afternoon waiting for you to find time to open the door? You know, when you came to me for a job, I happily gave you one, but every day you make me regret it!"

A tall man in a purple suit exited the limousine and looked around. He had a strong jaw, deep blue eyes, and shiny black hair. He was probably the best-looking man Sabrina had ever seen, and her heart began to race. That was, until he opened his mouth again.

"What is this? Heads are going to roll, Mr. Seven," the man fumed as he looked around.

"Yes, sir," Mr. Seven answered.

"I was told that this was taken care of last night. It's just lucky that I realize that everyone who works for me is an incompetent boob or we would never have known this was still out here until it was too late. My goodness, look at that rubbish sitting there in broad daylight. What do the Three think I pay them for? I can't have this nonsense going on right now. Doesn't everyone realize that the ball is tomorrow? Heads are going to roll, Mr. Seven."

The little man nodded in agreement. His boss looked down at Sabrina and Daphne and scowled.

"Look, the tourists are already here and they're leaving their filthy children unsupervised. They are children, right, Mr. Seven? Not just a couple more of your kind?"

Mr. Seven's dunce cap had slid down over his eyes. He lifted it and gazed at the two girls. "They're children, sir."

"The way they are dressed you would think they were circus folk. You worked in the circus for some time, didn't you Mr. Seven?"

The little man nodded.

"Why, there ought to be a law about unsupervised children. This is a crime scene and it's crawling with kids. Mr. Seven, let's make that a law, if that isn't too much trouble?" the man continued.

"No trouble at all, sir," said Mr. Seven as he took a spiral-bound pad and a pen from his jacket pocket and furiously jotted down his boss's instructions.

"See how easy it is to be a team player, Mr. Seven? I like your change of attitude. If you keep this up we might be able to get rid of that hat," the man said.

"That would please me, sir."

"Let's not rush things, Mr. Seven. After all, you still haven't given these children my card, which is incredibly frustrating, especially since we discussed this just last night. What did I tell you, man?"

"Give everyone your card. It's good networking."

"Indeed it is," the man replied, tapping his toe impatiently.

"So sorry, Mr. Charming, sir," Mr. Seven said as he rushed to the girls and shoved a business card into each of their hands. It was purple with a golden crown on one side and the words MAYOR WILLIAM CHARMING—HERE TO LEAD YOU written on it in gold lettering. Underneath the name were a telephone number, an e-mail address, and a Web site: www.mayorcharming.com.

"Now, what was I saying before I had to tell you how to do your job, Mr. Seven?"

But before the little man could answer, Sabrina stepped forward. If there was one thing she couldn't stand, it was a bully.

"You were saying there ought to be a law against unsupervised children," Sabrina said angrily. "There should be a law against talking to people like they are morons, too!"

"Yes, that's correct. See, Seven, if this carnival girl can pay attention to the conversation, why can't you? Why, she can't be more than eight years old, and certainly slow in the head," Mayor Charming said.

"I'm almost twelve," Sabrina shouted. "And I'm not slow!"

Mayor Charming seemed startled by her anger.

"Where are your parents, child?" he snapped.

"We're here with our grandmother," Daphne answered. Sabrina spun around on her sister angrily. The old lunatic was not their grandmother.

"How splendid for you," Mayor Charming sneered. "And who is your grandmother?"

Daphne pointed to Mrs. Grimm, who was busy taking notes on a little pad of paper.

"Relda Grimm is your grandmother?" the mayor growled between gritted teeth. "When will this cursed family die out? You're like a swarm of cockroaches!"

Mrs. Grimm looked over, saw Mayor Charming, and quickly came to join them.

"Relda Grimm, I just met your granddaughters," the mayor said, as his face changed from a scowl to a smile. "They're the spitting image of their grandfather."

He bent over and pinched Daphne on the cheek. "Hopefully, they'll grow out of it," he muttered.

"Mayor Charming, what brings you all the way out here? I thought you'd be busy planning the fund-raiser. It's in a couple of days, correct?" said Mrs. Grimm with a forced smile.

"It is not a fund-raiser!" Charming insisted. "It's a *ball*! And it is tomorrow night. But you know how the community is. If I don't investigate every little stray cloud, the flock gets nervous. But then again, I could ask you the same question. What is the famous Relda Grimm doing in the middle of nowhere looking at a broken house?"

He was right—it was a house that had fallen down. Sabrina saw pieces of furniture and clothing sticking out of the pile and an old afghan quilt swinging from a stick in the breeze.

"I don't know what the farmer expected with such shoddy workmanship. He's lucky to have crawled out alive," he continued.

"So there was a survivor?" Mrs. Grimm said, writing in her notebook.

"Here she goes, Mr. Seven. You can almost see the wheels spinning in her head. Relda Grimm, private eye, out to solve the case that never was," the mayor said. "See, that's the problem with you Grimms. You could never quite grasp that in order to solve a mystery there must *be a mystery* to solve. A farmer built a flimsy house and it fell down. It was an accident. Case closed."

"Then why did you call it a crime scene?" Sabrina piped up.

Charming turned and gave her a look that could have burned a hole through her. "You must have misheard me, child," he said between gritted teeth. "Mr. Seven, take down this note, please. New law—children should not ask questions of their elders."

As the little man scribbled furiously in his notebook, Mrs. Grimm said, "We both know why we're here, Mayor."

Charming's face turned red. He tugged on his necktie and adjusted his collar. "This is *none of your concern*, Relda."

Before the old woman could respond, Mr. Canis joined the group.

"Well, if it isn't the big bad . . ."

"Mayor Charming!" said Mrs. Grimm angrily.

"Oh, I'm sorry, I heard you were going by *Canis* now." Charming grinned and leaned in close to Sabrina and Daphne. "Do yourselves a favor, girls, and check Granny's teeth before you give her a good-night kiss."

"Do you think it wise to provoke me?" Mr. Canis said as he took a step toward the mayor. Despite Mr. Canis's quiet demeanor, the words seemed to unnerve Charming.

"That's enough!" Mrs. Grimm demanded. Her voice shocked the girls, but the effect on the two grown men was even more startling. They backed away from each other like two school-boys who had been scolded by a teacher.

"The dog has found something," Mr. Canis said gruffly. He placed an enormous green leaf in Mrs. Grimm's hand and her eyes lit up in satisfaction.

"Well, look at that, Mayor Charming, I think we've found a clue. There might be a mystery to solve here, yet," she said, waving the leaf in the mayor's angry face.

"Congratulations! You found a leaf in the middle of all these trees," Charming scoffed. "I bet if you could bring out the forensics team you might find a twig, or even an acorn!"

"It looks a lot like a leaf from a beanstalk," the old woman replied.

Charming rolled his eyes. "That proves nothing."

"Maybe, maybe not, but it does seem odd that a fresh green leaf is out here in late November," Mrs. Grimm said. Sabrina looked around at the trees. Every limb was bare.

"Listen Relda, stop meddling in our affairs or you're going to regret it," said the mayor.

"If you don't want me meddling, then you must really do a better job of covering up your mistakes." Mrs. Grimm placed the leaf inside her handbag.

The mayor scoffed and then turned to Mr. Seven. "Get the door, you lumpy bag of foolishness!" he shouted. The little man nearly lost his paper hat as he rushed to the car door. Within moments, the limo was spitting gravel behind it as it drove away.

"Girls, why don't we take a walk over to that hill and sit by the tractor? I'd like to see this site from above," Mrs. Grimm said. Daphne took the old woman's hand and helped her up a sloped embankment where a lonely tractor was parked. When they reached the top, the old woman plopped on the ground and caught her breath. "Thank you, *liebling*. Either the hills are getting steeper or I'm getting older."

"Who was that man?" Daphne asked.

"Let's just say he's a royal pain," Mrs. Grimm replied. "Mr. Charming is the mayor of Ferryport Landing."

"What's with the bad attitude?" Sabrina said. The mayor reminded her of the orphanage's lunch lady, who seemed to delight in telling the children they were getting fat.

"He gets a little territorial sometimes."

"He and Mr. Canis sure don't like each other," Daphne added.

"They have a long history," the old woman said. She picked a small, black disk off the ground. "How interesting." She happily jotted down a note in her notebook. "A lens cap, from what looks like a very expensive video camera."

"Maybe it's just junk or something the farmer lost," Daphne said.

"Maybe, or maybe whoever is responsible for all that damage wanted a record." Mrs. Grimm tossed the lens cap into her handbag.

Just then, a white van with the words ACTION 4 NEWS painted on the side pulled up. The doors swung open and a cameraman and a pretty reporter in a business suit jumped out. The reporter checked her hair in a compact mirror as the cameraman handed her a microphone. They eyed the pile of lumber and brick and then spotted the girls and the old woman sitting on the hill. In no time, they were standing before them.

"Hello ladies, I'm Wilma Faye from Action Four News," the reporter said as she shoved her microphone in Mrs. Grimm's face. "We were wondering if you might be able to tell us what happened here."

"Oh dear, am I on television?" the old woman asked.

"You will be," the reporter replied. "Tell our audience what you witnessed."

"Oh, we didn't see anything, I'm afraid," said Ms. Grimm. "We only just got here."

The reporter groaned and the cameraman lowered his camera.

"This is just great!" Wilma Faye complained. "Five years of journalism school, graduating with honors and at the top of my class, and I'm out here in Ferryport Landing, in the cold, covering a house that collapsed."

"I'll get some shots of the damage," the cameraman said as he hoisted his heavy video camera back onto his shoulder and walked down the hill to the rubble.

"Good idea," the reporter replied. "Let's get out of here as soon as possible."

"Sorry I couldn't be of any help," said Mrs. Grimm.

"Oh, it's not your fault. I just keep getting sent out to this town when there isn't any news."

"Yes, unfortunately, there's not a lot of excitement in Ferryport Landing," the old woman agreed. Wilma Faye nodded and headed back to the van.

When the news crew had left, Mrs. Grimm removed the large green leaf and an odd little box covered in knobs and lights from her handbag. She placed the leaf on the ground, then pushed a red button on top of the box and waved it over the leaf.

"What are you doing?" Daphne asked.

"I'm analyzing it. Very scientific stuff," the old woman said just as the machine let out a loud honking sound that could only be described as a fart. "Just as I thought, it's from a giant beanstalk."

"There's no such thing as giant beanstalks." Daphne giggled.

Mrs. Grimm pointed at the clearing below. "What do you see?"

"A house that fell down?" the little girl suggested.

"Yes, but what else? What is surrounding the house?"

Sabrina focused her attention on the rubble. What was so unusual about it? Nothing, really, except maybe for the large area of sunken ground that surrounded it. "The earth is mashed around it," she said.

"And what could cause something like that to happen?"

"I don't know. What do you think?" Sabrina said, after running through the possibilities.

"I think a giant stepped on it," Mrs. Grimm answered. "Find a giant beanstalk leaf and you'll probably find a giant."

Daphne began to laugh but Sabrina was horrified. The old woman was getting crazier by the second.

"Well, I better go down and have a second look," the old woman said as she climbed to her feet. She walked back down the hill and joined Mr. Canis at the pile.

"She's funny." Daphne giggled.

Funny in the head, Sabrina thought.

"I want to ride on the tractor!" Daphne cried.

She jumped up and pulled her sister over to it. Sabrina lifted the little girl onto the seat, who then grabbed the wheel and turned it, making *vroom vroom* sounds as she pretended to drive.

"Look at me, I'm a farmer," she said in a goofy voice. Sabrina looked up at her sister and laughed. Daphne was the funniest person she had ever met.

"What kind of food do you grow on this here farm, Farmer Grimm?" the older girl played along.

"Why, I grow candy on this here farm." Daphne laughed. "Bushels and bushels of candy. Just sent my crop to market last week. Got me a pretty penny, I did."

Sabrina smiled, but then a shadow covered her heart. Why did the old lady have to lie about who she was? Why did she have to make up crazy stories? Why couldn't she be normal? Her house was warm and comfortable and as long as Sabrina kept an eye on Mr. Canis they might just be OK. If the old woman wasn't a lunatic she'd make a perfect grandmother.

"Sabrina, look at the house," Daphne whispered. She had stopped playing and was staring at the pile below.

Sabrina looked down at the clearing but saw nothing new.

"Do you see what I see?" Daphne cried, pointing.

"What? What do you see?"

"Come up here, you have to see it from up here."

Sabrina crawled up onto the tractor and stood high on its hood.

"Do you see it?"

And then Sabrina saw what her sister was so excited about and her heart leaped into her throat. The indentation surrounding the broken-down house had a shape.

"It's a footprint," she gasped.

3

Mrs. Grimm and Mr. Canis were pulling a prank on them. It explained why Mrs. Grimm talked to the house and served her crazy food and why Mr. Canis said so little and acted so weird. They were trying to make the girls look stupid, which made Sabrina furious. And worse, the joke didn't seem to end. They spent the rest of the day traipsing over the field for more "clues," until Mrs. Grimm looked at her wristwatch and said they'd better get home for dinner.

At the house, Mrs. Grimm prepared a huge plate of meatballs for the girls, complete with purple gravy, the recipe for which she claimed she'd gotten from a Tibetan monk. Too hungry to resist, Sabrina cut a meatball in half to make sure there weren't any poison pills inside and, finding none, took a bite. It tasted like pizza. She devoured the plateful and was working on seconds when Mrs. Grimm joined them, placing a weathered old book on the table.

"So, we've got a mystery on our hands, *lieblings*. We should do some research. A good detective always does her research. Let's see. Giants. What do we know about them? Oh, here's one, 'The Tailor and the Giant,'" she said as she flipped through the pages.

"OK, you've had your fun," Sabrina said fiercely. "Don't you think we're a little old to fall for your joke?"

Mrs. Grimm looked up from her book in astonishment.

"You can't really think it was a giant!" Sabrina cried.

"Well, of course I do," the old woman replied without blinking.

"Granny, there's no such thing as giants," Daphne said between bites of meatball.

"Oh dear, I knew your father wanted to distance himself, but I never imagined he wouldn't have at least taught you the basics," the old woman said. "No wonder you two have been looking at me like I'm crazy."

"What are you talking about?" Sabrina cried.

"I'm talking about this," Mrs. Grimm said as she flipped the book to its first page.

"*Grimms' Fairy Tales*," Daphne read aloud.

The old woman flipped to the next page. On it were portraits of two very ugly men. "Do you know who these men are?" she asked. The girls looked at the portraits but said nothing. They didn't look familiar to Sabrina. "These men were Jacob and Wilhelm Grimm, also known as the Brothers Grimm. Wilhelm was your great-great-great-great grandfather," said the old woman as she pointed to the portrait of a thin man with a large nose, tiny eyes, and long hair.

"*Grimms' Fairy Tales*! The fairy-tale guys?" Daphne cried.

"Yes, *liebling*, the fairy-tale guys. But there is nothing in this book that's a fairy tale. This is a history book. Every story is an account of something that *really* happened."

The girls looked at each other, unsure of what to say.

"Back when Jacob and Wilhelm were alive, fairy-tale creatures were still living among people," Mrs. Grimm continued. "You could still wake up and find a giant beanstalk on your farm or pixies in your barn or see a group of knights fight a dragon. But things were changing. For a long time, a tension had been building between humans and fairy-tale creatures. Everafters were being persecuted, even arrested or forced into hiding, just because they were different. Magic was banned and dragons were captured and caged. The brothers realized that the age of fairy tales might be coming to an end, so they set out to document as many stories as they could, for posterity's sake. Some of the things they wrote about in their book happened hundreds of years before they were born, while others Jacob and Wilhelm witnessed themselves. Naturally, as they collected these tales, they made a lot of friends of Everafters."

"What's an Everafter?" Daphne asked.

"That's what fairy-tale creatures call themselves. After all, *fairy-tale creature* implies that they are all some sort of monster or animal. Many of them are human, or once were, before a spell changed them. They can be quite touchy about it.

"So, like generations of poor and persecuted before them, many Everafters decided to move to America. Back then so much of this country hadn't been settled that for a group of folks trying to keep a low profile it seemed like the ideal place to live and thrive. Wilhelm acted as their ambassador. He found ships and used his connections to buy five square miles on the Hudson River. The Everafters built this town on the land, more Everafters came here from all over the world, and for a long time everyone lived together in peace. But inevitably human beings started to move into Ferryport Landing, and soon the Everafters felt endangered again. Wilhelm tried to convince everyone that there was nothing to worry about, but a small and vocal group of rebels argued that it was just a matter of time before they would be persecuted again. They saw humanity as an infestation that needed to be rooted out at the source, and began tormenting the humans who had once been their friends."

"That's not nice," Daphne said.

"I agree, but fear can make people do terrible things. Wilhelm tried everything he could but the rebels' popularity and numbers were growing. It wasn't long before a plan was discovered by Wilhelm to conquer Cold Spring—the next town over—and make it part of Ferryport's territory. Desperate to prevent what would surely be an all-out war between Everafters and humans, Wilhelm went to the most powerful witch in town, Baba Yaga. Together they cast a spell on the town, preventing any of the Everafters from leaving."

"And then what?" Daphne asked. Sabrina watched her sister's widening eyes. She seemed to believe every word the old woman had said, and even if she didn't really, the little girl was happy enough here to want to believe.

"Then the problems really began . . . especially for Wilhelm," the old woman said. "You see, to get Baba Yaga to cast such a powerful spell, Wilhelm had to sacrifice something of his own. Magic always has a price and what the old witch wanted was what Wilhelm had taken from the Everafters—his freedom. It's a price that hangs over our family to this day. A Grimm must stay in Ferryport Landing, just like the Everafters, as long as the spell is intact. It's the reason I couldn't come to the orphanage and get you myself."

"Isn't there something that could break the spell?" said Daphne.

"Yes, there is," Mrs. Grimm said as she shifted in her chair. "The spell will be broken when the last member of this family is dead. When there are no more Grimms, the Everafters will be free."

"What a bummer," Sabrina said.

"Indeed," Mrs. Grimm said, ignoring Sabrina's sarcasm. "But we make the best of it, and so do most of the Everafters. They keep a low profile, buying homes and starting businesses. Some have families and have even given up their magical powers and possessions in hopes of living more normal lives. And, with a couple of exceptions, things have been pretty peaceful in Ferryport Landing between humans and Everafters. But just a look through Jacob and Wilhelm's book, and the books of Hans Christian Andersen, Andrew Lang, Lewis Carroll, Jonathan Swift, and countless other chroniclers of Everafters shows you how fragile the peace is, and that trouble could be right around the corner. So, like Wilhelm, we have the responsibility of keeping this pot from boiling over. We watch the town, investigate anything strange or criminal, and document what we see, so that when we are gone our children will know what we went through. Think of us as detectives. Someday I will pass all of this on to you, as your Opa Basil passed it on to me when he died. It is your destiny. We are Grimms and this is what we do."

"But why didn't you pass it on to Dad?" Daphne wondered.

"Your grandfather lost his life because of our responsibilities," the old woman said as she lowered her eyes. "Henry wanted something else for his children, so when your mother became pregnant with you, Sabrina, they left Ferryport Landing. He wanted to protect you and give you normal lives. Even if it meant telling you I was dead."

"Don't talk about my mom and dad like you knew them!" Sabrina shouted. The rage inside her was bubbling over. "I've sat here and listened to your silly story, but you're not going to tell a fairy tale about my parents."

The old woman was startled and tried to stammer out an answer, but Sabrina wouldn't let her. She had Mrs. Grimm on the ropes and she wasn't going to let her up.

"You are not our grandmother!" the girl raged. "Our grandmother died before we were born! My dad told us so."

"Your dad lied to you, *liebling*. Henry tried to run from his destiny. He didn't want this life for you, but it is your destiny as well. Your being here is evidence enough that it is impossible to escape. You will see the truth soon enough, and when you do we will prepare you for what lies ahead."

"My father never told a lie in his life," Sabrina cried.

The old woman laughed as she got up from the table. "It sounds like he hid more from you than the family history. I'm sure you need some time to let this sink in, and I have some things I need from upstairs. We're going to the hospital to see the poor farmer who owned that house. He might be able to tell us more about what he saw."

She left the room and went up the stairs, where the girls could hear the jangling of keys and knew she was opening her secret room.

"That woman is a lunatic," Sabrina whispered.

"She is not!" Daphne cried. "What's a lunatic?"

"A crazy person. She thinks people live in the woods, she's nailed all the windows shut, she talks to the house, and now she thinks fairy tales and giants are real. We can't stay here."

"What if I don't want to go?"

"You don't get a say. Mom and Dad put me in charge when they weren't around, and you have to do what I tell you to do."

"You're not the boss of me." Daphne crossed her arms in front of her chest and huffed indignantly.

"We're out of here as soon as I see a chance," Sabrina declared.

• • •

After dinner, they were off to the hospital, with Mr. Canis driving again. Asking the old woman questions was pointless, as the car was as loud as ever. Once they had arrived at the hospital and Mr. Canis had turned off the engine, Mrs. Grimm said to the children, "OK, let's review what we know so far, so we don't get confused. It's important for detectives to review their clues."

The previous night was catching up with Sabrina. She was so tired she didn't even have the energy to argue.

"First, a farmhouse was destroyed by what appears to have been a giant's foot. A footprint surrounded the destruction," Mrs. Grimm continued. "Second, a giant beanstalk leaf was found at the scene, a definitive sign of a giant. And it has been touched by a giant."

"How do you know that?" Sabrina asked.

"Because Elvis smelled its scent on the leaf."

"How does Elvis know what a giant smells like?"

"Because," Mrs. Grimm said, pulling the brown fabric out of her handbag that she had held under the dog's nose that morning, "he smelled this. It's cloth from a giant's trousers. Take a sniff."

Daphne smelled the piece of cloth and looked as if she might be sick. "E-gad!"

"Everything has its own particular scent, but giants are really stinky," the old woman explained. "Everybody and everything they touch will stink like them, too. I knew Elvis's nose would help us find a clue."

"This is nonsense," Sabrina said with equal amounts of scorn and exhaustion.

Mrs. Grimm ignored Sabrina's protests. "Of course, there's also the lens cap from a video camera we found on the hill overlooking the farm. My guess is the criminal wanted to videotape the giant when he arrived. And lastly, Mayor Charming showed up and he's . . ."

"Is Mayor Charming Prince Charming?" Daphne asked.

"Why, yes, *liebling*."

The little girl squealed in delight. "We met a celebrity!"

Mrs. Grimm chuckled, and then broke into a full laugh when she noticed the scowl on Mr. Canis's face.

"As I was saying, Mayor Charming showed up and tried to get us to give up our investigation," Mrs. Grimm continued. "If this were just an accident, he wouldn't have bothered to come by and check on it."

"When he first arrived, he was angry that someone he called *the Three* hadn't done a good job cleaning up the place," Daphne offered.

"*The Three* isn't a person, they're a coven of witches; Glinda the Good Witch of the North, Morgan Le Fay, and the gingerbread house witch, Frau Pfefferkuchenhaus. They work for the mayor. He calls them *magical advisors,* but they really just sweep whatever trouble there is under the carpet."

"I thought you said that Everafters gave up their magic," Sabrina said, hoping she had caught the old woman in a lie.

"No, I said some of them did, and in most cases, it was voluntary. I'm sure there's plenty of stuff hidden away in closets and attics all over Ferryport Landing," Mrs. Grimm replied. "Including, apparently, a magic bean I wasn't aware even existed. Let's go inside."

Ferryport Landing Memorial Hospital was tiny, at least small compared to the giant skyscraper hospitals Sabrina was familiar with in New York City. It had only two floors and no ambulances in front of the emergency room door. They left Mr. Canis in the car and, as they headed inside, passed a short, squat man and his two huge companions waiting by the hospital door. They were impeccably dressed in expensive suits, perfectly tailored to fit their extreme frames. The short man stared at Sabrina, sending a flash of heat to her face.

We look like idiots, Sabrina thought as she tried to tug her high-water pants down a little.

Inside, doctors and nurses rushed around the brightly lit hallways. The place smelled of cleaner and antiseptic, which tickled Sabrina's nose. The three Grimms managed to maneuver through the chaos and approach the information desk, where a portly receptionist sat talking on the phone. He had a large, round face and a toothy grin, and when he saw them, he put the phone to his chest and smiled.

"Can I help you ladies?"

"We're here to see Thomas Applebee. He was in an accident recently," Mrs. Grimm said.

"Oh, yes, the man whose house blew up. He's in room 222," the receptionist replied. "Popular fellow, he just had three people up to see him."

Mrs. Grimm cocked an eyebrow. "Indeed? Well, is there somewhere I should sign in?"

The receptionist handed the old woman a clipboard. Before she handed it back, she quickly pointed out three names on the list to the girls: a Mr. William Charming, a Mr. Seven, and a Ms. Glinda North had signed in ten minutes ago.

"Girls, we have to hurry."

They rushed down a hallway, through two double doors, and made a left, stopping at an elevator. Mrs. Grimm pushed the Up button several times.

"Why are we rushing?" Sabrina asked.

"Because Charming is here to erase the farmer's memory!" the old woman said as the elevator doors slid open and they stepped inside. They got out on the second floor, found room 222, and rushed inside.

On the bed was Thomas Applebee, a graying old man with his left arm in a sling and his right leg encased in plaster and held above the bed by a pulley system. Sabrina winced at how painful it looked and thought the poor man was lucky to be asleep. Standing over him were Mayor Charming, Mr. Seven (still wearing his insulting hat), and a rather chubby woman wearing a diamond tiara and a silver-and-gold dress. The woman was slowly emptying a bag of pink dust onto the sleeping patient. When she saw Mrs. Grimm, she dumped the contents all over the man and shoved the bag into her purse.

"Glinda, you've erased his memory," Mrs. Grimm cried. "I thought you were supposed to be a good witch."

The witch's face flushed red. She lowered her head and quickly made her way to the door.

"We all have to pay our bills, Relda," Glinda said as she walked out.

"Save your indignation," Charming added as he and Mr. Seven followed. "This is part of my job."

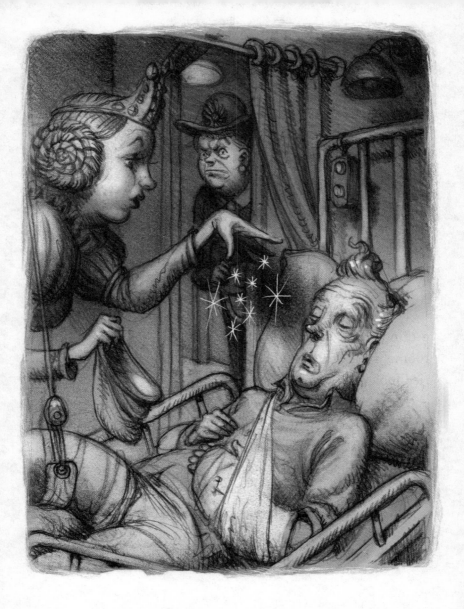

Mrs. Grimm looked discouraged. "He'll never be able to tell us anything," she said loudly, as if for the benefit of the three people who had just left. "And without an eyewitness account, we're never going to get to the bottom of this."

After several seconds, she poked her head out of the room.

"They're gone."

"What are we doing here?" Sabrina asked. She didn't feel comfortable waiting around in the hospital room of a man she didn't even know. Especially after people had been dumping what looked like the contents of a vacuum cleaner bag all over him.

"We're waiting."

"For who?" Daphne asked, but no sooner had she said it than a thin, frail woman with gray-streaked black hair entered the room. When she saw Mrs. Grimm and the girls, she got a worried look on her face.

"Mrs. Applebee, I'm Relda Grimm and these are my granddaughters, Sabrina and Daphne. We heard about the accident. Are you OK?" Mrs. Grimm said.

"Oh, I'm fine. Thank you for asking. Do you know my husband?"

"Oh, no, we're just concerned citizens and neighbors. I happen to do a little detective work from time to time and I was thinking I might be able to help. How is your husband?"

Mrs. Applebee gazed down at the broken man and smiled sadly. "To be honest, I'm a little worried about him. He was raving earlier. The doctors gave him a sedative to calm him down . . . Wait a minute, he's waking up," she said as he began to stir. He opened his eyes and looked at the three strangers in his room.

"Thomas, how are you feeling?" Mrs. Applebee asked as she sat next to his bed and rubbed his hand.

"Debra, who are these people?" the farmer asked his wife.

"They're with the police," Mrs. Applebee replied.

Mrs. Grimm stepped forward. "Not the police, dear. I'm a detective . . . of sorts. Mr. Applebee, my name is Relda Grimm, and these are my granddaughters. I'm very glad to see you weren't too badly injured, considering . . ."

"You three are detectives?" Mr. Applebee looked from Mrs. Grimm to the children, eyeing them suspiciously.

"Yes," Mrs. Grimm said, causing Daphne to practically swell with pride.

"Well, I think a crime has been committed, Mrs. Grimm," Mr. Applebee said.

"You do?"

"They should arrest whoever dressed your granddaughters this morning."

"Thomas, stop it! I think they look adorable," Mrs. Applebee cried. "I'm sorry, he's been a grouch since we got here. He doesn't like hospitals."

Sabrina looked down at her goofy outfit and seethed with anger. *Who would buy a girl who was almost twelve a shirt with a monkey on it?*

"Well, what can I do for you, Mrs. Grimm?" Mr. Applebee grunted.

"Do you remember anything about the accident?" the old woman said.

"What accident?" the farmer asked.

Mrs. Grimm frowned.

"What accident!" Mrs. Applebee exclaimed. "Thomas, the house has been destroyed and I found you lying in the yard."

"I don't know what you're talking about. There's nothing wrong with the house," Mr. Applebee argued.

"Oh, dear, the painkillers are really doing a number on you," Mrs. Applebee said, shifting anxiously in her seat. The farmer returned his wife's stare with an innocent look.

"Mrs. Grimm, I don't think my husband is up to discussing the case right now," his wife said.

"I understand. Perhaps you might have a moment to spare us, then?"

"Of course." Mrs. Applebee gestured for them to follow her into the hallway.

"So sorry to trouble you," Mrs. Grimm said to the farmer as they walked toward the door. "I do hope you feel better soon, Mr. Applebee."

Daphne stopped and turned to the injured man. "I like my outfit," she said and stuck her tongue out.

Mr. Applebee stuck his tongue out, too, and the little girl stomped out of the room.

"He's acting very odd right now," Mrs. Applebee said when they were in the hallway. "I'm considering taking him out of this hospital."

"Oh, I'm sure he's in good hands. So, you said he was raving about something," Mrs. Grimm prompted.

"Oh, it's silly. He swore he'd seen a giant."

"Oh, well, wouldn't that be a sight." Mrs. Grimm chuckled.

"But I have a different theory about what happened," Mrs. Applebee explained. "There was a British man out to the farm several times, asking us if we would rent the place to him for a couple of nights. He said he needed the field for a special event, but only for a couple of days. At first he was very friendly, but when Thomas refused he got quite nasty."

"Has he come back?" Mrs. Grimm asked.

"Well, that's just it. A week later he did come back and apologized for being so rude. He said he wanted to make it up to us so he booked us into a fancy hotel in New York City, all expenses paid, and tickets to a Broadway show. We hadn't had a vacation in years—farming is a tough business—so I accepted."

"How nice. Did you enjoy your vacation?"

"Not at all. When I got there I found that the hotel didn't have any record of our reservation and the tickets to the show were counterfeit," Mrs. Applebee said angrily.

"You say *you* found out. Didn't your husband go with you?" Mrs. Grimm said.

"Oh, no, Thomas doesn't care for the city much," Mrs. Applebee sighed, tears forming in her eyes. "I took my sister. We had to use our own money for a hotel and the only place with a room was infested with bedbugs."

"How dreadful," Mrs. Grimm sympathized. "Mrs. Applebee, this man's name didn't happen to be Charming, did it?"

"Oh no, it was Englishman," the woman replied, sniffing.

"What did this Mr. Englishman look like?"

"I'm sorry, I never saw him. Thomas had all the dealings with him."

"One last question, Mrs. Applebee. I'm sure you want to get

back to your husband. Do either of you own a video camera?" Mrs. Grimm took a clean handkerchief out of her handbag and offered it to the woman. Sabrina noticed that a soft, pink powder fell from the handkerchief as the woman wiped her eyes.

"No, we don't. Mr. Applebee is a little tight with the money, if you know what I mean." Suddenly, Sabrina noticed a change in the woman's face. It seemed to wipe itself of all emotion and her eyes drifted into a blank stare.

"I'm sorry, have we met?" Mrs. Applebee asked, her voice distant.

"No," Mrs. Grimm replied. "But I hear you had a wonderful time in New York City."

"OK," Mrs. Applebee said. Then she turned and went into her husband's room without saying good-bye.

Mrs. Grimm pulled her notebook out of her handbag and jotted down some notes. "So, the plot thickens," she said with a wide smile. "We can definitely say there was a giant, now."

"There's no such thing as giants!" Sabrina said, a bit louder than she meant to. The declaration echoed down the hospital hallway.

"Sabrina!" Daphne shouted.

"You heard the woman," Sabrina said in a much lower tone. "This Mr. Englishman wanted to rent their farm for some special event. When the farmer wouldn't agree, he lost his temper and blew the place up. Charming is probably trying to cover this up because he's in on it."

"Sabrina, I'm proud of you," Mrs. Grimm said as she led them into the elevator. "You have incredible skills of deduction. You looked at the clues and chose the most likely path to solve the crime. You're going to make a great detective. But how do you explain the footprint?"

"Listen, I don't know where you live, but my sister and I are here on Earth where things can easily be explained without having to consider giants. Maybe whatever Englishman used to blow up the house caused the ground to sink."

"Brilliant, but there's a loose end in your theory. When someone blows something up, usually pieces fly everywhere. This house looked like it had been squashed from above," Mrs. Grimm pointed out. The elevator stopped and the Grimms stepped into the busy emergency room lobby.

"The house was stomped on," Daphne said.

"That's my theory," the old woman said as they left the hospital. "And I know who is responsible."

"Who is it?" Daphne squealed.

"I think you'll enjoy it more if it's a surprise."

"Well, hello, ladies," a voice said as three men emerged from the deep shadows that lined the pathway to the parking lot. They were the same men in suits who had been staring at them when they entered the hospital. The small, dumpy one held an iron bar that he kept smacking into his gloved hand. The men on either side of him stood like huge, muscle-bound bookends to their much shorter leader.

"Good evening, gentlemen," Mrs. Grimm said calmly, despite the fact that one glance told Sabrina the men were trouble.

"We hear you've been asking some questions about a certain piece of property," the dumpy leader said. Sabrina saw that his nose had been broken in three places. She could tell he wasn't a man to mess with.

"Then you've heard correctly, young man," Mrs. Grimm said as she placed herself squarely between the girls and the thugs. Daphne grabbed her sister's hand and squeezed tightly, but Sabrina hardly noticed. She was too awestruck by the old woman's courage.

"Well, if you know what's good for you, then you'll just forget about the whole thing," the leader said with a wicked grin that revealed the absence of a front tooth.

"If I knew what was good for me, I wouldn't be in this line of work," Mrs. Grimm replied. "Now, if you'd be so kind to let us pass, I really must get my granddaughters out of the cold air."

"In a minute, Relda." The leader grinned. "We just want to make sure you understand what we're trying to say."

"I seem to be at a disadvantage, young man. You know my name, but I don't know yours. Or better yet, who the unfortunate employer is who hired the likes of you three."

The two big men grunted angrily, but the leader raised his hands to quiet them. "No need to get rude, Relda. We're just having a conversation, ya know, trying to avoid a confrontation."

"Boys," Mrs. Grimm said with the tone of someone who has lost her patience. "I want you to go back to your boss and tell him that he should know it takes more than three thugs to make me give up. Now, good night."

She tried to pass the men, but as she did, the leader grabbed her jacket and pulled her close to his fat face.

"Some people can't take a hint."

Mrs. Grimm pulled a little silver whistle from around her neck and blew into it, but no sound could be heard. When she put it back inside her dress, the bullies laughed.

"I'm warning you. If you don't let us pass you are going to regret it," she said. Sabrina's heart began to pound. How could Mrs. Grimm be so calm? These men were about to tear her apart!

"Lady, it's *you* who's going to have the regrets."

4

eave my grandmother alone!" Daphne commanded. Before Sabrina could stop her, the little girl rushed forward and kicked the dumpy man in the shin. He cried out in pain and rubbed his leg. Mrs. Grimm then hit him on top of his head with her heavy, book-filled handbag. He crumpled to the ground and groaned. Seeing how easily their leader had fallen to a little girl and an old lady, the two other thugs laughed.

"What are you laughing at?" the leader snapped as he crawled to his feet.

"Sorry, Tony, we didn't mean to laugh," one of the goons said.

"What are you doing?" Tony bellowed.

"What?" the tall one asked defensively.

"You told her my name. We all agreed we were going to keep our identities secret."

The tall one shrugged. "Sorry, Tony, I didn't think."

"Steve, you just did it again," the other thug pointed out.

"You did it, too!" Tony shouted. "You just told them Steve's name."

"Who cares?" Steve said.

"Because they can identify us to the cops," Tony complained as he turned his attention back to Mrs. Grimm. He raised his heavy crowbar above his head and snarled. "Now we have to kill them!"

"Easier said than done," a voice said from behind them. Sabrina and Daphne turned to see Mr. Canis emerge from the shadows with Elvis close behind.

"Look out, here comes her boyfriend." Steve laughed. "You want to handle him, Bobby?"

"Shut up! Both of you!" Tony shouted. "Why don't you idiots just give them our addresses and phone numbers, too!"

"If you run off now, no one will get hurt," Canis offered. His voice was powerful and hard but the thugs just chuckled. Even Sabrina could tell that frail old Mr. Canis wasn't going to be able to stop them. Sometimes he looked as if his own clothes were too heavy for him to wear.

Sabrina realized now would be a great time to grab her sister and make their escape, but it didn't feel right. The old woman and her feeble friend needed their help. She would have to do something herself—find a weapon—a rock, a stick—anything she could use to fight the men off. But the pathway was as clean of debris as it was of people.

"Girls, get behind Elvis, please," Mr. Canis said, taking their hands and pulling them back so that the Great Dane was between them and trouble.

"Enough of this. Get him!" Tony ordered, and Bobby and Steve lunged at Mr. Canis. Sabrina was sure they had seen the last of the old man, but he caught both of the men by the throat, one in each hand, and lifted them off the ground, holding them aloft as their feet dangled and kicked. Even more shocking was the loud, guttural growl the old man released when he tossed the two thugs, sending them sprawling across the cold concrete ground. For ten yards they thumped and bounced, groaning with each painful smack against the pavement.

"All right, if that's the way you want to play it," Tony threatened as he pushed Mrs. Grimm roughly to the ground. He swung his iron bar wildly at Mr. Canis and rushed forward, but the old man quickly stepped sideways and tripped him, sending the thug to the pavement with his friends. Tony leaped up and rushed at Mr. Canis again, only to feel the same painful results.

"Hurry girls, we should get to safety," Mrs. Grimm said as she got up and led them away from the fight. Elvis trotted along beside them, barking warnings at the goons not to follow. When they got to the car, Daphne climbed in but anxiously peered out the windows. After several minutes, Mr. Canis had still not joined them.

"We shouldn't have left him. There were three of them, Granny! He can't fight them all," the little girl said, with tears running down her cheeks. Before Mrs. Grimm could calm her down, the car door opened and Mr. Canis crawled in behind the wheel. He was completely unharmed, and oddly, he had a little grin on his face.

"See, *lieblings*? He's just fine," the old woman said. She turned to Mr. Canis. "The girls were worried about you."

The old man turned in his seat and looked back at Sabrina and Daphne. He was his same painfully thin, watery-eyed old self. Daphne leaned forward and planted a kiss on his cheek. His face turned red with embarrassment.

"Don't you ever do that again!" she commanded as she hugged him tightly and then sat back into her seat. Mr. Canis nodded in agreement.

"I, for one, am thrilled at what's transpiring," Mrs. Grimm

said, taking out her notepad and pen. She began jotting notes frantically.

Sabrina was shocked. "Thrilled? We were almost killed."

"Killed? Oh Mr. Canis, doesn't she remind you of Basil?" Mrs. Grimm tittered.

Mr. Canis nodded.

"No, I think we have cause to celebrate," the old woman continued.

"Why, did you find a clue?" Daphne asked.

"No, not at all."

"Then, what's to celebrate?" Sabrina said.

"We're getting close, *lieblings*. When they send the goons, the bad guys are getting nervous."

"So what now?" Daphne asked.

"We'll follow those goons back to their hideout."

"What? Why would we do that?" Sabrina cried, remembering Tony and his crowbar.

"Because they're going to lead us right back to their boss. Ladies, we're going on a stakeout."

• • •

Mr. Canis managed to find the thugs' car in no time and he trailed them at a distance (which had to be pretty great, considering the noise coming from Mrs. Grimm's old rust bucket), driving high into the hills overlooking Ferryport Landing. They passed no other cars, just a few deer wandering by the road in the fading light. But Sabrina wasn't enjoying the scenery. She was a nervous wreck. She had already worried about Mrs. Grimm's sanity, based on the ridiculous fairy-tale story she had told earlier that day. Now the crazy old woman had them chasing three dangerous men. She wanted to kick herself for not escaping when they had had the chance, and decided that she and Daphne would make a run for it as soon as possible.

Eventually, the thugs' car pulled into the empty driveway of a small mountain cabin. Mr. Canis turned the engine and lights off and let the car coast along the road until they found a dense growth of trees to park behind. When they came to a stop, Mrs. Grimm opened up her handbag, fumbled through it, and took out a pair of odd-looking binoculars.

"What are those?" Daphne asked.

"They're binoculars for nighttime. They're called infrared goggles. I thought they might come in handy tonight," the old woman said as she handed them to Daphne. "Want to take a peek?"

Daphne took the goggles and raised them to her eyes.

"Oh, that's horrible!"

Sabrina looked out the window but saw nothing. "What? What do you see?" she asked nervously.

"You." The little girl giggled. "Here, take a look."

The older girl stuck out her tongue and took the goggles from her sister. When she looked through them, the darkness became illuminated in green light, and she saw the three thugs going into the cabin.

"Let's see who else turns up," Mrs. Grimm said. "Sabrina, would you mind letting Elvis out? He probably needs to stretch his legs."

Sabrina handed Mrs. Grimm the goggles and opened the door. Elvis lumbered out, causing the car to make noises that sounded like squeals of delight. With the door open, the girls could have easily made a break for it, using the woods for cover as they made their escape, but Daphne was leaning on the front seat asking questions.

"Granny Relda, are all the fairy tales true?"

"Almost all of them, but some are just bedtime stories to get kids to go to sleep. For instance, a dish never ran away with a spoon, and no cow that I know of has ever jumped over the moon."

"How about the three little pigs?"

Mr. Canis shifted in his seat but said nothing.

"Yes, dear, they are real," Mrs. Grimm replied.

"How about Snow White?"

"Yes, indeed. In fact, she's a teacher at Ferryport Landing Elementary. We're going to have to enroll you two there in a couple of weeks. She's very sweet and, as you know, very good with little people like yourself."

"What about Santa Claus?"

"I've never met him, but I have it on good faith that he is alive and well."

"I've got a question for you," Sabrina said. "These stories were written hundreds of years ago. How could all these people still be alive?"

"Easy child, it's magic," Mrs. Grimm explained.

"Duh!" Daphne said to her sister, as if it were common knowledge.

Sabrina shot her an angry look, but the little girl ignored it.

"Granny Relda, have you ever seen a giant?" Daphne asked.

"Of course, *liebling*, I've even been to the giant kingdom on a couple of occasions. The last time I was nearly squished by the Giant Queen's toe." Mrs. Grimm laughed. "As an apology, she gave me that piece of fabric."

"Well, if there really are giants, how come we haven't seen any yet?" Daphne asked.

"There weren't any around until yesterday," Mrs. Grimm said. "Long ago, the Everafters realized that giants were just too unpredictable. They caused as much destruction when they were happy as they did when they were mad, and once they planted themselves somewhere it was impossible to move them. Imagine trying to plant seeds on your farm with a sleepy giant lying across it! When humans started moving into Ferryport Landing, everyone realized that giants were just too big to disguise. Of course, the giants didn't agree and refused to go back to their kingdom. Your great uncle Edwin and your great aunt Matilda tricked them into climbing their beanstalks, and once they were all up there, the townsfolk chopped the beanstalks down."

"What good would that do?" Daphne asked.

"No beanstalk—no way into our world. Of course, there were a couple of people who didn't much care for the plan. In the old days, people would plant magic beans and climb up the beanstalks just to steal the giants' treasures. Lots of people were foolish enough to try, but only one ever survived the ordeal," Mrs. Grimm said.

"Jack?" Daphne asked.

"You are correct, *liebling*. Jack robbed many giants and killed quite a number of them, too. In his day he was very rich and famous, though I hear he's working at a Big and Tall clothing store downtown, now. I can't imagine he'd be too happy doing that."

"Are you going to sit here and tell us that Jack was a real person?" Sabrina snapped.

"Was and is, my love," Mrs. Grimm replied.

"So, let's just say all this is true. If all the beanstalks were destroyed, how did a giant get down here?" Sabrina asked, confident that she had tripped up the old woman.

"Ah, *liebling*, that is indeed the mystery we are trying to solve. Whoever did it had to have a magic bean, and I thought we had accounted for all of them. It would help if we knew why they wanted to let a giant loose."

"I'll bet he was a big one, Granny Relda. Probably a thousand feet high!" Daphne exclaimed.

"Oh, sweetheart, he's probably no bigger than two hundred feet tall," Mrs. Grimm said.

Sabrina looked at her little sister in the moonlight and frowned. Daphne's eyes were as big as Frisbees. Sabrina was losing her little sister to the old lunatic. For a year and a half it had been just the two of them, and Sabrina had done everything she could to keep them together and safe. She had protected her sister from nasty Ms. Smirt, the horrible kids in the orphanage, and all those foster parents, and now she was unable to protect her from a crazy old woman.

Just then, Elvis let out a low growl.

"Someone's coming," Mrs. Grimm warned as headlights flashed behind them. "Everyone get down."

They all huddled under the windows as a car passed by and headed toward the cabin. When it was far enough away, they lifted their heads.

"I don't think he saw us," Daphne said.

The old woman lifted the goggles to her eyes.

"Well, Sabrina, we've got more evidence for your theory. That's Mayor Charming's car," Mrs. Grimm said. "I didn't expect to see him here."

Mr. Canis rolled his window down and sniffed the cool mountain air. Then, as if he had smelled something foul, his nose curled up. The odd thing was that Elvis, who was sitting outside of Mr. Canis's window, had the same expression. The two of them were smelling something they didn't like.

"Charming is knocking on the door," Mrs. Grimm reported.

Mr. Canis turned in his seat. "Child, open your door. The dog should get back into the car."

Daphne opened her door and called for Elvis, but the Great

Dane stood motionless, sniffing the air as if he was dedicating all his attention to it.

"They're talking," the old woman continued, still looking through her goggles.

"Get into the car, dog," Mr. Canis called sternly. Elvis turned to face him but kept sniffing.

"Wait a minute, Charming is running to his car. Something has got him spooked," Mrs. Grimm remarked. "And you won't believe who's with him!"

It was the perfect opportunity. The old woman was watching the house and Mr. Canis was distracted by Elvis. Sabrina grabbed her sister's hand, opened her car door, and pulled Daphne out.

"What are you doing?" Daphne cried.

"We're getting out of here this minute!" Sabrina replied, but before they could even take a step Elvis blocked their escape with his huge body.

"Come on, you big flea hotel. Get out of the way!" Sabrina shouted, but the dog refused to budge.

"Don't call him a flea hotel!" Daphne scolded. "He's sensitive!"

Elvis let out a horrible whine. It was followed by an earth-shaking thump that sent the girls tumbling to the ground.

"What was that?" Sabrina asked, trying to stand up.

"Girls, get into the car," Mr. Canis urged. His face looked serious and dark.

"We're not going anywhere with you," Sabrina cried as she got to her feet.

"*Lieblings*, please. Something is coming," Mrs. Grimm begged.

"Something is coming? What does that mean? Enough with the stories, OK?" Sabrina yelled. "You're just trying to scare us and give my sister nightmares so that maybe we'll be too frightened to leave you." It was almost as if the mini-earthquake had knocked something loose inside of Sabrina, an anger and frustration at being abandoned, drifting from foster home to foster home, always hoping for someplace where they could be happy, but finding that whenever they got close, it was tainted with some sort of craziness.

"Sabrina, we can discuss this at another time. Please get into the car," Mrs. Grimm pleaded once more.

"I don't want to hear another word about fairies and goblins and giants or Jack and the Beanstalk or Humpty Dumpty!" Sabrina raged as Elvis let out a shrieking howl. "I know the difference between reality and a fairy tale!"

But she had hardly finished her rant when something fell out of the sky. It was monstrous and encircled the car and lifted it off the ground. Sabrina couldn't believe what she was seeing, but it was there, right in front of her.

It was a hand—a giant hand.

Her eyes traveled up the arm, higher and higher, until she found a giant head and then immediately wished she hadn't. Boils as big as birthday cakes pocked the giant's greasy skin. A broken nose zigzagged across his face, and one dead white eye seeped puss while the other one was lined with the crust of sleep. Hairs as thick as tree trunks jutted out of his nose and hung over a mouthful of broken, misplaced, yellow-and-green teeth. He wore the hides of dozens of gigantic animals, including the head of what looked like a giant bear for a helmet. The dead bear's sharp fangs dug into his bald head, threatening to pierce his brain. His boots were made from more hides, and tangled in the laces were several unfortunate saplings.

The giant lifted the car up to his repugnant face and looked inside like a child inspecting a toy. With his free hand he picked his nose.

"Where is Englishman?" he bellowed. "Why does he hide from me?"

Sabrina couldn't see what was going on in the car as it was nearly two hundred feet off the ground. Were Mrs. Grimm and Mr. Canis even still alive? It was all so horrible that the two girls barely noticed that something had dropped from the car, landing with a clang at their feet.

"You cannot hide from me, Englishman!" the giant shouted as he lifted his enormous leg and stomped down hard on the little mountain cabin, flattening it like a pancake. Pieces of timber and stone sprayed into the air, just missing the girls. Sabrina and Daphne gasped. The three thugs—Tony, Steve, and Bobby—had been inside the cabin. There was no way any of them could have escaped.

Looking down at the destruction, the giant let out a sickening laugh. He stuffed the car into a greasy shirt pocket, lifted his other humongous leg, and walked away, carrying the remains of the mountain cabin in the treads of his boots. The earth shook violently and a ripple spilled across the land as if someone had tossed a stone into a pond to see it skip. Because of his mammoth stride, the giant completely disappeared over the horizon after just a dozen steps. Only the distant rumbling of his disastrous footfalls and the angry growls of Elvis remained.

The girls stood completely frozen. Competing with Sabrina's fear was another unsettling emotion—humiliation. Mrs. Grimm had been telling the truth the whole time and Sabrina had refused to listen. Sabrina had deliberately been a jerk to the old woman, and now she might never see her again to tell her she was sorry. She moved to comfort her sister, but Daphne pulled away. The little girl rushed over to pick up whatever had fallen from the car. It was Mrs. Grimm's handbag.

"She was telling the truth and you have been a big snot since the first minute. Tell me now if you think she's crazy," Daphne said furiously.

"I don't think she's crazy," her older sister said, but Daphne had already turned and was marching down the road. "Where are you going?"

"I'm going to rescue our family," the little girl called back without stopping.

5

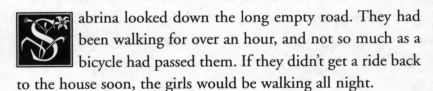abrina looked down the long empty road. They had been walking for over an hour, and not so much as a bicycle had passed them. If they didn't get a ride back to the house soon, the girls would be walking all night.

The time might have passed more quickly if there had been a little conversation, but for an hour, Daphne had marched ahead of Sabrina, refusing to speak. Even Elvis, who followed closely behind, was ignoring her, but since he was a dog, his silence was a lot easier to take. But Daphne hadn't been quiet for longer than five minutes since she was born. She was even a noisy sleeper.

"How was I supposed to know?" Sabrina cried. "Anybody would have thought she was crazy!"

"I didn't," Daphne said, finally breaking her silence.

"You don't count. You believe everything," Sabrina argued.

"And you don't believe in anything," the little girl snapped. "Why are we even talking? You don't care what I think, anyway."

"That's not true!" Sabrina said, but before the words had left her mouth she knew they were a lie. What Daphne thought hadn't mattered in a long, long time, at least not since their parents had deserted them. But it wasn't like Sabrina wanted it that way. She was only eleven and didn't want to have to make all the decisions for both of them. She would love to feel like a kid and not have to worry about whether they were safe. But that wasn't how things were. Unfortunately, she realized now, she had never considered what Daphne thought when it came to their best interests.

"Whatever!" Daphne muttered, and continued her angry march back to the house.

Elvis followed, sniffing the air wildly for the giant's stench. Sabrina could see that he took his guard dog duties seriously. Every little buzz and cracking sound had to be investigated. The dog darted back and forth, peering through the barbed-wire fence that separated the road from the endless forest. Once he was confident that the swaying limbs of the pines or the occasional rooting woodchuck were not a giant sneaking up on them, he trotted to the center of the road and put his huge nose back to work.

"This is ridiculous. We'll never get home if we walk," Sabrina said. Her feet were aching, and at the pace they were going they'd be lucky if they made it back to the house by nightfall the next day.

"You're not helping!" Daphne cried as she spun around. Her face was red and she had her hands on her hips.

"What do you want me to do?" Sabrina asked. "The old woman . . ."

"Our grandma," Daphne corrected.

"Whoever she is . . . just got carried off by a giant and we are trapped in the middle of nowhere. I'm sorry, but I've run out of ideas!"

Daphne's shoulders loosened and her expression sank. She walked over to a fallen tree trunk next to the road, sat down, and began to cry. Elvis trotted over and nuzzled her, licking the little girl's tears from her chubby cheeks, and adding his whines to her sobbing. Sabrina sat down beside her sister and put her arm around the little girl.

"You don't care if we ever find them," Daphne sniffled, pulling away. "Now you can run off like you planned with no one to stop you."

Sabrina thought for a moment before she responded. She had to admit to herself that running away was her first instinct.

"Daphne, that monster was real. We can't fight that by ourselves. Even if we knew where he carried them off to, I don't think we could get them back. What are a seven-year-old and an eleven-year-old going to do about a giant?"

"You're almost twelve," Daphne said, wiping her eyes on the sleeve of her fuzzy orange shirt. "Besides, you heard Granny Relda. We're Grimms and this is what Grimms do. We take care of fairy-tale problems. We'll find a way to save Granny and Mr. Canis."

"How?"

"With this," Daphne said, holding the old woman's handbag above her head.

Sabrina took it from her sister and fumbled through it. Inside were Mrs. Grimm's key ring, the swatch of fabric the old woman had said came from a giant, books, her notebook, and a small photograph. Sabrina pulled it out.

"Mom and Dad," she said, as surprise raced through her. It was a picture of their parents, young and in love. Their dad had his hand on their mother's very pregnant stomach and they were both grinning. Granny Relda stood next to them, beaming, while Mr. Canis was off to the side, stone-faced as ever.

It had been more than a year and a half since Sabrina had seen a picture of her parents. The police had seized everything during the investigation and promised that when it was over they'd get everything back. But when the cops gave up looking for her mom and dad, their promises faded away. Now Sabrina's bitterness toward her parents faded, too. She held the snapshot as if it was a delicate treasure. It was evidence that her parents had existed, that at one time she and her sister had been part of a family. And it was obvious, seeing Granny Relda and her father standing side by side, where her father had gotten his warm round face. She glanced at Daphne and saw that face in her sister, as well. She looked at her father's blond hair and recognized her own. Daphne had her mother's jet-black hair; Sabrina had her high cheekbones and bright eyes. How could her mom and dad have walked away from their family? Proof that they should be together was right there in their faces.

Daphne hovered over her sister to get a better view, tears still running down her cheeks. Sabrina turned the picture over. Someone had written, "The Family Grimm—Relda, Henry, Veronica, Mr. Canis, and the soon-to-be-born baby, Sabrina."

"Why did he lie to us about her?" Sabrina whispered as she tucked the family portrait safely into her pants pocket.

"I don't know," Daphne answered quietly.

"And what happens if we start to love her and she abandons us, too?" the older girl asked, trying to hide the hurt in her voice.

"Maybe she won't," Daphne said. "Maybe she'll just love us back."

The little girl wiped her eyes and dug into Granny Relda's handbag. She pulled out their grandmother's giant key ring. "She wanted us to have these keys. She wants us to go home."

If we can even get home, Sabrina said to herself as a light caught the corner of her eye. She looked down the road. There were headlights approaching.

The two girls got up from the log and brushed themselves off. "What should we do, stick out our thumbs?" Daphne asked.

Sabrina didn't know. They'd never hitchhiked before. In the past, whenever the girls had found themselves alone or on the run, they slipped under the turnstiles in the subway stations and traveled New York City's subterranean highway.

Sabrina stuck out her thumb and Daphne did the same. The car came to a screeching stop. It sat still for a moment, with its engine humming, blinding the girls with its high-beam lights so that they had to shield their eyes with their hands.

"Well, that was easy," Daphne said. "What's he doing?"

"I don't know," Sabrina said, stepping to the side. "Maybe he doesn't want to give us a ride."

Suddenly, the car let out a long, eardrum-rattling honk, followed by more engine revving. To Sabrina, it seemed as if the car were an animal, waiting for the right time to pounce on them. She recalled hearing stories about hitchhikers being killed by lunatics. Hitchhiking didn't seem like such a great idea anymore. She grabbed her sister's hand and pulled her off the road. As if in response, the car revved its engines again.

"Run!" Sabrina cried. Surprised, Daphne stumbled along beside her but did what she was told. The two of them raced back the way they had come, hand in hand. Elvis followed closely behind, turning his big head to bark out the occasional angry warning at the menacing car, but it had little effect on whomever was behind the wheel. The squeal of tires on asphalt told Sabrina that they were now being chased. The car honked again, sending a shocking jolt through her bones, and then suddenly it veered to the other side of the road. It sped up and passed the girls, then spun around, leaving black stains on the asphalt and the smell of burning rubber in Sabrina's nose. It was a police car, now stretched across the road, blocking the girls' escape.

The door opened and a short, stout, pear-shaped man stepped out. He wore a beige police uniform with shiny black boots, a billy club at his utility belt, and a wide-brimmed hat that fastened under his three chins. His face was puffy and pink with a nose that angled slightly upward, so that a person could see up his nostrils. On his shirt was a shiny, tin star that read FERRYPORT LANDING SPECIAL FORCES and a name tag underneath it that said SHERIFF HAMSTEAD.

"Girls, why are you running?" the sheriff asked in an unusually high-pitched voice that sent shivers into Sabrina's belly.

"We thought you were trying to kill us," Daphne said angrily. Sabrina flashed her a look, letting her know that she would do the talking.

"I see. Well, I'm sorry if I gave you two a start, but it's not safe for little girls like yourselves to be walking out here in the dark. These roads can be treacherous," the sheriff said.

"Treacherous?" Daphne asked.

"Dangerous," Sabrina explained.

"I got a call that you were out here, so I came looking," the portly man continued as he hoisted his sinking pants up around his waist. "Why don't you two hop into the squad car and I'll take you home?" He pointed to Elvis. "I don't know if we can put your horse in there, but we'll try."

"He's not a horse," Daphne said. Then, realizing the sheriff was joking, she added, "You can't tease him. He's very sensitive."

Hamstead leaned down and scratched Elvis under the chin. "Oh, I'm sure he is, aren't you, Elvis?"

The big dog growled and snapped at the sheriff's hand.

Hamstead pulled it away just in time, but then rubbed it with his other hand as if the dog had gotten a lucky bite.

"How do you know Elvis?" Sabrina said suspiciously.

"Oh, Elvis and I have met before. You must be Relda Grimm's grandchildren. I heard you were in town," the man said. "I'm the local sheriff, Ernest Hamstead."

"I'm Daphne," the little girl offered.

"Sabrina," Sabrina muttered.

"So, do you two need a ride home or are you trying to raise a million dollars for the March of Dimes?"

Sabrina nodded and Hamstead opened the squad car's backdoor. Elvis clumsily climbed in and the sheriff shut the door behind him. Sabrina and Daphne walked around the car and got in on the passenger's side of the front seat.

Sheriff Hamstead squeezed and shifted his way into the car, breathing heavily as if carrying a great burden. He had left the keys in the ignition (Sabrina guessed so that he wouldn't have to fish them out of his tight pants), so as soon as he was settled, he started up the squad car and headed in the direction of Granny's house.

"So, I assume you two have already concocted some elaborate scheme to get your granny and her friend back?" Hamstead asked. The girls looked at each other, unsure of what to say.

"So you know about this?" Sabrina asked, dumbfounded.

"Yep," Sheriff Hamstead said. "Hard to miss a two-hundred-foot giant carrying grandmas away into the night, don't you think? I don't want you two girls to worry. Your granny is a tough cracker. I've seen her in bigger jams than this one and besides, she's got the entire Ferryport Landing Special Forces Squad working on the case. I know you two have been trained for this kind of thing, but we like to take care of our own problems here in Ferryport Landing."

Daphne cupped her hand around Sabrina's ear. "Have we been trained?" she whispered.

"I don't know what he's talking about," Sabrina whispered back.

"Are you an Everafter?" the little girl said, returning her attention to the sheriff.

The sheriff looked over and winked a yes at Daphne. She squealed in delight. "Which one?"

Suddenly, the squad car's CB radio crackled to life. "Hamstead? Sheriff Hamstead?" a man's voice fumed. It sounded oddly familiar to Sabrina.

The sheriff seemed nervous. When he tried to pick up the handset, it fumbled in his sweaty hand before he finally got ahold of it.

"I'm here, boss. En route now," Hamstead said.

"That's fantastic news, Hamstead. Nice to know you can do something that's asked of you. If you care at all, I picked up our little troublemaker about a half an hour ago and he's sitting in a cell as we speak. So all I'm asking from you is to get those little trolls back to the mansion, ASAP! I can't have any headaches ruining tomorrow's festivities."

Sabrina's heart froze and as she looked at her sister, she saw the same horror reflected in Daphne's eyes. The voice on the police radio was Mayor Charming's! The car had come to a stop sign, and Sabrina knew they had to act.

"Daphne, do you remember that time Mr. and Mrs. Donovan took us to that three-day lima bean cook-off festival?" Sabrina asked casually, hoping the girl would remember the crazy foster couple they had lived with for three weeks the previous year. The little girl grimaced, obviously remembering the pickled lima bean pie Mrs. Donovan was so proud of, but then a light in her eyes told Sabrina she also remembered their daring escape. Sabrina slipped her hand into her sister's and quickly pulled on the door handle. Before Hamstead could react, the girls were out of the car and freeing Elvis from the backseat.

"Hey!"

The sisters ran to the side of the road where a five-foot barbed-wire fence lined the edge of the forest. There was no way to climb it; the barbed wire's sharp teeth would tear them apart. Their only chance was to try to scurry between the rusty wires to the other side. Desperate, Sabrina stood on one of the wires, reached down and grabbed a safe spot on the next highest one, and pulled upward as hard as she could, creating a hole her sister could crawl through.

"Go!" Sabrina shouted, carefully watching the portly sheriff struggling out of the car. Daphne scampered through the small gap to the other side. The little girl got to her feet and tried to mimic the trick she had just seen Sabrina do. The result was a small gap Sabrina couldn't possibly fit through.

"It's heavy," Sabrina coached Daphne, "you have to be strong."

"I am!" the little girl cried, pulling harder.

"Girls, you can't run!" Hamstead shouted angrily, as he finally freed himself from the car. Elvis positioned himself between Sabrina and the sheriff and barked a warning when the man took a step forward.

Sabrina got down on her hands and knees and tried to crawl through, but before she could get to the other side, Hamstead, dodging Elvis, was on top of her, grabbing her legs and trying to pull her back out.

"You're coming with me!" he squealed.

Sabrina kicked wildly and looked back into the sheriff's face, and what she saw bewildered her. Sheriff Hamstead was going through a disturbing metamorphosis. His already pug nose became a slimy pink snout. His round face puffed up to three times its size, and his ears turned pink and pointy and migrated to the top of his head. His chubby fingers melded into thick black hoofs, and his back bent over until he was literally on all fours. Hamstead had turned into a pig—an angry, determined pig in a policeman's uniform.

"I can't hold it any longer," Daphne cried, wide-eyed at what she was witnessing. Sabrina kicked one more time and felt her foot sink into Hamstead's gelatinous belly. His piggy face turned white and he fell onto his back, honking and gasping for air as his little legs flailed back and forth. Just as suddenly as he had changed to a pig, he changed back to a man.

Daphne's arms gave out and the barbed wire came down on top of Sabrina, snagging her pants. Daphne vainly tried to lift it again, but the taut wire barely moved.

"What are we going to do?" Daphne cried as Hamstead staggered to his feet. He rushed toward Sabrina, this time as a full man. Suddenly, Sabrina heard a series of notes, as if someone in the woods was playing a flute, followed by a buzzing sound that grew closer and closer. Sabrina peered through the trees nervously, remembering the music from the night before.

"They're coming, aren't they?" Daphne said, and before she finished the question a cloud of little lights zipped out of the forest and surrounded them. This time the lights didn't attack. Instead, they hovered as if waiting for instructions. Another note pierced the night air and the little lights buzzed into action, perching on the barbed wires that had Sabrina caught and, with a flutter of wings, pushing at the lowest wire and pulling the other one up, creating a hole big enough for Sabrina to scamper through. When she got to the other side, the little lights let go of the wires.

Hamstead, trapped on the other side of the fence, squealed in frustration and searched for an opening. He waddled back and forth, huffing and grunting, but found nothing that would allow his human or pig form to pass. Desperately, he got to his hands and knees and tried to squeeze through the wires. And that's when Elvis made his move. The big dog ran full steam right at Hamstead like some kind of fur-covered locomotive. He leaped onto Sheriff Hamstead's broad back and used it as a springboard. The sheriff let out a painful grunt as Elvis sailed effortlessly over the top of the fence and landed on all fours.

The chubby policeman quickly recovered. He stood up,

grabbed a fence post, and began to climb. Sabrina knew she had to do something. She grabbed another post and pushed all her weight against it. Discovering it was quite loose in the ground, she shook it back and forth as hard as she could, and the fence swayed uncontrollably.

"Hey, stop that!" Hamstead shouted nervously as he clung to the fence.

Daphne rushed to Sabrina's side and together they shook the fence even harder. Suddenly, with a loud tearing of fabric, Sheriff Hamstead's body thumped to the ground on his side of the fence. He groaned and let out an angry cry. After a moment, he picked himself up. Unfortunately, his pants had not survived the fall. They hung from the sharp teeth of the barbed-wire fence, leaving the sheriff in just a pair of droopy long johns. Defeated, he hobbled back to his car.

"He's leaving," Sabrina said as she followed her sister into the dark woods.

"He turned into a pig," Daphne whispered.

"I saw him," Sabrina replied. "But I think we have another problem."

The little lights waited patiently ahead of them. They darted into the woods and then came back out, as if they wanted the girls to follow them.

"What do you want?" Sabrina asked, and the lights shimmered and blinked an answer.

"Should we follow them?" said Daphne.

"I don't see that we've got much of a choice," Sabrina said, thinking the lights might attack if they didn't.

She took her sister's hand and they walked through the dark woods, with Elvis trotting closely behind. Low-hanging branches blocked their path, and with each step the girls had to dodge and weave to get through. Several times Sabrina walked into trees, feeling the prickly spindles of a pine or the crusty bark of an oak tear at her clothes and skin. The lights guided them, slowing down occasionally to see if they were keeping up.

"They're making sure we're following them," Sabrina said, wondering if it was a good thing or a bad thing. Soon, the girls stepped into a clearing. In the center was a pile of junk. An old refrigerator, a couple of burned-out microwaves, some abandoned teddy bears, and a broken toilet had been assembled into a massive chair. Sitting on the junk "throne" was a boy with a mop of blond hair that was tussled and dirty. He wore a pair of baggy blue jeans and a green hooded sweatshirt in desperate need of a washing, and in his hand he held a small sword. But most interesting was the golden crown that rested on his head.

"Pixies," he called to the little lights. "What have you found?"

The little lights erupted into a loud buzzing.

"Spies, you say?" the boy asked. "Well, what do we do with spies?"

There was more buzzing in response, and a wicked grin appeared on the boy's face.

"That's correct." He laughed. "We drown them!"

6

When the girls protested their kidnapping, the army of pixies surrounded them and delivered several stings. Nursing their wounds, the girls were forced to follow the odd boy farther into the woods.

"Where are you taking us?" Sabrina asked, but the boy just laughed.

Soon, they came to the end of the forest, where a tall fence blocked their way. Built into the fence was a door, and the boy pushed it open. The girls stepped through and found themselves standing in front of a tarp-covered swimming pool in the backyard of a two-story suburban-style house. Some pixies swirled around the tarp and lifted it off the pool, while others zipped off and returned with a rope. They stung

Sabrina's arms relentlessly until she put them behind her back, and then they tied the rope around her wrists.

The boy stuck the tip of his sword into Sabrina's back. He forced her onto the diving board. "You've made a terrible mistake, spy!" he shouted.

"We're not spies!" Sabrina exclaimed.

"Tell it to the fish!" the boy hollered, causing the little lights to make a tittering noise that sounded like laughter. Sabrina looked down at the pool and wondered how deep the water was. There was a diving board, so it had to be deep, and with her arms tied behind her she'd certainly drown if the icy water didn't freeze her to death first. She tugged at the ropes, but each pull just tightened them around her wrists.

"So, spy, would you like to repent your crimes before you meet your watery doom?" the boy asked.

"What crimes?" Sabrina cried, and then took a deep breath, certain he would push her in. But after several moments, nothing happened.

"The crime of trying to steal the old lady away from me," the mop-topped boy declared.

"Granny?" Daphne asked from the side of the pool.

"The one they call Relda Grimm."

"Relda Grimm is our *grandmother* and we're not trying to steal her. We're trying to save her!" Sabrina shouted.

"Save her?" the boy asked suspiciously. "Save her from what?"

"A giant," the two girls called out together.

Sabrina could sense their captor's confusion. She turned and found him talking to several of the little lights that hovered around his head.

"Well, of course it makes a difference," the boy replied, annoyed.

"We're trying to get home. We need to save her before it's too late," Daphne pleaded.

The boy groaned and quickly untied Sabrina's wrists. "Where did this happen?" he asked. "How big was the giant?"

But Sabrina didn't answer. Instead, she spun around, grabbed the boy by the shoulders, and heaved him into the pool, sending a splash of water and soggy dead leaves high into the air. The sword had slipped from the boy's hand as he fell, and with nimble fingers, Sabrina caught it. She leaped to safety on the side of the pool and waved the sword threateningly at the pixies.

"You're going to let us walk out of here," she demanded. There was no movement at first, but then they flew around the pool, making a laughing sound, as if they were chuckling at their leader's misfortune. Sabrina stood dumbfounded, unsure of what to do next.

A geyser of water shot high into the air, with the soaked boy riding its crest. When the water crashed back into the pool, the boy stayed aloft, several feet above Sabrina. Two huge wings had come out of his back and were flapping loudly. Oddly enough, the boy was laughing.

"You think this is funny?" Sabrina exploded. She began making jabs at the boy, who flew effortlessly away from her thrusts. "A kid and a bunch of flying cockroaches kidnapping girls and threatening to kill them? That's how you losers have fun?"

"Aww, we wouldn't have killed you. We were just fooling," the boy said.

"Well, if you're finished with your stupid, psychotic games, my sister and I have to rescue our grandmother," Sabrina declared. She took Daphne's hand and turned to leave. Elvis joined them, but Sabrina shot him an angry look. The dog had spent the entire episode sitting lazily by the pool as if nothing peculiar were happening. The Great Dane caught her eye and whined.

"You've only been in this town for two days and you've already lost the old lady," the boy said bitterly, as he floated into the girls' path.

"We didn't lose her, she was taken by a monster as big as a mountain," Sabrina argued.

"Well, if you've come looking for help, you've come to the wrong place," the boy crowed. "Rescuing old ladies is a job for a hero! I'm a villain of the worst kind."

"Good! We don't want your help!" Sabrina said angrily, tossing the boy's sword aside.

"I thought Peter Pan was one of the good guys," Daphne added.

The boy's face turned so red Sabrina thought his head might explode. "Peter Pan? I'm not Peter Pan! I'm Puck!"

"Who's Puck?" Daphne asked.

"Who's Puck?" the boy cried. "I'm the most famous Everafter in this town. My exploits are known around the world!"

"I've never heard of you," Sabrina replied. She spun around and started walking through the yard to the street, with her sister and Elvis following. After only a couple of steps, the boy was hovering in front of them again.

"You've never heard of the Trickster King?" Puck asked, shocked.

The girls shook their heads.

"The Prince of Fairies? Robin Goodfellow? The Imp?"

"Do you work for Santa?" Daphne asked.

"I'm a fairy, not an elf!" Puck roared. "You really don't

know who I am! Doesn't anyone read the classics anymore? Dozens of writers have warned the world about me. I'm in the most famous of all of William Shakespeare's plays."

"I don't remember any Puck in *Romeo and Juliet*," Sabrina muttered, feeling a little amused at how the boy was reacting to his non-celebrity.

"Besides *Romeo and Juliet*!" Puck shouted. "I'm the star of *A Midsummer Night's Dream*!"

"Congratulations," Sabrina said flatly. "Never read it."

Puck floated down to the ground. His wings disappeared and he spun around on his heel, transforming into a big shaggy dog. Elvis growled at the sight of him, but Puck didn't attack. Instead, he shook himself all over, spraying the girls with water. When he was finished, he morphed back into a boy.

As she wiped the water off her face, Sabrina was tempted to give the weird boy another piece of her mind, but they had wasted enough time with this "Puck." She took Daphne's hand in hers once more, and together they marched down the deserted street.

"I'm afraid the old lady is a goner!" Puck taunted. "You'll get no help from me. Like I said, I'm a villain."

"Fine!" Sabrina shouted back.

"Fine!"

Daphne turned on the boy. "You sent those pixies to attack us last night, didn't you?"

"Just a little fun," Puck replied.

"That wasn't very nice." The little girl gave him her best angry look and then turned to join her sister.

"I'm a lot of things, but nice isn't one of them," the boy called after them.

"Maybe we should team up with him? He could fly over the forest and spot the giant," Daphne suggested to Sabrina.

"Daphne, you saw what a lunatic he is. I don't want him to ruin whatever slim chance we might have."

• • •

The path to the front door of Granny Relda's cottage seemed like a walk up a mountain, and by the time they arrived at the house Sabrina was nearly asleep standing up. She took out Granny's key ring and felt the weight of a hundred keys jingling in her hand, singing their mysteries.

By the time all the locks were open, it seemed as if hours had passed. Elvis was asleep and drooling on the sidewalk, swinging his thick legs back and forth as he dreamed.

As Sabrina unlocked the final lock, she turned to her sister and smiled. "That's all of them." She twisted the knob and leaned into the door. Unfortunately, the door didn't swing open. In fact, it didn't budge at all.

"What's wrong?" Daphne said, sitting up. She had been resting on the ground with her head on Elvis's warm belly.

"It's jammed," Sabrina said, pushing her shoulder against the big door to force it open.

Daphne got up and walked over. "Are you sure you unlocked them all?" she said. Sabrina fumed. If she knew anything, it was how to unlock a door. They'd escaped from a dozen foster homes in the last year and a half. Locks were not Sabrina's problem. She took the cold doorknob in her hand and turned it, proving that she had unlocked it. She pushed hard but still nothing happened.

"Well, it's not opening. Maybe the back door," she said, preparing to circle the house.

"You've forgotten the secret," a familiar voice commented. Puck floated to the ground, his huge wings disappearing just as he landed.

"What do you want?" Sabrina demanded.

"I did a flyby, all the way up into the mountains. I found some tracks, but no giant," Puck said. "I sent some pixies to keep searching without me."

Sabrina turned the doorknob angrily, hoping the door would suddenly open so she could laugh as she slammed it in Puck's face. But again, nothing happened.

"You have to tell the house you are home." Puck sighed.

"Of course!" Daphne knocked on the door three times. "We're home," she said, repeating the same words the girls had heard Granny Relda say each time they had entered the house, and turning the doorknob. The door finally swung open.

"How did you know that?" Daphne asked Puck.

"The old lady and I are close. She tells me everything."

Elvis immediately leaped to his feet and trotted into the house, nearly knocking over the girls on his way to the kitchen. The girls followed, and Puck pushed his way in as well, closing the door behind him.

"Now, I know I'm one of the bad guys," the boy said, tossing himself into the fluffy recliner in the living room. "But the old lady does provide me with a meal from time to time. Not that I feel any loyalty, but if she were to get eaten by a giant, my free lunches would disappear. So, we should probably get started."

"We? What do you mean *we*?" Sabrina cried.

"Of course, you two will have to keep this to yourselves," the boy continued, ignoring Sabrina. "I do have a reputation as the worst of the worst. If word got out that the Trickster was helping the heroes . . . well, it would be scandalous."

The girls stared at each other, dumbfounded.

"First things first. I want you two to prepare a hearty meal so that I will have plenty of energy to kill the giant," Puck instructed.

"You've got to be kidding," Sabrina groaned.

"The old lady always makes lunch when a mystery is afoot. I know it's not the most glamorous work, but I think you two are best suited for domestic tasks."

"What does *domestic tasks* mean?" Daphne asked.

"The way he means it is *women's work*," her sister replied.

Daphne snarled at the boy.

"Besides, as your leader I need to save my energy for the battle," Puck insisted.

Sabrina's temper boiled over. "Leader! No one made you leader. No one even said they wanted your help!"

"You may not want it, but you need it," the boy shouted back. "The two of you can't even get into your own house. Do you think you'll strike fear into a giant?"

"Maybe if you two keep shouting, the giant will come to us," Daphne said.

Sabrina and Puck stared angrily at each other for a long moment.

"Who's hungry?" Daphne said. "I'm going to go do some domestic tasks for myself."

Sabrina was too hungry to fight any longer. Eating would clear her head. The three children raided the refrigerator and dug through the breadbox, grabbing anything and everything they thought they could eat. Puck seemed to share Daphne's big appetite; both of their plates were heaped with odd-colored food. The two also ate the same way—like hungry pigs, scarfing down anything that came close to their mouths. They were both working on seconds by the time Sabrina had made two Swiss cheese sandwiches and found what she hoped was just a weirdly colored apple.

"So, what's with the crown?" Daphne asked.

Puck's eyes grew wide. "I'm the Prince of Fairies. Emperor of Pixies, Brownies, Hobgoblins, Elves, and Gnomes. King of Tricksters and Prank-Players, spiritual leader to juvenile delinquents, layabouts, and bad apples."

The little girl stared at the boy with confusion in her face.

"I'm royalty!" Puck declared.

"So where's your kingdom?" Sabrina asked snidely.

"You're in it!" he snapped. "The forest and the trees are my kingdom. I sleep under the stars. The sky is my royal blanket."

"That explains the smell," Sabrina muttered.

The Trickster King ignored her comment and munched hungrily, tossing apple cores and whatever he couldn't eat onto the floor. A turkey bone soared from his hand and landed on a nearby windowsill.

"Puck, can I ask you a question?" Daphne said.

"You bet."

"If you knew Shakespeare, why do you look like you're only eleven years old?"

This was something Sabrina had been wondering about as well. Granny's explanation that magic kept the Everafters alive just wasn't making sense. Mayor Charming and Mr. Seven had to be hundreds of years old, yet they looked as if they hadn't aged at all.

"Ah, that's the upside of being an Everafter," Puck said. "You only get as old as you want to be. Some decided to age a little so that they could get jobs and junk like that."

"Then why didn't you?" Sabrina asked.

Puck shrugged. "Never crossed my mind. I plan on staying a boy until the sun burns out."

Sabrina thought that she'd like to see him running around in the dark as the earth froze over. She bit into her sandwich, only to discover that the Swiss cheese tasted more like hard applesauce.

"So, tell me what happened with the giant," said Puck.

While Sabrina ate, Daphne told the boy the whole sordid mess. She told him about the farmhouse that had been stepped on by the giant and how Mayor Charming had demanded that Granny Relda give up her detective work. How the farmer had spoken to a man named Mr. Englishman, and how a witch had erased the farmer's memory. She told about the gang of thugs that had attacked them outside of the hospital, and how, when they had followed the gang back to a cabin, they had spotted Charming again. Then she told him about the giant's attack, how he had killed the thugs, and how he had snatched up Granny and Mr. Canis.

Sabrina got up from her chair and went into the living room, where she stood in front of one of the many bookshelves.

"Books on giants . . . where would they be?" she said to herself. Puck and Daphne got up to join her, and together they scanned the bookcases.

"Look!" Daphne said.

Sabrina looked closely at the shelves Daphne was pointing to. They seemed to hold a collection of diaries. She took one down and read the title: *Fairy-Tale Accounts 1942–1965, by Edwin Alvin Grimm.*

"There's a book here for everyone in our family, I guess, including this one," said Daphne as she pulled one from the shelf and handed it to her sister. Sabrina almost dropped it when she eyed the title: *Fairy-Tale Accounts by Henry Grimm*. It was a book written by their father! She flipped through it, recognizing her dad's neat handwriting. She ran a finger along the short circles his words made, tracing his hand's movement from when he had put the words on paper. She turned more pages, feeling more of him in his words—not bothering to read, just taking comfort in knowing that he had once held the book.

"Let me see," Daphne said as she snatched the book from her sister's hands.

"You're wasting your time with these stupid books. I'm the smartest person I know and I've never read a book in my life. We should all be out looking," Puck said.

"If you want to go, there's nothing keeping you here," Sabrina said as she snatched her father's book back from Daphne. The two girls rushed to the dining room table and hovered over the slightly dusty journal. They flipped to the first page. A color photograph of Mayor Charming, dressed in royal gowns of purple-and-white silk, stared back at them. He wore a sapphire-and-diamond crown and a dazzling ruby ring on each finger. He smiled smugly, as if he thought very highly of himself.

Elvis sauntered into the room and licked Sabrina's hand. He spied Charming's picture and growled.

"Don't worry, Elvis! He can't get us now," Daphne said. Sabrina read aloud what her father had written.

July—Today we had another encounter with Charming. Mom and Dad discovered that he was attempting to buy a thousand acres of land on the eastern border of the town known as Old McDonald's farm. Where he got the money for such a big purchase came into question and Dad, of course, accused him of using his witches to conjure up phony cash. Charming huffed and demanded an apology. When Dad refused, the two of them got into a fistfight, which Charming got the worst of. (Dad has one heck of a left hook! KA-POW!) But the biggest surprise was Charming's freak-out. He swore he'd turn Ferryport Landing into his kingdom again, and he looked forward to the day when he could personally drive a bulldozer through our house.

"He's rebuilding his kingdom," Sabrina said as she flipped to the next page. There she found more interesting facts. "It's all in here. Listen to this."

December—Charming had given up the most when he

moved to America. He was forced to sell his castle, his horses, and everything he owned. One of the three ships Wilhelm had hired for the Atlantic crossing was used primarily to haul Charming's enormous fortune. The ship hit a sandbar off the coast of Maryland and sank, taking Charming's wealth to the bottom of the ocean. When he got to Ferryport Landing (changed from Fairyport Landing in 1910), he blew what was left on one bad investment after another: a failed diamond mine partnership with the seven dwarfs, a wholesale carpet company poorly managed by his business partner, Ali Baba, and a company that went bankrupt manufacturing something called a laser disc player. Being mayor doesn't pay much, and Dad believes that Charming runs a bunch of financial scams, both illegal and magical, just to keep the electricity on at the mayoral estate. That was until he came up with the greatest and most recent scam: the Ferryport Landing Fundraising Ball. Once a year, Charming invites the Everafter community to the mansion, and every year they throw money at him, trying to win his support for whatever political cause they have. The money obviously goes straight into the prince's pocket. I'd bet any-

thing that Charming is storing most of the money so that he can buy up the whole town and run it like his old kingdom.

"But what's that got to do with giants? And if he wanted to buy the farm, why did he send that Mr. Englishman to do the work?" Daphne asked.

"I believe that Mr. Englishman and Mayor Charming are the same person. Charming does have an English accent. He could have worn a disguise so Mr. Applebee wouldn't recognize him as the mayor," Sabrina said.

"I bet you're right!" her sister said.

"But where does the giant come in?" Sabrina wondered aloud.

"In the old days, giants and people used to work together all the time," Puck said, stealing the purple apple from Sabrina's plate and chomping on it.

"They did?"

"Oh yeah, giants are pretty dumb," the boy said. "From what I hear you can pretty much talk them into anything."

"He's right." Daphne was poring over a large book entitled *Anatomy of a Giant*. "I don't know what this word is," she said.

"How is it spelled?"

"A-L-L-I-A-N-C-E-S."

"It's *alliances*; it means to team up or join a group," Sabrina explained.

"It says that in olden days people used to form all-all . . ."

"Alliances."

". . . alliances with giants to destroy their enemies. People found that giants were very dumb and could be easily tricked."

"Charming's using the giant to scare people off their land. Anyone that won't sell gets squashed!" Sabrina cried.

"But you said he used Glinda to erase the farmer's mind, right?" Puck interrupted.

"Yes."

"Well, why would he do that? Why would he want the farmer to forget to be afraid?"

"And don't forget the lens cap," Daphne added. "If he were trying to scare them off, why would he want to videotape it? I don't think I'd want any proof of what I'd done if it were me."

Sabrina didn't have any more answers.

"Let me finish," her sister said, looking down at the book. "It also says that rarely do these all-all . . ."

"Alliances."

"Yeah, it says they usually backfire. In most cases, the human was eaten by the giant or dragged off to the giant kingdom to be a slave. There's a story here about a giant kidnapping a princess for an evil baron, and before the baron could collect a ransom from her family, the giant ate her," Daphne said quietly. "It says the townspeople used hound dogs to track down the giant because giants have a strong smell. When they caught him, he nearly killed the entire town before they could bring him down."

The girls spent a moment looking into each other's worried eyes. What if the giant had eaten Granny and Mr. Canis? What if he was eating them as they wasted time doing research?

"It says when giants got out of hand, the townspeople sent a hero to kill the giant for them," Daphne read. "His name was Jack and in his prime, he killed more than ten giants, stole treasure from the giant kingdom, and was world-famous."

Sabrina turned her attention back to her father's journal. She flipped through more of its pages until she found an envelope stuffed inside.

"What's this?" she wondered aloud.

Daphne got up from her chair and walked around the table to look.

"It says *To Sabrina, Daphne, and Puck. From Granny Relda,*" Sabrina said.

"See! I told you I knew her!" Puck cried.

"Read it," Daphne begged.

Sabrina tore open the letter and began to read.

Lieblings,

If you're reading this, then one of my investigations has not turned out the way I had hoped. I don't want you to worry, as I am very experienced with all kinds of things and can take care of myself, and I know a little kung fu. If for some reason I am unable to be there and you need my help, you should take my keys and enter the room you have been forbidden to enter. All the answers you need will be staring you in the face.

Love, Granny Relda

P.S. Don't give Elvis any sausage. It makes him gassy.

"She wants us to go into the room?" Puck said in amazement. "I've been trying to get in there since the day she told me it was off-limits!"

"Cool! That's where she got that giant-detector she used at the farm," Daphne cried. "I bet the place is filled to the ceiling with stuff we can use to rescue them!"

"Staring us in the face? What does that mean?" Sabrina said, but before she knew it, her little sister was halfway up the stairs with the key ring in her hand.

"Wait up!" Sabrina shouted, taking the stairs two at a time. By the time she got to the top, Daphne was already trying keys.

"I bet she's got a shrink-ray in here. We'll shrink him down to the size of an ant and stomp on him," the younger girl said.

"Hurry," Sabrina said.

Puck flew up the stairs and grabbed the keys out of Daphne's hands.

"Royalty first, peasant."

"She gave these keys to us," Sabrina snapped, snatching the keys from him.

"A set of keys you have no idea how to use!" Puck shouted, taking them back.

"Puck, give me those keys!"

"No!"

"Listen Puck, don't make me do something you're going to regret."

"I've fought tougher guys than you, Grimm. Though most of them had better-smelling breath!"

"WHAT IS GOING ON OUT THERE?" a voice suddenly boomed from behind the door. It startled them all so much that they fell backward onto the floor.

"Did you hear that?" Daphne whispered.

"Everyone heard that," Sabrina and Puck replied.

"KNOCK OFF THAT RACKET RIGHT NOW!" the voice shouted angrily.

"Maybe it's the sheriff? Maybe he got into the house some-how?" Daphne whispered.

"Hamstead would have just come down and grabbed us," her sister said. "Besides, Elvis isn't freaking out."

"Then who is it?" Puck said.

"Granny locks that door for a reason. If there's someone in that room, Granny doesn't want them going anywhere. They might be dangerous," Sabrina warned.

"I'm not afraid!" the boy cried.

"I have an idea," Daphne said. She took Puck and Sabrina's hands and led them back down the stairs and into the kitchen.

• • •

Within minutes, the girls and Puck were standing at the bottom of the stairs again. Each was wearing a metal spaghetti strainer as a mighty battle helmet. Daphne wore an ancient washing board on her chest and had duct-taped huge metal spoons to each kneecap as protection from unfair kicks. She held a frying pan as her weapon. Sabrina had a pressure cooker lid taped to her behind. She held a wok pan for a shield and a rolling pin for a club. She swung it, preparing to whack whomever might be on the other side of the door. Puck had his trusty sword in one hand and a car-rot peeler in the other. He'd found a couple of cookie pans to tape to his chest and back, and his feet were encased in oven mitts.

The big dog stood behind them with an odd, confused expression.

"We should send Elvis up first," Sabrina said.

"Good idea," Daphne replied.

Sabrina turned to the Great Dane. "Elvis, there's someone upstairs. Go get him!"

Elvis sat down on his hind legs and used his back paw to scratch his neck. If he understood the order, he wasn't letting on. Discouraged, Sabrina turned back to her sister and Puck. "We'll go together and sneak up on him."

They nodded in agreement, and all three took the first step up the stairs. Their "armor" clanged and knocked around, causing a tremendous racket. By the time they got to the top of the steps, Sabrina realized that a sneak attack was probably no longer realistic, so she went with plan B.

"Whoever is up here better leave, 'cause we're armed to the teeth. I wouldn't want to be you when we find you!" Sabrina shouted. Her threat was met with silence.

"Maybe he's gone," Daphne said hopefully.

"I say we bust the door down and skin him alive," Puck said loudly.

"There's going to be no skinning of anyone," Sabrina said as she fumbled in her pocket and pulled out the key ring. She started the tedious work of finding the right key, and soon one went in the lock and clicked.

"Just stay together and, most of all, stay calm. If we don't panic, we can take this guy ourselves," Sabrina said.

"On three," Daphne whispered, giving her frying pan a practice swing.

"ONE, TWO, THREE!" Sabrina screamed, pushing the door open and rushing into the room. The trio swung their weapons frantically, slashing at whatever enemy dared to face their deadly kitchen utensils. After several minutes, and zero deadly hits, Sabrina stopped and looked around the room. In the moonlight from the single window, she could see it was empty, except for a wood-framed, full-length mirror that hung on a wall.

Puck, who was lying on the floor laughing hysterically, roared, "STAY CALM, YOU SAY?"

"Where did he go?" Daphne said, as she peered behind the door and found no one.

"Maybe we imagined it," Sabrina said, scowling at the boy's laughter. "C'mon, let's get back to work."

She turned to leave, but Daphne said, "Granny's note said that all the answers we need would stare us in the face." She pointed at the mirror.

"It's just a mirror," her sister argued.

"It can't hurt to take a look!" Puck said, and trotted over to it. Sabrina switched on the room light and reluctantly joined him, followed by Daphne, and together they looked at their reflection.

"I think I see something," Daphne said.

"What? What is it?" Sabrina said.

"A booger. It's in your nose." The little girl laughed. "Gotcha, again!"

Puck laughed so hard he snorted, but then saw Sabrina staring and stopped abruptly.

"WHO ARE YOU?" a loud voice suddenly bellowed from within the mirror. Sabrina looked into its reflection and felt the hairs on the back of her neck stand on end. A face was staring out at her but it was not her own. Floating without a body, the face was that of a man with a bald head and thick, angular features. He stared at the children with eyes like blue flames flickering a mixture of rage and disgust, as if the children were rodents found munching on the turkey during Christmas dinner. Terrified, the children ran back toward the door, but a blue ray shot from the mirror, hit the door, and slammed it shut, trapping them inside.

"WHO ARE YOU?" the head bellowed. "TELL ME NOW OR I WILL KILL YOU WHERE YOU STAND!"

7

’d like to see you try," Puck said defiantly.

A six-foot-high circle of fire snaked around the group, trapping them inside. The flames licked at the pots and pans the children had hoped would act as armor, and managed to scorch Sabrina's hand. She pulled it close to her and rubbed the painful burn.

"I WILL ROAST THE FLESH FROM YOUR BONES!" the face threatened. Dark gray clouds framed the bulbous head in a violent thunderstorm. Lightning crackled around the face, exploding in light and sound with every twitch of its eyebrows. "Who dares to invade my sanctuary?"

Sabrina pulled Daphne close to her, while Puck stepped between them and the closest flame, thrusting his little sword into the wall of fire. "We're not invaders! We live here!" he shouted over the roaring fire.

The face cocked an eyebrow and looked at them sternly.

"You're the grandchildren?"

"Yes! Sabrina and Daphne!" Sabrina shouted.

"And Puck!" Puck chimed in.

Suddenly, the fire puttered out, as if someone had turned off a stove.

"Oh, thank goodness. I thought carnival folk had broken into the house," the head cried. "You can hardly blame me, three kids break into my room and they're dressed like escaped inmates from the Ferryport Landing Asylum. You may not have heard, but the whole circus-clown-meets-crazy-street-vagrant-look is so over."

Sabrina looked down at her outfit: the torn, bright-blue pants, the orange sweatshirt with the monkey, the pressure-cooker lid strapped to her behind. Her face flushed with embarrassment as she took off her spaghetti-strainer helmet.

"What are you?" Sabrina asked, regaining her composure.

"I'm not a what, I'm a who!" the face in the mirror croaked, looking deeply insulted.

"Then who are you?" Sabrina said impatiently.

"Tsk, tsk, tsk, why I'm the seer of seers, the visionary of

visionaries, the man who puts the fun in your reflection," he replied with a dramatic flourish.

Sabrina looked at her sister for help. Daphne had read more fairy tales than Sabrina, but the little girl returned her sister's glance with a dumbfounded shrug. The face in the mirror frowned, sensing that the girls were far from star-struck and, in fact, had no idea who he was.

"I'm the magic mirror!" the face snapped.

"We could have guessed you were a magic mirror," Puck muttered.

"Not *a* magic mirror! *The* magic mirror! 'Mirror, mirror, on the wall'?"

"From 'Snow White'?" Daphne asked.

"Is there another?" The face growled. "You can call me *Mirror*. Your grandma told me you were coming from New York City, though she didn't tell me she was giving you a set of keys."

"She didn't. Granny threw hers to us before she was carried off by a giant," Daphne explained.

Mirror's eyes grew wide with astonishment.

"Well, there's a sentence you don't hear every day." He chuckled. "And I suppose you are in the midst of a rescue plan?"

"They are," Puck said defensively. "I'm a villain."

"So, let's hear this thrilling plan," said Mirror.

"We haven't got all the details worked out yet," Sabrina said, trying to make herself sound older and more mature.

"You don't have a plan!" Mirror exclaimed.

"We're still working on it," Sabrina muttered. "We thought there might be something up here that could help us."

"You're just like Henry." Mirror sighed. "Ready to jump headfirst into an adventure, hoping he'd come up with a plan along the way."

The girl was shocked. *Headfirst* didn't sound like her dad at all. *My dad read the labels on cans of food before everyone could eat,* she thought.

"You knew our father?" Daphne exclaimed.

"Knew him? I was Henry's babysitter most of the time. I saw him off to the prom. I was even invited to your parents' wedding. They propped me up on my own seat. I am a member of this family, after all."

"Sorry, we didn't mean to offend you," the little girl said. "So if you're *the* magic mirror, what do you do?"

"I can show you anything you want to see; all you have to do is ask," Mirror said proudly.

"What are you talking about?" Sabrina asked with growing impatience. All this chatter was keeping them from acting. Who knew what that monster was doing to Granny and Mr. Canis.

"You got a question. I got an answer," the face bragged. "All you got to do is ask."

"Are Granny Relda and Mr. Canis still alive?" Daphne asked.

"Sorry, kiddo, that's not how it works. You have to ask me the right way."

"What's the right way?" Sabrina demanded.

"Well, if you're going to be cranky, then just forget it!" Mirror said. He jutted out his lower lip.

Puck swung his carrot peeler menacingly at the face, then realized what he was doing, and flashed his little sword. "Listen, Mirror, you tell us what we want to know or you're going to find yourself cracked and broken all over the floor!"

"You wouldn't dare!"

"Just see if I wouldn't!"

Daphne tugged on Puck's arm. Acting as the diplomat for the group, she apologized to Mirror. "We're just very eager to find our granny and Mr. Canis, and we don't understand what you are saying."

The face's expression changed to a huge smile. "Apology accepted. Now, like I was going to say before I was so rudely interrupted," he said as he eyed Sabrina disapprovingly, "you have to ask your questions in a special way to activate the magic. You have to . . ."

"Rhyme them!" Daphne interrupted with a happy cry.

"Bingo!"

The little girl turned to the other two. "We have to rhyme the question. Like, mirror, mirror, on the wall, who's the fairest of them all?"

A blue mist filled the mirror's surface and the face faded away, only to be replaced with the image of the most beautiful woman Sabrina had ever seen. She had black hair like Daphne's, and flawless, porcelain skin. She was standing in front of a class-room, teaching. Every boy in the class stared at her like a lovesick puppy, and there was a stack of apples on her desk.

"That would still be the lovely Snow White," Mirror said.

Just then, all the students got up from their seats and exited the room. When Snow White was finally alone, she tossed the apples into a garbage can and slid it under her desk.

"OK, how about this?" Sabrina said. "Mirror, mirror in a bee-hive, is Granny Relda still alive?"

The man in the mirror's face reappeared and he was frown-ing. "In a beehive?"

"All you said was it had to rhyme. You didn't say it had to make sense."

"Very well," said the face, and the blue mist returned. "Your grandmother is alive and well, for now."

"Where is she?" Daphne asked.

"Uh-uh. One question at a time, and that one didn't rhyme, anyway."

"Mirror, mirror we're just kids, can you show us where our grandma is?" Puck chimed in.

"Sorry, that doesn't technically rhyme," Mirror argued.

"It's close enough!" the children shouted.

Mirror frowned but misted over and, suddenly, Granny and Mr. Canis appeared in the reflection. They were climbing on top of their car, which was enclosed in what could only be described as a giant bag. Mr. Canis pulled the fabric down and the two of them looked over the edge. They were still in the giant's shirt pocket.

"They're alive." Daphne sighed with relief as the image zoomed out to show the giant. The ugly brute was asleep, lounging against a huge rock outcropping.

"He's up in the mountains," Puck said.

"You've probably tossed kids off of that very cliff," Sabrina commented.

"A few," Puck agreed, making Sabrina wonder if he was serious. "Look at the size of that beast. I'm going to need a bigger sword."

"We'll come with you," Daphne said.

"You aren't going anywhere," the boy replied. "The last thing

I need is a couple of girls bawling while I fight the giant. You two are staying here."

"What are we supposed to do while that's happening?" Sabrina asked.

"Women's work. You can clean up that mess in the dining room."

"Women's work!" the girls cried.

"Oh, you've said it now," Mirror warned Puck.

"If anyone's going up there, it's me!" Sabrina declared. "I can't expect some smelly kid who lives in the woods to save my grandmother. You couldn't even push me into a pool. You stay here and keep an eye on Daphne!" she commanded.

"'Keep an eye on Daphne?'" Daphne repeated indignantly. "I'm not staying here! She's my granny, too!"

"What you need is someone who has had experience with giants," Mirror interrupted.

"What we need is someone who can kill a giant," Sabrina said.

"Like the Big Bad Wolf," Daphne suggested.

"No, tougher than that."

"I'll do it!" Puck said angrily. It was obvious that the boy was offended at their lack of respect for his fighting skills.

"Mirror, mirror, what can we do, to rescue Granny from you know who?" Sabrina asked.

The mirror misted over once again, and this time when it cleared the children saw a man sitting in a jail cell. He had a boyish face with spiky blond hair and big eyes. He was lying lazily on a thin, ratty cot. He got up, walked over to a small window, looked out, pulled on the bars in a hopeless effort to free himself, and when he found them unbendable, scowled and returned to his dingy bed.

"You need the help of Jack the Giant Killer," Mirror said, as his face returned to the reflection.

"Jack the Giant Killer?" Sabrina asked.

"'Jack and the Beanstalk,'" Daphne explained. "He's the same guy."

"That guy sitting in jail has killed giants? I'm not impressed," Puck said, continuing his sulk.

"Granny said he was down on his luck," Sabrina said. "But I didn't think she meant *that* down. I guess it'll be easy to find him now."

"We passed the jailhouse on the way to the hospital," her sister pointed out.

"We do not need Jack," Puck fumed.

Suddenly, Elvis barked an angry warning from downstairs. It was followed by several loud knocks on the front door.

"Who's that?" Sabrina whispered.

"Mirror, mirror, one question more, who's that knocking on our door?" Daphne asked.

"Now you're getting the hang of it!" Mirror said as his face misted over. Outside of the house, two police cars were parked in the driveway. "It seems as if the local authorities have arrived."

"Hamstead's here," Sabrina said as the image revealed the fat sheriff hoisting up a new pair of pants in between angry knocks on the front door. An equally plump deputy with a thick handlebar moustache gestured for Hamstead to walk around the house, and together they did, revealing pink curly tails sticking out of the backs of their beige slacks.

"He brought friends," Daphne said as the image blurred, then reappeared from another angle. Another equally rotund deputy with a shock of bright, white hair tucked under his hat walked along the side of the house, trying to find an open window. When he got to the dining room window, he placed his face against it to peer in, only to fall over backward when Elvis lunged at him from the other side. The terrified deputy transformed into a pig, but changed back once he calmed down.

"Ferryport's finest, Sheriff Hamstead and his dim-witted deputies, Swineheart and Boarman," said Mirror.

"I can't believe the Three Little Pigs are working for the bad guy." Daphne sighed.

"I can't believe anyone still calls them the three *little* pigs." Mirror tittered. "That trio has been tipping the scales for as long as I can remember."

"Look at them, they're no match for us. Why, I could take the three of them by myself," Puck said so excitedly that his wings appeared and he flew off the floor. Sabrina pulled him back down by his sweatshirt sleeve.

"Ladies, this is the police. Open the door," the sheriff demanded through a megaphone in a tinny, amplified voice. "We can stay out here all night if we have to."

"What do we do?" Daphne asked.

"Nothing. They can't get in here," Puck replied.

"But we can't get out. We're trapped," Sabrina said, worried.

"What is this nonsense I'm hearing from you?" Mirror said. "You two are Grimms. Performing the impossible is what you do. Do you think your family could have survived this long with ogres and monsters running around if they couldn't find a way out of their own house?"

"OK, you're so smart, *you* tell us what to do," Sabrina snapped. "We came up here because we're looking for some help. Now there are cops outside who want to arrest us and, worse, who are keeping us trapped in here so we can't get out and save our grandmother and her best friend, who have been kidnapped by a giant!"

"You're asking for my help?"

"Yes! Do we have to rhyme it, too?"

"Not at all. Ask, my little wardrobe-challenged friends, and you shall receive," the face said. "I need your keys."

"What? Why?" Sabrina asked.

"Do you want some help or not? Give me the keys." The reflection warped, and a portion of the mirror's surface grew outward as if someone were blowing a bubble from the other side. It pushed out farther and farther, causing the reflection to shimmer and ripple until a hand was thrust through. Even Puck seemed unsettled by what he was seeing.

"C'mon, girl, I don't have all night," Mirror complained.

Sabrina put the keys into the hand and it disappeared into the bubble.

"I'll be right back," the face said as it vanished and the surface of the mirror flattened, returning to normal. After several moments, the face reappeared.

"I've got just the thing for you," Mirror said with a smile. Again, the surface of the glass rippled, and this time a dusty, rolled-up carpet came through. Once it had completely broken the surface, the carpet fell to the ground, where it unrolled before them.

Dazzling burgundy and gold threads formed an intricate pattern of symbols: moons, stars, flowers, sickles, and triangles, which seemed to shimmer as if they were woven from precious metal. Golden roped tassels hung from the carpet's edges. Sabrina thought it was the most beautiful rug she had ever seen.

"What's this?" Daphne said, stepping on the carpet. Suddenly it lifted off the floor and hovered in the air. The movement was so quick that Daphne fell onto her backside. "It flies!"

"Just a little thing your grandpa picked up during a trip to the Middle East. Maybe you've heard of Aladdin?" Mirror said proudly. "This is his flying carpet. Thought it might be the best thing for your little rescue mission. Just tell it the location of where you want to go and it'll get you there. Even if you don't know how to get there yourself."

"How do I make it go down?" Daphne asked, giggling, but no sooner had the question left her lips than the carpet fell to the ground, causing Daphne's "armor" to clang on the floor.

"When you're finished with it, I expect you to return it," said Mirror sternly as Granny's keys came back through the surface and fell to the ground. Sabrina picked them up.

"But how are we going to get out of the house?" Sabrina asked.

"Listen, cowgirl, I can't do it all for you. From what I hear, you're quite the expert at being sneaky. I suggest you cause a diversion," Mirror said.

"With what?"

"I don't know. What could possibly distract three pigs enough so that you could get away?"

Sabrina thought for a moment and then grinned. "I know exactly what to do."

• • •

The girls carried the carpet down the stairs and into the kitchen, where they laid it on the floor. They removed their "armor," and Sabrina opened the refrigerator. Granny's odd and abundant cooking filled the shelves. It would take an army to eat it all. The girls pulled out pies, cakes, oddly colored fruits, and several things Sabrina couldn't identify, and tossed them onto the carpet. Elvis sat by, drooling with hunger, obviously wondering what they were doing.

"Is this enough?" Daphne asked.

"I hope so," Sabrina answered. "Carpet, up!"

The carpet rose to her waist and hovered next to her. "Come!" she commanded, and the carpet followed them as they walked to the front door.

Daphne peeked out the window. "They're sitting on the hoods of their squad cars," she said. "Puck, are you ready?"

The boy entered the foyer. He had finished taking off the last of his own kitchen gear and now pulled a small flute from his sweatshirt pocket.

"You don't have to ask the Trickster King if he is ready," he said arrogantly.

"I'm ready," Daphne said to Sabrina. "But are you sure about this? The police are after us. Do you think going to the jailhouse is the smartest thing?"

"I don't see any other way," Sabrina said as she opened up the front door. Hamstead scrambled off the car hood.

"Finally, you two have come to your senses," he said as he and his deputies approached the house.

Sabrina looked down at the carpet full of food hovering next to them. "Carpet, go to the policemen," she said. The carpet rose into the air and floated gently toward Hamstead and his men, and as it got closer it began to have the effect Sabrina had hoped for.

"Food!" one of the deputies squealed as the carpet stopped at their feet. The smell of the cakes and pies sent a change through the two men, and soon both were in pig form, rooting wildly through the banquet the girls had built on the rug.

"Gentlemen, we have work to do here!" Hamstead shouted while eyeing a pan of baked beans the others had overlooked. Unable to resist, he quickly shape-shifted to his pig form and slopped around in the mess.

Puck hovered several feet in the air near the girls, clearly displeased with Sabrina's success.

Daphne looked up at him and smiled. "We couldn't do this without you," she said, earning a grumpy shrug. "As soon as Jack tells us how to stop that giant, we're going to need you to lead us again."

The boy puffed up with pride, and a huge smile sprang to his face. He winked at Daphne, and then zipped across the front yard until he was hovering directly over the squad cars. The gorging piggies didn't even notice him.

Sabrina, Daphne, and Elvis stepped out of the house, closing the door behind them. With nimble fingers, Sabrina went to work locking all the bolts on the door, while Daphne kept an eye on Hamstead and his men.

"They're disgusting," Daphne said, mimicking the pigs' grunting and oinking.

"OK, that's the last one," Sabrina said, inserting the final key. She turned it and heard the lock roll into place.

"Ready?" she asked, pulling up the zipper on her sister's jacket.

"Ready!"

Sabrina turned to the pigs. "Carpet, here!" she shouted.

Abruptly, the carpet pulled itself out from under the three pigs, sending them topsy-turvy and flopping across the yard. The food flew into the air and rained down on them with a great splat as the carpet itself glided across the yard and stopped at Sabrina's feet.

"Get them!" Hamstead shouted as he struggled onto his hoofs and then back into his human form. The deputies followed suit and in no time they were all running toward the girls.

"Excuse me, piggies," Puck called from above. He blew a low note on his flute and within seconds a wave of pixies flew out of the woods. He played another note and the little lights encircled the two parked squad cars.

"You know what to do," Puck called to the pixies and they went into action, effortlessly lifting each car. They carried them high over the house and into several large trees, where they squeezed them between the thick branches. The police officers snorted their protests, but the boy just laughed.

The plan was working, and it was time for the girls to go. They stepped onto the carpet.

"Hold on tight. We haven't actually ridden on this thing," Sabrina said. She and Daphne knelt down and each grabbed a side of the carpet. Elvis hopped on, too, and Daphne wrapped her free arm around his neck.

"Don't worry Elvis. I've got you," the little girl said.

The police had stopped watching the pixies steal their cars and were now closing in on the sisters. They were almost on top of them when Sabrina shouted, "UP!" and the carpet rocketed into the sky. The girls held on for their dear lives as the house, the yard, and even their street became smaller and smaller. Sabrina's stomach lurched as they found themselves shooting through a cloud.

"Carpet, down!" she said as the oxygen began to seep from her lungs. Just as quickly as the carpet rose, it fell. Daphne's pigtails lifted from the side of her head and floated next to her ears as the girls screeched back toward Earth, falling like a rock.

"CARPET, STOP!" Sabrina cried, inches before the carpet smashed onto the ground. She gasped with relief. Unfortunately, they had stopped right behind the three police officers, who were still searching the sky for the girls.

"Wait, we've forgotten something!" Daphne cried. "Carpet, take us to the front door."

"No!" Sabrina shouted, but it was too late. The magic carpet zipped off again, this time plowing into the group of portly police and knocking them down like bowling pins.

"What are you doing?" she demanded as the carpet screeched to a halt at the door of Granny's house.

"There's one more lock," Daphne said. She knocked on the door three times. "We'll be back!"

But the detour had given Hamstead and his men the time they needed to recover and they now had the carpet surrounded. Hamstead grabbed one of the tassels and smiled.

"OK, fun time is over, ladies," he said.

"Let go of the carpet," Sabrina demanded. Elvis echoed her protest with a low growl.

"Not a chance, girls! Now, let's head down to the station and . . ."

"I said, let go of the carpet."

"What are you going to do to make me?" Hamstead scoffed.

Sabrina and Daphne exchanged glances. Daphne tightened her grip on the carpet and gave an extra squeeze to Elvis at the same time.

"Carpet, up!"

The carpet shot into the sky, carrying the girls, Elvis, and a stubborn Hamstead with it. Hanging on with one hand, the sheriff desperately tried to climb on board as they soared high above the house.

"Take us down, right now!" he squealed.

Sabrina peeked over the side and smirked.

"I'm sorry, Sheriff, but you don't have a ticket for this flight. I'm afraid you're going to have to get off at the next stop. Carpet, we have an unwanted passenger. Get rid of him!"

The carpet bolted forward as if thrilled with the request. It zipped up and down and did wide loopty-loops that made Sabrina want to barf. She looked over at Daphne and Elvis, who both sat calmly on the carpet.

"If you just let go, it's a real easy ride," Daphne shouted over the whipping wind, but Sabrina wasn't convinced, and held on tightly. A small beetle flew into her mouth and she spit it out, gagging.

"A bug flew in my mouth!" Sabrina croaked. Daphne patted her hand sympathetically.

Unfortunately, Hamstead was still very much a passenger.

"Let go!" Sabrina shouted again, but the sheriff shook his head defiantly. Displaying its own stubbornness, the carpet darted over the house and began to skim the top of the forest. Hamstead smacked into limbs and skittered across the treetops.

"I'm not going anywhere," he shouted as the carpet found an opening in the forest and dove into it like a kamikaze pilot. Sabrina was sure the carpet was going to sacrifice them all to get rid of its unwanted rider, but just as it seemed they would all be splattered across the forest floor, the carpet leveled out and dragged Hamstead directly over some thorny bushes. Motivated by the pain, the sheriff struggled once more to climb on board. Elvis barked at him as Daphne tried to pry his fingers from the carpet's tasseled corner.

"Carpet, do something!" she cried.

The carpet soared between several trees and zipped along a rocky stream. It lowered itself to mere inches above the water,

dragging Hamstead along the muddy banks, and finally shaking him loose. He tumbled into the mud and sank up to his nose.

The carpet darted back and hovered above him. The sheriff crawled out of the muck, covered in swamp goo. A small frog leaped from his shirt pocket as he wiped filth from his eyes.

As the girls darted away on the carpet, Sabrina could hear Boarman and Swineheart rushing to their boss's aid.

"Boss, what are you fooling around in the mud for?" Boarman asked.

"Shut up!"

The girls soared out of the forest and high into the sky. There, Puck met them and flew alongside, laughing at the sheriff's misfortune.

"You keep them busy!" Sabrina shouted and the boy's mood darkened.

Daphne pinched her sister. "You have to talk to him like he's the leader. He needs to feel that he's important," Daphne whispered.

Sabrina was stunned by her sister's perceptiveness. "Sorry, Puck, I know you can handle them and we'll be back soon with all the information you will need," Sabrina said awkwardly. "We know you could kill the giant yourself right now, but a little insider information never hurts."

Again, Puck puffed up with pride. "Of course, probably a waste of time, but who knows? By the way, there's one more cop you have to deal with when you get there."

"Who?" Daphne asked.

"A nervous little man named Ichabod Crane."

"Not the guy from Sleepy Hollow?" Sabrina said.

"That's him. Since he nearly lost his head, he gave up teaching and became a cop. I guess his idea is that he's safer if he's around the police. He shouldn't be too much of a problem," Puck said, turning in midair and soaring away.

"How did you know that we could get him to do whatever we want if we pretended he's in charge?" Sabrina asked Daphne.

"It's what I do with you," the little girl replied. "You two are exactly the same."

"Carpet, take us to Jack," Sabrina said after she had stuck her tongue out at her sister.

The carpet darted on and glided above the little town. For the first time, Sabrina could see Ferryport Landing for what it really was—quaint. To the east of the town, the moon shone on the curve of the Hudson River, and old gas lamps lined the paths of a park along the water. More lights twinkled in the center of the town, where dozens of brownstone buildings clustered around Main Street. Sabrina could see people having a late supper in the railway-car diner and a last movie playing at the drive-in theater. Far off to the west of town, she could just make out the humped shapes of the tree-blanketed mountains.

As they got closer to Main Street, the carpet began to descend, dropping nearly a dozen feet at once and causing Sabrina's belly to flip. She looked at her sister and saw that she had wrapped her arms around Elvis and was squeezing the air out of the poor dog. They plummeted through the clouds, the girls screaming as the wind screeched past them, but just as they were feet from crashing onto the pavement, Sabrina managed to shout "Carpet, STOP!" and the carpet screeched to a halt. It took them several moments to realize that they hadn't died and that they were still screaming.

When they had calmed down, Sabrina looked around and saw that they were floating next to the window of a brick building. It had bars on it. Suddenly, a boyish-looking head with spiky blond hair appeared. It was Jack! He had beautiful blue eyes and a round face with a button nose, but he looked tired and in desperate need of a shave. He also had a painful-looking fat lip that had specks of dried blood around it.

"What is going on out there? Can't a man get some rest when he's in prison?" he shouted in a thick English accent. When he saw the girls, he lifted himself higher in order to see what they were standing on. Then he smiled.

"Well, young ladies. Who might you be?"

"Are you Jack?" Sabrina asked.

"That's the name I was given," he replied with a chuckle.

"*The* Jack?" Daphne asked. "As in 'Jack and the Beanstalk'?"

"Indeed I am, duck. But as you can see, I'm a little indisposed to be signing autographs." He laughed.

"We need your help!" Daphne cried.

"Well, I don't know if you happened to have noticed, but this isn't a country club I'm relaxing in. This is the county jail. Unless you need some help making license plates, I think you've got the wrong bloke."

"We need your help with a giant," Sabrina said.

Jack's eyes grew wide and a smile briefly lit up his features. Then he grew terribly serious and pulled his face closer to the bars.

"A giant, you said?"

"He's taken our grandmother," Sabrina replied.

"And we want her back!" Daphne added.

"Well, I don't blame you," the young man said. "But exactly how does a human go about getting themselves in trouble with a giant?"

"We're Sabrina and Daphne Grimm. Our grandmother is . . ."

"Relda Grimm," Jack interrupted with a smirk. "I should have guessed. Went and got herself in trouble with a big boy, eh?"

"Yes, she and Mr. Canis both," Daphne said.

"Canis, eh? Can't say I feel sorry about that," Jack growled. "So what do you want from me?"

"We were told you were an expert on giants," Sabrina answered. "We need you to tell us everything you can about how to stop this one and save our family."

"It's true, I am an expert on the big boys. Killed nearly fifty of them in my day," Jack boasted.

"The books said it was less than twenty," Daphne said.

"Don't believe everything you read, duck," said Jack. "I've sent more than my fair share of big boys to the grave. Why, there was a time when people used to call me *Jack the Giant Killer*. I was famous, oh yes. My name was once synonymous with bravery and daring. That was until the spell that trapped me in this barmy town."

"What does *barmy* mean?" Daphne whispered to her sister.

Sabrina shrugged. She was having trouble keeping up with Jack's accent.

"Now I'm taking any work I can. Do you know what the mighty Jack does for a living?"

Sabrina began to get nervous as the young man's face filled with rage. She knew the answer to his question but thought it best to lie. "No, I don't."

"I sell shoes and suits at Harold's House of Big and Tall," Jack exploded. "A lowly sales boy! I sat with kings. I drank the finest wines in the world. I filled my belly with exotic meats and socialized with the world's most interesting people and now, because of that cursed spell that keeps us here, I spend my days measuring inseams and helping people pick out insoles!"

"We're sorry," Daphne said.

"At least that's what I used to do. Today I quit!" Jack bragged. "I have a feeling Jack the Giant Killer's luck is going to change."

"So how did you end up in jail?" Sabrina asked.

"That miserable cur, Charming," Jack raged. "Runs this town like it's his own personal kingdom and wants to keep the rest of us as peasants."

"Did he give you the fat lip?" asked Sabrina.

"No . . . I had a disagreement with some business associates," Jack said, wiping his wound with a bloody handkerchief. "No worries. You can't keep a bloke like me down, can you? No-siree-bob! You can count on that!"

"Jack, I hate to interrupt, but we've really got to hurry. Is there anything you can tell us that will help?" Sabrina said.

"Oh, I'm going to be a big help to you ladies," he said with a confident grin. "Just as soon as the two of you break me out of jail."

abrina gasped.

"You want us to help you break out of prison?"

Jack nodded his head. "Quite right."

"How are we supposed to do that?" Sabrina asked.

"Easy, you go in through the front door and distract the guard. Then the little one here will hit him in the gob with a club or something and snatch his keys."

"I'm seven years old. I can't hit someone with a club, and not in the gob—whatever that is!" Daphne cried.

"Sure you can. Deputy Crane isn't going to put up a fight. He's daft in the head and jumpy as a flea. But if he does happen to put up a fight, all you have to do is hit him in the shins. He'll fall over like a sack of potatoes," Jack replied.

"She's not hitting anyone with a club," Sabrina said.

"Well, if saving your granny and her pal isn't that important to you, I can just stay in the nick."

Sabrina looked into Jack's hopeful face. How could this odd little man actually be the key to Granny and Mr. Canis's survival? It just didn't seem possible, but on the other hand, the note Granny had left told them that the mirror would have all the answers they needed. After two days of disbelieving everything the old woman had told her, Sabrina didn't feel like being proven wrong again, especially when so much was riding on the outcome.

"So girls, what's it going to be? If I could do it myself, I would have already, but the bobby took my lock-picking kit when he put the cuffs on me. Smart on his part, too. There isn't a door Jack can't open."

"You say there's only one deputy?"

"Yes," Jack insisted.

"And he happens to be Ichabod Crane—the guy from 'The Legend of Sleepy Hollow'?"

"Not so much a legend as a true story, but yes."

"We'll get you out of here, but we're going to do it my way," Sabrina declared. "No one is going to get hurt. Deal?"

Jack frowned but thrust his hand out the window. He shook Sabrina's and smiled. "So boss, what's the plan?"

"First, I'm going to need your shirt."

• • •

When Sabrina opened the front door to the police station, her heart was pounding faster than it had ever pounded. They were taking a huge chance, especially with Sheriff Hamstead and his deputies searching for them. By now Crane had to know the girls were on the loose. Two kids dressed in bright-orange monkey sweatshirts, flying around on a magic carpet with a two-hundred-pound Great Dane weren't going to be too hard to spot. On the upside, what they were about to do was the sneakiest thing the girls had ever tried. It was nice to be challenged every once in awhile.

When the door swung open, Sabrina half expected to find Hamstead, Boarman, and Swineheart waiting for them. But luckily, the station was empty except for a tall, painfully thin man with a gigantic hooked nose, thin lips, and an Adam's apple that bobbed up and down. Ichabod Crane looked just like the story had described him, and he was fast asleep, sitting in a chair with his feet propped up on his desk.

Sabrina found the light switch and flipped it off, drowning the room in murkiness. She gestured behind her and the carpet drifted in, hovering two feet off the ground and carrying its own Headless Horseman: Daphne, sitting on Elvis's back and wearing Jack's shirt so that her head was hidden inside.

"He's going to figure this out," Daphne whispered.

"It's our only shot," Sabrina replied. She crouched down behind an empty desk and cupped her hands around her mouth. She used her feet to kick the door shut and it slammed so loudly the poor man fell backward over his chair. Once he was on his hands and knees, he rubbed his eyes and looked around in the dark.

"Hey, who turned out the lights?" he called in a whiny, high-pitched voice.

"Crane!" Sabrina moaned in the deepest voice she could produce. The carpet slowly drifted across the room, carrying its headless passenger.

"You!" the deputy cried in horror. "You're supposed to be gone!"

"I have returned," Sabrina croaked. The dark room was creating a very believable nightmare. Crane scurried around the room, hiding behind desks and chairs the best he could.

"Crane, you cannot hide from me. I am the Headless Horseman. I see all!"

The deputy screamed and continued to crawl, but the carpet hunted him slowly around the room.

"I'm a law enforcement officer now!" Crane shouted, trying to muster all his courage. "A defender of the peace. I can arrest you for . . . for . . . riding a horse without a head. That's a serious crime in this town," he cried.

"Your laws mean nothing to me. I've come for something, Crane, and I will have it!" Sabrina bellowed.

"What do you want?" the deputy cried.

"Your head!" Sabrina groaned.

Crane burst into tears. "No! Please, not my head!" he begged.

"Very well, if not your head, I'll take something else."

"Anything, anything. Whatever you want!"

"I want the keys to the jail."

Crane was silent for several moments.

"Why do you want the keys?"

"Would you prefer I take your head instead?" Sabrina moaned just as an unlucky bounce of the carpet knocked Daphne off Elvis's back. She fell to the ground, knocking a trash can into a radiator. The sound couldn't have been more appropriate, but Daphne was down for the count. Unable to see, she flailed in her costume, causing more commotion and sending a computer crashing to the floor.

Crane, who seemed to think this was part of the Headless Horseman's attack, shouted, "Here, the keys!" and tossed them at Daphne's feet.

"Now go, or I will change my mind!" Sabrina said. Crane

leaped to his feet and ran, not noticing Sabrina as he rushed out the station door. Once she was sure he was gone, Sabrina stood up and turned on the lights. Daphne was still rolling around, unable to see anything.

"Get me out of this," the little girl cried. Sabrina unhooked the top buttons and Daphne's head popped out. Elvis, who had stepped off the carpet, was ready with a lick to her face.

"You were very convincing." Sabrina laughed as she helped her sister to her feet.

Daphne reached down and scooped up the keys. "Let's get him out of here."

Sabrina rolled up the carpet, flung it over her shoulder, and the two girls raced to find Jack's cell.

Down a long hallway at the back of the building were two jail cells. The one on the left was empty, but the one on the right held Jack. He stood with his arms reaching through the bars as the girls entered the room.

"Give me the keys," he pleaded, but before they could, Elvis lunged angrily at the cell. Growling and barking wildly, the big dog sniffed and snarled at Jack.

"Elvis, it's OK, he's a friend," Daphne said, which seemed to calm the dog down, but still his nose was sniffing and at full alert.

Sabrina handed Jack the keys and he sorted through them.

"Corking! I told you it would work," he bragged.

He found the right key, stuck it in the lock, and turned it from inside. The door clicked and he pushed it open.

"Crane ran like he'd seen the devil himself," Sabrina said proudly.

"I've seen the devil, and you're not him," a voice said from down the hallway.

Sabrina turned and found Deputy Crane standing in the doorway, blocking their exit. He was so angry he was shaking.

"Listen, Crane, just let us pass and no one will get hurt," Jack said.

"Get back in your cell, Jack," the deputy ordered, pulling his billy club from its strap and swinging it threateningly.

"Sorry, Ichy. I wish I could help you but I've just been hired for a rescue mission. Now, are you going to let us pass or are we going to have to get rough?" Jack threatened.

Daphne grabbed his undershirt and yanked on it. "You promised, no one gets hurt."

Jack scowled. "I wouldn't hurt him . . . badly," he said.

"Do your worst!" Crane stammered as he backed up a step.

"Crane, I mean it. I'm not staying in this jail."

"Bring it on, you *washed up has-been*."

Jack laughed. "That's what I am? A washed up has-been? I'd

watch what you say, Ichy. Things can change in the blink of an eye."

"Not in Ferryport Landing, Jack."

The two stared at each other for a long time. Sabrina could almost feel the heat and rage in their eyes.

"Carpet, let's wrap this up!" Jack commanded and the carpet lifted off Sabrina's shoulder. It darted down the hallway and, like an anaconda, wrapped Crane inside it. He fumbled and fought but couldn't break free.

Jack walked over to the rug and patted it lightly.

"Nothing personal, Ichy, but destiny awaits," he said. He grabbed an end of the carpet and pulled it roughly, causing Crane to spin away like a top. After several rotations, the skinny man collapsed to the floor, overcome by dizziness. Jack set the carpet on the floor and stepped onto it.

"All right, ladies," he said as he extended his hand to help the girls onto the rug. Elvis rushed to join them and stood like a guard between the girls and Jack.

"Carpet, up," Sabrina said, and it rose a few feet and then sank slowly back down like a balloon with a hole in it.

"Why aren't we going up?" Sabrina cried.

"We must be too heavy!" Jack groaned. "Can we lose the hound?"

Elvis answered him with a threatening snarl.

"Very well. Carpet, take us to the Grimm house!"

Though it was weighed down, the carpet didn't lack any of its speed. It zipped along, three feet off the floor, down the hallway, through the main room, and out the front door of the police station. It sailed across the parking lot and made a left into the street, causing a pickup truck to screech to a stop. As they passed, the girls waved a friendly "sorry" gesture to the bewildered driver.

"That was almost too easy," Jack said. But no sooner had he puffed out his chest than the sound of a police siren wailed in their ears. A moment later, a police car turned the corner and raced in the group's direction. Ichabod Crane was behind the wheel.

"Tenacious, isn't he?" Jack said.

"Tenacious?" Daphne asked.

"It means persistent," Sabrina said.

"And what does *persistent* mean?" Daphne asked.

"It means he's not going to give up."

"And I wouldn't have it any other way," Jack assured them. "Carpet, faster!"

Close behind, Crane turned on his squad car's flashing lights.

"Is this the best idea?" Sabrina shouted, holding on to an end of the carpet as they sailed between cars and ran through a red light. "We're attracting a lot of attention!"

"It's about time this little burg saw some action!" Jack cried out happily. "Ferryport Landing, you haven't seen anything yet!"

Sabrina heard a horrible crunching sound behind them and turned back to see what could have made such a loud noise. What she saw stole the breath from her lungs. The road behind them began to rise, like a massive wave rolling in from the ocean. It was followed by another horrible crunching sound.

"What's happening?" she cried as she watched parked cars get tossed aside like toys.

"We're in luck, ladies," Jack said. "We've already found our giant."

Suddenly, a giant foot planted itself in the middle of Main Street. The impact caused windows in nearby businesses to shatter. The ground exploded and a gas main underneath the street burst, shooting flames high into the air.

"What do we do?" Daphne said.

"We have two choices. Stand and fight and die a horrible, messy death, or run," Jack said.

"Carpet, get us out of here!" Sabrina shouted, and the little rug jumped in speed.

Unfortunately, the giant was not discouraged by how fast the group was making its getaway. A single stride put the monster right behind them, even when the rug increased its speed again. And with every step the big monster took, the pavement crumbled beneath him. Electrical wires snapped, spraying sparks everywhere. The few drivers on the road at that early hour lost control of their cars and crashed into buildings. Jack turned to see the chaos and a broad grin came to his face.

"Finally, this is getting interesting." He laughed.

The carpet took a sharp left turn and Sabrina felt lucky that she hadn't tumbled off, when she noticed that Daphne was no longer sitting next to her. In fact, Daphne was hanging from the back of the carpet, holding on desperately with both hands.

"Jack!" Sabrina cried. The spiky-haired "legend" reached down and grabbed the little girl by the back of her sweatshirt and pulled her onto the carpet.

"Blimey! This is better than a roller coaster." Jack laughed as he sat the girl safely on the carpet.

Daphne hugged her sister. It was the first time Sabrina had ever felt her sister shake from fear. She didn't like it.

"We're going to get ourselves killed," she shouted as the carpet narrowly missed being crushed by a delivery truck filled with chickens.

"Nonsense, we can't die like this. We're immortal," Jack replied.

"You're immortal, we're not. We have to get off this road," Sabrina demanded.

"I see. Must be quite a pain to be human, but the carpet picks the route." Just then an eighteen-wheeler pulled directly into their path and stopped.

"CARPET, UP!" everyone shouted. The carpet slowly rose, sputtering as if it were the little train that couldn't.

"We're not going to make it!" Sabrina shouted.

"Lie down flat," Jack commanded.

"You can't mean what I think you mean!"

Jack nodded, and the two girls reluctantly lay on their backs.

"Elvis, play dead," Daphne said, and the dog lay on his side. The little girl turned a worried face to her sister. "He's not going to do what I think he is, is he?"

"CARPET, DOWN!" Jack shouted, and the carpet fell from the sky until it was literally skidding across the pavement. Its momentum carried the group underneath the truck to the other side and down the street. When they sat up again, the young man was already laughing—until he looked up and saw the street cleaner barreling toward them.

"CARPET, UP!" they all shouted and the little rug struggled higher, narrowly missing the boiling-hot water and sharp bristles the machine used to scour the street. The carpet continued to rise until it had cleared the vehicle. Sabrina sat up and turned around. Ichabod Crane was out of his car, angrily ordering the owners of the eighteen-wheeler and the street cleaner to move. Unfortunately, the traffic problems did little to stop the giant. It's monstrous foot soared high above the commotion and landed only yards from the carpet.

"THAT THING IS GOING TO KILL SOMEONE," Sabrina shouted. "Carpet, we have to get away from the main road!"

The carpet made an abrupt turn toward Ferryport Landing's farm community. The giant followed closely behind and the little rug dodged each deadly footfall. Several times the ugly brute reached out to squash the group in his hands, but each time the carpet zipped out of his reach. He grunted and roared at them, but eventually became exhausted by the chase and gave up, shaking his fist into the air and roaring with frustration.

"Don't cry, big boy," Jack shouted to the giant as he disappeared behind them on the horizon. "You'll be seeing me again, very soon!"

• • •

As the magic carpet coasted up the driveway, it was barely six inches off the ground and had lost all of its kick. When the group finally stepped off of it, the beautiful little rug dropped to the ground and rolled itself up, just as it had been delivered to the girls. Daphne leaned over and picked it up gingerly, the way one would a tired kitten, and cradled it in her arms.

"Poor thing is all worn out," she said, cooing.

Sabrina looked toward the forest. Hamstead's squad cars were still perched in the tall trees behind the house, but he and his men were nowhere to be seen. Reaching into her pocket, Sabrina removed Granny Relda's enormous key ring and began the tedious job of unlocking all the bolts. Jack watched attentively until she had unlocked every one. Before Sabrina could say the magic words that gained them entrance, Daphne pulled her aside, cupped her hand over her big sister's ear, and whispered, "Should we let him in?"

It was a fair question. Every time they had broken one of Granny Relda's rules they had regretted it, but they were in a tough situation. Jack was probably the only person in the world who could confront a giant, and he had offered to help.

"I don't think we have much of a choice," Sabrina whispered back. She made a fist and knocked on the door. "We're home."

Jack cocked an eyebrow in confusion.

"Family tradition," Sabrina said in hopes of throwing him off. "Granny does it and it makes Daphne laugh so I picked it up, too."

Daphne faked a laugh.

Jack shrugged. "Whatever."

"What's he doing here?" Puck said as he floated down from the sky.

Jack turned around and eyed the flying boy, whose huge wings flapped hard to allow him to hover over them.

"He's offered to help," Daphne explained, but this time her diplomacy was falling on deaf ears.

"Help us do what, try on some big pants?" Puck sneered, taking a jab at Jack's recent job. "You weren't supposed to bring him back."

"Listen, you little brat, I'm the only hope you've got," Jack replied. "Two little girls and a garden gnome aren't going to stop a giant."

"Who are you calling a garden gnome?" Puck said, pulling his flute from his sweatshirt. "My royal army knows how to deal with insolent peasants."

"Boys!" Sabrina and Daphne cried in unison. "That's enough!"

Puck and Jack backed off. The girls looked at each other. Apparently, there was a bit of Granny in them both.

"What happened to Hamstead and his deputies?" Sabrina asked.

"Charming came by and picked them up," Puck said, staring

a hole into Jack. "I sat up on the roof and watched him scream at them for half an hour. It was hilarious."

"Good, we could use a break," Sabrina said, turning and opening the front door.

Elvis rushed past her and into the kitchen, returning a moment later with Granny Relda's handbag. He dropped it at the girls' feet and began to snarl at it. The girls ignored him. Daphne headed into the living room, set the carpet tenderly on the floor, and plopped down, exhausted, into a chair. She pulled a book out from underneath the cushion she was sitting on and tossed it aside.

"So, this is the famous Grimm house," Jack said as he wandered from room to room, lifting up photographs and snooping around. "Oh, I wish I had my camera with me. No one will believe I was actually inside."

"Make yourself at home, please," Sabrina said. If Jack heard the sarcasm in her voice, he pretended not to and continued his snooping.

"So girls, where can I take a kip?" he asked.

Daphne looked at Sabrina for a definition but Sabrina shook her head.

"I have no idea what that means."

"You know, hit the sack?" Jack said.

"You want to go take a nap?"

"I'm zonked."

"We didn't break you out of jail so you could camp out in our house."

"Kids, I was on a lumpy jail cot all night. I need to get some rest, and besides, my big plan can't go into effect until tomorrow night, anyway."

"What big plan?"

"Right now, it's best that we don't discuss it." Jack fell onto the couch and stretched his arms behind his head.

"He doesn't have a plan!" Puck snapped.

"Yes, I do!" Jack replied. "We'll talk about it later. I just need a couple of hours of shut-eye." He closed his eyes and drifted off to sleep.

Puck looked at the girls, turned, and stomped outside, slamming the door behind him.

"What do we do now?" Daphne said sleepily.

"I suppose we might as well get some rest, too," Sabrina said, seeing her sister's head bob. She scooped her grandmother's handbag off the floor and set it on the table, then gently urged Daphne out of her chair. Elvis whined at the girls.

Sabrina turned and whispered into the dog's ear, "Elvis, keep an eye on Jack."

The dog's eyes reflected an understanding, and he seated himself like a stone guardian, watching the sleeping man. The two girls went up to their bedroom. It had been a long day.

• • •

Sabrina didn't remember falling asleep, but when she woke up she was still in her clothes and it was already nine o'clock in the morning. She crawled out of bed, leaving her snoring sister alone, and walked down the hallway. She heard a sound from Granny Relda's room and decided to investigate, but when she opened the door, no one was there.

She stepped inside and noticed a framed photo on the old woman's dresser. It was of Granny and Grandpa, hugging happily under an apple tree. As usual, Mr. Canis was standing nearby. His face seemed slightly out of focus and the camera flash had turned his eyes a bright blue color. Sabrina reached into her pocket and pulled out the photo she had found in Granny Relda's handbag. Comparing the two, she found the same odd effect over Mr. Canis. Sabrina was surprised she hadn't noticed it before.

"What are you doing in here?" Puck's voice asked. It startled Sabrina and she dropped both the picture and the framed photo to the ground. Luckily, the glass didn't break.

Sabrina looked around the room, searching for the boy, but didn't see him. "Where are you?"

"Up here, ugly," said Puck.

Sabrina looked up and nearly screamed. A housefly the size of Elvis was sitting upside down on the ceiling above her. But its enormous size wasn't nearly as disturbing as its human head, which had shaggy blond hair, a gold crown, and a mischievous grin. Apparently, Puck had a whole bag of disturbing tricks.

"What are you doing in here?" Sabrina demanded.

"Uh . . . it's the only quiet room in the house," Puck replied. "Besides, I know you and Jack have got your big plans. Wouldn't want to get in the way."

"Could you come down here?"

Puck suddenly morphed back into his human form and fell clumsily to the bed below.

"You're being a baby," Sabrina said. "Jack wants to help, and you can't stand not being the center of attention."

"Whatever," the boy replied. "But when he gets you into trouble, don't be angry when I remind you that I told you so."

"You got a better plan, then let's hear it, 'cause all I've heard from you is the never-ending buzz of your flapping lips," Sabrina snapped. "My parents ran out on me and Daphne almost two years ago. We've been through the wringer and have been bounced around for far too long. I admit, when we met Granny Relda I didn't want anything to do with her. But now that I know she's the real deal, I'm going to do whatever it takes to get her back. I've lost one family. I'm not losing another. So if you have a better idea, then I'm all ears!"

"Don't look at me," Puck said. "I've made no promises to the old lady. She knew I wasn't a good little boy when we met."

Sabrina was taken aback by his insensitivity. "So you couldn't care less what happens to her?"

"I've learned one thing in this life of mine. Look out for yourself. Everyone else will just end up disappointing you."

"So you won't help?"

"I'm not one of the good guys," Puck said.

Suddenly, the sound of Elvis's barking filled the room. Sabrina peered into the hallway. There, she saw Jack fighting with Elvis, who was shredding the man's pants in his angry teeth.

"Get this beast away from me! He's rabid," Jack begged.

"What are you doing up here?" Sabrina asked, suspiciously.

"I was coming up to wake you."

Daphne entered the hallway rubbing sleep from her eyes. "What's going on?"

"The Giant Killer is prowling around the house looking for something to steal," Puck said. "Your savior has sticky fingers."

"Shut your mouth, you dirty little hooligan," Jack shouted.

"It'll take more than your words to make that happen, you thieving barn rat."

"Elvis," Daphne said as she patted the angry dog on the head—her touch seemed to have a calming effect on him—"take a chill pill."

Elvis released Jack's pant leg from his teeth.

"Thank you," Jack said, eyeing his mangled trousers. "So, are you ready to hear my plan?"

Sabrina looked at Puck, hoping the boy might reconsider and help them, but he sneered and looked away.

"Yes, we're ready," she replied.

Puck said nothing. He walked down the stairs and out the door, slamming it behind him.

"We don't need him, anyway," Jack said. "Is anyone hungry? Let's have some breakfast!"

He rushed down the stairs and into the kitchen, the girls following behind. They watched as he rifled through the contents of the refrigerator.

"There's nothing to eat in this house," Jack complained. "I could really go for some bubble and squeak or some bangers. Do you kids think you could cook up some steak-and-kidney pie for me?"

The girls stared.

"I hear noises coming from his mouth but they don't sound like words," Daphne said.

"Maybe he's having some kind of fit," Sabrina said.

Jack rolled his eyes, snatched up some leftovers, and ate greedily.

"Let me tell you kids," he said, his mouth full, "prison food is terrible."

"We'll take your word for it," Sabrina said.

While Jack ate, the girls took turns telling him how Granny Relda and Mr. Canis had been kidnapped. Sabrina told him her theory about Mayor Charming being the mysterious Mr. Englishman, and how she thought he was using the giant to scare people off their land.

"So, tell us your plan," Daphne said as Jack finished his breakfast.

"I'm still working out the details."

Both the girls flashed Jack an angry look.

"Don't worry!" he said defensively. "It's going to be brilliant."

Sabrina had had enough. She got up from her seat and grabbed the telephone.

"We helped you escape from prison so you could help us save our grandmother and all you have done is eat our food and drool on our sofa," she raged. "If you can't do it, then I'm just going to call Deputy Crane and let him know you're ready to go back."

"Put the phone down and relax," Jack said calmly as he helped himself to another chicken leg. "You think tracking down a giant is easy? Giants have survived thousands of years being as big as they are and they've learned a few things about staying out of sight when they need to. Now we can traipse through the woods, cut down the forest, and drag the Hudson River, but the fact is that if a giant doesn't want to be found, he's not going to be found."

"You're talking in circles," Sabrina complained.

"What I'm saying, duck, is that we have to be smarter than a giant to catch a giant. You said it yourself, that the mayor was try-ing to cover up what happened to that farm. It's no secret he wants to buy up the entire town. What better way than to get a giant to scare off the landowners who won't sell? So when your family started snooping around, he sent the big boy after you. He's got your granny and now he's after the two of you. All the evidence you need was chasing us down Main Street yesterday."

"Go on," Sabrina said, as she set the phone back in its cradle.

"Knowing Charming, he's got a map of Ferryport Landing in his office, with all the property he's after and where he's going to send the giant next. All you have to do is sneak into his office during the ball tonight, find the map, and see where the giant's next target is. Then we show up, the giant shows up, I do what I do, and bingo-bango, we kill the big boy and save your grandmum."

"That's your big plan?" Sabrina cried.

"You got something better? I know that sneaking into the ball doesn't sound as exciting as burning down the forest and waiting for the giant to run out, but I've always had a mind that tells me the easiest way is the best way."

"There's one big problem, though," Daphne spoke up. "The mayor and the police are looking for us. We're going to have a tough time sneaking into the place."

"Oh, girls, you're going to go right through the front door and no one is even going to notice," Jack said confidently.

After he had eaten, he insisted the best way to digest a meal was to follow it with another kip. As their "hero" rested, the girls frantically searched the books for anything that might help. Eventually, they came upon one of their grandfather Basil's many journals. Inside, he had sketched out a rough plan of Charming's estate.

The mayor's mansion was a sprawling several-story palace with dozens of rooms. Their grandpa had given estimates of room sizes, locations of various windows, and even an indication of a wall he believed held a secret door. But Grandpa hadn't seen all of the house, and many parts of the drawing were labeled with question marks. Sabrina noticed he had paid extra attention to possible escape routes—apparently, Grandpa had been a bit of a sneak as well.

Sabrina carefully studied the map and did her best to commit it to memory. When Jack finally woke up, several hours later, he found the girls ready to get started.

"The first thing we need is the magic mirror," Jack said.

"I don't know what you're talking about," Sabrina said, stealing a look into Daphne's eyes.

"Girls, I know Relda has the magic mirror. Everyone knows that. Why do you think the front door has a dozen locks on it?"

Sabrina took the keys out of her pocket and led her sister and their guest up the steps. Once they arrived at the mirror's room, she inserted the key and unlocked the door. As before, the face in the mirror was filled with rage at the invasion.

"WHO DARES?" he bellowed.

Jack strolled in without a care, followed by the girls.

"Turn off the drama, Mirror," he scoffed.

"Oh, it's you," Mirror mumbled.

"Of course it's me. I'm the bloke you call when you have a big problem, and these girls have a really big problem," Jack bragged.

"And where is the carpet?" the face in the mirror asked Sabrina.

"Sorry," she said. She walked to the doorway and called for it. After a couple of minutes, the carpet floated limply into the room.

"What have you done to it?" Mirror cried as the carpet fell to the floor and once again rolled itself up.

"I think we had too many people on it," Daphne explained as a hand broke the surface of the mirror and snatched the carpet from the ground.

"It's nearly unraveling in my hand," the face wailed as he babied the rug. "Poor little carpet, look at how they treated you."

"Too many years hanging on a wall in the Grimm house have made you a real sourpuss," Jack commented.

"How can I help you?" Mirror asked, brushing off the insult.

"We need to sneak into Charming's mansion tonight and we need some disguises," Jack said.

"Not a problem at all."

"And we need the slippers."

Mirror frowned. "Absolutely not," he stammered.

"Listen, this house is going to be surrounded with the police any minute now. Ali Baba's carpet isn't going to get us into Charming's mansion. We need the slippers," Jack argued.

"Mrs. Grimm would not approve. The slippers were entrusted to this family so they would never fall into the wrong hands," Mirror replied.

"You can trust me," said Jack.

"Didn't you used to have your own magic items? What happened to the Cloak of Darkness?"

"I lost it in a game of poker."

"You lost a cloak that turns you invisible in a poker game? What about the Shoes of Swiftness?"

"I hocked them."

"The Cap of Knowledge? The Goose that Laid the Golden Egg?"

"Lost the cap in a game of dice. And I accidentally left the window open one day and the goose flew off."

"I suppose you sold the Sword of Sharpness?" Mirror grumbled.

"No, I still have the Sword of Sharpness," said Jack indignantly. "I just misplaced it. It's in my flat somewhere. The point is, we need the slippers. If you won't let me have them, then let one of the girls wear the shoes. It doesn't make any difference to me."

"What slippers?" Sabrina shouted. She was tired of their bickering.

"Dorothy's slippers," Jack and Mirror shouted.

"Dorothy from *The Wizard of Oz*?" Daphne exclaimed.

"Yes," Jack said impatiently. "They can transport you anywhere you want to go, all you have to do is . . ."

"Click three times!" Daphne cried. "Gimme the slippers!"

"Girls, I have to warn you. The slippers are very powerful magic. People have died trying to get them. There are still those . . . some in this town . . . who would slit your throats to possess them," Mirror said.

"Enough of this," Jack said, and then he did something that shocked Sabrina. He stepped into the reflection and pushed the man in the mirror aside.

"How dare you!" Mirror shouted.

"C'mon kids, keep up!" Jack said as his face appeared in the reflection.

The girls were unsure of what to do. Daphne reached up and curled her hand into her sister's. Sabrina squeezed softly and the two of them took a tentative step through the mirror. It was a cool sensation, almost as if they had been caught in a summer rainstorm, and when they finally opened their eyes, a brilliant glimmering light flooded their pupils. What they saw made Sabrina queasy. It wasn't natural. It just wasn't possible.

Sabrina had expected to walk into a reflection of the room they had been in. After all, the mirror was a mirror. But she couldn't have been more wrong. Instead she found herself in a long, wide hallway that reminded her of Grand Central Station. It was vast, with a vaulted ceiling and endless archways of glass and steel. Glowing marble columns held up the ceiling, which rose hundreds of feet above them. Breathtaking sculptures of men and monsters lined the hall. And along each wall were hundreds of doors of all shapes and sizes, some no bigger than a rabbit, others a hundred feet high. Some were wooden, others steel, and still others seemed to be made from pure light. Sabrina looked down at Granny Relda's key ring and realized what all the keys were for. Yet another of Granny's eccentricities had a legitimate explanation.

Even more startling than the gigantic room they were standing in was the man who lived in it. The face in the mirror was no longer a disembodied head, but a short, chubby little man in a black suit and tie.

"Keep your hands in your pockets, Jack," the man insisted.

"Mirror, I am shocked. Don't you trust me?" Jack said.

"I trust you about as much as the person who gave you that fat lip," said Mirror.

"What is this place?" Daphne asked.

"It's an arcane-powered, multi-phasic, trans-dimensional pocket universe," Mirror replied.

"A what-who?"

"Your grandmother calls it the world's biggest walk-in closet." The little man sighed. "It's a sort of holding area for dangerous and valuable items. I call it the Hall of Wonders, and you're not supposed to be in here."

"Oh, Mirror," Jack said. "We've learned one of your secrets. Don't worry, I'm sure you have a million more."

The little man's face flushed with anger. His fists clenched and he looked as if he might hit Jack, but the giant killer just ignored him.

"All right, Mirror, where are the slippers?" Jack asked impatiently.

"This way," Mirror said, gesturing for them to follow. He walked down the long hall past many doors. The plaque on one read FAIRY GODMOTHER WANDS while the next read TALKING PLANTS. As they continued down the hallway, they found more doors labeled: POISONOUS FRUITS, DRAGON EGGS, IMPOSSIBLE ANIMALS, WISHING WELLS, CRYSTAL BALLS, CURSED TREASURE, SCROLLS AND PROPHESIES, and on and on and on. Passing one massive door, the group jumped as violent pounding from within threatened to knock it off its hinges. Something on the other side wanted out, something named GRENDEL.

The group pressed on down the hallway where they finally stopped at a door that read MAGIC SHOES.

"Here we are," Mirror said reluctantly. "But I must once again remind you that magic is dangerous. There's a reason why the Everafters asked this family to look after all of these things. Magic in the wrong hands only leads to chaos."

"We'll be careful," said Sabrina as she knelt down to the lock. It was a simple one that would take a skeleton key, but Granny's key ring had dozens of skeleton keys. Sabrina tried the first one and it failed. She tried another; still nothing.

"Let me try," Jack said impatiently.

"I've got it," Sabrina snapped. She turned another key, and this time the lock opened. The door swung wide and everyone entered.

The room was simple, but its contents were amazing. Along the walls were hundreds of pairs of shoes: cowboy boots, woven sandals, wooden clogs, leather moccasins, and many more, all displayed on wooden shelves. Some of the shoes seemed as if they had been made for animals, while others were big enough for the entire group to stand in. One golden pair had downy, white wings that flapped as if the shoes were alive, and another glittering pair were made of pure glass.

Jack picked up the pair of shoes with wings, but the little man promptly smacked his hand and snatched them from his grip. After replacing the shoes, Mirror crossed the room, picked up a pair of sparkling silver slippers, and handed them to Sabrina.

"Try to take better care of these than you did the magic carpet," he said gruffly.

If these were the famous ruby slippers, they were more silver than red, though in the light Sabrina saw hints of a warm, rosy color. She couldn't figure out what they were made of, but if forced to guess, she would say they were tinfoil.

"Put them on, child," the little man said.

"They're way too small," Sabrina said as she eyed the shoes.

"One size fits all, duck," Jack said.

Sabrina yanked off her sneakers and slid her foot inside one of the slippers, which magically grew in size and fit her foot perfectly. Once she had the other one on, an odd energy crept up her legs and filled her whole body.

Just then, Jack darted out of the room and across the hall.

"Jack!" the little man shouted after him, but Jack didn't listen. When they finally found him, the giant killer was eyeing a door with a plaque that read MAGIC BEANS.

"I can't believe you have a whole room of them!" he shouted with glee.

"We might be bending the rules on the slippers, but those are off-limits to the likes of you!" Mirror said.

"How about a peek?" Jack pleaded. He suddenly looked like a lost little boy. "These things are part of my past. Can't a man take a walk down memory lane?"

Sabrina could see his expression, and all at once she felt sorry for him. Jack was a man whom the whole world had loved. He had seen amazing things and lived life to the fullest, but being trapped in Ferryport Landing had put an end to all of it. It dawned on Sabrina that Ferryport Landing might have been the home of many of the world's fairy-tale creatures, but it was also a prison they were never allowed to leave. It didn't seem right.

Sabrina pulled out the keys, knelt down, eyed the keyhole, and within seconds opened the door. Jack pushed past her into the tiny room, where a single mason jar sat on a table. Inside it was a collection of little white beans.

Jack gasped and picked up the jar. "There must be a hundred of them."

Mirror snatched the jar out of his hand and placed it back on the table.

"These things are dangerous. If you dropped them on the floor we'd be ear-deep in giants."

Jack scowled for a moment and looked as if he were ready to fight for his treasure, but he took a deep breath and his anger vanished, only to be replaced with a boyish grin.

"Thanks, Grimms, you don't know what you've done for me," he said.

Mirror hurried everyone back through the door.

"Well, ladies, now that we've got the shoes, we need the proper disguises," Jack said. "I think a little fairy godmother magic will do the trick."

"Wands are over here," Mirror said, leading them down the hallway. They stopped at the door labeled FAIRY GODMOTHER WANDS and Sabrina unlocked it. Inside, a small black cauldron sat on a tiny table, with several skinny sticks popping out of the top. Mirror reached into the pot and removed one that had a glittery glass star on the end, and handed it to Sabrina.

"The first magical item your family ever had to confiscate," Mirror said.

"I remember old Wilhelm Grimm trying to get that away from her." Jack laughed. "Girls, I'll say one thing about your family. They are brave. Fairy godmothers are sweet as pie on the outside, but try to take away their wands and they can get downright mean."

"Indeed," Mirror said.

"How does this work?" Sabrina asked.

Mirror frowned. "I can't believe your father!" he cried. "I'd hoped that your mother, Veronica, might at least give you the basics behind his back. Very well, this is the changing wand used by Cinderella's fairy godmother. It will alter your clothes, shoes, even your bodies, in any way you want."

"Charming's ball is going to be filled to the rafters with Everafters," Jack said. "You're going to go in as one of them."

Daphne smiled. "I know what I want to be! I want to be the Tin Woodsman!"

"Are you sure, honey?" the little man in the mirror asked. "Tin is so last season."

Daphne nodded enthusiastically.

"Very well, it's your fashion funeral," he said. "Sabrina, just say 'Tin Woodsman,' make three small circles with the wand, and then tap her on the head."

"OK," Sabrina said. "Tin Woodsman!" She made three awkward circles in the air and then smacked her sister on the head with the wand. Daphne squealed in pain and rubbed the spot, but as she was rubbing, a miraculous change began to occur. Her skin took on a silvery tone. She grew several feet taller and her clothes faded, only to be replaced by gears and joints. Her hair retreated into her scalp and a shiny funnel took its place. Sabrina blinked her eyes to be sure they weren't playing tricks on her, but she knew they weren't. Her sister had become the Tin Woodsman.

"That hurt," Daphne cried as her hand scraped against her new metallic head. Hearing the screech of metal in her ears, she looked at her hand and squealed in delight. She walked around the hall, squeaking with every step. "Look at me!"

"Spitting image," Jack said.

Daphne took the wand from her sister. "OK, who do you want to be?"

Sabrina was stumped. She realized she had to choose wisely. She needed to be inconspicuous at the ball, someone small and unnoticeable, and someone who could be very, very sneaky.

"OK, I was thinking . . ."

"I know, Momma Bear!" the little girl interrupted and before Sabrina could stop her, she had performed the circles and was cracking her big sister on the head.

Sabrina felt the transformation immediately, as if her body was being inflated. Her clothes disappeared and were replaced with a bright, pink-and-white polka-dotted dress that ended well above her knee. She looked down at her humongous arms and groaned as hair exploded from every pore. Fangs burst from the top of her mouth and razor-sharp claws sprang from her fingernails and toenails. She could feel them scratching at the insides of the ruby slippers, which had expanded to fit her new size-twenty-six feet. When the transformation was complete, Daphne giggled.

"You did that on purpose!" Sabrina growled.

"You are so cute!" Daphne cried as she threw her metal arms around her sister and gave her a big hug. "I could just eat you!"

"Well, no one's going to see the two of you coming," Jack moaned, though it was obvious he found the whole thing funny.

"Girls, you realize there's a timer with this magic. When the clock strikes nine o'clock, you're going to change back. Do you understand?" Mirror lectured.

"Nine o'clock? I thought it was midnight. Cinderella had until midnight," Sabrina argued.

"Cinderella was seventeen years old. You are eleven. There's no way your grandmother would approve of you staying out until the wee hours of the morning."

"We're trying to save her life," Sabrina pointed out.

"Still, children should not be allowed out that late, thus, your magic wears off at nine," Mirror said.

"That doesn't give us much time, it's seven o'clock right now," Jack said, eyeing his wristwatch.

Mirror took the wand from Daphne and put it back into the pot. He led the group out of the room, closed the door, and, when Sabrina couldn't manage, locked it with Granny's keys.

"One last thing," Jack said. "You don't happen to have any walkie-talkies in this place, do you?"

9

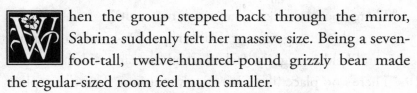

hen the group stepped back through the mirror, Sabrina suddenly felt her massive size. Being a seven-foot-tall, twelve-hundred-pound grizzly bear made the regular-sized room feel much smaller.

"I'll never get through the doorway," Sabrina worried.

"You won't have to," Jack said as he stepped through the reflection. "Just click those heels together and you'll go anywhere you want. But before you do, you'll need these."

Jack held three walkie-talkies. He opened Sabrina's handbag and stuffed one inside, then slid open a panel in Daphne's tin frame and popped in the other. He kept the third for himself.

"These will help you keep in touch with me."

"You're not going in with us?" Sabrina asked.

"Are you kidding?" Jack cried. "I'm on Ferryport Landing's

'Most Wanted' list by now. Even if I disguised myself, Charming is sure to have security that can sniff me out. I can't take the chance. I'm going to stand outside the mansion and direct you. When you find the map of Charming's next target, we'll go save your grandmother and Canis."

"OK," Sabrina said, looking down at the slippers on her huge, furry feet. "I just click them together?" she asked, feeling ridiculous.

"Three times," Daphne cheerfully reminded her.

"There's no place like Charming's mansion?"

Jack nodded in agreement. Daphne put her hand on Sabrina's arm and held on tightly. Jack reached over and did the same.

"There's no place like Charming's mansion. There's no place like Charming's mansion. There's no place like Charming's mansion."

The last thing Sabrina saw was Elvis trotting into the room. In his mouth he had the piece of fabric Granny claimed was from a giant's pants, as well as a big scrap of Jack's pants. He spit them out on the floor and whined for attention, but suddenly there was a pop and the lights went out. Sabrina's ears filled with a squeaky sound, like someone was slowly releasing the air from a balloon, and when the lights came back on, the three of them were standing in front of Charming's estate.

It was the biggest house Sabrina had ever seen, with several stories and marble columns like the ones on the White House framing a golden front door. A coat of arms depicting a lion fighting a snake decorated the front of the house. The lawn was immaculately trimmed and bordered by stone paths and clipped shrubbery. A statue of Prince Charming surrounded by admiring woodland animals rose out of a fountain in the middle of the lawn. Several hulking attendants with green skin and oversized muscles—parking valets—waited by the circular driveway, opening car doors, taking keys, and driving the cars away.

A car pulled up in front of the house and a blond woman in a blue bonnet and puffy dress got out. She reached into the backseat for a long white staff with a curled end. Before the attendant could close the door for her, half a dozen lambs tumbled out and eagerly followed the woman inside.

"Little Bo Peep," Daphne cried. "Can you believe it?"

"OK, girls, I'm going to stay out here and let you know if the cops show up. Keep your radios on and try to stay inconspicuous," Jack said.

"I'm a grizzly bear in a dress," Sabrina muttered.

"Charming's office is on the second floor," Jack continued. "I'd mingle with the guests for a while, work the crowd, and find your way up there without attracting attention."

"Oh, is it that easy?" Sabrina said.

"Once you find the map, pop yourselves back down here and we'll go find your giant," Jack finished. He gave them a thumbs-up sign and disappeared into some nearby trees.

"He makes it sound so simple," Sabrina grumbled to Daphne.

A line had formed as guests waited to be announced, so the girls walked to the back of it. In front of them were a large man and his wife, having some kind of argument.

"Isn't there a line for the rich people?" the woman groaned.

"Maybe if we had gotten here earlier we'd be inside already," the man grunted. His voice was slurred and Sabrina thought he might be drunk.

"I wanted to look nice for the ball," the woman said defensively.

"You wanted to look nice for the prince," he muttered.

"Are you going to harp on that, again?" The woman sighed. She turned and noticed Sabrina and Daphne. Her cheeks flushed red and she forced a sheepish smile to her face. Even in her embarrassment, the woman was radiant. Her beautiful amber hair cascaded in curls down her neck and her bright-green eyes sparkled in the light, competing for brilliance with her pearly white smile.

"Good evening," she said politely.

Her husband turned to see who she was speaking to, and the agony of his face was revealed. His features were pushed flat, giving him a cat-like appearance, accentuated by the mane of hair that framed his face. Long fangs crept out of his mouth and hung down nearly to his chin. But his most horrible feature was his eyes, bright-yellow slits that blinked at them fiercely. Sabrina knew exactly who they were—Beauty and the Beast.

"Good evening," the Beast grunted. "Nice to see you, Woodsman. How on Earth did you and Momma Bear come to be acquainted?"

The girls weren't prepared for questions and stood dumbfounded.

"You're such a gossip," Beauty scolded. "What Poppa Bear doesn't know won't hurt him."

Several more guests joined the line. Sabrina turned around to see a small white rabbit in a vest clutching an old-fashioned chain watch in his paw. He looked at the time and stuffed the watch back into his vest pocket.

"For once, we are not late." The White Rabbit sighed with relief. His companions were three mice wearing black sunglasses and carrying canes.

"Always the worrywart," one of the mice said as he tapped his cane against the ground.

"I told you we would make it," the second added.

"Someday I'd like to smash that watch of yours. All that worrying about time is going to give you a heart attack," the third mouse concluded.

"I believe in being punctual," the White Rabbit said defensively.

"Have you heard the news?" the second mouse squeaked to the crowd.

"No, I want to tell. I heard it first," the first mouse cried. "Relda Grimm has been carried off by a giant!"

The folks in line gasped in surprise and turned their attention to the little mouse.

"Are you sure?" the Beast asked.

"Maybe you'd prefer an eyewitness," the first mouse cried. "I may be blind, but my hearing is just fine."

The Beast rolled his eyes.

"A giant? That's impossible," Beauty exclaimed.

"I didn't believe it, either, but it's true," the White Rabbit replied. "The giant has been stomping around all over town scaring the humans to death. The Three are working overtime, showering the town in forgetful dust. Be prepared to dig deep, my friends. The damage is extensive and forgetful dust costs a pretty penny. You all know Charming's going to ask us to foot the bill."

Sabrina hung on every word.

"If she's dead, we might actually be able to leave Ferryport Landing!" Beauty cried, unable to hide her excitement. "Has anyone tried?"

"The barrier is still intact," said the third mouse, almost stumbling over a pebble as he stepped forward with the moving line. "We tried it this morning."

"Well, I wouldn't get your hopes up about Relda meeting an untimely demise," the White Rabbit said. "I'm sure Canis will save her. He always does."

"Oh, that's not going to be a problem this time," the third mouse chirped. "The giant carried him away, too!"

"Two birds with one very big stone," the second mouse sang with glee.

"So, it's just a matter of time," the Beast said.

"Maybe not," the second mouse said. "I hear they've found the granddaughters."

Everyone groaned.

"I thought they had died!" Beauty said.

"No, just missing. Apparently, whatever carried off their parents didn't get them," the White Rabbit said.

"I'm sorry," Sabrina interrupted. "But did you say the girls' parents had been carried away?"

"The family thinks they abandoned them, but I've heard whispers that Henry and his wife were kidnapped," the Beast answered.

Sabrina and Daphne shared a stunned look.

"But it's not all bad news," the first mouse said.

"Indeed?" Beauty asked.

"I hear they're already trying to rescue their grandmother. Can you believe it?" said the White Rabbit. "Two kids taking on a giant! The whole family will be pushing up daisies by morning."

"That's the dumbest thing I've ever heard, and when it comes to the Grimms, that's saying something," the Beast said.

The crowd laughed.

"Momma Bear, you must be so excited," Beauty said, taking Sabrina's heavy paws into her delicate hands. "Soon, you'll be reunited with your family. Are they still hiding out in that Romanian zoo?"

"Uh . . . yes, that will be wonderful," Sabrina muttered, doing her best not to swat Beauty across the yard and then stomp the rest of them into paste. The talk of her parents had caught her attention.

"Do you know who kidnapped the parents?" said Sabrina.

"Who cares?" the White Rabbit replied.

"You people are horrible," a voice said from behind them.

Sabrina turned around and saw a beautiful, dark-skinned woman with dazzling green eyes. She wore a diamond tiara and a beautiful evening gown. She looked at the group in front of her with disgust.

"Briar Rose," Beauty said nervously. "I think you may have stepped into the middle of a conversation and misheard something."

"I heard all I need to hear," Briar Rose said.

The crowd shifted uncomfortably and turned away from her accusing stare while Sabrina's mind filled with possibilities. Could it be true? Their parents hadn't abandoned them? Could someone have kidnapped them?

Soon, Sabrina and Daphne were almost at the front of the line. Mr. Seven stood at the door, this time without his pointy "idiot" hat. He announced Beauty and the Beast and the couple disappeared into the chattering party inside.

"Good evening," Mr. Seven said as he opened the door for them. He cupped his hands together and yelled, "Momma Bear, escorted this evening by the Tin Woodsman," as the girls entered the room.

The mansion was a spectacular display of wealth and taste. A crystal chandelier hung from the ceiling and a beautiful red-carpeted staircase led up to a large landing, where four men played violins. The room was already crowded with people, animals, and monsters of all shapes and sizes—Everafters as far as the eye could see. They wandered around, talking and drinking champagne. Some laughed at jokes while others argued politics. A very ugly couple of trolls dressed in evening wear danced to the music, and several hulking waiters hurried around the room, extending trays of appetizers to guests. No one seemed to be bothered that there were ogres and winged people hobnobbing with talking animals, so Sabrina's worries that people would notice a man made of metal and a bear in a polka-dotted dress quickly dissolved.

"Sabrina, all of the Everafters wish we were dead," Daphne said.

Sabrina looked around the room. Every fairy-tale creature she had ever read about seemed to be here: Cinderella and her fairy godmother, the Mad Hatter, Mowgli and Baloo. Even Gepetto was off in a corner chatting with Ali Baba. And Sabrina knew they all hated the Grimms. As unsettling as it was, Sabrina could understand why. Even though Ms. Smirt had dumped the girls into some awful foster homes, Sabrina and Daphne knew they could always run away. For the Everafters there was no escape, and it had been that way for almost two hundred years. *It must be torment for them,* she thought.

"Where should we start?" Daphne asked.

They needed to get into the mayor's office, but they also needed to know where Charming was while they were doing it. Sabrina looked around the room, but he wasn't present.

"Let's just stay out of the way and keep our ears open. Once we know where he is, we'll make our way upstairs. For now, let's mingle."

The two walked awkwardly around the main room, gawking at the various literary celebrities and capturing bits of conversations.

"So she's not coming?" a dwarf said to a huge black panther. The panther licked its paw and hungrily eyed Sabrina.

"She never comes," the panther said. "If I left him at the altar, the last place I'd want to go is the man's house. I think it's very respectful of Snow White not to show her face here."

"But it was almost four hundred years ago. The man has been married at least half a dozen times since," the dwarf said. "Cinderella, Sleeping Beauty, and Rapunzel are all here. If they can move on, then Snow White surely can. This community is important."

"Ladies and gentlemen, we're pleased that you could attend the Ferryport Landing one hundredth annual community ball," Mr. Seven shouted from the top of the red staircase. The musicians laid down their instruments and everyone turned their attention to the mayor's assistant. "Allow me to introduce your host for this evening. Your mayor, his majesty, Prince Charming."

The violinists immediately broke into a stately song as a pair of double doors at the top of the stairs swung open. The crowd burst into applause as Charming waved and descended the staircase.

He was all smiles, shaking hands with everyone he met, kissing women on the hands, even if they were ugly witches or even uglier stepsisters, and calling everyone by name as he glided around the room. Mr. Seven followed closely behind him, handing out business cards.

"What do you say, Woodsman?" Charming asked, taking Daphne's hand and shaking it vigorously.

"Hello," Daphne seethed, unable to hide her contempt.

Charming reached over, took Sabrina's massive hairy paw, and placed a kiss on it.

"Momma Bear, as lovely as ever," he said with a wink. "I hope the two of you are having a wonderful time."

"We are, thank you," Sabrina said sharply. Maybe she had acquired some of the bear's aggressiveness along with its body, because for the second time that night she thought she might like to swat someone with her paw. One quick swipe and she could probably take Charming's head clean off his shoulders.

Instead, she smiled and did her best to curtsy, imagining how ridiculous this move looked from a twelve-hundred-pound bear.

"Please eat, drink, have a wonderful time. This celebration is for us," Charming said as he swept on to the center of the room.

"Friends, I am so happy that you could all attend the annual ball," he continued. "Each year we gather together as a community to toast our hard work and, most importantly, our patience."

Charming's words sent a frustrated rumble through the crowd.

"But once again, your support is needed to continue to build our community," he said. "There is still work to be done and we need your help to maintain services, to fund our fine police force, and various other community endeavors. So, I ask you, when you contribute tonight, give deeply. In fact, give until it hurts, or I'll put you all in jail!"

For a moment there was complete silence, and then, a broad, boyish grin sprang to Charming's face. The crowd burst into nervous laughter.

Suddenly, a woman pushed through the crowd. Her face was white with powder, as was the long wig she wore on her head. She had used a black pencil to accentuate her eyebrows and lips, and had drawn a large black mole on her left cheek. She wore a royal gown, decorated with large red hearts, and next to her stood two armed guards who, much to the girls' amaze-ment, were playing cards.

"Prince, what are you doing about the giant?" the woman demanded.

The crowd grew silent but Charming merely smiled at her.

"Your majesty, it is such an honor to have the Queen of Hearts here at the gala," he said.

"You haven't answered my question," the queen snapped, eye-ing the crowd to make sure all were paying attention. "I think the community deserves to know what you are doing to protect this town and if the money we give each year at this party of yours is well spent."

"Every Everafter can rest assured that my administration is on top of the problem," the prince said. "The sheriff and his deputies have been searching the forests and I have my best witches busy casting locator spells. And if that doesn't work, well, I'll just go lock up the next two-hundred-foot man I see."

The crowd chuckled at his joke.

"That's all fine and good, Charming," the queen replied. "But one must ask how a giant got loose in the first place. This kind of thing would never have happened in Wonderland. When I was ruler, people knew better than to try such shenani-gans. You have to be firm with the criminal element."

Some of the crowd muttered in agreement, but Charming only smiled wider.

"Well, Queen, let's not go losing our heads over this," he said. The crowd roared with laughter, causing the Queen of Hearts to turn red with rage. "It's just one giant, and . . ."

"I've heard a rumor that you are actually controlling this giant," Sabrina said, hardly believing the words came from her mouth.

"Momma Bear, I never pegged you for a gossip," the prince replied. "Did this nasty little rumor you heard carry more information? For instance, why I would want a giant smashing up the town?"

"So you could buy the land back cheap and rebuild your kingdom," Sabrina replied.

Charming's face turned pale. "Nonsense," he muttered.

"What if the Grimms hear of this?" said the Queen of Hearts.

"Relda is already aware of it. The giant has carried her off," the prince informed her.

The crowd roared in shock.

"Relda Grimm is in the hands of a giant?" the queen cried.

"As is Mr. Canis," Charming added.

The crowd was silent and then a spattering of applause broke out. Many of the Everafters shook hands and patted one another on the back, while others looked worried and upset.

"Canis will finally get what's coming to him," a troll cheered.

"Take that back!" Daphne screamed. Sabrina tried to pinch her to be quiet, but her paws slid off her sister's tin body.

"People, unfortunately, this celebration is turning into a town hall meeting," Charming called above the noise. "If you have any further concerns I want you to know that my door is always open . . . between the hours of eight and eight fifteen every morning. Please call for an appointment. For now, let's dance, drink, be merry, and most of all, be ourselves, free of the disguises we all wear to fit into this pathetic, boring little town. The night is young, and by the grace of magic, so are we."

Charming's words were followed by another lively tune from the violinists and the festive mood soon returned.

The girls mingled in the crowd, barely able to contain themselves whenever they heard angry, threatening words about their family from the mouths of characters they had grown up loving. It seemed that the only topic of conversation tonight was how wonderful the world would be if the Grimm family dropped off the face of the Earth. When the clock struck 8:45, both girls had heard enough. It was high time they made their move.

"I have to get upstairs," Sabrina said to Daphne. "If we stick around here any longer we're going to change back, and these people will probably kill us. Find somewhere out of the way and warn me on the walkie-talkie if Charming is coming."

"Good luck," Daphne said, wrapping her hard metal arms around Sabrina and hugging her.

Sabrina navigated through the crowd. As she approached the steps, she thought she'd finally found her opportunity. That was until Sheriff Hamstead stepped in her way.

"Young lady, you are under arrest," Hamstead said.

Sabrina wondered what she should do. She could probably knock the sheriff down with one swing of her big bear paw, but everyone would see. Running away didn't seem like an option, either.

"For being the prettiest lady at the ball," the sheriff continued.

"Uh, thank you," she stammered, somewhat confused.

"Wonderful party, don't you think?" said Hamstead as he transformed to his true pig self.

"Yes," she said. "Could you excuse me? I have to visit the ladies' room."

Hamstead apologized and let her pass. Sabrina lumbered up the stairs until she reached the top. She walked past the violinists and down a long hallway. Once she was out of sight of the crowd, she made sure no one was following, then reached into her purse and pulled out the walkie-talkie, awkwardly switching it on with her big paws.

"Jack, I'm upstairs," she said.

"Good job, duck. His office is the last one—" Jack said, his voice popping and crackling.

"I can barely hear you. Say again," Sabrina said.

"It's the last one on the right!" Jack repeated, still sounding distant.

Sabrina walked down the hallway. When she got to the end, she found the door Jack had spoken of. She opened it, and standing before her was another seven-foot grizzly bear ready to pounce. Sabrina screamed, but the bear did nothing. In fact, it didn't even twitch. Sabrina realized it was stuffed.

The room was dedicated to Prince Charming's hunting trophies. Several mounted deer heads, a stuffed fox, and a wild boar overlooked Charming's immense desk. A rattlesnake sat on top of it, poised and ready to strike. What portions of the walls weren't covered in dead animals were hung with portraits of the prince done in various artistic styles. There was even an abstract portrait in which his nose was on his forehead.

"Creepy," Sabrina whispered to herself. She reached for her walkie-talkie and pushed the button again. "I'm in."

"The coast is clear down here," Daphne's voice said. "Charming is busy talking to a raccoon in a tuxedo. That's so crazy!"

"Look for a map or something like that," Jack's voice squawked through the box. "Charming keeps records of everything."

Dozens of files and reports littered the top of the mayor's desk, including an unfolded map of the town. Someone had circled areas in red and written "reported sightings" next to them.

"Jack, are you there?" Sabrina said into the walkie-talkie.

"Yes," his voice crackled.

"I found a map with some circles on it, but there's nothing that says the exact time or location of a meeting. In fact, to me it looks like Charming's trying to track the giant as well."

"I doubt it . . . that . . . homes . . . too." Jack's voice broke up.

"Jack, I can't hear you. Try to get closer," Sabrina said, but there was no response.

"Daphne, I've lost Jack somehow. I'm going to take the map. What is Charming doing?" Sabrina asked.

But there was no response from her sister, either. Sabrina looked around the room. In the corner was a television. Hooked to the back by wires was a video camera, and on the television's screen was a frozen image of the Applebee farm. Sabrina crossed the room and found the remote control. She picked it up awkwardly and after several difficult seconds managed to get her giant paw to press the Play button.

The screen came to life with the most amazing scene. A giant beanstalk was exploding upward from the ground, soaring high into the sky and disappearing off the top edge of the TV. Within seconds, an enormous body came crawling down it and the sight sent shivers through Sabrina. It was the giant she had met the day before. It stomped down on the little Applebee farmhouse just as Mr. Applebee leaped out the door. Granny had been right. The lens cap did mean someone—Charming— had taped the whole violent episode!

"Daphne, I found a tape in Charming's office that shows the giant destroying the farmhouse. Now we have proof that he and the giant are working together," Sabrina said.

But before she could finish her sentence, the door burst open and the Tin Woodsman was pushed inside. Behind her was Charming, looking murderous. He slammed the door and took a crossbow from the wall, where it was hanging like a piece of art.

"I'm sorry," Daphne apologized. "He snuck up on me before I could warn you."

"Who are you?" he demanded.

"I'm Momma Bear," Sabrina lied.

"Is that so?" Charming sneered. "That would be interesting, since it's almost December and you should be three weeks into your hibernation by now."

"I didn't want to miss such a lovely party," Sabrina stammered.

Next to the door sat a quill of arrows. Charming selected one, inserted it in the crossbow, and pulled the bowstring back. Then he aimed it at Sabrina's heart.

"I'm going to give you until the count of five to tell me who you are or your head is going to join the others on my wall," he threatened coolly.

10

’m not playing any more games with you people,” Charming said. “I’ve told you already I’m not interested in joining the Scarlet Hand. Your revolution is not for me.”

“We don’t know what you’re talking about,” Daphne cried.

“One,” Charming began counting.

Sabrina looked over at the clock. There were only seconds left before the magic would wear off, but more than the five Charming had promised them.

“We’re Relda Grimm’s granddaughters,” she blurted out desperately.

“Two.”

“We used a magic wand to change our shape so we could

sneak into your house," Daphne cried. Oily tears leaked from her eyes.

"Three."

"We're not part of any revolution!" Sabrina begged. "We just want our grandmother back!"

"Four."

"We're not lying to you!" Daphne sobbed.

"Five."

Sabrina closed her eyes tightly and awaited her death, wondering if she would be stuffed like the other bear in Charming's office or if her body would change back after her heart had stopped beating. But when nothing happened, after a few more moments, Sabrina bravely opened her eyes. She and her sister had magically transformed back into their normal states. The only evidence of their disguises was the oily smears on Daphne's cheeks.

"Ladies, I could toss you into jail and throw away the key for what you've done," Charming said, removing the arrow from his crossbow. "You've used a magical item to help a known criminal escape from jail, infiltrated an Everafters party without an invitation, impersonated Everafters, committed espionage against a government official, broken into my home, put the Ferryport Landing Ball in serious jeopardy, and ruined two pairs of Sheriff Hamstead's pants."

"We didn't ruin your stupid party," Sabrina argued.

"If that crowd downstairs sees the two of you here, the top of this house will fly off," Charming replied. "The only way we're going to prevent a mob is to have Hamstead toss you in some old sacks and carry you out the servants' entrance. He can take you down to the jailhouse and let you cool off in a cell."

Sabrina lunged for the video camera. The wires came with it and the image of the giant faded from the television screen.

"We're not going anywhere without our grandmother and Mr. Canis," Sabrina said. "This tape is all the evidence we'll need. How do you think those people downstairs are going to feel knowing you intend to buy up this town and smash anyone that gets in your way?"

Sabrina expected Charming to fight for the tape, but instead he only laughed.

"You are just like your parents." Charming chuckled. "Henry was always shooting his mouth off before his brain could catch up and Veronica was the suspicious one. What an unsettling combination you are."

Suddenly, something moved in the window. Sabrina turned her head, but nothing was there. "Did you see that?"

"See what?" Charming asked as a giant, puss-filled eye peered into the house.

"ENGLISHMAN!" a booming voice growled, shaking the windows in their frames.

"That!" the girls shouted.

Charming calmly picked up the phone on his desk and dialed a number. "Mr. Seven, are you aware that there is a giant outside?" he said into the receiver, as if he were informing a waiter that there was a hair in his soup. "Oh, you didn't know. Well, now you do . . . No, this isn't some kind of emergency drill . . . Well, I agree, we should do something about it before the guests panic. Maybe you should send the witches out to put a protection spell on the house . . . Well, of course it's a good idea!"

Charming slammed the phone down, crossed the room, and dragged both girls roughly out of the office and down the hall.

"Where are you taking us?" Sabrina demanded.

"Keep your heads down and don't say a word," the prince sneered. "I'm taking you outside."

An acidy fear rose up in Sabrina's throat as they stumbled out of his office and into the second-floor hallway. "You can't take us out there with that thing!" Sabrina cried, pulling at Charming's vise-like grasp.

"You wanted to find your grandmother. Well, her ride just showed up," he said.

"HELP!" Sabrina cried as they turned a corner and headed

down a long hall toward the back of the house. Daphne took her sister's cue and called for help as well, causing many of the guests to look up and see what was happening.

"Those are the Grimm children!" an orangutan shouted angrily.

"No need to let it ruin your evening," said Charming, with his toothy smile. "I have the situation under control."

"They're spying on us!" the Queen of Hearts gasped. "Off with their . . ."

"They aren't spies, my friends," the prince said as he changed course and pulled the girls down the stairs with him into the angry crowd. "Please, go back to the celebration."

But before he could get the words out of his mouth a horrible crunching sound filled the room. The partygoers looked to the ceiling, only to see it ripped away right before their eyes. Pieces of plaster fell down around everyone and a collective scream erupted among the Everafters.

"The sky is falling! The sky is falling!" a chicken cried as it raced for the door, only to get caught in a stampede of terror when the hole in the roof was replaced by the giant's horrible, gnarled face, breathing its rancid, rotten-egg breath down on the crowd.

The Queen of Hearts ran to a nearby window, threw open the curtains, and tried to climb out. Her playing card attendants rushed over in time to catch her from falling over. The rest of the crowd ran in all directions, and the panic gave Sabrina and Daphne a chance to break Charming's grip. They rushed into the crowd and ducked between legs and feathers as all sorts of unusual creatures rushed around them.

"Where is the murderer?" the giant bellowed.

"He's not here, big boy. The murderer is not here," Charming shouted as he turned to face the monster.

"Liars! You protect him," the giant growled. "I smell his murderous blood. He released me only in hopes of killing me but my fate will not be like that of my brothers and sisters. He is here and I will have him."

Charming looked up the staircase to the violinists, who were scattered in fear. "I didn't tell you to stop playing," he said, snapping his fingers at them. Bewildered, the musicians went back to their overturned chairs, set them upright, and began playing music as if a giant wasn't staring down at them.

"Fe, fi, fo, fum, I smell the blood of an . . ."

"I think we've all had enough of your temper tantrum," Charming interrupted. Suddenly, three figures fluttered into the air and hovered around the giant's head. One of them was an ugly old woman darting through the air on a broom; the second was a strikingly exotic beauty dressed all in black, who levitated off the ground; and the third was a blond lady inside a silver bubble. As she floated by, Sabrina recognized her as Glinda from the hospital. All three had magic wands that they waved threateningly at the giant. The monster swatted at the witches, but they weaved and bobbed out of the way of his massive hand. The ugly witch waved her wand and a rocket of flame shot out of it and exploded on the giant's chest, searing his shirt and causing him to scream in agony.

"Stop!" Daphne cried. "Our family is in his pocket!" The little girl broke away from her sister and ran outside. Sabrina, followed by Charming, rushed after her.

The witches had flown out of the hole in the roof and now continued their assault.

"Leave while you can, Giant!" Charming shouted.

The second witch raised her wand and a stream of lightning fired out of it, hitting the giant in his face. The giant roared with pain and raised his hands to block the bolt. A charred, black smear was added to the other ugly features on his grizzled face.

Glinda waved her wand and a spray of ice froze the giant's backside and continued to cover the rest of his body. Within seconds, the massive man was encased in an ice tomb, but soon cracks appeared and, with flexing muscles and a powerful roar, the giant broke free. Enormous chunks of ice rained down on the parking lot, flattening an unlucky car.

The doors of the mansion were thrown wide and a dozen men rushed out past the girls. Each was in a purple tunic embroidered with a red lion on the chest. Swinging their swords wildly in the air, they roared a war cry as they rushed toward the giant. At the front of the attack was a man Sabrina instinctively knew to be King Arthur. The knights charged the giant's feet, and together they whacked angrily at an exposed big toe. The giant roared at the assault and stomped his feet angrily, trying to squash his attackers. Each of the men was lightning quick and dodged the giant's blows, managing to strike at his exposed ankle in the process. Shrieking in pain, the giant quickly turned and fled.

Charming knelt in respect as the king and his knights turned to face him.

"I am indebted to the Knights of the Round Table. Thank you, Your Highness," Charming said.

"Your thanks will not be enough, Charming," King Arthur barked. "The beast destroyed my car. Trust that you will find a repair estimate in the mail this week."

Charming scowled, but as the party guests filed out of the half-destroyed mansion, he forced a smile. Mr. Seven rushed to the prince's side, carrying a large black pot he held out to the approaching crowd. "Friends, who says nothing exciting ever happens in Ferryport Landing?" The prince chuckled. But this time his wit and charm fell on angry ears. The people passed him, returning his laughter with disgusted looks.

"Is this what we're paying you for?" the White Rabbit said as he hopped past.

"People, there's no need to leave," Charming said. "We'll have the mansion back to its old self in just a matter of moments. There's plenty of food and drink and we've even arranged a door prize."

"As the elected leader of this community, I would have thought you'd take the safety of your constituents much more seriously," a Bengal tiger said as he stalked past them.

"I assure you, Shere Khan . . ." But the tiger didn't stop to hear Charming's assurances.

"Well, if you all must go, please don't forget to donate to the Ferryport Community Fund," the prince continued, kicking Mr. Seven, who immediately held the pot higher so that everyone could see. But not a single penny was added to the donations.

"I do believe this town is in need of some new leadership," the Queen of Hearts said, as she left. Charming said nothing as he watched the last of his guests drive away.

"Put the pot down, Mr. Seven," he said. The dwarf slowly lowered the empty pot and took a peek inside.

"We want our grandmother and her friend," Sabrina demanded.

"This is all your fault!" Charming shouted as he turned on them.

"What?"

"You two brought him here."

"If you can't control your giant, then maybe you shouldn't be working with one," Daphne advised.

"I'm not working with any giant. Only a fool who wants to be someone's lunch would make a deal with a giant," Charming said.

"That's a lie," Sabrina yelled. "He's one of your goons, just like those guys you met at the cabin."

"Ladies, I am nobility. I don't have goons. Those men don't work for me. I was there to arrest them and their boss."

"Well, if you're not their boss, who is?" Sabrina demanded.

Charming snatched the video camera from Sabrina's hand. He opened a side panel where a small LCD screen folded out. Then he rewound the recording, pressed the Play button, and handed the camera back to the girls.

The image was shaky at first but then suddenly it cleared up as the person holding the camera set it down on the hill that overlooked Applebee's farm. Four men were talking to one another.

Two of them were extremely tall, another was short and fat, and the fourth couldn't be seen. It was obvious who the other three were—Bobby, Tony, and Steve—the goons who had attacked the family at the hospital. Finally, the fourth figure stepped in front of the lens, leaned down, and grinned broadly. It was Jack.

"That's evidence we found on Jack when he was arrested. He wanted a tape of himself killing a giant," Charming cried. "It had nothing to do with the farmhouse. In fact, he admitted he thought the farmer had left town."

Jack laughed wildly at the camera, held up a small white bean, and then rushed down the hill. Soon, the familiar footage of the beanstalk and the destruction of the giant played again.

"So, you're not trying to buy up the town to rebuild your kingdom?" Daphne asked.

"On the contrary, I *am* trying to buy up this town," Charming said. "But there are better ways to get what you want than to let a giant loose on the countryside."

Sabrina didn't know whether to be furious with his admission or respect his honesty.

"So why did you send the sheriff after us?" Daphne asked.

"He was supposed to pick you up and take you somewhere safe until we could hunt down the giant and find your grandmother," Charming said.

"Every Everafter in this town wishes we were dead," Sabrina said. "Why would you want to help us?"

"I have my reasons."

"I'm confused," Daphne said. "Why would Jack bring us here and tell us this story about you being the bad guy?"

"And why did he want to stay in contact with these, if he was just going to take off?" Sabrina said, handing Charming her walkie-talkie.

"Because, if he kept you busy he could go back to your house," the prince said.

"But he can't get in. He doesn't have the keys," Sabrina replied.

"He doesn't need the keys," Daphne gasped. "We didn't say 'good-bye' to the house when we left. We used the ruby slippers. The house is unlocked."

Hamstead, in his human form, came rushing out of the mansion.

"I've got the deputies chasing the giant," he said. "He's heading into the woods in the direction of Widow's Peak."

"Good job," Charming said. The sheriff beamed with pride.

"We've also searched the grounds. There's no sign of Jack," Hamstead continued. "But we did find this."

He held out Jack's bloody handkerchief.

"So the giant would smell him and come running," Charming said. "You might as well join your men, Sheriff. The girls and I will call you if we need you."

"Where are you going?" Hamstead asked.

The prince took Sabrina's arm and urged Daphne to do the same. "We're going back to the Grimm house. I have an unsettling notion of what our giant killer is up to," Charming said.

Sabrina clicked her heels together.

"There's no place like home. There's no place like home. There's no place like home."

Instantly, the girls and Charming were standing outside of Granny's house. The front door was wide open and through the doorway they could see that Jack had ransacked their home. They walked inside. Bookshelves were tipped over, furniture was overturned, and even the couch cushions were thrown aside. He had searched through every kitchen cupboard, emptied closets, and destroyed antiques. But his crimes against the house weren't what was bothering Sabrina. What hurt her was that she had been tricked. In the last year and a half, Sabrina had learned to be street-smart and savvy. She was the one who was supposed to pull fast ones on people. She was the queen of the sneaks and she had been suckered.

Suddenly, the telephone rang. She picked up the receiver and said hello.

"Hello, this is Wilma Faye at Action Four News. I'm following up on a tip we got about a half hour ago. A Mr. Englishman said there would be a murder on Widow's Peak tonight. We've already got a camera crew on their way but we were hoping we might be able to speak to Mr. Englishman first," the woman begged.

"No, he's not here," Sabrina replied.

"Well, if you see him please tell him that we are very intrigued by the story and will have a camera team and reporter there as he requested," the woman continued. Then, with a click, she hung up.

"That was a reporter," Sabrina said. "Jack called them and told them there was going to be a murder on Widow's Peak tonight."

"This is exactly what I was trying to prevent. He's going to kill a giant on television so he can be famous again," Charming said. "When the world sees that, this little town will be turned upside down by reporters. There's too much here to explain. We've got to stop him."

"Elvis!" Daphne cried suddenly. The giant dog was nowhere to be seen. Daphne shouted his name and, after several painful moments of silence, a low bark could be heard from upstairs.

Daphne rushed up the steps, followed by Sabrina and Charming. She threw open the door to Mirror's room and found Elvis lying on the floor in a small puddle of his own blood. He had a serious cut on his belly but he barked happily when he saw the girls. Daphne knelt down and kissed the dog gently on his nose. When she lifted her face, tears were pouring down her cheeks.

"He hurt Elvis," the little girl sobbed.

"Girls, we have to find Jack," Charming said coldly. "We don't have time for this mongrel."

Sabrina and Daphne looked at the man as if he were a moldy sandwich that had slowly turned to soup in the bottom of the refrigerator. The prince groaned and took his cell phone from his pocket. He dialed a number and sighed impatiently.

"Mr. Seven, I need you to send one of the Three to the Grimm house. The door is open so they can come right in. There's a dog that needs medical assistance . . . Yes, a dog . . . a D-O-G. No, Mr. Seven, I don't know what's wrong with him, maybe a broken rib . . . No, Mr. Seven . . . Yes, Mr. Seven . . . Mr. Seven, if you don't stop asking me questions, I'm going to feed you to this dog."

Sabrina eyed the man suspiciously and Charming caught her gaze.

"And Mr. Seven, my orders are that whichever one of the

witches comes, she respect this house," Charming added. "No snooping."

Daphne wrapped her arms around the prince's neck and hugged him as he hung up his phone.

"Thank you," she sobbed and, for a brief moment, Charming seemed to enjoy the hug, but then he pulled away from her.

"You're ruining my suit," he replied, wiping his lapel clean of the girl's tears. "We should check the mirror."

Sabrina gazed over at it. The little man who was usually in its reflection was missing.

"Mirror!" Charming shouted.

"You have to step through it," said Sabrina.

"I'm aware of how it works," the prince said impatiently. "I used to be engaged to one of its former owners."

He stepped into the reflection and disappeared. Sabrina followed closely behind, leaving Daphne to nurse Elvis.

The little man known as Mirror was lying on his side on the cold marble floor, barely conscious and covered in bruises. Charming knelt down to him and lifted the pudgy man's head. Mirror slowly opened his eyes and grimaced in pain.

"He was too strong and fast for me. I couldn't stop him," Mirror groaned.

"What did he take?" Charming asked.

"I tried to fight him off but he just laughed at me. You wouldn't believe how quick he is," Mirror complained.

"Focus, man! We need to know if Jack took anything."

"He took the beans," Mirror replied.

"How? He doesn't have a key," Sabrina asked, reaching into her pocket and pulling out Granny's key ring.

"I forgot to remind you to lock the door after you let him take a peek at the jar," said the little man.

"I don't get it," Sabrina said. "If killing the giant will make him famous again, what does he want with the beans?"

"It's insurance. If his fame starts to fade, he'll let another giant out with another one of those beans. The giant will kill people and destroy things and then Jack will come to the rescue," Charming explained.

"But how is he going to find the giant in the first place?" Sabrina asked. "We haven't been able to find him and he's two hundred feet tall."

"He's not going to have to find it, it's going to find him," Charming answered. "Giants have a great sense of smell, especially when it comes to blood. That's why the giant showed up at the mansion. Jack left his bloody handkerchief and the giant could smell it. It's amazing, really, that they can smell anything over their own stink. If one touches you, you can't wash off the odor for weeks."

Suddenly, Sabrina thought of the two pieces of fabric Elvis had brought into the room just before the group had left for Charming's mansion. One was Granny Relda's cloth from the giant, the other was a piece of Jack's pants. *Elvis was trying to warn us that Jack had been near a giant,* Sabrina realized. She was a terrible detective—she couldn't recognize a clue when it was offered to her by a two-hundred-pound Great Dane. She wanted to kick herself, but she had to focus on what Charming had said.

"But if giants have such great noses, why didn't this one attack us here? Jack was in our house for hours," she said to Charming.

"Protection spells. If Relda is anything, she's careful. We have one on the jailhouse, too," he replied.

"So, what are we going to do?"

"Mirror, I'm going to need something," Charming said.

• • •

Sabrina unlocked the door labeled MAGICAL ARMORY and let the prince inside. The room was filled with all types of weapons—bows and arrows, swords, a nasty-looking pole with a spiky metal ball attached by a chain, and hundreds of others. Some things were obviously magical, as they glowed or hummed, while most were just shining with horrible possibilities.

Charming pointed to a sword on the wall. "That's the one," he said.

Mirror hobbled into the room with a worried face. "I find this very unwise. There is already one Everafter running around with magic; this town does not need a second. Especially with Excalibur. Any person whose skin is pierced by its blade is a goner. Even the tiniest scratch will kill you."

Sabrina took the sword off the wall and held it in her hand. It was long and wide, with a jewel-encrusted handle. An odd tingle raced through her when she held it with both hands. She felt powerful, the way King Arthur must have felt when Excalibur belonged to him.

"Sabrina, is this someone you can trust?" Mirror asked.

"No, he's not," she said. "I've heard what this town thinks of my family and what my death might mean for your freedom. How do I know you won't just stab me in the back when I'm not looking?"

"Grimm, I am not your friend," Charming said. "I resent your family for the life they have forced me to live for the last two hundred years and I resent you for the future that you represent. And if I were doing this for your worthless family, you would probably be right. But I'm not doing this for you. I'm doing it for me. As much as Baba Yaga's spell has trapped me in Ferryport Landing, it has also benefited me. I have power here. I have wealth and respect. If Jack shows the world that giants and fairy tales are real, then life in this town will change and my position as its ruler . . . I mean mayor, might be challenged. Therefore, you and I are in an unusual situation. Tonight, I am your ally, and I will help you save your grandmother and Canis. If that is the only solution, then so be it. But rest assured, Grimm, tomorrow I am your enemy again."

Sabrina looked up into his eyes and saw that he was being honest, even if his brand of honesty made her sick to her stomach. Could she trust him? She reached into her pocket, took out the picture of her family, and gazed at their faces—her mother and father, Mr. Canis, and finally, Granny Relda. She had to do something to get the old woman back. She wasn't going to lose her family all over again. She took the heavy sword and handed it to him.

Mirror continued to protest, limping along, as Charming and Sabrina exited the room and returned through the mirror. Daphne was waiting for them with Elvis. They gently carried the dog into the hallway and then Sabrina carefully locked the door to Mirror's room.

"You stay here with Elvis," Sabrina ordered her sister.

"No way!" Daphne cried. "We're Grimms, this is what *we* do!"

"This is dangerous."

"Whatever," the little girl said, grabbing Sabrina's hand tightly.

Sabrina surrendered, hooked her finger into Charming's pocket, and clicked Dorothy's shoes together.

"There's no place like where Jack is," she said.

"Sabrina, wouldn't these shoes take us to wherever Mom and Dad are?" Daphne wondered aloud. Sabrina's eyes grew wide with possibility.

"We can save them next," her sister said happily.

"All right," Sabrina said, clicking her heels together. "There's no place like where Jack is. There's no place like where Jack is."

The lights went out and the familiar squeaky wheeze filled Sabrina's ears. In a split-second, Charming and the girls were standing in the woods on Widow's Peak. They had little time to adjust to their new surroundings. Sabrina looked above her and saw the giant's massive foot preparing to crush them all.

They managed to leap out of the way but the aftershock tossed them around as if they were on a sinking ship. The ground split apart, sending stones and soil into a gaping crevice where the group had once stood.

The giant leaned down to get a better look at the three people scurrying at his feet. He reached to snatch them, but a flaming arrow zipped from the tree line and landed in the side of the giant's face. The monster cried in pain as he plucked it from his cheek, only to have a second and third arrow pierce his chin.

"Stop it, Jack!" Sabrina commanded. "There are people in the giant's pocket and if you kill him they'll die when he falls!"

Jack peeked his head out from behind some branches in a nearby tree and laughed.

"Oh, it's not time to kill him yet," Jack shouted, remaining safely hidden in the trees. "I'm just trying to get him good and angry."

"We know about the reporters, Jack," Charming said. "We're never going to let that happen."

Jack fired several more arrows into the giant's face, landing a painful shot to the monster's lower lip. The giant raged as he tried to pluck it out. While the giant was busy, the young man dropped out of the tree and landed as nimbly as a cat.

"Blimey! Charming and the Grimms on the same side? I never thought I'd live to see the day," he said. "Has the prince turned traitor like that worthless mongrel Canis?"

"The only allegiance I have is to myself," Charming said as he waved Excalibur in the air. "Now, we can do this the easy way or the hard way. But the result will be the same. You're going back to jail."

"Sorry, Prince, but I've spent my last day in the Ferryport Landing lockup. My fans await," Jack said, loading another arrow into his bow and firing it at the giant. It pierced the skin between two fingers of the giant's left hand, and he shrieked. Overcome with rage, the giant swept his arm across the tops of the forest trees, cracking many ancient cedars in half. A sizable chunk of one fell from the sky and nearly hit Charming in the head.

"Oh, he's angry now." the giant killer laughed, loading his arrow again. This time he aimed it at Charming.

"Jack, don't!" Sabrina cried.

"I was hoping it wouldn't have to come to this," he said as he lined up his arrow with Charming's heart. "But don't worry. I promise to have them spell your name correctly in your obituary."

He released his arrow and the girls watched it soar through the air at Charming. Daphne screamed and squeezed her sister's hand, knowing Jack's aim was true. But something happened the girls didn't expect. Charming lifted Excalibur slightly and the arrow bounced off its metal blade and fell to the ground. Jack was flabbergasted.

"What luck you have!" he cried.

"Try again and see if it was luck," the prince said, stepping forward with the sword.

With hands like lightning, Jack fired another arrow and Charming deflected it with similar results. Jack pulled three arrows from his quill and lined them up together on his bow. He fired them all at the same time. Sabrina watched in amazement as Charming guided Excalibur to block each from their deadly course.

"I can do this all night," the prince bragged, but just then the giant's monstrous hand swung down and hit him from behind. Excalibur was knocked free of his grip and fell at Sabrina's feet. Charming was sent sailing through the forest, landing painfully against a tree and slumping to the ground.

Jack pulled more arrows from his quill, lit them with a lighter Sabrina recognized from Granny's kitchen, and fired five off with furious speed. Each landed in more of the giant's sensitive spots. The painful barrage was enough to get the giant to back off, giving the young man an opportunity to turn on the girls. He put another arrow into his bow and aimed it at Sabrina.

Instinctively, Sabrina reached down and snatched Excalibur from the ground. It was incredibly heavy and bulky but she swung it around in the air the best she could.

"And what do you think you're going to do with that, duck?"

Jack scoffed as he stepped toward her. "Grimms aren't killers. You don't have it in you!"

"Well, we're kind of new at this job. If we break a couple of rules, that just goes with the learning process," Sabrina said with as much bravery as she could muster. Her courage was short-lived. As Jack got closer, she noticed something painted on his shirt. It was a red hand, just like the one the police had found in her parent's abandoned car. It sent a chill through her body.

"You took my parents," Sabrina said.

Jack looked down at the red hand and smiled. "No, girl, I didn't, but I know who did. The Scarlet Hand has plans for them."

"Where are they?" Daphne cried.

He laughed.

"You know, I grew up reading about you," Sabrina said, trying to keep him busy. "You had a very exciting story. You climbed the beanstalk, killed the giant, and captured the treasure. Lots of kids think of you as a hero."

"But not you?"

"Once, but not now. Now that I've met you—the real Jack—I see what a rotten person you are. That's what you're famous for now, Jack. Not being a giant killer, but being scum."

"Give me the sword, girl, so I can cut your tongue out with it," he threatened.

"Daphne, I want you to run away and get some help," Sabrina said. She knew she couldn't deflect Jack's arrow and didn't want her sister to see her die.

"I won't do it," Daphne insisted.

Jack pulled his bowstring back further and, just as he was about to fire his arrow, the giant's foot came down on top of him, giving the man only a split second to leap out of the way.

Daphne grabbed her sister's hand and together they raced into the forest, dodging trees and branches. Jack followed closely behind, and worse, the giant strode after him. Its first step landed several yards behind them.

An arrow whizzed by and impaled itself into a nearby tree.

"That was a warning shot, ladies," the young man shouted as he loaded another arrow. "I'm quite good with this thing."

Suddenly, the two girls were slipping down the side of a hill and into an ice-cold creek. Another arrow splashed in the water at Sabrina's feet as they pulled themselves out of the stream and continued to run. With now-frozen feet, they did their best to avoid the jagged rocks that littered the forest floor, but soon Sabrina took a tumble and fell end-over-end across the ground.

She tried to stand up and quickly realized she was missing something—her left shoe—Dorothy's left slipper—lay glistening in the moonlight behind her. It had fallen off.

"C'mon," Daphne begged as she tried to help her big sister to her feet, but Sabrina crawled desperately toward the shoe. It was their only chance of finding their parents. She used her arms to pull herself along the ground, knowing that Jack would fall upon her at any second. But before she could reach it, the giant's foot came down hard on top of the slipper. The vibrations shook the girls and sent them tumbling. When the giant lifted his foot, the shoe was gone; the only thing remaining was a piece of glistening fabric that turned to dust in Sabrina's outstretched hands.

Heartbroken, Sabrina pulled her sister behind a huge oak tree and the two of them rested.

"Don't worry, I'll think of something," she said, squeezing her sister's hand.

But the sound of a monstrous crash drowned Sabrina's answer and flooded the forest. Splintering wood and damp soil rained from the sky as the tree they stood next to was violently uprooted.

The two girls looked up into the face of death towering above them and felt its hot, pungent breath blow their hair back from their scalps. *What's happened to our lives?* Sabrina wondered.

The giant tossed the tree aside and then reached down with his grubby hand to pick them up, but just as he did, Sabrina thrust Excalibur into the air. The giant's hand plunged into its blade, and suddenly his eyes lit up in surprise.

"What was that?" he asked softly. He stood up as if he was in a daze, unsure even of where he was. The anger in his face melted away, replaced by a sort of calm curiosity, and he began to wobble on his feet. Unable to keep his balance, he sailed backward, landing flat on his back and crushing an acre of forest beneath him. A thick cloud of dust rose above his body and settled down all around them. Half a pound of soil landed in Sabrina's blond hair.

And then, all was still.

"I didn't mean for that to happen," Sabrina said, looking in horror at the sword still clutched in her hand.

"Granny Relda and Mr. Canis?" Daphne whispered as tears filled her eyes.

Jack rushed through the brush and saw the giant, lying dead on the ground.

"You've killed him," he said angrily. "*I* was going to kill him!"

"It's over, Jack," Sabrina said.

"It's not over until I say it is," Jack raged. "I'm going to be famous again, but for another reason. Tonight, the Everafters of Ferryport Landing are going to find they are suddenly free from the spell that has kept them in this mercilessly boring town for two centuries. With your grandmum now dead, the spell turns to the last living Grimm. Some might be patient enough to wait for you two to die of old age, but I am not. This ends tonight."

11

ack rushed forward and violently shoved Sabrina to the ground. Daphne lunged at him, but she received the same treatment. Sabrina had dropped Excalibur in the fall and Jack quickly picked it up, admiring its blade for a moment and then readying himself to bring it down on Sabrina's head.

"They're going to have a parade in my honor for this," the young man said with a sick smile.

Suddenly, a loud, wheezing honk filled the night. Jack spun around. In the giant's breast pocket, a wonderful thing appeared: Two headlights blinked to life. An engine roared, backfired violently, and then, with a squeal of tires, the family car ripped through the pocket and sped along the giant's body. At the wheel was Mr. Canis and, next to him, Granny Relda, safe and sound. The car soared over the giant's gelatinous belly, down his leg, and hit his huge kneecap, sending the car sailing into the air. It landed several yards away from Jack and the girls and skidded to a stop. The engine puttered out, the lights went dim, and the car doors opened. Granny Relda stepped out with a very concerned face.

"Jack, what is the meaning of this?" she asked.

The young man pulled the mason jar of beans out of his jacket and held it up.

"It's about this, old woman. It's about capturing my rightful place in the spotlight," Jack said.

"Those days are over," Mr. Canis said, as he stepped out of the car.

"Maybe for you, traitor," Jack snarled. "But I've got bigger plans than selling shoes and measuring hemlines. These beans are going to make me a hero again. But for that to happen, some things have to change around here."

"What are you suggesting?" Granny Relda asked.

"The Grimms have to die."

"You know I won't allow that, Jack," Mr. Canis said.

"I've been killing giants since I was a lad. I suspect I won't have too much trouble with an old mutt like you."

Mr. Canis looked over to Granny Relda. Something passed

between them—a sort of question and answer that only the two of them shared. Granny Relda nodded in approval and Mr. Canis took off his hat.

"If you want to sic your dog on me, Grimm, then do it. But I'll have my destiny either way," Jack said, putting the jar of beans back into his jacket and swinging Excalibur around menacingly. "I've been waiting for this for a very long time."

Mr. Canis smiled in a way Sabrina could only describe as eager. Once again, she was sure he was doomed. The old man had managed to take out three overweight goons, but could he handle a lightning-fast slayer of giants carrying a sword that killed anything it touched?

Jack charged wildly, screaming into the air, but before he could even swing the deadly sword, a change came over Mr. Canis. His shirt ripped off his chest as his body doubled in size. His feet snapped and stretched as they transformed into paws. Hair sprang from every inch of skin, fangs crept down over his lips, his nose extended out, replaced by a snarling snout, and the tops of his ears twisted into points and raised to the top of his head. But most disturbing were his eyes, as they changed into an achingly bright blue color. The same color Canis's eyes were in the picture Sabrina had found of her family. The transformation was complete. Mr. Canis had turned into a wolf the size of a rhinoceros.

"Bring it on, little man," the Wolf snarled, as it jumped up on its back legs. Sabrina could hear a hint of Mr. Canis's voice in the Wolf's growl, but the way he said the words held nothing of her grandmother's feeble old friend's calm. The Wolf's voice was full of viciousness.

The Wolf charged at Jack and sent him hurtling backward into a tree, giving the young man no time to recover as the Wolf savagely sunk its teeth into Jack's right arm. Jack screamed in agony. With the Wolf on top of him, he couldn't swing the deadly sword. The best he could do was hit the beast on the head with Excalibur's handle. The Wolf backed away, slightly dazed, and then licked its lips.

"Bad news for you, Jack," the Wolf barked. "I know your taste now, and I like it."

In the commotion, Granny held out her arms for the girls and they ran to her side.

"Everything will be fine," Granny consoled them.

"You didn't tell us Mr. Canis was one of them," Sabrina said.

"Oh, didn't I? Yes, Mr. Canis is the Big Bad Wolf," Granny said as she kept her eyes on the fight.

"The Big Bad Wolf?" the girls cried.

The Wolf lunged at Jack, ripping his chest with its razor-sharp claws. Jack swung back and punched the beast in the

face, but the Wolf just chuckled. Desperately, the young man jumped up, grabbed a tree branch, and used it to catapult himself at the Wolf. The force sent them both tumbling over each other, leaving Jack on top.

"When I kill you, this town is going to erect a statue in my honor," Jack boasted. "How does it feel to know that your own kind wish you dead?"

"Not nearly as bad as it must feel to know they don't care if you are alive," the Wolf snarled as it rolled over on top of Jack. "Maybe they'll notice when I leave your rotting corpse hanging in the town square. That is, after I've eaten all the juicy parts."

Jack thrust his knee into the Wolf's belly, knocking the wind out of it, and giving the young man the chance to throw the beast off. He crawled to his feet and picked up Excalibur.

"Even the tiniest scratch will send you on your way, mongrel," Jack warned. He rushed forward, pushed the beast against a tree, and held the lethal blade to its neck. "Perhaps they will now call me Jack the Legend Killer, as well."

Sabrina looked to her grandmother and saw the worry in her face. She knew Jack was going to win, and then he would turn on them. How would the three of them fight him off? But suddenly, above the snarling and fighting, she heard an odd sound, as if someone had just played some notes on a flute. At first,

Sabrina thought she might have imagined it, but then a swarm of pixies darted out of the woods and surrounded Jack. He cried in pain with every little sting and soon blood began to leak from all over his body.

"No one likes a bragger," Puck said as he floated down from the trees and rested on a branch above the fighting.

"Puck!" Daphne cried. "You really are a hero!"

"Hush, you'll ruin my reputation," Puck replied.

In vain, Jack tried to brush the pixies off, swatting at them wildly with little result and dropping the sword in his struggle.

"Old lady, are you well?" Puck asked as he floated to the ground. "I tried to tell Sabrina that Jack couldn't be trusted but she wouldn't listen. She's very stubborn and stupid."

"I'm sure Sabrina had her reasons, Puck," Granny replied as she winked at her granddaughter. "But before we can celebrate, Jack has a jar in his coat we need."

Puck smiled, took out his flute, and played a quick, sharp note. One lone pixie left the others and buzzed around the boy's head.

"We need to get that jar away from him," Puck said. The little light blinked as if to say yes, and zipped into the storm of pixies tormenting Jack. Suddenly, a small group of them flew into his jacket and collectively carried the jar of magic beans away.

"No!" Jack cried in panic, swatting and swinging wildly at the pixies. Seeing his prize carried off, he desperately grasped for the jar, only managing to knock it to the ground, sending shards of glass and beans in all directions.

"Oh, dear," Granny gasped.

The Wolf fell over as if it was having a fight with itself.

"I'm not going back inside, old man!" the beast bellowed. It groaned and complained as it transformed back into Mr. Canis. The old man was exhausted and broken. He had a worried look on his face.

"We have to get the children out of here," Mr. Canis gasped.

Suddenly, the Action Four News van came careening through the woods and stopped. The doors slid open and Wilma Faye got out, followed by her cameraman. The reporter fixed her business suit, checked her hair in a small compact mirror, and then turned to face the girls.

"Girls, I'm Wilma Faye from Action Four News. We heard there was a story out here tonight," the woman said, but her words were drowned out by a horrible rumbling. The little white beans were taking root. They dug deep into the forest's soil and instantly a hundred little green sprouts popped out of the ground. The sprouts grew at an alarming rate, becoming vines and then stalks that jockeyed among one other for space.

They soared higher and higher into the air until it seemed they would touch the moon itself.

The cameraman tapped Wilma Faye on the shoulder and the reporter turned around.

"What is it?" she said impatiently.

The cameraman pointed up and Wilma's eyes followed. Above her were dozens of angry giants quickly climbing down the beanstalks. The cameraman pointed his camera into the air, flipped a switch, and a bright light mounted on the camera lit up their faces.

"Are you getting this?" Wilma asked, panicking.

"I'm getting it!" the cameraman shouted.

"What have you done?" Jack bellowed.

"You wanted giants, Jack. You're going to get your wish," Granny Relda said, as the first giant planted a foot on the forest floor. Dozens and dozens of them followed, all in all nearly a hundred, knocking over trees that had been growing for centuries. Each one of the giants was uglier than the last and all of them had murder in their eyes.

One of the most gnarled of the bunch stepped forward. It let out an ear-shattering roar and pounded on its chest.

"Fe, fi, fo, fum, I smell the blood of that murderous Englishman!" the giant bellowed at Jack, sending his hair flapping behind him.

"I didn't kill your brother, it was the girl," the young man cried, pointing a shaky finger at Sabrina. "Sabrina Grimm killed him!"

The giants looked down at Sabrina with suspicious eyes. One ducked his head down, shoving it into the girls' faces. His nostrils blasted hot air into their clothes.

"Lies!" the giant bellowed, spraying Sabrina and Daphne with its hot, snotty breath. "These are children. They could not kill one of us!"

As the giant swooped down and grabbed Jack in his huge, grimy hand, Granny Relda stepped forward. "What do you plan on doing with him?" she asked the giant, as if she were talking to an ordinary person.

"Crush his bones to paste and eat him with some bread, Grimm." The giant grunted. "Or maybe we will pull his little limbs off one by one and see if he screams."

"You'll do nothing of the sort," Granny Relda replied. "Take him to your queen. She'll decide what to do with him."

"Help me, Relda!" Jack cried. "Don't let them take me!"

Granny Relda lowered her eyes. "I cannot deny them their justice. I only hope they are more merciful with you than you have been with them."

Jack saw the futility of his words, and calmed himself, then he laughed, almost insanely. "Do you think I did this all on my own?" he ranted. "Where do you think I got the first magic bean? They've got Henry and Veronica. The Scarlet Hand is coming and your days are numbered!"

The giants ignored Jack's threats and turned back toward their beanstalks. A few leaned down and gingerly picked up their dead brother. They carried him on their shoulders as they climbed up the beanstalks and disappeared into the cold night air, just as three squad cars roared into the clearing with lights and sirens going. Flying high above the police were Glinda in her bubble and Hansel and Gretel's Frau Pfefferkuchenhaus on her broom. They sent a stream of fire that lit the bases of the beanstalks, setting them all ablaze.

Hamstead got out of his car and, along with Boarman and Swineheart, rushed to the family's side.

"I hope that you are OK, Relda," Hamstead said.

"Of course, thank you very much, Sheriff," Granny replied.

"You've got some pretty smart grandchildren," Hamstead said, smiling at Puck, Sabrina, and Daphne. "Not ones to let a man explain anything, and not so easy on my wardrobe, but I suppose they're pretty smart."

He reached his hand out and Sabrina shook it. Daphne did the same.

"In the future, kids, remember, we're the good guys," Hamstead said. "If you'll excuse me, I have to confiscate a little evidence."

The sheriff looked at Mr. Canis and nodded his head.

"Wolf," he said with an odd respect.

"Pig," Canis replied, returning the gesture.

Hamstead excused himself again and approached the cameraman and the reporter. He said something to them and they immediately began to argue. The portly sheriff grabbed the camera and tried to remove the videotape inside. He managed to take it out and break it in half, but got several whacks on the head from Wilma Faye's microphone for his efforts.

"What about the reporters?" Daphne asked.

"Glinda will make sure they don't remember a thing," Charming said as he entered the clearing. He was rubbing his head and placing his phone back in his pocket.

Mr. Canis stepped closer to the family as Charming stopped in front of the girls.

"Relda, your grandchildren are as meddlesome as you are," the prince continued. "But they were helpful in putting an end to Jack's plan."

"Your Majesty," Relda chirped happily, "are you suggesting that the Grimms might be useful in this town?"

"Hardly," Charming growled. He turned to the girls and

looked at them darkly. "Remember what I said about tomorrow, children." He spun around and made a beeline for the sheriff.

Daphne and Sabrina hugged their grandmother around the waist and burst into a torrent of happy tears. Granny Relda leaned down and covered the girls in kisses.

"*Lieblings*, are you OK?" she asked.

This time, Sabrina didn't feel like pulling away from the old woman. This time, Granny's hug felt like home.

"I'm OK," Sabrina said, fighting back more tears.

"We're sorry we almost got you killed," Daphne said. "We're not very good detectives."

"Nonsense!" Granny Relda laughed as she led them to the car. "You rescued Mr. Canis and me and managed to prevent a serious catastrophe. I say the two of you are first-rate detectives. We should celebrate. Does anyone have any ideas?"

Sabrina eased back into her seat. "I'd really just like to get out of these clothes," she said, looking down at the monkey hanging from the tree on her sweatshirt.

HANG IN THERE, it read.

• • •

Elvis woke the girls the next morning with loving licks on their faces. Luckily, Jack had not hurt the dog too badly. His ribs were bruised and he would have to wear a bandage on his side until the veterinarian could remove his stitches. But the only thing that seemed to truly hurt was Elvis's pride. Daphne apologized to him for not paying attention to his clue and promised that his opinion would always be considered in the future.

Granny greeted them at the dining room table with more of her unusual culinary treats. That morning, they enjoyed blue scrambled eggs, some little orange nuts, home fried potatoes soaked in sparkly green gravy, and wedges of tomato. Mr. Canis was still in his room and Puck was nowhere in sight.

"Is Mr. Canis OK?" Daphne asked.

"He will be," Granny Relda replied. "I'm sure he'll be happy to hear you are concerned."

"Where's Puck?"

Granny Relda smiled. "He'll be here soon."

After breakfast, the three Grimms went to the mall and bought the girls a dozen outfits apiece. Even Granny found a new hat with a sunflower on it that matched a yellow dress she said she hadn't worn in years. Sabrina suggested they burn their orange monkey sweaters and blue heart-covered pants but Daphne refused. Granny took Sabrina aside and apologized for the outfit, saying that Mr. Canis might not have been the right choice to shop for girls. After all, he was color-blind.

When they got home, Granny had presents for them. The girls unwrapped them quickly and found they each had a brand-new, cloth-bound book, just like the one in which their father had kept his journal. The covers had their names stenciled in gold with the words FAIRY-TALE ACCOUNTS above them. When Sabrina opened hers, she found there was nothing inside, only hundreds of blank pages.

"As your father and generations of Grimms before him did, it is your responsibility to put on paper what you see, so that future generations can know what you went through," Granny said. "We are Grimms. This is what we do."

The rest of the day, the girls scribbled what had happened into the books. They picked each other's brains for anything they might have forgotten and when they were finished, Sabrina tucked the picture of her family inside her journal's pages. Together, the girls rushed downstairs and placed their books alongside their father's on the shelf reserved for their family.

"Girls, I'd like to show you something else," Granny said. The girls followed her up the stairs, where she unlocked Mirror's room. The little man's face was in the glass again and he smiled when the old woman and the girls entered.

"Good afternoon, Relda," Mirror said.

"Good afternoon. I do hope you are feeling better," Granny replied.

"Much better. The bruises look worse than they felt," Mirror said.

"That's nice to know," the old woman said. She turned to the girls and took their hands. "Would you like to see your parents?"

Sabrina's heart nearly jumped from her chest.

"Is it possible?" she asked.

Granny turned back to the mirror. "Mirror, mirror, near and far," she said aloud. "Show us where their parents are."

The mirror misted over and two figures slowly appeared in the reflection. When the mist cleared, Sabrina saw her parents, Henry and Veronica, lying on a bed in a dark room. They were very still, with their eyes closed.

"They're dead," Sabrina said, before she could stop herself.

"No, not dead," Granny Relda corrected her. "Just sleeping."

"We lost one of Dorothy's slippers," Daphne cried. "We could have used them to rescue Mom and Dad."

Sabrina's face flushed with regret.

"*Liebling*, don't you think I have tried the slippers and everything else inside the mirror?" Granny Relda sighed. "This Scarlet Hand, whoever they are, used strong magic to take your

mom and dad away from us, but we aren't going to give up. We'll find them, I promise."

The girls wrapped their arms around Granny Relda and hugged her tightly. Sabrina and Daphne sobbed, both tears of happiness that their parents weren't dead and tears of despair that they didn't know where they were.

"I hope you'll let me into your family until we can all reunite," Granny said, breaking into tears herself.

Suddenly, there was a knock at the downstairs door. The old woman took a handkerchief from her pocket and wiped the girls' eyes. Then she wiped her own and stuffed the hankie back into its home.

"Come girls, we have guests," she said as she exited the room. The girls watched the image of their parents slowly fade from the mirror and then stood for a moment, staring at their own reflections.

"We're home now," Sabrina said to her sister.

"Well, duh!" Daphne giggled.

The two left the room and closed the door behind them. Then they ran down the stairs to the foyer. Puck was already inside, carrying several boxes filled to the top with old toys, junk, and several dead plants. Behind him were Glinda, Hamstead,

Boarman, and Swineheart.

"What are the police doing here?" Sabrina asked.

Glinda, Boarman, and Swineheart walked past them into the dining room and spread a huge roll of papers onto the table. When Sabrina got a closer look, she realized they were blueprints.

"What's all this?" she asked.

"We're putting an addition on your house," Hamstead said as his expression turned to a sly smile. "This house isn't big enough. You need another bedroom right away. Relda asked us for our advice. Before we went into law enforcement, we used to be in construction."

"I'm getting my own room," Sabrina squealed happily. "I haven't had my own room in a year and a half."

Daphne looked insulted and stuck out her tongue.

"Oh, Sabrina, we're not building you your own bedroom, yet," Granny apologized. "No, we need another room because . . ."

"I'm moving in!" Puck interrupted. He shoved his box of junk into Sabrina's hands and joined the witch and the deputies looking over the plans.

"He's lying, right?" Sabrina said hopefully. "You wouldn't let that stinky freak move in here with us?"

"I think it's great!" Daphne cried.

"Girls, he may not be my real grandson," Granny replied, "but I love him like he was my own."

Daphne took her sister's hand and smiled. "I have a feeling we're going to have a lot more to write in those books."

Sabrina scowled.

To be continued . . .

THE SISTERS GRIMM

THE UNUSUAL SUSPECTS

· BOOK TWO ·

For the friends who shaped my life:
Michael Madonia, Michael Nemeth, Todd Johnson,
Ronald Schultz, Ed Kellett, and Heather Averill Farley

THE SISTERS GRIMM

THE UNUSUAL SUSPECTS

SABRINA SCRAMBLED THROUGH THE DARKNESS *armed with a shovel and using the cold, stone walls as a guide. Each step was a challenge to her balance and senses. She stumbled over jagged rocks and accidentally kicked over an abandoned tool, sending a clanging echo off the tunnel walls. Whatever was waiting for her in the labyrinth knew she was coming now. Unfortunately, she couldn't turn back. Her family was somewhere in the twisting maze and no one else could help them. Sabrina prayed they were all still alive.*

The tunnel made a sharp turn, and around the corner Sabrina spotted a distant, flickering light. She quickened her pace, and soon the tunnel opened into an enormous cave, carved out of the bedrock of Ferryport Landing. Torches mounted on the cave walls gave the room a dull light, not strong enough to dissolve the black shadows in every corner.

Sabrina scanned the cave. A few old buckets and a couple of shovels leaned against a crumbling wall. She started to retrace her steps when something hit her squarely in the back. She fell hard on her shoulder, dropping her shovel. Searing pain swam through her veins, followed by a throbbing ache. She could still move her fingers, but Sabrina knew her arm was broken. She screamed, but her cries were drowned out by an odd clicking and hissing sound.

As she crawled to her feet, Sabrina grabbed the shovel and swung it around threateningly, searching the room for her attacker.

"I've come for my family," she shouted into the darkness. Her voice bounced back at her from all sides of the rocky room.

Again, she heard clicking and hissing, followed by a cold, arrogant chuckle. A long, spindly leg struck out from the shadows, narrowly missing Sabrina's head. It slammed against the wall behind the girl, pulverizing stone into dust. Sabrina lifted the heavy shovel and swung wildly at the leg, sinking the sharp edge deep into the monster's flesh. Shrieks of agony echoed through the cavern.

"I'm not going to be easy to kill," Sabrina said, hoping her voice sounded more confident to the monster than it did to her own ears.

"Kill you? This is a party!" a voice replied. "And you're the guest of honor."

1
THREE DAYS EARLIER

et's get this party started, already!" Sabrina complained under her breath as she rubbed the charley horse in her leg. She and her seven-year-old sister, Daphne, had been crouching behind a stack of Diaper Rash Donna dolls for nearly three hours. She was tired, hungry, and more than a little irritated. For a week they had been on this "stakeout" and it was beginning to look as if they had wasted another perfectly good night of sleep. Even Elvis, their two-hundred-pound Great Dane, had given up and was snoring on the floor next to them.

Of course, how Sabrina wanted to spend her time wasn't really considered, she had learned, especially if there was a mystery afoot. Their grandmother loved a good mystery, so when Gepetto complained that his toy store had been robbed every night for two weeks, Granny Relda volunteered herself and the sisters

Grimm to help the police catch the crooks. Sabrina wondered what an old woman, two kids, and a sleepy dog could do that the expensive security cameras and motion detectors the old man had installed couldn't, but once Granny sunk her teeth into something she wouldn't let go.

In most towns, the police do not rely on an old woman, two kids, and a sleepy dog to solve crimes, but Ferryport Landing was no ordinary town. More than half of its residents were part of a secret community known as the Everafters. Everafters were actually fairy-tale characters who had fled Europe to escape persecution. Settling in the little river town almost two hundred years ago, they now used magical disguises to live and work alongside their normal neighbors. Ogres worked at the post office, witches ran the twenty-four-hour diner, and the town mayor was the legendary Prince Charming. The humans were none the wiser—except the Grimms.

As fantastic and thrilling as it sounded to live among fairy-tale characters, it wasn't a dream come true for Sabrina Grimm. Being the last in a long line of Grimms (descended from the famous Brothers Grimm), she and her sister had had the family responsibility of keeping the peace between Everafters and humans thrust upon them no less than three weeks ago.

And it wasn't an easy job. Most Everafters saw the Grimms as the bane of their existence. A two-century-old magical curse had trapped the Everafters in Ferryport Landing for all eternity, and the girls' great-great-great-great grandfather Wilhelm was responsible. Trying to prevent a war between Everafters and humans, Wilhelm had aligned himself with a powerful witch named Baba Yaga and together they had cast the spell over the town. The Everafters' freedom could only be returned to them when the last Grimm had passed away, and so far, the Grimms were alive and kicking. Yet even with that kind of baggage, Granny Relda had made a few genuine friends in the community. Sheriff Hamstead was one of those friends. The rotund policeman with the Southern charm was actually one of the three *not-so-little* pigs. Lately, he had turned to the family for help with Ferryport Landing's unsolved cases.

And here the Grimms were, leg cramps and all, waiting for someone or something to make its move. After five long nights, Sabrina's patience had worn thin. There were things she should have been doing, important things, that didn't involve hiding behind Etch-A-Sketches and cans of Silly String stacked miles high for the Christmas season. Sabrina reached into her pocket and pulled out a small flashlight. She flicked its switch and a tiny focused beam illuminated a book sitting at her feet. She picked it up and started reading. She didn't get far.

"Sabrina," Daphne whispered. "What are you doing? You're going to give us away. Turn off that light."

Sabrina grumbled, slammed the book closed, and set it aside. If *The Jungle Book* held any clue to rescuing their parents it would have to wait. Sabrina's little sister had taken to detective work the way a dog does to a slice of bologna. Like their grandmother, Daphne loved every minute of it—the stakeouts, the long hours. She was a natural and took her new job quite seriously.

Suddenly, there was a rustling sound across the room. Sabrina quickly shut off her flashlight and peered over the stack of dolls. Something was moving near a display for a hot holiday toy, Don't Tickle the Tiger. Daphne poked her head up and looked around, too. "Do you see anything?" the little girl whispered.

"No, but it's coming from that direction," Sabrina whispered back. "Wake up Sleepy and see if he smells anything."

Daphne shook Elvis until he staggered to his feet. The big dog had recently had bandages removed after a run-in with a bad guy's boot, and was still a bit sluggish. He looked around as if he didn't remember where he was.

"You smell any bad guys, Elvis?" Daphne asked.

The dog sniffed the air. His ears rose and his eyes grew wide. He let out a soft whine to let the girls know he *had* smelled something.

"Go get 'em, boy!" Daphne cried, and the big dog took off like a rocket.

Unfortunately, that was when Sabrina realized that Elvis's leash had wrapped itself around her foot. As the dog howled wildly and tore through the store, the girl was dragged behind him, knocking over stacks of board games and sending balls bouncing in all directions. They emptied boxes of puzzle pieces and sent an army of Slinkys slinking across the floor. Sabrina struggled to grab the leash, but every time she got close to freeing herself, the dog took a wild turn and sent her skidding.

"Turn on the lights!" Daphne shouted.

"Hey, let me go!" a voice cried out.

"What's the big idea?" another one shouted.

Elvis circled back around, and Sabrina slid into a pile of what felt like sticky leaves. Some clung to her arms and legs and one glued itself to her forehead.

When the lights finally came on, Elvis stopped, stood over Sabrina, and barked. The girl sat up and then looked down at herself. There she was, in the center of Gepetto's Toy Store, covered in sticky glue mousetraps, each of which had a tiny little man, no more than a couple of inches high, stuck quick in the glue.

"Lilliputians," Sabrina said.

"I knew it!" Granny Relda said, appearing from around a stack

of action figures. The old woman, dressed in a bright blue dress and a matching hat with a sunflower appliqué sewn into it, had the nerve to laugh. When Sabrina scowled at her, she tried to stop, but couldn't.

"Oh *liebling*," she giggled in her German accent.

Daphne rushed over and tried to pull one of the traps off of Sabrina's shirt but found it was stuck tight to her sister, as were a dozen or so Lilliputians.

"Who is the sick psychopath that came up with this idea?" one of the Lilliputians shouted indignantly.

Granny leaned down to him and smiled. "Don't worry, a little vegetable oil and we'll have you free in no time."

"But I'm afraid you're under arrest," Sheriff Hamstead said as he stepped out from behind a stack of footballs. His puffy, pink face beamed proudly as he tugged his trousers up over his massive belly. The sheriff was always fighting his sinking slacks.

The Lilliputians groaned and complained as the sheriff went to work yanking the sticky traps off Sabrina's clothes.

"You have the right to remain silent," Hamstead said. "Anything you say can and will be used against you in a court of law."

"Ouch!" said Sabrina as the sheriff tugged the glue-trap from her forehead.

"I'm not talking, copper," one of the Lilliputians snapped. "I'll let my lawyer do the talking when we sue you for police brutality."

"Police brutality!" Sheriff Hamstead exclaimed. Unfortunately, when the portly policeman got angry or excited, the magical disguise he used to hide who he really was stopped working. Now his nose vanished and was replaced by a runny, pink snout. Two hairy pig ears popped out of the top of his head and a series of snorts, squeals, and huffs came out of his mouth. Hamstead had nearly completed the change when the security guard from the next store over wandered in.

"What's going on in here?" the guard said with a tough, authoritative voice. He was a tall, husky man with a military-style hair cut. He puffed up his chest and pulled a billy club from a loop on his belt. He eyed the crowd as if he were fully prepared to deal with a gang of crooks, but when he saw the pig in a police uniform hovering over a dozen tiny men in glue traps, his confidence disappeared and his club fell to the floor.

"We forgot some of the shops have their own security guards," Granny Relda said softly as she reached into her handbag and approached the stunned man. She blew some soft pink dust into his face and his eyes glazed over. She told him he'd had another usual night at work and nothing out of the ordinary had occurred. The security guard nodded in agreement.

"Another night at work," he mumbled, falling under the forgetful dust's magic.

Sabrina scowled. She hated when magic was used to fix problems, especially when the problem involved humans.

• • •

"The glue traps were a brilliant idea," Sheriff Hamstead said as he drove the family home in his squad car. Granny sat in the front, enjoying his praise while Sabrina and Daphne were in the back, jockeying with Elvis for seat space. Hamstead had locked the Lilliputians in the glove compartment and whenever their complaining got too loud, he would smack the top of the dashboard with his puffy hand and yell, "Pipe down!"

"I'm just glad we could be of some help," Granny Relda replied. "Gepetto is such a nice old man. It broke my heart to hear he was being robbed, and with Christmas only two weeks away."

"I know the holidays are hard on him; he misses his boy," Hamstead said. "It's hard to believe that in two hundred years no one has heard a peep from Pinocchio."

"Wilhelm's journals claim he refused to get on the boat," Granny replied. "I suppose if I had been swallowed by a shark I wouldn't be too eager to go back to sea either."

"I thought it was a whale," Daphne said.

"No, hon, only in the movie," Granny replied. "It's just a

shame he didn't tell his father. By the time Gepetto discovered he wasn't on board, they were too far out to turn back."

"Well, I really do appreciate your help with this," the sheriff said. "The mayor's been cutting budgets left and right these days and I just didn't have the man power or money to catch the little thieves myself."

"Or make sure that the security guard was off duty so we didn't have to mess with his brain," Sabrina grumbled.

"Sheriff, the Grimms are always at your disposal," Granny Relda said, ignoring Sabrina.

"I appreciate that, Relda, and I wish I could give you the credit for the arrest, but if Mayor Charming found out we'd been working together, my backside would be one of those footballs in Gepetto's store," Hamstead said.

"It's our little secret," Granny Relda said with a wink.

"How is Canis?"

Granny shifted uncomfortably in her seat. Both Sabrina and Daphne watched her closely, wondering what their grandmother would say.

"He's doing just fine," the old woman replied, forcing a smile.

Sabrina couldn't believe what she had just heard. In the short time they had known the old woman, Granny Relda had never told a lie. Mr. Canis was not "fine" by a long shot. Three weeks earlier, Granny's constant companion and houseguest, Mr. Canis, had transformed into the savage creature known as the Big Bad Wolf. Since then, no one had seen him. He had locked himself inside his bedroom while he fought to put back his real-life inner demon. Every night, Sabrina and Daphne had heard the old man's painful moans and labored breathing. They would be woken by one of his horrible cries or the sound of him slamming against a wall. Mr. Canis was far from "fine."

"That's good to hear," Hamstead said, though even from the backseat Sabrina could spot the look of doubt on his face.

"I want my phone call," a little voice cried from the glove compartment. "We were framed!"

The sheriff banged heavily on the dashboard. "Tell it to the judge!"

Soon, Sheriff Hamstead pulled his squad car into the driveway of the family's quaint, two-story yellow house. It was very late and all the lights were off. Sabrina opened her door and Elvis lumbered out, still wearing two Lilliputian-free glue traps on his giant behind. It was bitterly cold, and Sabrina hoped the two adults wouldn't blabber on. Granny could talk a person's ear off. But the sheriff just thanked them again and excused himself, claiming he had paperwork piling up back at the station.

At the front door, Granny took a giant key ring out of her

handbag and went to work unlocking the many locks. Once Sabrina had believed Granny Relda was just a paranoid shut-in, but in the last three weeks she had seen things that she would never have dreamed possible and now understood why the house was locked so tightly.

Granny Relda knocked on the door three times and announced to the house that the family was home, making the last magical lock slide back and the door swing open.

After cookies, and some vegetable-oil swabbing for Elvis, Granny Relda said, "Get cleaned up and hurry to bed. You've got school tomorrow. I've kept you up too late as it is."

"Actually, Granny," Sabrina replied. "I think I'm coming down with something. I'd hate to go to school and get everyone sick."

Granny grinned. "Sabrina, it's been three weeks. If you two don't go to school tomorrow they are going to put me in the jailhouse. Now, up to bed."

Sabrina frowned, forced a cough to make the old woman feel guilty, and then marched up the steps. Couldn't Granny see there were more important things to do than go to school?

• • •

Long after Daphne had drifted into a steady, snoring sleep, Sabrina crawled out of their four-poster bed in the room that had once been their father's. His model airplanes still hung from the ceiling and an old catcher's mitt rested on his desk. She knelt down on her hands and knees and pulled several dusty books and a key ring out from under the bed before climbing to her feet again and creeping silently into the hallway.

Sabrina was very good at creeping. In fact, she'd have said she was an expert. A year and a half in and out of an orphanage and foster homes had taught her how to step lightly on hardwood floors and avoid creaky beams. In the past she had used these skills to escape from one bad situation after another. In eighteen months, the sisters Grimm had run away from more than a dozen foster families. Some of the families had used them as personal servants while others expected them to be punching bags for their own obnoxious children. These days the girls didn't want to run away. Granny Relda had given them a home. But being sneaky still had its advantages. Especially when Sabrina was doing something she knew her grandmother would disapprove of.

When Sabrina reached the door at the top of the steps, she sorted through her own growing collection of keys and found the long brass skeleton key that fit it. Once it was unlocked, she took a quick look around to make sure no one was watching, and then stepped inside.

The room was empty except for a full-length mirror that hung on the far wall. A single window allowed enough moonlight into the room for Sabrina to see by. She stepped up to the mirror and her reflection appeared. Her long blond hair and blue eyes glowed a ghostly milky blue, but Sabrina wasn't here to admire herself. Instead, she did what most people would think was impossible—she walked directly into the glass and disappeared.

The mirror was actually a doorway that led to an immense room Sabrina knew as the Hall of Wonders. In many ways it reminded Sabrina of Grand Central Station in New York City with its incredibly long, barrel-vaulted ceiling supported by towering marble columns. There were literally thousands of arched doorways on either side of the hall. Each door was labeled with a little brass plaque that revealed what was behind it: talking plants; giant living chess pieces; Babe, the Blue Ox; and thousands more impossibly interesting magical items and creatures, all collected by the Grimms for safekeeping. Granny called it the world's biggest walk-in closet. Sabrina had started to see it as her only hope.

She scanned the hall and spotted a lonely figure sitting in a high-backed chair several yards away. She headed in his direction.

"Mirror," the girl said to the short, squat man. "I think I've found something useful."

Mirror, as he was called, was a balding man with deep angular features and thick, full lips who lived inside the mirror. His was the face that had proclaimed Snow White "the fairest one of all" to the Wicked Queen. When he spotted Sabrina, he set a celebrity magazine he had been reading down and got up from his chair.

"I thought you'd given this up," he said.

"Granny's had us pretty busy," Sabrina explained. "So, let's get started."

"What? No *hello*? No *how are you*? *How's the family*?" the little man complained.

"Sorry, Mirror, I don't have a lot of time."

"Apology accepted. So, kiddo, what's on the agenda tonight?"

"I found this thing in Burton's translation of *The Arabian Nights*," Sabrina said, opening one of her books and handing it to Mirror. He didn't even bother to look at the page.

"Listen, blondie, I assure you, if we had a jinni's lamp I'd have a lot more hair on my head and we'd all be living in Hawaii. Sweet-ums, don't you think that if your grandmother had access to that kind of power, your parents would have already been found?"

Sabrina frowned. She would spend the whole day researching ways to rescue her parents from their kidnappers, and every night, Mirror would shoot her ideas down one by one.

"Fine," Sabrina replied, handing Mirror another book she had opened already. "What about this?"

Mirror looked down at the book, flipped it to view its cover, and smiled. "L. Frank Baum, huh? Follow me, little cowpoke. I think we might just have that one in stock."

The little man spun around and headed down the long hallway. "The Golden Cap is one of the most interesting things the Wicked Witch ever owned, yet most people are more fascinated by her broomstick," he continued.

"I've been reading as much as I can," Sabrina replied, doing her best to keep up with Mirror's quick pace.

"Oh, I have no doubt about that," the little man said, spinning around on the girl. "So, you know how it works?"

"Yes, I put it on and the monkeys come. They'll do whatever I want them to."

"The only downside is the monkey smell," Mirror said. "That's a stink that never quite goes away."

After a short hike, Mirror stopped at a door labeled MAGICAL HATS and reached out his hand. Sabrina handed him her key ring.

"You're building quite a collection," he said disapprovingly. "Does your grandmother know you've been swiping her keys and making copies?"

Sabrina shook her head no.

"Well, you've got one for this door," he said. He opened the door and went inside. As Sabrina waited in the hall, she could see him rummaging through the room. He made quite a racket moving things around, knocking over a helmet in the process, which rolled across the floor with a clatter. Soon he returned with a gold-colored hard hat, which held a can of soda on each side. Tubes ran out of the cans and dangled below the chin strap. On the front of the hat the words EMERALD CITY GREEN SOX were printed in big green letters. Mirror dusted it off and handed it to Sabrina.

"This is the Golden Cap the Wicked Witch of the West used to summon the flying monkeys?" she said in disbelief.

"The Witch was a huge sports fan," Mirror replied. "The magic instructions are inside."

"You've got to be kidding me," Sabrina said as she read them.

"Afraid not."

The girl scowled and put the hat on her head. Following the ridiculous instructions, she lifted her right leg and began the crazy spell. *"Ep-pe, pep-pe, kak-ke."*

Mirror turned away and snickered.

"Don't laugh, I feel stupid enough," Sabrina said, lowering her leg and lifting the other. *"Hil-lo, hol-lo, hel-lo."*

"I wish I had a camera." The little man giggled.

"Ziz-zy, zuz-zy, zik!" the girl said, now standing on both feet. Suddenly, her ears filled with the sound of a hundred flapping

wings. Monkeys materialized out of thin air. They gathered around their summoner, grinning and beating their black wings. Sabrina understood immediately why Mirror had warned her about the monkey smell. They were a ripe bunch. She thought she might gag when one of the monkeys, wearing a beanie with a bright blue ball on top, took her hand and gave it a sloppy kiss.

"What is your bidding, master?" it asked in a deep, unearthly voice. Sabrina hadn't gotten used to talking animals yet. They made her nervous.

"OK, uh, Mr. Monkey . . . uh, I need you to go fetch my parents," she commanded.

The monkeys screamed and clapped their hands as if she had just promised them bananas. Their wings started to flap and they leaped into the air. But instead of disappearing as Sabrina expected, they zipped around the hall, flying in all directions, as if they weren't sure which way to go. The leader floated back down to the girl. He had a confused expression on his face.

"What's wrong?" Sabrina asked.

"Great magic blocks our path. Your wish cannot be granted," he said, and as quickly as he and the others had appeared, they were gone.

"Why not?" Sabrina shouted, angrily. She took the obnoxious magic hat off her head and shook it, but the monkeys did not return.

Mirror gave her a sad, pitying smile but Sabrina couldn't bear to look at it. She was exhausted and angry and not a single step closer to finding her parents. How many more dead ends could she come up against?

She forced a smile and handed the Golden Cap back to Mirror. The little man nodded and put it inside its room, shutting the door and locking it behind him.

"Thanks, anyway." She sighed as she took her key ring and silently walked away. She stepped through the portal without looking back and found herself alone again, in the empty room. Crossing the floor, Sabrina suddenly stopped, turned, and looked at herself in the mirror's reflection.

"Mirror?" she called out, softly. A blue mist filled the glass and the little man's squat, muscular head peered out at her.

"Want to take a look?" he asked.

Sabrina nodded.

He winked. "You know how it works."

"Mirror, mirror, near and far, show me where my parents are," the girl said. Once again, the mirror's surface changed. As the little man's face disappeared, Sabrina's parents, Henry and Veronica Grimm, appeared instead. They were lying on a bed in the dark, fast asleep.

Sabrina looked at her parents' faces and sighed. Her father had a round, warm face like her sister's, framed with blond hair. Her mother, Veronica, was beautiful, with high cheekbones and jet-black locks. They looked vulnerable lying there surrounded by darkness.

"I won't let another Christmas go by without you. I'll find a way to bring you home," Sabrina said as she reached out to touch them. Her hand dipped into the magic mirror's reflective surface and her parents' image rippled the way a pond does when a stone is thrown into it. Sabrina stared at them until they faded away.

"Same time tomorrow night?" Mirror said as his face reappeared.

"See you then," Sabrina said, wiping the tears from her cheeks and flashing Mirror a hopeful smile. The little man nodded and his face faded away.

The girl tiptoed back down the hallway, but just as she reached her bedroom she heard a painful groan coming from the room opposite. Mr. Canis was having another difficult night. Sabrina stood in the hallway listening to his painful breathing. She imagined that at any moment the door might explode and the Big Bad Wolf would catch her up in his jaws. What would they do if the Wolf beat Mr. Canis and got loose? What if the old man wasn't strong enough to keep him inside?

But Mr. Canis wasn't the only Everafter she had doubts about lately. The charm of living in a community where fairy god-mothers and cowardly lions were her neighbors had worn off and Sabrina was beginning to view the Everafters with suspicion. After all, one of them was responsible for kidnapping her parents. She had decided to keep an eye on them all until her parents were home—Mr. Canis included.

"Go to bed, child," a voice growled. "Or are you going to huff and puff and blow the door in?" The voice startled Sabrina—it sounded like a combination of Canis and the Wolf—and she quickly darted into her bedroom and closed her door tightly. Leaning against it, she realized how dumb she had been. Of course he could smell her through his bedroom door.

2

here were three things that Sabrina took great pride in: one, she had successfully arm wrestled every boy at the orphanage (including two extremely humiliated janitors); two, she wasn't afraid of heights; and three, she wasn't a sissy. But when one wakes up to find a giant hairy spider crawling on one's face, one should be allowed to throw a hissy fit. Which was exactly what Sabrina did.

And her bloodcurdling scream caused Daphne to wake up, see the spider, and scream, too. Daphne's scream just made the whole thing that much more horrible for Sabrina, so she screamed even louder, which caused the little girl to scream at her sister's scream, resulting in a mini-concert of hysteria that went on and on for about five minutes.

Granny Relda burst into their bedroom with Elvis at her side.

Granny's gray hair, still streaked with its former red, was rolled up in huge curlers and tucked underneath a sleeping cap. She wore a bright blue nightgown patterned with little cows jumping over little moons and her face was covered in a mossy-green mud mask that she swore kept her looking young. But her mud mask was not nearly as startling as the deadly sharp broadsword she held in her hand and the fierce battle cry that bellowed from her throat.

Scanning the room for attackers, the old woman said, "My goodness, *lieblings*—what is the matter?"

"That!" Sabrina and Daphne shouted in unison, pointing at a black tarantula the size of a baked potato that had leaped off the bed and now clung to a nearby curtain. Its eight long, hairy legs and vicious-looking pinchers clicked and snapped as it climbed up the drapes.

"Oh, children, it's just a spider," Granny Relda said as she crossed the room and picked the creepy-crawly thing up with her bare hands. Daphne squealed as if she had been the one to touch it and crawled under her blanket to hide.

"Just a spider?" Sabrina cried. "You could put a saddle on that thing!"

"He's South American I believe," Granny said, petting the spider like it was a kitten. "You're a long way from home, friend. How did you find your way here?"

"Like you have to ask!" Sabrina cried.

"Now, now," the old woman said. "It's just a harmless spider."

Elvis trotted over and sniffed the creature. The tarantula raised up two legs and hissed at the Great Dane, causing the usually fearless hound to leap back and yelp in surprise.

"Is it gone yet?" Daphne's muffled voice came from under the covers. "Has it been squished?"

"Girls, Puck's just being a boy. Brothers do these kinds of thing to their sisters all the time," Granny said soothingly.

"He's not our brother!" Sabrina shouted as she crawled out of bed and stomped across the room toward the door.

"Where are you going?" Granny Relda asked.

"To tell Puck's face what my fist thinks of him," the girl said, marching past the old woman and out the door.

"Don't leave me in here with the spider!" Daphne begged, but her sister ignored her plea. Puck was long overdue for a sock in the nose and Sabrina was just the person to give it to him.

Puck, like Mr. Canis, was an Everafter, a four-thousand-year-old fairy in the body of an eleven-year-old boy. Rude, selfish, smelly, and obnoxious, the boy had been taunting Sabrina since he had met her. He'd dumped a bucket of paint on her, rubbed her toothbrush in red-pepper seeds, filled her pockets with bloodworms, and put something in her shoes that still made her shudder when she recalled its smell. Puck also had a slew of magical pranks. He could shape-shift into any animal and several inanimate objects. Sabrina couldn't count how many times he had morphed into a chair and then pulled himself out from under her when she sat down. Why Granny Relda had taken to him was beyond comprehension, especially with his well-documented history. Everyone from William Shakespeare to Rudyard Kipling had warned about Puck's exploits, yet Granny treated him as if he were one of the family and had even invited him to live with the Grimms. Now Sabrina was determined to make the "Trickster King" wish he had declined the invitation.

She marched down the hall to his bedroom. No one had been in Puck's room since it had been built. Glinda the Good Witch and the Three Little Pigs used nails, hammers, and magic to create it and when it was finished, the rude boy hadn't bothered to invite anyone in to see the final result. So, when Sabrina opened the door and stepped inside, she was amazed by what she found. Puck's room was impossible.

There were trees and grass and a stone path and a waterfall that spilled into a lagoon. There was an actual sky with clouds and kites where the ceiling should have been. In the center of a clearing was a wrestling ring in which a kangaroo wearing boxing gloves and shorts sat lazily waiting for his next challenger. A roller coaster sailed on a track above Sabrina and an ice-cream truck sat off to one side. In the center of it all was Puck, perched on an enormous throne, wearing his stupid golden crown. He was eating an ice-cream cone that held half a dozen different flavored scoops, all of which were dripping down his arm.

Poor Sabrina was so astonished by her surroundings that she failed to notice the metal plate at her feet. When she stepped onto it, she triggered the release of an egg, which rolled down a narrow track and fell onto a rusty nail that cracked its shell in half. The egg then emptied its drippings onto a skillet, which triggered the striking of a match that ignited a gas burner. Soon, the egg was popping and crackling as the heat from the flame cooked it, causing steam to rise, which, in turn, filled a balloon that rose into the air. The balloon was connected by a string to a small lever that tipped a bucket of water into a drinking glass sitting on the high end of a seesaw. The seesaw tilted downward from the weight, untying a rope that held a heavy sandbag. The sandbag fell to the ground and hit a bright red button and then it all came to a stop.

And, unfortunately, that's when Sabrina noticed the bizarre contraption.

"What the—?" she said aloud but just then a buzzer drowned out her voice and the girl was catapulted off the metal plate and up, up through the air and then down, down into a large vat of goo, causing an enormous splash.

"Doesn't anyone knock around here?" Puck complained when Sabrina finally fought her way to the surface.

"What is this stuff?" she cried, as she struggled through the vat of thick white mush in which several dark chunks floated. The stink of it nearly made Sabrina barf.

"It's a big tub of glue and buttermilk, of course," the boy said, as if it were obvious. "With some bread-and-butter pickles added for flavor. It's quite stinky."

"You're going to pay for this, Puck!" Sabrina screamed as she climbed out of the tub. She wiped her face as well as she could and flared her nostrils.

"There she is, Miss America," the prankster sang. He tossed his huge ice-cream cone into the wrestling ring and the boxing kangaroo lapped it up happily. Then the boy jumped into the air and two massive pink-streaked insect wings sprang from his back. Soon he was soaring high above Sabrina.

"Just like an Everafter to use magic to run from a fight! Come down here, you smelly little freak," Sabrina shouted.

"With our fists?" Puck cried indignantly. "Human, I'm royalty. A prince fights like a prince."

His wings flapped loudly as he flew across his forest room to a nearby table. He scooped up two swords and flew back to Sabrina, tossing one at her feet as he floated effortlessly to the ground.

The girl grabbed her weapon and held it confidently. It was made of wood, like Puck's, but it would still hurt if she got a good whack at him.

The two children circled each other. Sabrina wasted no time thrusting her sword at the boy, who immediately floated several feet off the ground and spun easily, dodging her attack. While she was off balance, Puck flew toward her, trying to strike her arm. But Sabrina shifted her weight, swung her sword, and hit him on the top of his head.

"Dirty little snotface!" the boy cried as he rubbed his sore noggin. "Someone's been learning."

"Charge me again and you'll see what else I've learned, horse-breath!" Sabrina threatened.

Puck flew at her, swinging his wooden sword toward her

shoulder, only to have it blocked by Sabrina's sword. She took a swipe at his belly, missing him by less than an inch.

"*Tsk, tsk*. Looks like you haven't learned the most important lesson of all." He laughed. "Always protect your butt."

Puck spun around and smacked Sabrina on the backside with his sword. The blow felt like the sting of a dozen honeybees, but Sabrina would never give him the satisfaction of hearing her cry out in pain.

"You're as slow as you are ugly," the boy taunted.

"You miserable little stink-pig!" Sabrina screamed, wildly slashing at him. He easily dodged each attack, leaping and flying out of the way, even flipping over her head. When he landed, he jammed his sword into her back and chuckled.

"Too bad, you're dead," he said. "You've got to get a hold of that temper. It beats you every time."

Sabrina tossed her sword down angrily and spun around on him with her fists clenched. Seeing that she meant to knock his head off, Puck did what anybody would do when facing an angry Sabrina Grimm—he ran. She chased him around the lagoon, through some heavy brush, out the other side, and right into Granny Relda. The old woman stood over them, and her expression, or what they could see of it behind her beauty mask, was disapproving.

The mask seemed to make a big impression on Puck.

"Old lady!" he cried—he always called Granny Relda by that name. "Your face! You've been cursed by a hobgoblin!"

"*Lieblings*, that's enough of this nonsense," Granny said as the dirty boy scampered to his feet and hid behind her.

"First of all, in my defense, the chain saw was propped on the door and was only supposed to scare her," he said. "If someone got hurt, it wasn't my fault."

"Puck, we're talking about the spider," Granny Relda said.

"Oh, the spider. How did it go off? Were they scared out of their wits?" he asked. "Which one of them wet the bed?"

"I know you didn't mean any harm," the old woman said. "But the girls do have school today and it would have been nice to have a quiet, chaos-free morning, for once."

Puck looked into her face as if she were speaking another language. "And what would be the fun in that?"

"Let's back up!" Sabrina demanded. "What chain saw?"

Granny ignored the question and took the boy's hand. She placed the tarantula into it and smiled kindly. "Let's put this somewhere safe."

Puck took the spider and rubbed its furry back softly. "It's OK, little guy. Did the big ugly girl scare you? I know, she's gruesome, but you're safe now."

Sabrina growled.

"What's going on in here?" Daphne said from the doorway. The little girl rubbed the sleep out of her eyes and then looked around. "Holy cow!"

"Daphne, move off the plate you're standing on," her sister warned, but the little girl just gawked at Puck's room.

"You've got an ice-cream truck," she cried as the roller coaster whipped along its track above her. "And a roller coaster!"

"Daphne, listen to me," Sabrina shouted, but the egg was already cooking. The balloon was already floating upward.

"Sabrina, why do you look like a booger?" the little girl asked as the seesaw fell. The alarm sounded and, just as it had done to Sabrina, the catapult fired Daphne into the air and sent her flailing into the vat of goo. When she landed, she struggled to stand up and wipe the slime from her face.

"What is this?" she asked.

"Glue and buttermilk!" Puck shouted.

"And bread-and-butter pickles," Sabrina added, picking a squishy slice of pickle from behind her ear and tossing it to the ground.

Daphne's face curled up in confusion as if she couldn't get her brain around the idea. Then a huge smile came to her face.

"I want to do it again!" She laughed.

Granny Relda helped Daphne out of the sticky soup.

"Look at us," Sabrina said. "We can't go to school today!" Suddenly, her anger at Puck faded. *We can't go to school today! I can do more research!* she thought.

"Oh *lieblings*, you've already been out for three weeks. I don't want you to get too far behind," Granny said, eyeing the girls and fighting a smile that eventually won the battle.

"We'll just go tomorrow, then," Sabrina suggested.

Before Granny Relda could respond, Mr. Canis appeared at the door, fully dressed in his oversized suit. He looked exhausted and feverish, even more frail than before his transformation, which was startling. He looked like he could use another three weeks in bed.

"The children have a guest," he said, leaning unsteadily against the doorframe.

"Thank you, Mr. Canis," Granny Relda said sounding quite motherly. "You go and get your rest."

The old man nodded and shuffled back toward his room.

"Who's here to see you?" Puck said enviously.

Sabrina shrugged and turned to follow Granny Relda downstairs, with Daphne and Puck following eagerly. As the family entered the living room they spotted a skinny old woman in a drab business suit standing by a bookshelf. She picked up a book with her bony hand and scrutinized the title. Sabrina knew the book. It was called *Mermaids Are People, Too*. The skinny woman tossed it aside and turned to face them, and before Sabrina saw the woman's face, she knew who it was.

"Good morning, girls," Ms. Smirt said. "Did you miss me?"

3

inerva Smirt hadn't changed since the last time the
girls had seen her. The caseworker was still ugly and
tired-looking. Her bones still poked out of her
clothes as if they were trying to escape her body, and she still
had the same angry scowl on her face that she'd had when she
left them on the train platform three weeks before. She gazed
over her long hooked nose and studied the family scornfully.
Puck cringed when her eyes swept over him.

"My, my, my," she said disapprovingly.

"Ms. Smirt, what a pleasant surprise," Granny Relda said
without much conviction. "It's so nice to see you again."

"Girls, get your things," Ms. Smirt said, staring into the old
woman's eyes. "You're going back to the orphanage."

Daphne slipped her hand into her sister's and squeezed so hard it hurt.

"What in heavens for?" Granny Relda exclaimed.

"Because, Mrs. Grimm, you've been completely negligent," the caseworker barked.

"What does *negligent* mean?" Daphne asked.

"It means she's a failure," Ms. Smirt said, interrupting Sabrina, who usually answered Daphne's vocabulary questions. "It means she's refused to do what the state requires of her. It means she is unfit!

"You two haven't had a day of school since you arrived," the caseworker continued. "I sent your grandmother a letter reminding her about the *law*, but I never heard back. So I sent another, and then another, and then another. But, still I heard nothing, so because your granny can't find the time to put pen to paper and assure me that you two will be educated, I had to get on a five a.m. train and sit next to man who sniffed his own armpits over and over again, for two hours. Imagine how thrilled I am to find out that not only have you two *not* been in school for a month, you obviously haven't seen a bathtub or a bar of soap, either!"

"Who is this woman?" Puck asked.

"Her name's Minerva Smirt. She was our caseworker from the orphanage," Sabrina answered.

"Cranky old buzzard, isn't she?" the boy replied.

Sabrina smiled. *Puck sure has his moments,* she thought.

"And who are you supposed to be?" Ms. Smirt asked, turning her angry face toward the boy. "The king of snot-nosed delinquents?"

Puck smiled. "Finally, someone who has heard of me!"

"This is my nephew visiting from . . . uh . . . Akron, Ohio," Granny said as she snatched Puck's crown off his head. "Ms. Smirt, I assure you the girls were going to go to school today. We've gotten a little sidetracked with visiting and such."

The truth was that Sabrina and Daphne had made every excuse to avoid school. After the family had foiled a plot by Jack (of the beanstalk story) to release giants into the world so he could kill them and regain his fame, the girls convinced their grandmother they needed some time to recover. Then Sabrina had come down with a *mysterious* stomach flu that Daphne conveniently got the next week. A series of stubbed toes, allergic reactions, dizzy spells, bronchial attacks, and food poisonings had continued to keep them out of the classroom, giving them time to do what they both thought was more important—research. Granny's immense and disorganized library of books on all things magical probably held the key to finding and rescuing the girls' parents, missing now for almost two years. The sisters Grimm were in agreement for once: School could wait until Henry and Veronica Grimm were home.

"You understand, Ms. Smirt," Granny Relda continued. "After all, I haven't seen Sabrina since she was a week old."

"And now you aren't going to see her until she's eighteen," the caseworker said. She grabbed the sisters roughly and pulled them toward the door. "Girls, we've got a train to catch. We'll send for your things."

Just then, Elvis trotted into the room. He spotted Ms. Smirt and his usually happy face instantly turned ferocious. He charged the caseworker, sending her tumbling backward over a pile of books, then stood over her, bearing his teeth and growling.

"Get this thing away from me or we'll be making a stop at the pound, too," Ms. Smirt shouted, waving a book at the dog in a fruitless attempt to intimidate him. Granny Relda stepped forward to help the woman, but Sabrina and Daphne stopped her. Instead, the girls stood on either side of the dog and looked down at their caseworker.

"Call him off!" Ms. Smirt demanded.

"Not until you understand what's going to happen today," Sabrina said. "My sister and I are going to go upstairs and get cleaned up. We're going to get dressed and then you are going to take us to school. Then you are going back to New York City, alone."

"You don't get to make the rules, young lady," Ms. Smirt snapped.

"Then we'll just let you and Elvis work out your problems on your own," Daphne said, patting the big dog on his head. "I guess you could probably make a run for it, but you won't get far. Elvis can smell evil."

Elvis barked viciously.

Ms. Smirt stared at the girls for a long moment and then furrowed her brow. "Go get ready for school," she snarled.

• • •

Despite her delay tactics, Sabrina was actually looking forward to her first day of the sixth grade. School offered her something that Granny Relda's house didn't—normal people. She would be surrounded by dull teachers and glassy-eyed kids, watching the clock tick slowly, and she would be as happy as a pig in mud. When you lived with a flying boy and the Big Bad Wolf, a little boredom was welcome.

Sabrina had even planned how her first day would go. She would melt into the crowd and do her best not to draw any attention to herself. She wouldn't join any clubs or raise her hand, but would drift through the day like an invisible girl. She would find some kids to befriend and they would sit together at lunchtime and maybe pass notes in class. Just like normal kids. It was going to be one long, dull, happy experience.

Unfortunately, Smirt was ruining Sabrina's plan. It's hard to be just another face in the crowd when you're being dragged down the hallway by your ear. Not that it was entirely Ms. Smirt's fault that Sabrina was getting attention. Even after three vigorous washings, the girl's hair was still full of goo from Puck's booby trap. It stuck out in a thousand different directions like a hungry octopus. Daphne, on the other hand, had sculpted her hair into an old-fashioned beehive style that spiraled high on her head. Inside the sticky tower, the little girl had inserted several pencils and pens, a ruler, a protractor, two gummy erasers, and a package of peanut-butter crackers for later. By the time the girls got to the principal's office, Sabrina was sure every kid in the school thought that Ferryport Landing Elementary was now enrolling escaped mental patients.

"Excuse me, I'm Minerva Smirt from the New York City Department of Child Welfare," Ms. Smirt said, pounding impatiently on a bell that sat on the counter of the school office. Two middle-aged secretaries were busy spraying bug spray at something in the far corner of the room. The one with the thick glasses leaned down and smacked whatever it was with a magazine, while the chubby one stomped on it like an Irish folk dancer.

"I think it's dead," the chubby one said as she bent over to get a better look.

Smirt rang the bell again, and the two women looked at her as if she had just come in with a flamethrower.

"I'm in a hurry," the caseworker said. "I need to enroll these two orphans."

"We are not orphans!" Sabrina and Daphne said. Ms. Smirt pinched them each on the shoulder for arguing with her.

The bespectacled secretary crossed the room and snatched the bell away. Once she had tossed it into a drawer, she looked up at the caseworker and frowned.

"I'll see if our guidance counselor, Mr. Sheepshank, is available," she said as she eyed the children in bewilderment. Shaking her head, she stepped over to a door and knocked on it lightly.

"Sir, we have some new students . . . I think," the secretary said, turning back and eyeing the girls' odd hairdos.

"Yes! Yes! Please bring them in," a happy voice called. The secretary ushered the trio into the office and closed the door.

Mr. Sheepshank was a little man dressed in a green suit and a bow tie with smiley faces on it. He had a round, full, friendly face with freckled cheeks as red as his hair. When he smiled, little wrinkle lines formed in the corners of his glittering eyes.

"Good morning, ladies. I'm Casper Sheepshank, your school counselor," the man said cheerily. "Welcome to Ferryport Landing Elementary."

Mr. Sheepshank took Ms. Smirt's hand in his and shook it vigorously. The caseworker blushed; and she did something Sabrina had never seen before: She smiled.

"I'm Minerva . . . Minerva Smirt from the New York City Department of Child Welfare," she said.

"It's a pleasure to meet you," the guidance counselor replied. "And who are these lovely ladies?"

"Introduce yourselves, girls," Ms. Smirt said, giggling.

"I'm Sabrina Grimm," Sabrina said. Sheepshank seized her hand and gave her the same joint-jarring treatment he had given to Ms. Smirt.

"I'm Daphne Grimm," Daphne chirped.

"Grimm? You wouldn't happen to be related to Henry Grimm?" the counselor asked.

"He's our dad," Sabrina said.

"He went to school here with us, too," Mr. Sheepshank said. "I remember him quite clearly. He was always getting into trouble. I assume I can expect more of the same from the two of you?"

Unsure of how to respond, the girls said nothing. After a long, uncomfortable pause Sheepshank chuckled and winked at Sabrina. "Just a joke, ladies. Your father was a model student."

"The girls were in my custody for a year and a half until we placed them here in Ferryport Landing with their grandmother, Relda," Ms. Smirt explained. "Unfortunately, Mrs. Grimm has not taken their educations seriously and they've been out of school for a month."

"Better late than never." The counselor laughed as he pulled some paperwork out of a desk drawer, and began to write.

"Casper," Ms. Smirt said, unbuttoning the top button of her shirt. "I wouldn't be able to sleep at night if I didn't warn you about these two. They are quite a handful. I tried to place them in good homes more than a dozen times, and each time it ended in chaos and grief. Nothing was ever good enough for them. They ran away from one foster home just because they were asked to help around the house."

"It wasn't a house! It was a stable," Sabrina said defensively.

"A pony got into my suitcase and ate all my underpants," Daphne added.

"They're also very argumentative," Ms. Smirt said, reaching under the desk and giving each girl a hard pinch on the leg.

"Well, Ms. Smirt," Mr. Sheepshank said, smiling warmly at

the girls. "Here at Ferryport Landing Elementary we like to set our sights on the future. Our motto is 'Everyone deserves a second chance.'"

"Well, I'll tell you, Casper, as a professional who's worked with children for almost twenty years, I'd say a second chance is the last thing a child needs. What most of them need is a swift kick in the . . ."

"Thanks for the warning, Ms. Smirt," the counselor interrupted.

"Please, call me *Minerva*," the skinny woman purred. "You'll need their transcripts of course. I could bring them up Friday. It's just a two-hour trip. Maybe we could discuss their files over dinner."

There was a long, uncomfortable silence. Mr. Sheepshank blushed and then shuffled some papers on his desk.

"Bring them up? All the way from New York City? That's not necessary. Just drop them in the mail when you get a chance," he said, staring down at his paperwork. "Well, I better get these girls started. I trust you can find your way out, Ms. Smirt?"

The caseworker shifted in her chair and her face turned red with frustration. "Of course," she said. She reached into her handbag and took out a card. "Here's my card if you need any help with them. My home phone is on there, too."

Sabrina gazed down at the caseworker's handbag. When she spotted a book entitled *Finding Mr. Right,* the unsettling truth about what she was witnessing revealed itself. Ms. Smirt was flirting. An image of the two grown-ups kissing burned into Sabrina's permanent memory and she shuddered as if she had just witnessed a car crash.

But what was really bothering Sabrina was the odd feeling forming in her own heart. She felt pity for the cranky old woman. Sabrina might not have had much experience with boys, but it was obvious Mr. Sheepshank wasn't into Ms. Smirt, even though the caseworker kept on trying.

"Well, Susie . . . Debbie, I'm off," the skinny woman said as she got up from her chair.

"Sabrina," Sabrina said. Her sympathy vanished.

"Daphne," Daphne added.

Ms. Smirt stopped and turned at the door. "Maybe we'll talk again, Casper . . ."

Mr. Sheepshank smiled but said nothing. He only stared at her as if he were a deer caught in front of a speeding truck. After several way-too-long, painful moments of silence, Ms. Smirt stepped into the hallway.

"Be good girls," the caseworker said as she closed the door. "Or I'll be back."

"Well, I suppose we should get you two to class," said Mr. Sheepshank as he rose from his desk and led them back into the hallway. "Ladies, the first day of school can be difficult for some students. But I want you to know that if there are any bumps in the road—for example, someone you can't get along with or a teacher who's given you too much homework—then I'm the man to come to. Feel free to stop by my office anytime you want. My job is to listen and my door is always open."

Sabrina liked Sheepshank's attitude. She'd been in a dozen schools in the last two years and no one had ever spoken to her the way their new counselor did. While everyone else lectured about learning responsibility and the value of hard work, he seemed to understand how hard it was to be a kid.

"Mr. Sheepshank!" a man shouted from the other end of the hall. He had a German accent not unlike Granny Relda's. "We are due for a conversation!"

The man rushed toward them. He was a tall, dark-haired man in a gray suit. He had a long, lean, ruddy face that made his crooked nose look enormous. Because he was upset, his big bushy eyebrows bounced around on his forehead like excited caterpillars.

"Children, this is your principal, Mr. Hamelin," the guidance counselor said, ignoring the man's frustration. "Mr. Hamelin,

I'd like to introduce you to our new students, Sabrina and Daphne Grimm."

"My grandmother says hello," Daphne said.

Principal Hamelin cocked an eyebrow, aware now that the girls knew who he really was. Granny Relda had told them there were two Everafters working at Ferryport Landing Elementary: Snow White, who was a teacher, and the principal, aka "The Pied Piper of Hamelin." The girls knew his story. Using his magical bagpipes, Hamelin had enchanted a thousand rats to follow him out of town and into the ocean, where they drowned. Granny had explained that Hamelin had gotten his job based on his leadership skills. If he could lead a bunch of rodents, he could handle a school full of kids.

"Of course, of course," Hamelin said, forcing a smile onto his face. "Welcome to Ferryport Landing Elementary. I needed to discuss the . . . uh . . . textbook shortage with Mr. Sheepshank, but it can wait. I hope you'll help them settle in, Casper?"

"My pleasure, Mr. Hamelin," the counselor replied, leading the girls down the hallway. Soon, they stopped in front of a classroom and Mr. Sheepshank patted Daphne on the shoulder. "This is your class."

The girls peered through the window in the door and saw a woman so stunningly beautiful Sabrina could hardly believe it.

Her jet-black hair and porcelain skin were hypnotic. Her eyes were a dazzling blue and her teeth were so white they were nearly blinding.

"Daphne, your teacher's name is Ms. White," Sheepshank said.

Daphne put the palm of her hand into her mouth and bit on it. It was an odd little habit she had when she was very excited.

"I'm so happy," the little girl said giddily, "I might barf."

Ever since Granny Relda had told them that Snow White was a teacher, Daphne had prayed on hands and knees each night that she would be placed in the legendary beauty's class. It looked as if someone had been listening to the little girl's prayers.

"Don't put any crayons in your nose," Sabrina joked as Mr. Sheepshank led her sister into the room. Daphne stuck her tongue out in reply.

As the guidance counselor introduced Daphne, Sabrina studied the teacher through the open door. Snow White and Mr. Hamelin were both Everafters. Could they be trusted? Suspicion clouded Sabrina's mind and anger flowed over her. Maybe Snow White and the Piper were in on her parents' disappearance. Maybe they were working together to kidnap her and her sister next.

"Sabrina, are you feeling OK?" Mr. Sheepshank asked. The girl hadn't noticed him step back into the hall. She nodded.

"Yes, just got a headache," Sabrina replied. It wasn't a lie. Her head was pounding.

"Check with the school nurse if it doesn't go away," the counselor instructed, as he directed her down the hall and up a flight of stairs. On the second floor was another long hallway full of classrooms. They stopped at the first door and Sheepshank opened it. He turned to Sabrina and gave her a warm smile. "I think this might just be the perfect homeroom for you."

"Mr. Grumpner," he said as he stepped into the classroom. "I'd like to introduce you and the class to a new student. Her name is Sabrina Grimm. She and her sister just moved to Ferryport Landing from New York City."

"She looks like she stuck a fork into a light socket," a boy called from the middle of the room. He was short with wiry black hair and big bug eyes. A few kids snickered, but most of the class seemed to be asleep, or about to doze off.

"Toby, shut up," the teacher growled. The boy's face turned red with rage and he looked as if he might actually get out of his seat and charge at the old man. A pretty girl with platinum blond hair and big green eyes put her hand on the boy's arm and it seemed to calm him down.

Grumpner turned his attention to Sabrina. He was an old man with saggy jowls and thin, charcoal-colored hair. To the girl, he looked like a deflating birthday party balloon you find in the garage a week after the fun is over. He frowned.

"Sit," he said gruffly as he pointed to several empty desks in the last row. Then he turned back to the guidance counselor. "Sheepshank, what is wrong with these kids?" he demanded. "Half of them are asleep and the other half are between naps!"

"I'm sure you'll find a way to get them motivated, Mr. Grumpner," the counselor said, as he waved to Sabrina and left the room. "After all, you're one of our finest teachers."

The compliment did little to calm the old man down.

"Open your books to page one forty-two," Grumpner growled, as he walked down the aisle and tossed a ratty text-book onto Sabrina's desk. She opened it and looked for page 142, but it and dozens more pages had been ripped out.

"You need to read this page carefully, morons," Grumpner threatened. "Tomorrow you're going to have a quiz on it."

Sabrina slowly raised her hand.

"What is it, Grimm?"

"That page has been ripped out of my book," she stuttered.

Grumpner's face turned red. Even from the back of the room, Sabrina could spot a throbbing vein on his forehead, preparing to explode. Luckily, the old grouch was distracted by a short, pudgy boy running into the classroom. He rushed past the teacher and hurried down Sabrina's aisle, where he slipped behind a desk and opened a book.

"Wendell!" Grumpner bellowed at the top of his lungs. The chubby boy looked up from his desk, wiped his nose with a handkerchief, and looked genuinely surprised by the teacher's anger. It took all of Sabrina's willpower not to break out laughing at the boy's dumbfounded expression.

"Yes, Mr. Grumpner," Wendell replied.

"You are late, again," the teacher said.

"I'm sorry. I forgot to set my alarm clock," the boy said meekly.

"You forgot?" Grumpner exploded. "Well, that's just great! I bet you didn't forget breakfast this morning! Everyone can see that! Maybe we should cover your alarm clock with candy and French fries; then you'd never forget to set it!"

"I said I was sorry!"

The old man stomped down the aisle and roughly pulled the boy out of his seat. He dragged him to the front of the room so everyone could see his humiliation.

"Do you know why you are always late, Wendell?" Mr. Grumpner asked. "It's because you are a worthless fat-body. Isn't that right?"

This woke up the class, who roared with laughter. Toby, the bug-eyed boy, nearly fell out of his chair giggling.

"Well, I'm sure I could stand to lose a little weight, but I wouldn't go so far as to say . . . !" but the chubby boy never got to finish. Grumpner shoved a piece of chalk into his hand and spun him toward the chalkboard.

"And you are going to write it until the end of this class. You may think that because you're the principal's son you don't have to play by the rules, but I'm not afraid of your father. I have tenure. Get started!"

Wendell turned to the chalkboard and wrote I AM A WORTH-LESS FAT-BODY. The students roared with laughter again, but Sabrina barely noticed. She was too stunned by what Mr. Grumpner had said. Wendell was the principal's son—the child of an Everafter? Sabrina had never imagined that the Everafters might have children or that they would send them to a school where all the other kids were human. She gazed around the room, watching the rest of the class laugh at the boy as he scrawled the mean sentence over and over again. Could any of them be Everafters, too?

• • •

As Sabrina drifted from class to class, she began to realize that Mr. Grumpner wasn't the only teacher on the verge of a nervous breakdown. In fact, the entire sixth-grade faculty was a collection of bullying, screaming nightmares. They shouted through most of their classes, dishing out detentions like scoops of ice cream. Not that Sabrina could really blame them, though. The kids in her classes were real pains in the butt. They slept through the lectures and none of them had done their homework.

Even in gym class, the kids staggered around exhausted. Unfortunately for them, gym class turned out to be the one place you really needed to be alert. Their teacher was Ms. Spangler. Spangler the Strangler, as the kids called her, was a bulky little woman with a ponytail and an evil glint in her eye, who apparently knew how to teach just one game—dodgeball. Sabrina had played dodgeball many times at school in New York City. She considered herself to be pretty good at it; she remembered being the last kid standing many times, so in Ms. Spangler's class, when the first rubber ball smacked her in the head and made her brains rattle in her skull, she knew that something about this dodgeball game was different.

Getting knocked out of the game early gave Sabrina a chance to study the other kids. It was easy to see who the dangerous ones were—the only two really playing the game. Sabrina recognized one as the giggling idiot Toby, from her homeroom class, but the other was a knuckle-dragging hulk with ratty hair. To be honest, Sabrina wasn't sure if it was a boy or a girl; all she knew was that Toby and It were vicious. Together, they whipped balls at the other kids at alarming speeds. When a kid fell down, the duo would pummel him or her mercilessly with the hard rubber balls. Even worse, Ms. Spangler encouraged the craziness. She ran around the gymnasium blowing her whistle and pointing out the weaknesses of the players to Toby and the big It, urging them to target the pudgy, small, slow, and awkward. Whenever a kid was hit and eliminated, Ms. Spangler clapped happily, like a child on Christmas morning.

There was only one other kid in the class who had the energy to defend herself. Sabrina recognized her, too. The pretty blond from Sabrina's homeroom managed to duck out of the way of several shots, dodging and jumping until she, too, was struck and tossed out of the game. She joined the battered kids waiting on the sidelines. When she spotted Sabrina, she smiled and waved. It was the first act of kindness Sabrina had experienced the whole day.

By lunchtime, Sabrina was bruised and belittled, but her main concern was Daphne. Sabrina could handle a screaming teacher or a bully, but her sister was only seven. This school would eat her alive.

Once Sabrina had her tray of food, she searched the cafeteria for her little sister, fully expecting Daphne to be huddled in a corner bawling her eyes out. She was stunned to find her sitting at a table packed with bright-eyed, happy kids, all hanging on her every word. As Sabrina approached the table, the children exploded with laughter watching her sister pull a ruler out of her big beehive hair.

"Daphne, you are the funniest person I have ever met," one of her little friends said.

"Are you OK?" Sabrina asked her sister.

Daphne smiled and nodded. "Time of my life."

Daphne was the hit of the second grade and Sabrina wasn't about to take it away from her. Instead, she trudged through the cafeteria looking for an empty table. She thought she had found one, but just as she was about to sit down, two kids quickly slipped into the seats as if she weren't there at all. She moved in the direction of another deserted table but the same thing happened again. Sabrina was starting to wonder if she could eat standing up, when she felt her feet come out from under her. Her tray flew forward, sending her lunch splattering across the cafeteria. She slammed to the ground hard, pounding her chin into the cold floor, and saw little lights explode in front of her eyes.

Standing over her was the It from gym class. The kid was ape-like, with long, thick arms, a hulking body, and an under-bite.

When Sabrina spotted the little pink ribbon sticking out of Its knotted hair, she finally realized It was a girl.

"Ooops," the girl grunted. Toby, the bug-eyed weirdo, was standing next to her, laughing.

As embarrassed as she was, Sabrina wasn't at all surprised. She had been bullied before. The orphanage had been like a prison at times, and the new kids always got the worst of it until they proved they could give as well as they got.

"You did that on purpose," she said as she calmly got to her feet.

"What are you going to do about it, Grimm? Cry on me?" the big girl laughed.

"If you know my name, then you should know I don't cry," Sabrina said, clenching her fist tightly and then socking the girl in the face. As the big goon fell backward, Sabrina's dreams of dull school days fell with her. For when she turned to look around the cafeteria, the sleepy-faced kids from her class were now wide awake and in awe of her.

"You shouldn't have done that," Toby hissed.

"You're exactly right," a voice shouted. A meaty hand grabbed Sabrina's arm and dragged her away. It was Mr. Grumpner and the vein on his forehead was throbbing.

"She started it," Sabrina cried.

"And I'm ending it," Grumpner shouted back.

• • •

Sabrina sat in Mr. Sheepshank's hot, windowless office waiting for her punishment. The mousy secretary with the thick glasses told her that the guidance counselor would be with her as soon as he was available. Three hours later, he still hadn't shown up.

Sabrina sat and reflected on her day so far. Apparently, the sixth grade was a nightmare, and no one had been courteous enough to let her know in advance. She thought it would be all books and tests—not guerilla warfare. The kids were hateful. The teachers were despicable. It was just like being back in the orphanage.

By the time Mr. Sheepshank and his smiley-face bow tie showed up, Sabrina was seething with rage. Mr. Grumpner followed him into the office, looking indignant, and the two men sat down.

"So, Sabrina," the counselor said. "Do you want to tell us why Natalie is in the school infirmary with a black eye?"

"I'll tell you why!" Mr. Grumpner growled, nearly jumping out of his seat. "This one is trouble."

Mr. Sheepshank sat back in his chair and licked his lips as if he were preparing for a big meal. "Go on, Sabrina, what happened?"

"That ugly freak tripped me on purpose," Sabrina said, wiping the sweat from her brow.

"That's what *she's* saying," Grumpner interrupted. "I saw the whole thing."

"If you'd seen the whole thing, then we wouldn't be sitting here!" Sabrina snapped, surprised by how quickly her anger had boiled over. Her head was starting to pound again. Maybe she was getting sick.

"Listen to that attitude," her teacher bellowed. "I don't know how school works in the big city, but in my classroom you will respect me or else!"

"Yeah, I've seen what 'or else' means in your classroom," the girl said. "I've seen how you teach children to respect you. You insult them, make fun of them, and drag them around. I dare you to try it on me! I just dare you!"

Mr. Grumpner backed away as if he had just stumbled upon a hornet's nest. "Are you going to let her talk to me like that?" he whined to the counselor.

"I believe that letting your feelings out is healthy," Mr. Sheepshank said. "Sabrina has a right to defend herself."

"Save your new-age psychobabble," the teacher grumbled. "What are you going to do to punish her?"

"Punish me?" Sabrina cried. "I didn't start the fight!"

"Mr. Grumpner, I think we need a breather," the counselor

said as he rose from his chair. He crossed the room, took the grouchy teacher by the arm, and led him to the door. "If you spot any more slug-fests, please be sure to bring them to my attention immediately."

"You didn't tell me what you're going to do with her," Grumpner argued, but Mr. Sheepshank just pushed him out of the room and closed the door in his face. "Discipline is the backbone of education!" the teacher shouted through the door. "We'll see what Principal Hamelin thinks about this!"

The guidance counselor ignored the teacher's threat and returned to his chair with a broad smile. "Interesting first day you are having," he said.

"I didn't start that fight but I'm not going to let someone pick on me, either," Sabrina said.

"I'm not asking you to," Sheepshank replied. "I think Natalie got what she had coming to her. She's been pushing kids around since kindergarten. I bet it felt pretty good to knock her down."

Sabrina was stunned. Adults always said you should try to talk out your problems first. "Aren't you supposed to tell me that fighting isn't the answer?" she asked.

"Let's just pretend I did," Mr. Sheepshank continued with a wink. "Sabrina, I know being in the sixth grade isn't easy. There are lots of things that aren't fair, like a bully picking on you. It's a natural human emotion to get angry. So what are you supposed to do? Bottle it up? Well, we all know what happens when you shake up a bottle of soda. It explodes all over the place when you open it. I think feelings are the same way. You've got to let them out when you're having them or you're just going to explode later on."

New-age psychobabble or not, Sabrina liked what Mr. Sheepshank was saying. She'd hadn't had an adult actually listen to her so well in a long time. In fact, he seemed almost eager to hear her thoughts.

"I think we'll forget all about this," the counselor continued. "You've been sitting here for several hours and have had plenty of time to think about what happened."

Sabrina got up from her seat, then paused and asked, "Mr. Sheepshank, does it get any better?"

He laughed. "I wish I could say it does, but don't worry, someday this place will be nothing but an ancient memory."

Sabrina looked up at the clock. School had been over for five minutes. Daphne would be waiting.

"I have to go meet my sister."

"Of course," Mr. Sheepshank said. "But before you go, I just want to remind you that my door is always open. I'm a pretty good listener."

Sabrina nodded. "I'll see you tomorrow, then," she said.

"I'm on the edge of my seat," the guidance counselor replied.

The girl nodded and stepped into the hallway. Natalie, the bully, was waiting by some lockers. Her left eye had a black-and-purple bruise around it. When she spotted Sabrina, she turned and punched a locker door. The impact was so great it dented the door badly. Happy with her handiwork, the big goon smiled, pointed at Sabrina, and shuffled down the hallway.

Great, I've been here less than eight hours and I already have a mortal enemy, Sabrina thought. *I wonder what Tuesday will be like?*

"Don't worry, Sabrina. Tomorrow's a new day," a voice behind her said. Sabrina spun around and found the pretty blond girl from her homeroom and gym class.

"That's what I'm worried about."

The girl laughed. "I'm Bella," she said. "And don't worry, not everyone's like Natalie."

Just then, Daphne rushed down the hallway to meet them. She had her coat and mittens on, and a couple of books under her arm.

"I've had the greatest day of my entire life!" she screamed as she hugged Sabrina tightly. "We spent the first part of the morning making papier-mâché hats, and then when the hats were dry we put them on and learned about what kind of people might have worn them. I had George Washington's hat."

The little girl paused to catch her breath.

"Daphne, this is Bella," Sabrina said, introducing the two. "She's in my homeroom."

"You made a friend?" Daphne said, giving her sister another hug. "Oh, I'm so proud of you!"

"Cute kid," Bella said, giggling. "I gotta get going. See you tomorrow."

Sabrina nodded and watched the girl disappear down the hallway. Maybe there was a chance of having a normal friend, after all.

"Did you know that George Washington didn't really have wooden teeth? That's a myth. Ms. White said his teeth were made from ivory and bone, 'cause . . ." Daphne paused and looked around. Then she cupped her hand around her sister's ear and finished her sentence. ". . . she actually knew him. But she didn't tell the class that, she just told me."

Then Daphne pulled away and returned to her normal, excited tone. "Then we learned all about chimpanzees. Did you know that chimpanzees aren't actually monkeys? I didn't know that. Chimpanzees are so punk rock."

"Punk rock?"

"You know, cool."

"Where did you hear that?" Sabrina laughed.

"Julie Melphy. She's in my class. She's very punk rock," her sister replied.

"That's stupid."

"You're stupid," Daphne shot back. "And very un-punk rock! How was your day?"

"Horrible," Sabrina grumbled. "Come on, I have to go get my coat from my locker. It's upstairs."

The girls climbed the steps to the second floor just as Toby came running down them. He nearly knocked them over.

"Out of the way, lightning-bolt head," he shouted then laughed his annoying little laugh. He ran past and disappeared down the hall.

That kid is so un-punk rock, Sabrina thought.

The sisters reached Sabrina's locker and she went to work on the combination. If there had been anything good about the day it was that at least she had been assigned a locker near her homeroom. She wouldn't have to trudge through the halls in the morning with all her books.

"What kind of class are you in?" Daphne asked as she peered through the window into Grumpner's room.

"What are you talking about?" Sabrina said as she put on her coat and closed her locker.

"Look," her sister said, pointing into Sabrina's homeroom.

Sabrina gazed through the window. The room looked as if a tornado had gone through it. Desks and chairs had been tossed around and there was an odd, white substance covering everything. She opened the door and the girls stepped inside. The white substance hung from the ceiling in strands like silky ribbons. It fluttered in the icy wind that blew in from a broken window. In the center of the room, a large sack of the junk was suspended from the ceiling, slowly swaying in the breeze.

"Don't touch anything," Sabrina said, tugging at a strand that had attached itself to her coat.

"What's that thing hanging from the ceiling?" Daphne asked as her sister crossed the room to look. Sabrina grabbed a nearby chair, pulled it close to the sack, and climbed onto the seat.

"Something's inside it," she said as she yanked at the layers of sticky stuff that formed the sack. Soon, something began to reveal itself from deep inside—something with a face. "It's Mr. Grumpner," she whispered. The old man was as purple as an eggplant and his once puffy face was gaunt and drained. "He's dead."

"Awww, man! That's so gross!" Daphne cried unhappily.

"What could have done this?" Sabrina wondered.

"Probably whoever left that," the little girl said, pointing at the far end of the classroom.

Sabrina turned to see what her sister was referring to. On the chalkboard was another horrible but familiar sight. Someone had dipped his or her hand into a can of paint and pressed it on the wall. The handprint was bright red.

4

The school doors flew open and a dark-haired man in a purple suit strutted in with his head in the air. He swaggered down the shiny hallway with a dwarf and an obese police officer bringing up the rear. When Sabrina spotted the group, she groaned. Mayor Charming was not one of her favorite people.

To anyone else, Mayor Charming might have seemed like a run-of-the-mill politician, but Sabrina knew better. Mayor Charming was really Prince Charming, the dashing romantic hero of a dozen fairy tales. But, as Sabrina knew firsthand, *Charming* was only his name. The mayor could be an obnoxious, rude know-it-all, and he had a particular disdain for Sabrina's family. In a nutshell, he hated the Grimms.

Racing to keep up was Mr. Seven, the mayor's diminutive side-kick. Seven was actually one of the original seven dwarfs and acted as Charming's driver, assistant, and whipping boy. Behind him was Sheriff Hamstead, who did his best to keep up with the others while trying to hoist his pants up at the same time.

"So, let's go through this one more time," the mayor said to his followers with an air of condescension. "Who's doing all the talking?"

"You are," Hamstead and Mr. Seven said in unison.

"And why is that?"

"Because we are numbskulls."

"See how easy that was?"

"But what if I see something suspicious? I am the sheriff, after all," Hamstead argued.

Charming came to a halt and spun around on his heels. "Are you going to make me get out the idiot hat? 'Cause it sounds like someone wants to wear the idiot hat!"

"I don't," Mr. Seven said.

The sheriff frowned and shook his head.

"Good," Mayor Charming snapped. He took a deep breath and looked up to the ceiling as if someone were watching from above. "OK, let's relax. Let out all the anger and frustration. You are a great mayor. Smile."

Suddenly, a smile sprang to Charming's face and he started down the hallway again. The mayor was a master at the phony, toothy grin, but it slid off his face when he spotted Sabrina and Daphne.

"What are they doing here?" he moaned.

"They found the body," the sheriff explained.

"The sisters Grimm found the body and no one told me?" Charming said.

"You told us not to talk," Mr. Seven said defensively.

The mayor bit down on his lower lip and mumbled a variety of curse words Sabrina had never heard before. He reached into his pocket, took out a folded piece of paper, and handed it to Mr. Seven, who looked down at it and frowned. The dwarf unfolded it, revealing a pointy paper hat, and put it on his head. Someone had written IDIOT in big black letters on the front of it. Mr. Seven lowered his eyes in humiliation.

"Howdy, Mayor," Daphne said happily. Even though Charming considered the Grimms his eternal enemies, Daphne had a soft spot for him. The mayor had helped the family stop Jack the Giant Killer, but most important, he had been kind to Elvis when the big dog was injured. Since then, the little girl had been convinced that deep down Mayor Charming was one of the good guys.

"Sheriff, let's make a new law. Children who cannot stay out of the way go to jail," he said through gritted teeth.

"You're so funny," Daphne said, smiling into the mayor's face. The little girl grabbed Charming's necktie, yanked him down to her level, and gave him a smooch on the nose. The anger melted from the man's face only to be replaced by confusion. He pulled away from the girl as if he had accidentally touched a hot stove.

Principal Hamelin rushed down the hall to join them. "Mayor Charming, Sheriff Hamstead, this is such a terrible tragedy. I just want you two to know that the faculty will cooperate in every way we can. I just feel horrible about this."

Charming smiled and shook the principal's hand, vigorously. "I appreciate that, Piper. We'll get to the bottom of this and be out of your hair as soon as possible," he said. "I assume you don't have any more of these running around the building?" He waved his hand at the girls as if he were trying to shoo away a couple of annoying houseflies.

"You mean children?" the principal said. "Oh, no. It happened at the end of the day and most of them were already on their way home."

"Sheriff, let's take a look," Charming said, gesturing to the door of Mr. Grumpner's classroom.

The two men tried to enter the room at the same time and

got jammed in the doorway together. They squirmed and shoved but were trapped until Mr. Seven came up from behind and pushed them into the room.

"I thought we weren't going to do that anymore," Mr. Charming said, maintaining his phony smile in front of everyone. Hamstead muttered an apology and immediately took a camera from his pocket. He snapped pictures of the unusual crime scene and Mr. Grumpner's disturbing corpse.

"He was found about ten minutes after the last bell," Principal Hamelin offered.

"I see," said Charming as he yanked some of the sticky stuff off a desk.

Sheriff Hamstead stepped close to the body to take more photos. He pulled aside a strand of the sticky substance to get a better look at Mr. Grumpner's face. "Looks like the blood has been drained right out of him."

"Maybe it was a vampire!" Daphne cried.

"There's no such thing as vampires," Charming muttered.

I used to think there was no such thing as you, Sabrina thought.

"Sheriff, do you have any idea what happened to him?" the principal asked.

"Well," Hamstead said as he put his camera away, "if I had to hazard a guess I'd say . . ."

"Spiders," Charming interrupted. "A whole bunch of spiders murdered him. There are so many cobwebs here I'd say it took hundreds of spiders to make them. Looks like they came in through the window."

"It's too cold for spiders," the sheriff argued, but when the mayor flashed him an angry look, the portly policeman zipped his lips.

"And what would the spiders' motivation be?" Sabrina asked.

"How should I know?" Charming said. "Maybe Mr. Grumpner stepped on one and its family wanted revenge."

"Spider revenge?" Sabrina asked.

"I don't hear anyone else with a better theory," Charming snapped.

Suddenly the door opened and Granny Relda and Mr. Canis entered the room.

"Oh, I have a theory," Granny Relda said, scanning the room. "It was a monster."

Daphne ran to the old woman and wrapped her arms around her.

"We found something gross," the little girl cried, burying her face into the old woman's bright green dress. Granny bent down and kissed her on the forehead.

"A monster!" Charming growled. "You've had some insane theories in the past, Relda, but monsters?"

"You're right, Mayor," the old woman said sarcastically. "Ferryport Landing has fairies, witches, robots, and men made out of straw, but monsters? Now I've really lost my marbles!"

Charming scowled. "Well, have your look around. I know I can't stop you."

"Thank you, Mayor," Granny Relda said. She crossed the room to Sabrina and took her by the hand. "Are you OK, *liebling*?"

Sabrina nodded.

Granny patted her on the head and walked over to the broken window. Among the glass was something long and black. The old woman gingerly moved the glass aside with her fingers and plucked the object off the ground. It was a feather.

"Gentlemen, I believe I have found a clue," she said.

Sheriff Hamstead took the feather and eyed it closely. "Looks like crow to me," he said. "There's a couple more there under the windowsill."

Mr. Canis took a deep sniff of the air. "It is crow."

"They probably blew in with the wind," Charming said, snatching the feather from the sheriff's pudgy hands. He tossed it to the floor as if it were meaningless.

"We found a clue, too!" Daphne said proudly. She pointed at the red hand painted on the chalkboard.

Hamstead, Charming, Mr. Seven, and Principal Hamelin peered at the red hand closely. Each of them had a worried look on his face.

"It's just like the one the police found in my parents' abandoned car," Sabrina said. "Or maybe that blew in with the wind, too."

Charming scowled and rolled his eyes at her. "Probably just a prank."

"A prank?" Sabrina and Daphne cried.

"Mayor Charming, that's the sign of the Scarlet Hand," said Granny Relda.

"There's no such thing as the Scarlet Hand," he said. "Hamstead has done a thorough investigation and we've concluded that Jack invented the whole thing."

Sabrina couldn't believe her ears. Charming knew the Scarlet Hand was real. He had admitted to the girls that the shadowy criminal group of Everafters had approached him. And this was before they'd heard Jack brag about being a member. Why was he now lying about its existence?

Before Sabrina could confront him, the door opened and Snow White entered. It didn't seem possible, but Ms. White was even more beautiful up close.

Mayor Charming rushed to block her view of Mr. Grumpner's corpse, but the teacher had already spotted it.

"So, it's true," she gasped.

"Snow, you shouldn't see this," Charming said softly.

"I'm fine," Snow White said, but the mayor ignored her. He took her by the hand and led her into the hallway. Sabrina and Daphne shared a glance and pushed through the crowd, eager not to miss a second of this royal soap opera.

The mayor pulled the teacher into his arms as if she needed comfort, and for a brief moment she seemed to enjoy it, but then she pulled away.

"Billy," Ms. White said, "what did that to him?"

"Try to put it out of your head, Snow," Charming said. He put his hand on her shoulder and looked deep into her eyes. It was hard to believe that the usually obnoxious mayor could be so tender. "I've got my best men on it."

The others filed out of Grumpner's classroom and Sheriff Hamstead took a roll of yellow police tape from his jacket. He draped an X over the door to keep anyone else from entering.

"Snow, I don't want you to get involved in this," the mayor said. The teacher flashed him an irritated look, but then nodded. She turned and bent down so that she was at eye level with Daphne.

"Are you OK?" she asked.

"Don't worry about me," the little girl answered. "We see this kind of thing all the time."

Mayor Charming turned to the sheriff. "Mr. Hamstead, could you make sure my fiancée . . . I mean Ms. White, gets home safely," he said, blushing over his mistake. As Snow White stood up she smiled softly, but the bright red blush on her cheeks flashed like a police siren on her pale skin.

"I'd be happy to," Sheriff Hamstead said, extending his arm to the beautiful woman. He escorted her down the hall and she stopped to gaze back at Charming before they left.

"So, what's next, *Billy*?" Sabrina said, before she burst into giggles. Daphne and Granny Relda joined her. Even Mr. Canis cracked a smile. Suddenly, a loud, goofy laugh was heard behind them. When they turned they found Mr. Seven nearly falling over with laughter.

"*Billy*," Sabrina continued. "That's just precious. It's so sweet I'm going to get a cavity."

"I think it's romantic," Daphne said, doing her best to stop laughing.

"Enough!" Charming shouted, silencing everyone's giggles. "This is a crime scene. Relda, take your rug rats and your mangy mongrel with you or I'll have you arrested."

"Watch your words, Prince," Canis growled as his eyes turned icy blue, showing everyone that the Wolf was just below the surface. "Someday you're going to wake up and find someone has taken a bite out of you."

"Relda, I believe there's a law in this town about keeping animals on a leash," Charming said.

The men stared at each other for a long moment and then, suddenly, Canis's eyes changed back to watery gray. The old man looked exhausted and his face grew pale.

"That's quite enough of this nonsense," Granny said, stepping in between the two men. Every time Charming and Canis were in a room together they were at each other's throats, but the old woman had a way of making them feel foolish. They stepped back and lowered their eyes like two squabbling schoolboys who had just been disciplined. "It's time to go."

The family exited the school and found their ancient black jalopy in the parking lot. The beat-up monstrosity was in desperate need of a tune-up and its long-neglected shocks groaned and complained as each person climbed inside. Elvis was in the back, snuggling under a huge blanket, and didn't even bother to lift his head when the girls got in. Daphne wrapped her arms around the dog's neck and gave him a big wet smooch on the forehead.

"I missed you today," she announced.

Elvis tucked his head under his blanket and hid.

"What's the matter with him?" the little girl asked.

"He's pouting. He doesn't like to be left in the car," Granny Relda said as she jotted something into her notebook.

"Awww, my little baby," Daphne said, trying to pull the two-hundred-pound dog onto her lap like an infant. She showered the Great Dane in kisses. "Is somebody sad? Did somebody get left in the car? I won't ever leave you in the car."

Elvis gave her a lick on the cheek and the girl giggled.

Granny spun around in her seat with a delighted look on her face. "*Lieblings*, you know what all this means?"

Sabrina groaned. "We're in the middle of a mystery?"

"Isn't it exciting?" the old woman cried.

"Yes, and pointless," the girl argued. "You heard Charming and his ridiculous spider theory. He knows the Scarlet Hand killed Mr. Grumpner, but instead he lies about it. Grumpner was a human, so Charming couldn't care less. Why should the Everafter mayor and the Everafter police department do anything at all? No, they'll just cover up his death, and we'll run into one dead end after another."

"We are Grimms and this is what we do," Daphne said.

"Exactly right, little one. We are Grimms and part of what we do is make sure that this kind of thing doesn't go unpunished. We'll just sit here until everyone is gone and then we'll go back inside and have a look ourselves," the old woman said. "I have a feeling there are a lot more clues in that room."

Suddenly, Mr. Seven was tapping on the car window. He motioned for Granny Relda to roll it down and looked around nervously.

"Good evening, Mr. Seven."

"Mayor Charming has requested your presence at the mansion."

"You mean *Billy*?" Granny said, turning in her seat to wink at the girls.

The dwarf chuckled. "He has something he wishes to discuss in private."

Granny Relda and Mr. Canis shared a suspicious glance. After a moment, Mr. Canis nodded his approval.

"Tell Mr. Charming we'll be there," the old woman said.

The dwarf nodded and walked over to the mayor's long white limousine. He buffed the silver stallion on the hood with his shirtsleeve then climbed onto the stack of phone books on the driver's seat, and soon the limo was pulling away.

"Are you sure you're feeling up to this?" Granny said, putting her hand on the old man's shoulder. Mr. Canis nodded. He started the car and it sputtered to life with a series of backfires that Sabrina was sure could be heard in the next town.

They followed Charming's limo through the quiet country roads of Ferryport Landing. Sabrina gazed out at the sleepy little river town that her great-great-great-great grandfather Wilhelm Grimm had founded. Anyone driving through it would think it was just another boring little town. They would never know that many of the residents were princes, pigs, witches, and fairies, all in disguise. And on the rare occasions when one of the really big Everafters caused trouble, such as one of the giants or dragons, the endless acres of firs, Chinese maples, and oak trees that surrounded the town acted as an excellent cover from prying eyes. In addition, the invisible magical barrier that Wilhelm and the witch Baba Yaga had constructed around Ferryport Landing meant no Everafter, no matter how big, could leave the area. As for the humans who lived in town, they were none the wiser. The Everafters were too good at covering up their magic and mischief. Sabrina often wished she were oblivious, too. Ferryport Landing was a perfect place to live, unless you knew that it was all a lie, and the lie kept Sabrina from getting comfortable in her new life.

As they pulled into Charming's sprawling estate, Sabrina realized the mayor was the only person in town she could trust. He was corrupt, but at least he was upfront about it. He planned to buy the town piece by piece and recreate the kingdom he had given up when the Everafters came to America. He didn't care if you liked it or not and he didn't care if you thought it was wrong. Charming could always be counted on to do what was right for himself. He might not have any morals, but at least he was consistent.

Mr. Canis parked the car and turned off the engine. The last time Sabrina had been at the mansion it had been lit up like a Christmas tree for the Ferryport Landing Ball, an annual event for which the Everafter community came together to be themselves and to celebrate. Without all the glitz and glamour, Charming's mansion looked vacant. The lights were off and the fountain, which featured a lifelike sculpture of Charming, was drained and full of dead leaves.

"Mrs. Grimm, if it's OK with you I believe I will stay here," Mr. Canis said as he opened the car door for Granny Relda. "I'm feeling a bit tired and I suspect Charming will only make it worse."

"Of course, Mr. Canis," Granny Relda said. "I don't believe Mayor Charming poses any threat to us."

Elvis whined when he saw that the family was leaving him in the car.

"Elvis, we're not leaving you in the car. We're putting you in charge of it," Daphne said. The dog lifted his huge ears as if he was listening very carefully. "It's a really important job. You have to stay and guard Mr. Canis. Don't let anything bad happen to him."

Elvis barked, confirming his orders. He sat up in the backseat and watched out the windows for any would-be attackers. As the Grimms approached the mansion, Sabrina looked back and noticed Canis doing something very odd. The stick-thin man climbed on top of the car and sat Indian-style on the roof. He closed his eyes and rested his hands on his knees.

"What's he doing?" Sabrina asked.

"Meditative yoga," Granny replied, as if this were the natural response. "It's helping him remain centered and calm. Keeps the dark stuff at bay."

Of course, the Big Bad Wolf does yoga, Sabrina thought. *Why did I even bother to ask?*

The trio stood on the front steps of the mansion, but before Granny could ring the bell, Mr. Seven opened the door and ushered the family inside.

"Good evening," he said and, without offering to take their coats, he turned and raced up the staircase. "I'll get the mayor."

"What do you think he wants?" Daphne wondered.

"Hard to say," Granny Relda said. "The mayor is full of surprises."

"Maybe he felt like he didn't get to insult us enough at the school," Sabrina muttered just as Charming appeared at the top of the steps. Sabrina watched him grimace, then take a deep breath as he came down to join them.

"This conversation must be an absolute secret," he said as he stood before them. He leaned down and pinned a shiny tin star on Sabrina's coat. It looked like the kind sheriffs wore in old black-and-white western movies. She peered down at it and read the words FERRYPORT LANDING SPECIAL FORCES DEPUTY OFFICER.

"What's this?" she asked as Charming pinned a similar star onto Daphne's coat. The little girl looked at it and smiled. "Look at me! I'm a cowboy!"

"May I?" Charming said to Granny Relda. The old woman hesitated but finally agreed and he pinned the star on her dress, too.

"I don't think I understand what is taking place, Mayor Charming," Granny Relda said.

"I'm deputizing you," he said uncomfortably. "Raise your right hand and repeat after me."

Charming raised his right hand and waited for the Grimms to do the same. Sabrina stared blankly at the man, wondering if maybe he was pulling some kind of prank on them.

"Don't make this harder on me than it has to be," he begged.

"The town needs your help. You know it and I know it. Can't that be enough?"

"You want our help?" Sabrina said.

"I know you've been helping Hamstead," the mayor said. "For some reason the sheriff thinks you will be able to help with this case."

"Mayor Charming!" Granny Relda exclaimed. "I never thought I'd see the day when you would come to this family for anything."

The man lowered his right hand and groaned. "Do you think I would ask you if it wasn't absolutely necessary? I swore I'd see your family rot before I asked for your help, but drastic times call for drastic measures."

"What are you talking about?" Sabrina demanded impatiently, but as she waited for the mayor to answer, she noticed something odd about the mansion. It was filthy. Several curtains in the ballroom had fallen and lay in heaps on the floor. A giant red stain had ruined a polar bear rug lying near the fireplace. The carpet on the stairs needed a good vacuuming and a bucket sat on the floor collecting rain from a giant patched-up hole in the ceiling. Half a dozen overflowing bags of garbage sat by the door waiting to be taken out and a thick layer of dust covered everything, including a full suit of armor that leaned precariously against a wall.

"What happened here?" she asked.

"You happened here!" Charming snapped. "You and your smelly sister ruined the only fund-raising event this town has each year."

Daphne raised an arm to smell her armpit. She crinkled her nose and lowered her arm quickly. "I'm not that bad," she said.

"You crashed an invitation-only party, brought a giant here, which nearly destroyed the mansion and several cars in the parking lot, and worst of all, you made me look like a fool in front of the town's biggest donors," the mayor said. "We didn't raise a penny. The town is broke."

"We know what the fund-raiser is *really* for," Sabrina replied. "You want to use the money to buy the whole town. Why don't you just dip into the money you've conned out of everyone for the last two hundred years?"

"You dare question my honor?" Charming growled. "I haven't taken a penny out of this town. The rumors about my finances are greatly exaggerated. Relda, do you believe I would live like this if I didn't have to?"

Granny Relda gazed around the room. "No, I don't," she answered.

"Services had to be cut drastically. Transportation, education. I've even had to fire the crew of workers who polish statues of me in the park. Mr. Seven has agreed to a substantial cut in pay and I haven't taken a salary in weeks. I had to lay off three-fourths of the town's police force, which, since there were only four police officers to begin with, leaves me with Hamstead. The sheriff works hard and he's smart as a whip, but he's only one pig. We're stretched too thin, and we just don't have the resources to investigate a crime, let alone a murder committed by the Scarlet Hand. I need your help, and since most of this is your family's fault, I think it's your responsibility."

"So now the Scarlet Hand exists, huh? Why did you lie about it back at the school?" Sabrina asked.

"Because I don't need the citizens of this town to panic. If word got out that there was a terrorist group killing people, there would be chaos in the streets. Hamstead can barely keep up now with speeding tickets and jaywalkers. Your family has proven to be good detectives: you're persistent and lucky and stubborn," Charming continued. "If *you* don't stop whatever did that to the teacher, then it won't get stopped."

"Why do you care what happens to a human teacher?" Sabrina said. "I thought you hated humans."

Charming said nothing.

"You don't want anything bad to happen to Ms. White," Daphne cried. "You are in love with her. You want to kiss and hug her!"

"Nonsense!" the mayor shouted. "I can't have terrorists running around the elementary school, even if I approve of who they're killing."

"You want to write her love notes," the little girl persisted. "You want to hold her hand in the park and look at puppies in the pet store."

"Is there an Off button for this one?" Charming asked Granny Relda.

The old woman grinned at the mayor. "You haven't answered the questions."

"All right!" Charming surrendered. "Snow has a knack for getting in trouble. I would sleep better at night knowing she is safe."

"Of course, we'll do what we can," Granny Relda assured him.

"What are you going to do for us?" Sabrina asked.

The old woman looked at the girl in horror. "*Liebling*, we would never take payment for helping folks."

"Granny, finding the killer is going to take a lot of time—time that we could use to find Mom and Dad," Sabrina argued.

"What can I do?" Charming said. "I can't exactly send Hamstead to search everyone's homes."

"No, but you have connections we don't," said Sabrina. "People *will* talk to you. *Maybe* there is something we could use, something magical lying around we don't know anything about. Use your imagination, *Billy*."

Charming thought for a moment. "You have my word."

He raised his right hand.

"It'll have to do," Sabrina said as she raised her hand as well. Granny Relda and Daphne did the same.

"I do solemnly swear to protect and serve the inhabitants of . . ."

"What does *inhabitants* mean?" Daphne interrupted.

"It means the people who live in a particular place," her sister answered, noting Charming's impatient face.

"Why didn't you just say *the people*, then?" the little girl asked.

"Let him finish, *lieblings*," Granny Relda said.

"I do solemnly swear," Charming started over, "to protect and serve *the people* of Ferryport Landing to the best of my ability. I vow to protect the peace, secure the safety, and uphold the rule of law."

The Grimms repeated what he said, word for word, and then lowered their hands.

"You are now officially deputized under the laws of Ferryport Landing," the mayor said, as he pulled out a set of keys and handed them to Granny Relda.

"What are these?" Granny said, looking down at the key ring.

"Keys to the school," Charming said. "You'll need them to get inside."

Granny smiled and handed the keys back to the mayor. "I've got my own set, thanks," she said. Charming scowled and shoved the keys back into his pocket.

"Well, I'd love to keep this happy event going all night, but as you know, I can't stand you people," he said, leading them to the door. As his hand clutched the knob, he turned and looked the girls in their eyes. "Snow is important to me. I would appreciate you keeping a close eye on her."

"No problem, *Billy*," Daphne replied, wrapping her arms around the mayor and hugging him tightly. "It's sooooo romantic!"

Charming sneered, opened the door, and forcefully shoved the family outside.

"You should really tell her that you love her," Daphne said, right before the mayor slammed the door in her face.

• • •

Sabrina had been to a lot of schools in the last year and a half, and they all had a few things in common. Every one of them had a couple of grouchy teachers, a bully, a bully's punching bag, a weird cafeteria lady, a bathroom that everyone was afraid to go into, and a librarian who worshiped something called the Dewey Decimal System. None of those schools, however, had a teacher-killing monster scurrying through its hallways. And they said New York City had everything.

Granny Relda was convinced that a monster—maybe working with the Scarlet Hand—had killed Mr. Grumpner. Not knowing exactly what the monster looked like or where it might be now was doing a number on Sabrina's nerves as her grandmother led the girls through the darkened hallways of the school. The long shadows cast by the setting sun looked like dinosaurs and invading aliens. Every little creak sounded like the tread of Bigfoot or a swamp monster. And worse, Grumpner's bloodless purple face appeared every time Sabrina closed her eyes. All she wanted to do was run back to the car and hide under Elvis's blanket, but Granny insisted they take another look at the crime scene. For once, the girl wished Mr. Canis was by their side, but the skinny old man had chosen to stay with the car and meditate in the freezing cold. Luckily, Granny had relented to Elvis's begging and the big dog now trotted down the hall beside them.

"Mr. Canis looks terrible, and for him, that's particularly bad," Sabrina said to the old woman as they crept along.

"In the past he has been able to tap into the Wolf's strengths without losing himself," her grandmother explained, "but this time he made a complete transformation and worse, he tasted human blood. It's been a very long time since that has happened and the Wolf is not going to be put away without a fight. Don't worry, children. Mr. Canis will win this battle."

"And if he doesn't?" Sabrina asked.

"He will. I'm sure he'll be happy that you are concerned for his well being."

I'm more concerned about waking up in his belly, Sabrina thought.

When they got to Sabrina's homeroom, the crime scene tape and Grumpner's body were already gone. The broken window had been replaced and all the cobwebs were cleared away. Even the blood-red hand painted on the chalkboard was gone. Other than some misplaced desks, there was no evidence of the gruesome scene they'd witnessed only hours before. Principal Hamelin had obviously cleaned the place up.

"Whatever it was didn't catch him by surprise," Granny Relda said, pushing a desk back into its row. "The way these desks are scattered it looks like Mr. Grumpner tried to fight back."

Sabrina shuddered as she imagined her teacher fighting off his attacker. Whether it was a giant spider or a thousand little ones, the fact was that the man's death had been a nightmare for him. Even a grouch like Grumpner didn't deserve to die so horribly.

"Why are we here now?" Daphne asked, as they walked into the classroom. "We'll never find anything in the dark."

"Some of the best clues are found in the dark," Granny said. She crossed the room and opened Grumpner's desk drawers. They were empty except for the bottom one. Inside was a picture of the teacher and a woman. They were on a pontoon boat enjoying an afternoon on the Hudson River. Grumpner and the woman each had a glass of champagne in their hands and were toasting each other.

"His wife?" Sabrina asked, as Granny showed her the picture. "I can't imagine that Mr. Cranky found anyone to marry him."

"He was probably a very different man at home," the old woman replied. "You told me once you thought your father was too careful, but the Henry Grimm I know threw caution to the wind. There are many sides to us all."

"His wife must be very sad." Daphne sighed.

Granny sighed, too. "I suppose she is."

"Well, we found a picture," Sabrina said, eyeing a shadow in the corner that looked like the boogie man. "Can we go now? This place is giving me the willies."

"Don't be scared," Daphne said. "I'm a police officer, ma'am. I'll protect you." She leaned down and struggled with her belt, then walked around the room mimicking Sheriff Hamstead's bowlegged gait.

Sabrina laughed so hard she snorted.

Granny reached into her handbag and pulled out a familiar pair of infrared goggles. "Don't worry, *lieblings*, I'm hurrying," she said as she put the goggles over her eyes and looked around the room, finally focusing on the floor. "Ah-ha! Children, come and take a look."

The girls hurried to their grandmother. Daphne took the goggles and looked down at the floor. "That is so punk rock!" she said.

Eager for a turn, Sabrina snatched the goggles away from her sister and peered through their special lenses. They revealed ghostly white footprints—the last traces of the late Mr. Grumpner.

Granny Relda reached down and ran her finger across the floor. When she lifted it, there was white powder on it. "The plot thickens," she said, holding her chalky finger up to Sabrina's eyes. "Mr. Grumpner's feet were covered in some kind of dust."

A bit of the dust floated up into Sabrina's nose and she sneezed violently.

"Gesundheit," Granny Relda said.

"They come from out in the hallway," Sabrina said, opening the door and following the glowing footprints.

"Notice anything about the steps?" her grandmother asked, following closely behind.

"They're very far apart," the girl said. "Three of my steps are equal to about one of his."

"That's because he was running," the old woman informed her. Sabrina was impressed. Granny Relda was a natural detective, and Sabrina wondered if she'd ever be as smart. The footprints came from the stairs to the first floor and the girl headed in that direction until suddenly the infrared goggles were snatched off her head.

"Hey!" she complained, as she turned on her little sister. "If you wanted to wear them, all you had to do was ask!"

Granny and Daphne said nothing. They were looking at the ceiling with odd expressions. Sabrina followed their gaze and what she saw sent a shock down to her toes. Hanging upside down above them was a fat, frog-faced creature. Its head and feet were amphibious, with slimy, bumpy skin and a puffed, bulbous pouch under its lower lip, but it had the arms, legs, and body of a human being. It was the creature's long sticky green tongue that had snatched the goggles off Sabrina's head, and now it dragged them in and out of its mouth as if it were wondering whether they might make a good snack. Eventually it spit them out at Sabrina's feet, spraying sticky saliva all over the girl's pants.

"Uh, no thanks. You can keep them," Sabrina said, wiping the goop off her jeans.

The frog monster let out an odd, feminine giggle, and puffed up its huge air sack. Sabrina had seen frogs do just the same thing on TV. It was something they did when they were preparing to eat and she suddenly had the feeling that she was on the menu.

"Run!" she cried.

The Grimms and Elvis spun around and ran back down the hallway, but the monster leaped off the ceiling and landed in front of them, blocking their path.

"I spy with my little eye," the frog-girl gurgled, "something dead."

5

ranny Relda swung her handbag at the frog-girl and cracked her on her forehead. The monster groaned and fell to the ground. Sabrina had seen what sort of stuff the old woman kept in her purse—everything from spy goggles to rolls of quarters—so she knew it packed quite a wallop. It would take the frog-girl a while to get up—if she got up at all.

Not wasting any time, the Grimm women spun in the opposite direction and raced down the stairs. Elvis followed close behind, clumsily navigating the steep steps and barking threateningly.

"If we're lucky," Granny Relda said through winded breaths, "that thing will be too afraid of Elvis to come after us."

"And if we aren't?" Sabrina asked as she helped her grandmother down the last of the steps. Unfortunately, the old woman didn't get a chance to respond. The frog-girl bounced down the steps and onto a nearby wall, sticking like a suction cup.

Elvis stood his ground, baring his teeth at the monster, daring her to come closer.

"Your puppy isn't very nice," the frog-girl croaked. "But he'll digest in my belly as quickly as the three of you."

Daphne stepped forward and flashed her shiny new deputy's badge. "You're under arrest for . . . for . . . being gross!" she stammered, but the frog-girl was not impressed. She lunged for the little girl.

Sabrina grabbed her sister's hand and dragged her down the hallway toward the exit. The monster followed by leaping back and forth from wall to wall, gaining ground with each jump. By the time the Grimms reached the exit, the frog-girl was right behind them. She shot her thick tongue out and wrapped it around Daphne's arm, dragging the little girl back into her clutches.

Elvis leaped viciously at the creature, but it jumped to the ceiling and hung upside down out of his reach.

"Let her go!" Sabrina shouted as she desperately reached for her sister. The frog-girl let out a sickening giggle and continued to dangle Daphne right above Sabrina's grasp. The little girl struggled and squirmed and finally reached into her beehive hairdo. She yanked a protractor from her sticky locks and stabbed the frog's tongue with it. The monster shrieked and Daphne fell, knocking Sabrina to the ground.

"And you didn't like my hairdo," Daphne said to her sister as she quickly helped her to her feet and the two ran to the exit doors with Granny Relda and Elvis close behind.

"Start the car!" Sabrina shouted as they sprinted across the school lawn. Mr. Canis opened his eyes and, without pausing, climbed off the roof of the car. Within seconds·the old jalopy roared to life, grinding metal on metal and shaking violently. The junker's obnoxious concert had never sounded so good to Sabrina.

"What happened?" Mr. Canis asked as Elvis, Granny, and the girls clamored into the car, but no one got to answer. Something slammed onto the roof. It was so loud they all jumped, except Mr. Canis, whose only reaction was to look up and raise a questioning eyebrow.

Just then, a slimy green hand smacked the driver's side window. Sabrina and Daphne screamed. Granny Relda whooped in astonishment and Elvis growled and bared his teeth. But Mr. Canis just took a deep breath, put the car into drive, and floored the gas. The car's tires squealed and the jalopy rocketed into the street, skidding across the country road before some quick steering set it on the right course.

"Oh, I do wish I could drive." Granny Relda groaned. "I used to love situations like this."

"You know very well the police took your license away," Mr. Canis said, steering from one side of the road to the other in hopes of dislodging their stowaway. Unfortunately, nothing the old man did had any effect on the monster and it continued to beat violently on the roof.

"I got a couple of speeding tickets." Granny shrugged.

"You were arrested fourteen times for reckless endangerment. Several neighborhood groups banned you from driving on their streets. The German government said that if they ever caught you in a car in Berlin again you would be hanged," the old man corrected.

"Oh, Mr. Canis," Granny begged. "No one has to know. Besides, this isn't getting us anywhere."

He shook his head.

"Please!" she pleaded.

Mr. Canis slammed his foot on the brake and the car screeched to a halt. The frog-girl tumbled down the hood and bounced along the road for several yards until she stopped. She let out a terrible moan and then lay still.

"Let's stay off the major roads," the old man said, opening his door and getting out.

Granny squealed with delight and scooted over to the driver's seat. As they switched places, Sabrina watched the grotesque frog-girl stir, slowly get to her feet, and stare at the car. Even with her bizarre, twisted face, the murderous rage in her eyes was clear.

"Children," Mr. Canis said as he turned to face the sisters. "Put on your seat belts."

The girls eyed each other nervously and hurried to strap themselves in. Unfortunately, the ancient seat belts that had been installed in the car were torn, so Mr. Canis had used ropes to improvise. Sabrina helped Daphne tie hers into a knot around her waist and then went to work on her own.

Just as their ropes were secure, the monster leaped into the air and came down violently on the car's front end. The impact was so great, the car's back end lifted a full six feet off the ground, then came down violently. The monster leaned forward to get a better look through the windshield and then licked her wide lips.

"Going somewhere?" She laughed.

Elvis whined and crawled under his blanket as Granny floored the accelerator and the car lunged forward. The monster tumbled over the hood, up the windshield, over the roof, onto the trunk, and fell off the back end of the car.

"She's gone!" Sabrina cried, just before the freak hopped back onto the trunk. It laughed at them through the rear window.

"She's back," Daphne cried, diving under the blanket with Elvis.

Granny made a sharp left onto an old dirt road and pressed hard on the gas pedal. The ancient car screamed in protest, but held up its end with a burst of speed so powerful Sabrina felt the g-force pushing her body into the seat springs. Despite the incredible speed, the frog-girl held on with little effort and pounded angrily on the rear window. The massive blows caused a thick crack in the glass.

"Turning right!" Granny shouted from the driver's seat, just before she made the turn. Elvis tumbled over the girls as the car banked to the right, but the maneuver didn't seem to shake the monster.

"Turning left!" Granny shouted and Elvis tumbled to the other side of the car, landing heavily on Sabrina's belly and knocking the wind out of her.

The frog-girl smacked the window again, and this time it exploded, sending chunks of glass into the backseat. Several large

portions of the window stayed attached, but the monster pulled them off effortlessly and tossed them into the road.

Sabrina pushed Elvis off of her and fought to fill her empty, burning lungs. As she struggled, the frog-girl reached into the backseat with her big sticky hands, unfastened Daphne's rope belt, and snatched the little girl right out of her seat. Still choking and gasping for air, Sabrina grabbed desperately at Daphne's ankle and tried to pull her back inside the car, but the frog-girl's grip was too strong.

"She's got Daphne," she gasped, but Mr. Canis had already sprung into action. He rolled down his window and pulled his upper body out of the car.

"There's no need to hurry, old man," the frog-girl screamed over the wind. "You'll die soon enough."

A ferocious roar echoed back at the monster and Sabrina could see her eyes grow wide with surprise.

"You're one of us?" the frog-girl cried. "And you fight for the life of a filthy Grimm! You're the traitor. I should have known you by your stink."

"Put the child back into the car," Sabrina heard Mr. Canis demand, even over the roaring engine.

"The traitor gets no favors!" The frog-girl laughed. She reached into the backseat with her free arm and grasped for

Sabrina. Sabrina squirmed and slapped at the disgusting hand, but it still managed to snatch her sweater and drag her out the window as well.

"I'm not going to tell you again, beast," Mr. Canis threatened.

"I've heard stories about you, traitor," the monster croaked. "The Big Bad Wolf—trying to make amends for all the bad things he has done. You'll fail, old-timer! Your heart isn't in it! But no matter, I'll give you the dignity of knowing you died trying!"

Mr. Canis was too far away to do anything. Sabrina knew if she and her sister were going to survive, they were going to have to save themselves.

"Daphne, do you remember Mr. Oberlin?" Sabrina shouted, hoping her sister had not forgotten this particular foster father.

"From the Bronx?" the little girl asked.

Sabrina nodded.

The disgusted look flashing across her sister's face told Sabrina that her plan wasn't the little girl's favorite. Regardless, Daphne nodded and together the sisters leaned down and bit the frog-girl hard.

The monster shrieked in agony and let go of Daphne. Sabrina grabbed her sister and together they scrambled back into the car. The frog-girl huddled on the trunk, clutching her wounds.

"What happened?" Granny Relda said, still pushing hard on the gas.

"It appears I am not the only one in our home with fangs," Mr. Canis said, climbing back into the car.

"You've got to get rid of this thing," Sabrina shouted as she wiped the horrible taste out of her mouth with her shirtsleeve. A bit of the goo was on her chin and her shirt stuck to it like it was a powerful glue. Daphne was also busy rubbing the monster's taste off her tongue onto her sleeve. Again, the frog-girl reached in through the window, but Elvis snapped at her hand and the monster pulled it back.

"Don't worry, *lieblings*," Granny said as she made a rough turn onto a gravel road. "I have a plan."

Sabrina looked through the windshield and saw a sign blocking the road ahead. It read DANGER! BRIDGE UNSAFE! GO NO FARTHER! Worse was what was beyond it. In the distance was an old, rundown country bridge covering a rocky stream. One look at it told Sabrina that a mouse wouldn't be able to cross the bridge safely, let alone Granny Relda's ancient two-ton monstrosity on wheels.

"What's Granny's plan?" Daphne said, smacking at the frog monster's hand as it snatched at her through the window.

"You don't want to know!" Sabrina replied.

The car crashed through the old wooden sign and it exploded around them. A giant chunk slid over the roof and by the sound of the pained groan, smacked the monster in her head. The collision was enough to knock the frog-girl off the car and she tumbled painfully to the ground.

Unfortunately, Granny didn't stop driving, and when the jalopy raced onto the beginning of the rickety bridge, Sabrina knew they were in trouble. Creaking beams and snapping wood drowned out the car's backfires and grinding gears. The old bridge tilted to the left just as the car reached the halfway point, and she saw a sight that nearly gave her a heart attack. The middle of the bridge had collapsed, leaving a giant hole no car could ever get across. And Granny wasn't slowing down.

"Granny, we're not going to make it!" Sabrina shouted, battling the roaring engine to be heard.

"I love pancakes, too," the old woman shouted back.

I hate this car, Sabrina thought to herself.

Granny Relda floored the accelerator, the engine screamed, a flame shot out of the car's muffler, and suddenly they were soaring over the gaping hole. They landed hard on the other side and raced onto the road just as the bridge buckled and collapsed into the rocky stream below.

After several yards, Granny brought the car to a stop. She shut off the engine.

"That took care of the ugly little beast." Granny laughed as she turned around to face the girls. "How exciting was that? Were you excited? I'm having the time of my life!"

Everyone remained speechless, except for Elvis, who whined softly. Granny Relda didn't notice; she continued to jabber on like a little kid who had had too much sugar before bedtime.

"Oh, boy, did Froggie get the surprise of her life," she continued, smacking the steering wheel proudly. "You put Relda Grimm behind the wheel and things get done."

The old woman turned back around and prepared to start the car again but everyone shouted *"No!"* in unison. Mr. Canis snatched the keys out of the ignition. Sabrina saw the disappointment in her grandmother's face. The old woman slowly got out of the car and Mr. Canis slid over into the driver's seat. As she got in on the passenger's side, Granny Relda crossed her arms and pouted. It reminded Sabrina of something Daphne would do.

"My driving isn't that bad, is it?" the old woman asked.

"Yes!" everyone shouted.

• • •

Once the house was unlocked, the family staggered inside, with Sabrina quietly cursing one of the worst days of her life.

Puck was sprawled across the couch. He had moved the books away from the television and was watching it with the sound all the way up. The boy was surrounded by three delivery pizza boxes, empty bags of chips, a leaky carton of ice cream, and a two-liter bottle of soda from which he was currently drinking. On his belly was a can of spray cheese and when he saw the family limp into the house, he put down the soda and lifted the cheese can, spraying an enormous portion into his mouth. Then he gargled with it. Once he had swallowed the greasy orange junk food, he let out an enormous belch that actually rattled the windows.

"Old lady!" he crowed. "You've been hiding this magic box from me! You can see other worlds on it. I just watched a man and his talking sports car jump across a river!"

Sabrina felt her exhaustion turn instantly to anger. From their expressions, she could see the rest of the family felt the same way. While they had been hunted by a frog monster, Puck had had the best day of his life. Fate was cruel.

"What?" he said defensively, noticing their glares.

Granny started dinner and patiently explained to Puck what had happened to them. The boy seemed to think Mr. Grumpner's murder was fascinating and was terribly depressed that he hadn't seen the frog-girl.

"Was she ugly?" he asked. "Why is it that I miss all the fun?"

"I guess you just don't have our luck," Sabrina grumbled.

"I hope the two of you washed," he said to the girls. "Frogs give you warts and it sounds like the one you fought off was mighty big. I wouldn't be surprised if you wake up in the morning and find you are one giant brown wart."

Daphne's eyes grew as big as saucers. "Nuh-uh," she said.

"Sorry, kiddo, but if you hurry and take a bath it might not be too late!" Puck advised.

The little girl rushed out of the kitchen and could be heard running through the house and up to the bathroom.

"You shouldn't tease her like that," Sabrina said, vigorously washing her hands at the kitchen sink.

"Puck, do you know the Widow?" Granny Relda asked as she got up to stir a pot of soup on the stove.

"Of course," Puck replied. "Queen of the crows."

"Go get her," Granny Relda said.

"Why?" he asked. "Are we going to cook her?"

"Of course not," Granny said, horrified. "I have some questions for her."

"Since when does the Trickster King act as your messenger, old lady?" the boy asked.

"Since he started living under her roof," Mr. Canis growled.

He slammed his fist down hard on the kitchen counter, causing the sugar bowl to lose its lid. "This is serious business, boy. Now go!"

Puck eyed Canis stubbornly. "Villains do not run errands!"

The old man's eyes turned ice blue and a bit of his Wolf voice came out. "I'll show you a villain, Trickster."

Glistening wings sprang from Puck's back and flapped loudly. He flew quickly through the house and slammed the front door as he left.

Mr. Canis leaned against the kitchen doorway and tried to catch his breath. This was the first day he had been out of his room in three weeks and it hadn't been an easy one. If the old man was struggling with keeping his emotions in check, the last four hours had been an incredible test.

"Mr. Canis," Granny said, rubbing the old man's back with her palm. "Go and rest."

"There may be more danger," Canis insisted.

"Old friend, I already have three children arguing all the time," Granny Relda scolded, "I do not need another."

The old man nodded and shuffled out of the kitchen.

"Who's the Widow?" Sabrina asked.

"Hans Christian Andersen wrote about her in 'The Snow Queen.' She's an old friend," Granny said. "She might be able to shed some light on the crow feathers we found. She's sort of an expert on birds."

"So you don't think the frog-girl killed Mr. Grumpner?" Sabrina said.

"No, *liebling*, frogs don't make webs," the old woman said.

"Neither do birds."

"True. But the birds may have seen something."

• • •

When dinner was ready, Granny and the girls met in the dining room. Daphne's skin was red from scrubbing and her hair was wrapped up in a big white towel. The family took their seats and Granny served herself and the girls some hot soup and buttered rolls. The soup tasted like warm butterscotch pudding but Sabrina was so hungry she didn't have the strength to make her usual complaint about her grandmother's weird food.

Between slurps of soup, the old woman jotted some notes in her notebook.

"Well, then, it looks like we've got two monsters on our hands, now," Granny Relda said. "One frog-girl . . ."

"An a ian ida," Daphne mumbled between bites of bread.

"What?'

Daphne swallowed. "And a giant spider," she repeated and then immediately stuffed another oversized bite into her mouth.

"I agree," Granny Relda said. "Charming was way off on his 'army of spiders' theory. I think it was one big one."

"Don't forget the broken window," Sabrina said. "That's how it got inside."

"Maybe," Granny replied.

"You don't think so?" the girl asked.

"The glass was all over the floor, so something came through that window, and by how spread out the shards of glass were, I'd say it came in fast."

"*Urds,*" Daphne mumbled, with a mouthful of soup.

"Right, the birds," Sabrina said. "The black feathers were underneath the window. But that's where I get confused. Why would birds have come into the room?"

"Birds eat spiders," Granny Relda explained as she stood up and crossed the room to a pile of books stacked next to the radiator. She tugged at a couple in the middle of the stack and sent the rest tumbling to the ground. She left the fallen pile where it was and returned to the table. Granny wasn't much of a housekeeper.

"This book is just about everything ever written on giant monster spiders," Granny Relda said, setting it in front of the girls. "It's a bit dry, and the author has an unhealthy fear of certain animals, but it might be helpful."

Sabrina eyed the book, entitled *Magical Mutations of Insects*,

Reptiles, and Kitties. She opened the cover and saw a crude drawing of a giant kitten chewing on several screaming farmers. She flipped to another page and a thin pamphlet fell out. She picked it up and examined it. The cover read *Rumpelstiltskin's Secret Nature.*

"What's this?" she said, leafing through it. The pages were filled with tiny, neat writing.

"I've been looking for that for ages," Granny said. "That's a book your great aunt Matilda Grimm wrote."

Daphne took the pamphlet. "Rumpel . . . rumpel . . . what's this say?"

"It's called *Rumpelstiltskin's Secret Nature,*" her grandmother said, taking the booklet from the little girl. "Matilda wrote a lot about Rumpelstiltskin. You could say she was one of the few fairy-tale specialists in this family. She had dozens of theories on why Rumpelstiltskin kept trying to trick people out of their first-born children. You should read it when you get a chance."

"I'll check this out later," Sabrina said, setting the mutations book aside.

"Anyone for more camel hump soup?" Granny Relda asked as she got up from the table.

"This is made from a camel's hump?" Sabrina cried, dropping her spoon as images of a sweaty, flea-covered camel danced around in her mind. She'd seen one at the Bronx Zoo with her father and could still smell its rank breath years later. She felt sick.

"Actually, it's two-hump camel soup but I only use the second hump," Granny Relda explained. "The first hump is a little tough, and besides, it's the second hump that has all the flavor."

The girls stared at the old woman as if she were playing an elaborate joke on them, but Sabrina could see from her expression that she was serious. Of course, Daphne clapped her hands happily, and cried, "I'll have more! And this time make sure there's some extra hump in there!"

Sabrina slowly pushed her nearly empty bowl away just as there was a knock on the front door. Granny, who was on her way to the kitchen, stopped and rushed to answer it, with the girls following right on her heels. There on the porch stood a humongous black crow. Its eyes and beak bobbed nervously, and its squawk was ear-shattering. On one of its legs was a black ribbon, and when it saw the family it dipped its head in what Sabrina guessed was a bow of respect.

"Good afternoon, Widow," Granny Relda said to the bird.

"Good afternoon to you, Relda Grimm," the crow croaked in a scratchy yet feminine voice. Daphne squealed in glee, but Sabrina's stomach did a flip-flop.

More talking animals, ugh.

"Do you know that little brat you sent plucked a feather out of my behind and laughed?" the crow continued.

"I am very sorry," Granny Relda apologized. "I haven't seen you as a crow in some time."

"Well, the boy said it was important, so I did the bird thing. Normally, I'd take the seven down to the forty and get off at Miller Road, but you know that disaster with all the orange cones, and right now the eighteen is backed up for miles. At this time of night flying is really the quickest way," the bird croaked.

"Your English is coming along very well," Granny Relda commented.

"Thank you," the crow cawed. "Some of the others refuse to speak anything but Crow-ish, but I say you have to adapt. It's good to learn new things. I've even been surfing the Web."

"What fun," Granny said with a smile. "I was wondering if you had heard about the human that was killed today at the elementary school?"

"Yes, I have," the Widow replied. "Want to know how I know?" Granny nodded.

"A little bird told me," the crow said. For a moment, there was silence. "Get it? *A little bird told me*?"

"That's very funny," the old woman said, as a pained smile

crossed her face. Sabrina rolled her eyes, but Daphne laughed so hard she snorted.

"Oh, I like the little one." The crow chuckled. "You gotta have a good sense of humor to live in this town."

"The death was very suspicious," Granny Relda said, trying to steer the conversation back to the murder. She took one of the black feathers they had found in the classroom out of her handbag and held it out to the bird. "This was at the crime scene."

"I've heard rumblings in the flock," the Widow said, eyeing the feather.

"Rumblings?" Granny Relda asked.

The bird hesitated and looked around as if someone might be listening.

"Some of the crows claim they blacked out. They say they can't account for about fifteen minutes of the day," the crow whispered. "The ones I talked to said they heard music and suddenly they were all standing around the school yard, unsure of how they got there. Sounds like the piper is back to his old games."

"That would be unfortunate," Granny said.

"But I don't think it's your biggest problem," the crow continued. "Someone's sent you a message and I'm warning you, Relda, you don't want to mess with the Scarlet Hand."

"I don't know what you're talking about," said the old woman. "What message?"

"It's all over your house, Relda. Whatever you've gotten involved in this time has attracted the attention of some very bad people."

Sabrina and Daphne ran down the porch steps and looked up at the house. On the windows, roof, and even on the chimney were red-paint hands, just like the one they had found on the chalkboard in Mr. Grumpner's room.

"Who did this?" Sabrina asked.

"We've only been home for an hour," Daphne added.

The Widow hopped down the steps and flew up into the air. "Keep your nestlings close," the crow squawked as it disappeared over the tree line.

"Girls, get back into the house," Granny Relda said sternly.

6

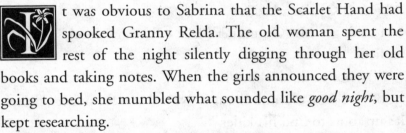

t was obvious to Sabrina that the Scarlet Hand had spooked Granny Relda. The old woman spent the rest of the night silently digging through her old books and taking notes. When the girls announced they were going to bed, she mumbled what sounded like *good night*, but kept researching.

While Daphne brushed her teeth, Sabrina ran her head under the bathtub faucet and washed her hair for the fourth time that day. She wrapped it up in a towel, and the girls headed for their bedroom. Daphne put on her favorite pair of footie pajamas and pinned her deputy's badge to them. After buffing it into a shine, she went to their father's desk, which the little girl was slowly converting into a beauty parlor, and took a hairbrush from one of its drawers.

"Can I?" she asked. Sabrina nodded and her little sister climbed up on the bed, took the towel off of the older girl's head, and ran the brush over her long blond hair. For some reason, brushing Sabrina's hair helped calm Daphne down so that she could go to sleep. After finding a dead body, being attacked by a frog-girl, nearly dying with Granny behind the wheel of the car, and having the house vandalized right under their noses, Daphne would be brushing for a long time, Sabrina suspected.

"You OK?" she asked.

"I can't get Mr. Grumpner's face out of my head," Daphne replied.

"Try not to think about it."

"But we have to think about it. Now that we're police officers, it's up to us to find his killer."

"I think we should let the sheriff handle this one," Sabrina said.

"We can't. We made a vow. Besides, the town needs us to solve the mystery. We are Grimms and this is what we . . ."

"What we need to *do* is find Mom and Dad," Sabrina interrupted.

"We'll find them," her sister said.

"I don't know how. We've been here for three weeks and have

spent all our time catching Lilliputians and killing giants. Isn't it time to start putting Mom and Dad first?"

"The mayor needs our help."

"And while we're busy doing the mayor's job, Mom and Dad are still missing," Sabrina snapped. "How do we know that Charming isn't responsible?"

"He wouldn't do that."

"He's an Everafter, Daphne! Everafters can't be . . ."

"What?" Daphne said. "Everafters can't be what?"

"Trusted!" Sabrina exploded.

Her sister looked at Sabrina as if she didn't recognize her. It was an expression more hurtful than any word the little girl could have said.

"It's obvious an Everafter kidnapped our parents and it's also obvious that an Everafter is behind Grumpner's murder," Sabrina tried to explain.

"Sabrina, they aren't all bad."

"All the ones I've met," the older girl insisted.

Daphne set the hairbrush on the nightstand, crawled under the covers, and turned her back on her sister.

"I don't like you very much, right now," she whispered.

"You'll see I'm right soon enough," Sabrina said.

She stared up at the ceiling, waiting for Daphne to respond, but the little girl remained quiet. Sabrina told herself she didn't care. Daphne wasn't going to make her feel guilty. She'd worry about being tolerant and accepting when their mother and father came home.

"Good night," she whispered, but her sister said nothing. Sabrina snatched a copy of *The Blue Fairy Book* off the night-stand and opened it to page one. Maybe there was something in the book, some kind of magic she could use to find their parents.

• • •

Once the house was quiet, Sabrina grabbed her set of keys up from under the bed, snatched a book off her nightstand, and headed to Mirror's room. When she walked through the portal, she found him with a reflective silver card under his chin and a tanning lamp shining in his face. On a nearby table he had a pitcher of margaritas and a bottle of suntan lotion. When he saw Sabrina, he smiled and flicked off the lamp.

"Just in time, kiddo," the little man said. "I'm roasting over here. How was your first day of school?"

"Oh, the usual. The kids made fun of me, I punched a bully, and a teacher was murdered by a monster," Sabrina replied.

"Sixth grade isn't how I remember it," Mirror said, reaching over to a table and pouring himself a fresh drink. "Sorry, I'd offer you one but you're a bit young. How about a Shirley Temple?"

"No thanks," Sabrina said.

"I remember my school days. It wasn't easy for a shy talking mirror, but I managed. Trust me, starfish, it gets better the day after."

"The day after what?"

"The day after you graduate," Mirror said. "Are you feeling OK? You look flushed."

"I think I'm getting sick," the girl said, holding her hand to her forehead to check for a fever. "I've been getting headaches all day and I've been a cranky jerk to almost everybody."

"Sounds like puberty to me. If you think school is tough now, wait until you start getting zits."

"So, you're sure I'm not sick?"

"Completely, kiddo. I remember when your dad went through it. He was in a fistfight every day for two weeks. I remember one time he got your grandfather so angry the old man chased him up a tree." Mirror laughed.

"So, this is normal," Sabrina said. "I thought I was going crazy."

"I didn't say you weren't going crazy," the little man responded.

"I just said you were growing up. The two are not mutually exclusive. So, did you just come to chat or are we going on a magic hunt again tonight?"

Sabrina sheepishly held out a book about King Arthur's powerful wizard, Merlin.

"Come on, kiddo," Mirror said, sounding resigned, and Sabrina followed him down the hall.

• • •

Early the next morning, Sabrina awoke to a thundering racket, followed by a series of thuds and crashes that knocked a picture off her bedroom wall. Something was going on at the end of the hallway that sounded like a fistfight and Sabrina knew there could be only one source of the chaos—Puck. She eyed the clock and saw that it was only five a.m. and her blood began to boil. Five a.m. was too early for his nonsense.

Of course, Daphne slept through the noise, snoring away as if nothing was happening. The little girl could sleep through World War Three. The only thing she wouldn't sleep through was breakfast.

Sabrina leaped out of bed and marched down the hallway. The day before had taught her not to just barge into his room, so she banged on the door angrily instead. After several moments, she realized that the tremendous noise she heard wasn't coming from inside Puck's bedroom, but from the bathroom down the hall. Fearing her grandmother had fallen in the tub, Sabrina rushed to the bathroom door, grabbed the knob, and flung the door open just as a nearly naked eleven-year-old boy ran past her.

"Puck!" Granny Relda cried. "Come back here!"

Mr. Canis leaped to his feet and rushed past Sabrina, chasing the boy, who had fled downstairs.

"What's going on?" the girl asked, as she peered into the bathroom. It was a complete disaster. The bathtub was surrounded by a dozen empty bottles of shampoo and what looked like the wrappings of at least twenty bars of soap. The inside of the tub was filled with an oily black sludge that slowly spiraled down the drain. On the toilet basin was a plate where four fat worms, several dead beetles, a hand grenade, and thirty-six cents in change had been collected.

"Puck is having his bath . . . his eighth bath," Granny Relda said, partly exhausted and partly annoyed. "You've let him out and now he's probably in the woods rolling in who knows what . . . *again*!"

"He's taking a bath?" Sabrina said. Puck hadn't taken a bath since he'd moved into the house and his unbearable stink had ruined many a meal for the girl. One whiff of his nauseating aroma was all anyone needed to realize that the Trickster King and soap were bitter enemies.

"Not that I'm complaining, but why is he taking a bath?" she asked suspiciously.

"We felt it was necessary, under the circumstances," said Granny Relda. Sabrina noticed the old woman was wearing plastic gloves to protect her hands.

"Circumstances? What circumstances?"

But Granny's explanation was interrupted by Mr. Canis, who stomped back up the stairs with the boy in his arms. Puck squirmed and kicked the entire way.

"This is rubbish!" he shrieked as the old man dragged him back into the bathroom and wrapped him in a clean towel.

"The tub is clogged again," Granny Relda said. "I suppose we could try another round on the teeth while it drains."

Sabrina eyed the bathroom sink where four worn-down and abused toothbrushes had met their doom. Several tubes of toothpaste littered the floor. Each had been thoroughly emptied of all its cavity-fighting protection.

"Will someone please tell me what is going on in here?" Sabrina demanded.

Puck turned and smirked at the girl. A devilish gleam sparkled in his eyes and he temporarily ceased his indignant protests.

"Guess what, piggy! I'm going to school with you today!" he shouted as he kicked the door closed in her face. "I'm going to be your bodyguard!"

• • •

"Yes, you absolutely do need a bodyguard." Granny Relda argued with Sabrina as she tried to pat Daphne's hair down with her hand. The little girl had molded her still glue-soaked locks into a pointy Mohawk that stood about a foot and a half above her head. Finding little success, Granny gave up and turned her attention to serving each girl glow-in-the-dark waffles for breakfast. "We've got two monsters running around in the hallways."

"But why him?" Sabrina cried. Her own hair had become super curly after her multiple shampoos, producing an almost perfect globe shape, like a big yellow tennis ball. "Why don't *you* come?" she said to her grandmother. "You could use a fairy godmother wand to change yourself into a kid."

"I'd look like a kid, but I'd still be an old lady," said Granny. "This way if something happens, then at least there's someone around who can fight."

"Actually," Daphne said, shoveling half a glowing waffle into her mouth, "I think it's a great idea. He's our age and none of the kids will know who he is."

Sabrina shot her sister a betrayed look, but the little girl didn't see it. She was obviously still angry and refusing to make eye contact with her.

"Oh, no! They won't notice him at all until he turns into a monkey and throws his own poop down the hallway," Sabrina said. "And it's not like the kids aren't going to notice the fifteen layers of crud he has under his pits. He smells like Coney Island after a clam-eating contest."

"Excuse me?" Puck inquired. The boy had slipped into the room without anyone seeing him. Sabrina turned to give him her usual nasty look, but when she saw how he had transformed, she dropped her fork. Puck was clean, shiny, and blond. He'd been scrubbed from head to toe. His leaf-infested, raggedy hair was neat and combed and his teeth sparkled like diamonds. Even his ever-present ratty green hoodie and jeans had been retired and replaced with black cargo pants, a striped baby blue rugby shirt, and brand-new sneakers.

"Puck! You're . . . you're . . ." Sabrina stammered.

"You're a hottie!" Daphne shouted.

Sabrina hated herself, but she had to agree. Puck, the shape-shifter, the royal pain-in-the-rear, had transformed into a cute boy. Sabrina couldn't help but stare, even when he caught her.

"Yes, it's true," he said as he took a seat. "Please, don't hate me because I'm beautiful."

Granny placed a plate of waffles in front of him and he shoved them into his mouth with his bare hands. Whatever spell he had cast on Sabrina quickly faded as she watched him pour some maple syrup down his throat and take a bite out of a stick of butter.

"Puck," Granny Relda groaned as she wiped syrup off the boy's face. "Use a fork. You don't want to have to take another bath, do you?"

"So you ran the garden hose over him. What about the insanity on the inside?" Sabrina asked, still doing her best not to look at him. Puck grinned at her and his big green eyes made her want to cry. She couldn't like Puck! He was disgusting! He wasn't even a real boy!

"Don't worry, old lady," he said with a grin. "I'll behave. Besides, who's going to notice me with these two and their hair?" Suddenly, his head morphed into a donkey's head. He brayed and laughed and spit all over Sabrina.

"Puck, sweetie, no shape-shifting at the table," Granny Relda lectured.

"Just getting it out of my system," the boy said, transforming

back to normal. Sabrina wanted to die. Even when he was being disgusting, he was cute.

Puck looked over at Sabrina, who was wiping his spittle off her face. "Hey ugly, is that your face or did your neck throw up?"

Sabrina was horrified. Did he think she was ugly? Why would he say such a horrible thing in front of everyone? And then it dawned on her—this beautiful boy sitting across from her was still Puck the Trickster. He was the boy who had dumped her in a tub of goo and put a tarantula in her bed. Puck was still Puck, even after a makeover.

"This is ridiculous," she said. "You're sending him because of all this Scarlet Hand message business, when we all know he's the one who did it."

"You think I made all those handprints on the house?" Puck asked.

"Who else?" she cried. "You're the so-called Trickster King. You were pretty mad when Granny sent you to get the Widow. You decided to get your revenge by scaring us. Why not add a little terror to your bag of pranks?"

"I think the glue and buttermilk is seeping out of your hair and into your itty-bitty brain," the boy snapped.

"I believe him," Daphne declared. "He always admits when he does stuff. He's proud of it."

Sabrina turned to her and fumed. Once again, her own sister had taken Puck's side against her.

"Well, I'm pretty proud of my right hook," Sabrina shouted, returning her attention to Puck. "Why don't you come over here and I'll show it to you."

"*Lieblings*!" Granny shouted. The children spun around to face the old woman. Her face was flushed and her little button nose was flaring. "Enough with the shouting!"

"He started it!" Sabrina shouted.

"She started it!" shouted Puck.

"Puck is going to school with you," Granny Relda said firmly. "End of discussion."

Everyone sat silently for a moment, staring down at their breakfasts.

"By the way, marshmallow," Puck said to Daphne, breaking the silence. "How many warts did you find this morning?"

The little girl rolled up her sleeves and showed the boy her arms. "Not one!"

Puck sighed. "That's a shame."

"Why?"

"Well, if you were going to have little ones they would have already shown up. You could put some cream on them and they'd go away in a day or two. But the really big ones take a couple days to show. Those are the kind that end up on the tip of your nose or growing out of your neck. You have to have surgery to get rid of those."

Daphne shrieked and jumped from her seat. In no time she was running up the steps to the bathroom again.

"You better scrub harder this time!" Puck shouted to the little girl.

"How is Captain Maturity going to keep an eye on both of us at the same time?" Sabrina asked. "Daphne and I aren't in the same grade."

"Puck is there to watch you, Sabrina. Daphne will be safe with Snow White," Granny replied. "Snow's a good friend and has volunteered to keep her eye on your sister."

"Don't worry, old lady," Puck crowed. "I'll keep this one out of trouble."

• • •

Granny Relda, Canis, and Puck headed off to meet with Principal Hamelin about enrolling "his majesty" into the sixth grade. As Puck was an Everafter, Granny decided an Everafter should take care of his enrollment and bypassed Mr. Sheepshank entirely. Sabrina was fairly sure the boy was a moron, so she wondered what Granny had planned if the principal decided Puck should be in kindergarten.

Sabrina had assured her grandmother that she could walk to homeroom alone, but regretted the decision when someone grabbed her from behind and dragged her into the girls' restroom. When she spun around, ready to sock her attacker, she found Bella with a brush and some hair spray in hand.

"You need some serious help," the blond girl said, ushering her over to the mirror, turning her around, and going to work on her hair with the brush. "How did you get your hair this way?"

"It's a long story," Sabrina said sheepishly.

Bella tugged and pulled with her brush, coated Sabrina's head with hair spray, and then tied the unruly mane up with a pink rubber band. To Sabrina's surprise, Bella had done something in seconds that Sabrina had been trying to do for herself for two days. She had made Sabrina look normal.

"It'll hold until lunch," Bella said, handing Sabrina her brush and can of hair spray. "After that, well, we may have to call in a professional."

Sabrina was so happy she could have cried. "Thank you."

"Don't thank me," Bella said. "You have the seat in front of mine in science class and with that head of hair there was no way I was going to be able to see the film strip."

Sabrina laughed. It felt good when Bella joined her. Just then, the bell rang.

"We better get to class," the blond girl said. "Old battle-ax will be mad if we're late."

"Didn't you hear?" Sabrina said. "Our teacher was killed last night."

"I think the fumes from the hair spray are affecting your brain. I saw her walking down the hall just a couple of minutes ago."

"Her? Our teacher was a him," Sabrina said.

But Bella had already rushed out of the restroom.

Sabrina walked down the hallway and prepared herself for the sadness and confusion the other students would be feeling when they discovered Mr. Grumpner was dead. She assumed there would be a ceremony to honor their murdered teacher. The school had probably brought in some grief counselors to console them and answer questions. Everyone would make a giant condolence card and sign it for Mr. Grumpner's wife and family. But when she stepped into the classroom, there were no tears running down faces, there were no confused, broken-hearted kids, there was not a single sad face.

In fact, the kids acted as if nothing had happened at all. Like the day before, they were sleepy and bored. Sabrina was shocked. Sure, Mr. Grumpner had been a bitter pill to swallow but he was still a human being and he had died a horrible death. Didn't anyone care?

Bewildered, Sabrina went to her seat, sat down, and scanned the room for anyone who might need someone to talk to. Across the room, Bella smiled and gave her the "thumbs up" gesture.

Has the world gone insane? Sabrina wondered to herself. *A man died in this classroom less than twenty-four hours ago and they're acting like it's just another day!*

A roly-poly woman lumbered into the room and set a handful of books down on Grumpner's desk. She had flaming red hair, done up in a bouffant, and a makeup job that looked as if it had been applied with a paintball gun. Something about her seemed oddly familiar.

"Good morning, class," she said. "Yesterday we were talking about transitive verbs. Let's pass your homework forward and see how you did at identifying them."

Sabrina was dumbfounded. *Homework?*

"Grumpner didn't assign any homework," Sabrina said to the sleepy girl next to her.

"Who's Grumpner?" the girl asked, taking out her assignment and handing it up the aisle.

The teacher glanced around the room, absorbing the faces of

her students. When she spotted Sabrina, her smile suddenly dissolved and was replaced with a bitter scowl. It was then that Sabrina recognized her. Sabrina had seen her when she and Daphne had snuck into the Ferryport Landing Ball—the Queen of Hearts.

"Grimm," she snapped. "A word, please."

Sabrina reluctantly got up from her desk and joined the woman at the front of the room. She had never actually met the queen, but after reading *Alice's Adventures in Wonderland*, Sabrina was familiar with her notorious disciplinary tactics. More than a few citizens of Wonderland had lost their heads when the queen lost her temper. Looking into the woman's face, it seemed to Sabrina that her own head might be next on the chopping block.

"Child, I know what you are up to," the queen said in a low voice.

"I'm not sure what you mean."

"You've come here to spy on me," the woman said. "Well you can tell that old busybody grandmother of yours that she's wasting her time."

"I'm not spying on you," Sabrina said. How dare the woman accuse her of such a thing? The queen didn't even know her.

"I know it drives you Grimms crazy that there are Everafters working around human children."

"I swear I'm not here to spy. I'm eleven. I have to go to school. It's the law," Sabrina snapped. She looked around the room and noticed that even some of the drowsy kids were listening to their conversation. She flushed with anger and embarrassment.

"A likely excuse, but I'm watching you, child. You step out of line just once with me and it's . . ."

"It's what, off with my head?" the girl interrupted as anger flooded over her. She realized she was shouting, but she couldn't help herself. "You're a paranoid old kook. If you want to start off like this on your first day, be my guest!"

"First day?" the queen said nervously. "Sabrina, I've been this class's teacher since the beginning of the year. Don't you remember?"

Suddenly, everything made sense. The reason no one was upset about Grumpner's murder was because no one remembered him. Grumpner had been erased! The Everafters had covered the entire town in forgetful dust and wiped him from everyone's memory. The only reason Sabrina remembered him was because her house was covered with protection spells that kept the family safe from magical attacks.

She didn't know why she was so surprised. The lousy Everafters were always making inconvenient things disappear. When something got in the way, it vanished. Just like her parents. Just like her entire family, if the Everafters got the chance.

"You erased him!" Sabrina shouted, unable to control her anger. "You wiped him away, just like that! Just like you did with my parents, but I won't let you do it again. You tell your dirty Everafter friends that I'm going to find my mom and dad. And I'm going to find who killed Mr. Grumpner, too!"

The queen's face reeled in horror. Sabrina had betrayed an unspoken rule of Ferryport Landing—never reveal the truth! She looked up at the nasty teacher's face, hoping the queen could see that she was tired of secrets. Daphne was right. Mr. Grumpner's murder needed to be solved, if only to show the Everafters that they couldn't get away with their tricks anymore.

Suddenly, Wendell, the boy who had been late for school the day before, rushed into the room. He looked confused for a moment as he spotted the queen, then he recovered and hurried down the aisle to his seat, an odd, chalky dust trailing behind him. He sat down awkwardly and hid his face in his textbook.

Sabrina's eyes watered and she sneezed loudly as the cloud of dust settled to the floor.

"Cut it out, Grimm," Toby cried from across the room. "You're spraying your cooties all over the place."

Sabrina turned on the boy, walked down the aisle, and grabbed him by the shirt collar. Still full of rage, she shouted, "Shut your mouth you little bug-eyed freak!"

Toby stared into her face and just smiled.

"Mrs. Heart, I'm sorry to interrupt," a voice said from the doorway. Sabrina spun around and saw Principal Hamelin. "I'd like to introduce a new student."

"Take your seat, Ms. Grimm," the queen said between gritted teeth. The angry girl marched back to her desk.

"Mrs. Heart, class, this is Robin Goodfellow," the principal said as Puck marched into the room, waving and bowing as if he were a movie star.

"*Taa-daa*," Puck sang. "Please, don't make a fuss."

"Robin is here all the way from Akron, Ohio, and he'll be staying with Sabrina Grimm's family," Hamelin announced.

"Robin Goodfellow?" the queen muttered knowingly. It was obvious to Sabrina that the teacher recognized the boy.

Puck winked at her. "That's my name, don't wear it out," he crowed.

"Take a seat in the back. There's one near your friend."

The boy looked around the room. "Is that the only seat available? The Grimm girl tends to have a very foul odor," he said with a wicked grin. "She's a real stinker."

The half of the class that wasn't asleep roared with laughter and Sabrina blushed.

"And she's got quite a temper, too," the queen replied. "Sorry, Mr. Goodfellow. If the rest of the class has to suffer, so do you."

The students roared again.

"So, Mrs. Heart, he's all yours," the principal said and left the room.

Sabrina's head was pounding and she had a fever. How had she gotten so angry so quickly? Mirror was right. Puberty was really screwing with her head and if she didn't get control over it she was going to be the school weirdo forever. She glanced around the room and noticed that kids were staring at her. How humiliating the whole thing had been. The only kids who didn't seem to care were the ones who had slept through it all and Wendell. The chubby little Everafter boy had been busy reading and keeping his head down the whole time Puck was being introduced by the principal, almost as if he'd wanted to avoid his father's gaze. There was something unusual about the boy. His feet were covered in white chalk. It had made Sabrina sneeze, just like the dust they had found in Mr. Grumpner's footprints. This odd boy with the runny nose had been in the same place their murdered teacher had been.

"Ms. Grimm," Mrs. Heart said—she had come down the

aisle and was standing over Sabrina with her grade book in hand—"No homework today?"

Sabrina's eyes flared as they met the queen's. "I didn't know we had any homework today," she snapped.

"That's a shame, Ms. Grimm," the teacher said with a wicked smile. "I'm going to have to give you a zero."

The girl met her grin with a bitter scowl.

"Since you're having trouble keeping up with your assignments, maybe we should set up some special time for you to get them done," Mrs. Heart said. "I'll see you in detention this afternoon."

"What's a detention?" Puck asked.

"It means I have to stay after school for an hour," Sabrina whispered

"An hour!" The boy laughed. "That's the most twisted, depraved punishment I have ever heard of. I've been here for five minutes and it's already an intolerable agony!"

"Well, then, *Mr. Goodfellow*, maybe you should join her," Mrs. Heart suggested.

"Your Majesty!" Puck cried, leaping from his seat. He threw his arms around the woman and wailed. "Show some mercy!"

The Queen of Hearts waited patiently for Puck's dramatics to end and for the students to stop giggling. When he released her, the teacher spun around and headed to the front of the classroom.

"Now, class, let's talk about past participles," she said, turning toward the chalkboard. On the queen's back was a sheet of paper that read I KISS GOATS. The kids who were awake fell over themselves laughing.

The teacher spun around and flashed the class a mascara-heavy evil eye. She turned back to the board and the class exploded again.

"Anyone who wants to join Ms. Grimm and Mr. Goodfellow tonight in detention, just keep it up," she shouted.

By the time the bell rang, the entire class was looking at Puck as if he were a rock star.

"Hilarious!" one kid snorted as the students emptied into the hall. Puck absorbed their praise like a greedy sponge and agreed with each one wholeheartedly that he was indeed a genius. But Sabrina had no interest in Puck's groupies. Her eyes were fixed on Wendell, who now hurried down the hallway, followed by a cloud of dust. She rushed after him.

"Hey, stink-pot," Puck said, breaking away from his followers. "You're not supposed to leave my sight."

Sabrina didn't reply. Instead, she darted through crowds and dodged open lockers as she trailed the chubby boy through the over-packed hallway. He raced down a flight of stairs and slipped through a door. By the time Sabrina caught up, he had already slammed the door behind him. The sign on it read BOILER ROOM.

"Where are you going?" Puck asked, grabbing Sabrina's wrist and pulling her back before she could open the door.

"I think that boy knows something about Grumpner's death," she replied, reaching for the door.

"You're not supposed to go anywhere without me."

"Well, you're here now, let's go."

"I don't feel like it."

"Puck, it's the boiler room. I bet it's dirty and gross in there," Sabrina said, trying to play to the boy's biggest weakness—filth. "I bet there's a greasy floor you could roll around on."

Puck's eyes lit up and he nodded vigorously. It was nice to see that she could manipulate him when it was important. She reached for the doorknob again, but before she could turn it, a muscular, grizzled-looking man stepped in her way.

"Where do you kids think you're going?" he asked. He was tall and strong, with arms as big as tree trunks and a chest as wide as the family car. It was obvious that he hadn't shaved in several days and could probably use some sleep. His blue coverall uniform had a patch on it that told everyone his name was Charlie and the smell coming off of him told everyone his uniform needed a trip to the laundromat. But it was the mop slung over his shoulder that told her this was the school janitor, and the boiler room was his domain.

"I was looking for my next class," Sabrina lied.

"In the boiler room?" Charlie laughed, spraying his cornedbeef-and-cigarette breath all over her. "Ain't nothing in there but a bunch of mops and brooms."

"My mistake," she said. She turned around and together she and Puck headed down the hallway. She snuck a peek back, hoping Charlie had moved on, but he was still there, leaning against the door.

"I could lure him upstairs and push him out a window," Puck offered.

"No, we can't do that. We'll come back later. For now, just go to your next class," Sabrina replied. "Where is it?"

She snatched his schedule out of his hand and looked at it. "Puck, you're in all my classes!"

"The old lady and Canis negotiated it with the principal," the boy explained.

Sabrina knew what kind of negotiating Mr. Canis could do. Now Sabrina would have Puck practically riding on her back.

There were several kids walking behind them and one of them laughed loudly and said, "Hello, Smelly Stink-pot."

Sabrina spun around to see who had insulted her but the kids just walked away.

"Smelly Stink-pot? What does that mean?" Sabrina asked Puck.

"Who knows?" he said. "Kids can be cruel."

It would be hours before Bella stopped her in the hallway and removed a sign that had been taped onto Sabrina's back. It read, PLEASED TO MEET YOU, I'M SMELLY STINK-POT!

• • •

The rest of the day, Sabrina and Puck kept a watchful eye out for Wendell, but it seemed as if the boy had disappeared. During a break between classes, Puck even rushed outside and summoned some pixies with his flute, to look for their chubby suspect. As Sabrina and Puck waited for word back, they went from one class to the next, and in each the Trickster King did his best to humiliate his housemate. Unlike a normal kid, Puck didn't bring pencils or a notebook to class; he brought what he called the essentials: a squirt gun, stink pellets, a shock buzzer, and his personal favorite—a whoopee cushion. Now, to Sabrina, fart jokes were so old-fashioned. She believed kids were pretty sophisticated in the twenty-first century. It would take more than an obnoxious noise to get a modern kid laughing.

Unfortunately, Sabrina was wrong. Puck let the whoopee cushion go in every class, making it seem as if Sabrina were having intestinal issues, and the kids just thought it got funnier and funnier. Eventually, he added a little acting to his routine, pretending to gag on Sabrina's imaginary fumes. When this proved to be wildly popular as well, it quickly evolved into an elaborate death scene, which ended with Puck shaking in convulsions on the floor. His performances, and Sabrina's threats of a serious beating, helped the two rack up an impressive five detentions apiece by midday. At the rate they were going, Sabrina suspected they would be in detention until they were twenty-five.

So, as they headed for gym class, she smiled, knowing revenge was within her grasp. Puck was about to get what he had coming to him.

"OK class," Ms. Spangler said as she tossed a ball back and forth between her hands. "We've got a new student today. His name is Robin and he says he's never actually played dodgeball."

Even from across the room, Sabrina could see Toby's and Natalie's eyes light up with excitement. Bella, who was standing nearby, leaned over to her. "Your friend is in serious trouble."

Puck waved to everyone, unaware that attention was the last

thing he wanted in this class. Once everyone got an eyeful of him, Ms. Spangler divided the class into two teams. Puck and Sabrina found themselves standing next to each other.

"How do you play this game?" he asked.

"People throw balls at you," she said. "If they hit you, then you're out."

"Let me get this straight. The object of this game is to hit someone with a ball. Can you hit them in the head?"

Sabrina nodded, eyeing the opposing team to avoid a sneak attack.

"And you can hit them as hard as you want?"

"That's actually encouraged. But be careful—if they catch it you're out."

"Does anyone ever catch the ball?"

"Rarely."

"How diabolical!" Puck cried. "It's so twisted, it's brilliant! Are you any good at this 'dodgeball'?"

"I used to be," Sabrina grumbled, staring at the two children directly across from her on the other team, Toby and the big goon Natalie, who were staring back at her with evil grins on their faces. They were like vultures, waiting to take a bite of her.

Ms. Spangler blew her whistle and the insanity began.

A ball whizzed past Sabrina's head and smacked into Bella.

Sabrina was surprised. The day before, the girl had been so agile, but now it seemed like Bella had actually stepped into the ball, as if she wanted to be knocked out of the game.

The blond girl shrugged her shoulders. "Good luck," she said to Sabrina, as she made her way over to the sidelines. Sabrina looked up to see Toby and Natalie. Both were grinning. Toby winged his ball straight at her head and just before it smashed her in the nose, Puck reached over and caught it.

"Toby's out!" Ms. Spangler shouted. Dejected, the boy scowled and sulked over to the sidelines.

"Now what do I do with it?" Puck asked.

"Throw it at somebody," Sabrina said impatiently.

Puck wound up, ready to smack Sabrina right in the face with the ball.

"Not me, you idiot!" she cried, pointing at the opposite team. "Them!"

Puck threw his ball at a red-haired boy standing close to the front. It rocketed across the room like a missile, hit the red-headed kid in the chest, and sent him flying backward ten yards. The class stopped playing and let out a collective gasp.

"Kevin is out!" Ms. Spangler said, unsympathetic to the boy's obvious injuries.

Every kid looked at Puck as if he had just suggested adding

another day to the school week. Even kids on his team seemed afraid of him, and when the game resumed, Puck was public enemy number one.

Balls came from every direction and the boy managed to duck, jump, and somersault around every one. He bent in impossible directions that no normal human being ever could. He stood on his hands and let balls fly between his feet. He taunted everyone, which only made them want to smash him in the face even more, but every effort failed. When the already sleepy kids were thoroughly exhausted, Puck began to collect their weak tosses. In no time he had collected almost every ball and had laid them at his feet. When the kids realized what he had done, they whimpered. Even Natalie let out a little cry.

Puck picked up the first of his collection and winged it at a boy standing nearby. The ball hit the kid so hard he slid across the floor and out the gym doors. Puck picked up another ball, and another, and another, tossing them at impossible speeds. A tall skinny girl was hit so hard her shoes flew off her feet. One ball hit a group of kids, bouncing off of one and then hitting the next and the next, until they all tipped over like bowling pins. Even Ms. Spangler got cracked hard in the back and nearly swallowed her whistle. By the time it was over, Sabrina, Puck, and Natalie were the only ones left standing.

"No boundaries!" Ms. Spangler said.

"What's that mean?" Puck asked.

"It means we can go after her," Sabrina said, pointing at Natalie.

He clapped his hands like a happy baby. "School is awesome!" he shouted. He picked up a ball and handed it to Sabrina.

Sabrina was so happy she could have kissed Puck. Quickly shaking off this thought, she helped him stalk the big girl around the gym. Natalie huffed like an angry bull.

"If you know what's good for you, you'll drop those balls right now," she threatened them.

"You're probably right," Sabrina said, tossing the ball at the girl as hard as she could. It smashed into the side of Natalie's face and she fell down. Sabrina had knocked the bully down for the second time in two days.

"Natalie is out!" Ms. Spangler shouted. "No sides!"

Sabrina turned to congratulate Puck, just as a ball crashed into the side of her face and sent her reeling. The class cheered and Puck raised his hand in triumph.

"I won!" he cried. He raised both arms into the air and ran around the gym shouting, "Victory lap!"

Sabrina could already feel her lip swelling.

• • •

By the time lunch rolled around, Sabrina was ready to strangle the boy. So when she saw Daphne's smiling face in the cafeteria, it was like seeing a rainbow. The little girl was surrounded by her classmates, who, as they had the day before, looked at her as if she were a movie star. When Daphne spotted Sabrina and Puck, she excused herself and joined them at a table in the far corner of the room.

"How has your day been?" she asked.

"It's been horrible," Sabrina said.

"Tell my sister I wasn't talking to her," Daphne said to Puck. "I was talking to you."

Sabrina rolled her eyes. "How long are you going to be mad at me?"

"Remind my sister that I just said I was not talking to her," the little girl said to Puck.

Puck grinned. "The squirt says she isn't talking to you."

"Get over it!" Sabrina cried.

"Tell my sister when she stops being a snot I will get over it."

"She says when you stop being a disgusting booger-crusted freak she will honor you with a conversation, but until then, shove off," Puck said.

"This is ridiculous," the older girl said, staring down at her serving of not-too-green green beans.

"Ask my sister what *ridiculous* means," Daphne said.

"She wants to know what . . ."

"I heard her!" Sabrina growled at the boy. "It means you are being silly! It means you are being a baby!"

"Tell my sister that I'm rubber and she's glue and whatever she says bounces off me and sticks to her."

"Your sister says . . ."

"Puck!" Sabrina shouted. She turned back to her food and took a bite of something she thought might be chicken. It wasn't even close.

"Well, if you're not going to talk to me, then you won't know that I've found a clue," she said.

Daphne's face lit up as bright as the sun. "What kind of clue?"

"Are you done with the silent treatment?" her sister asked.

"Depends on how good the clue is."

"You know those dusty footprints we were following last night? Well there's a kid in my homeroom whose feet were covered in the same dust."

"What did you do?" Daphne asked, interested despite herself.

"I tried to follow him, but he slipped into the boiler room," Sabrina said. "We're going to have to come back after everyone's gone and do some snooping."

Daphne smiled and hugged Sabrina.

Puck sniffed the creamed corn on his tray. He reached down with his bare hand and scooped some up. Then he licked it with his tongue. "Any of those disgusting warts show up, yet?"

"Ms. White told me that you don't get warts from touching frogs," the little girl growled. "Not even frog-girls."

"Ahh, I'm sorry to see that little joke die." The boy sighed as creamed corn dripped down his wrist and onto his clean shirt. "I had you completely freaked out."

"Hardy-har-har, Puck, you are so un-punk rock," Daphne said, turning her attention to her sister. "So, what's the plan?"

"First, you have to get a detention," Sabrina said as she eyed her gray hamburger.

"What?" Daphne cried.

"Puck got us in trouble, so we have to stay after school. Since the two of us have to stay, you might as well get in trouble, too. We should try to stick together."

"How am I supposed to get a detention?" the little girl asked.

"I don't know! Insult your teacher or something."

"I can't do that to Ms. White!"

"Yes you can. Be annoying!" Sabrina suggested. "You do it to me every day."

Daphne looked as if she was going to cry.

• • •

When the children met at the end of the last period, Daphne was back to giving Sabrina the silent treatment. Sabrina asked her how she'd managed to get detention, but she wouldn't answer. Sabrina shrugged. If she worried every time her sister got mad at her, she'd never have time to do anything else. Daphne would get over it. The important thing was that they were all together. Nothing bad could happen when they were together.

They walked down the hallway toward the detention room and Puck was nothing but complaints.

"I can't believe I have to be subjected to this torture," he whined. "I am royalty. To say anything I do is inappropriate in school is just foolish. Everything I do is majestic and regal."

"So when you were picking your nose in Mr. Cafferty's class, that was regal?" Sabrina asked.

"Absolutely," he said. "Back home people stand out in the freezing rain for days just to hear a rumor that I picked my nose."

"Ugh," was all Sabrina could say to Puck's disgusting conversation.

"This detention is going to be horrible. I've heard stories. Some kids go into that class and never come out, and the ones that do aren't the same."

"Aren't you being a little dramatic?"

"Not at all," Puck insisted. "From what I hear, this detention is a house of horrors."

Sabrina rolled her eyes and opened the detention room door. Immediately she put her hand over Daphne's eyes. Mrs. Heart lay in one corner of the room. Snow White struggled to her feet in another, and in the center was a skeleton in shredded coveralls with a name patch still visible—Charlie. The killer had left one identifying mark on the fabric of the coveralls—a bright red handprint.

"See, I told you!" Puck said proudly.

"It's gross, isn't it?" Daphne asked, turning into her sister's arms and hiding her face in Sabrina's sweater.

"Yes, it's gross," Sabrina whispered.

"I guess this means we don't have detention," Puck said.

Daphne pulled herself away from her sister and rushed to Ms. White. The teacher didn't look seriously injured, but was dizzy and disoriented. The children helped her to her feet and sat her at one of the desks in the classroom. Sabrina kneeled down to check on Mrs. Heart. She was breathing normally, but was out cold.

"What happened, Ms. White?" Sabrina asked.

The teacher looked confused and mumbled, but only one word was distinguishable: "Wendell."

Suddenly, there was a loud thump outside the window, followed by a painful moan. The children ran to the window and Sabrina stuck her head out. Below her was Wendell. The boy had jumped out the window, tumbled end over end, and was climbing to his feet.

"Hey!" she shouted. The boy looked up and his face went pale. He darted off toward the woods as fast as his chubby little legs could carry him.

Puck's enormous wings burst out of his back. "I'll get the little piggy."

Sabrina grabbed his arm before he could fly away. "Someone might see you," she cried, dragging the boy back from the window. Instead, she crawled out herself, dropping five feet before landing safely on the ground. Daphne followed and her sister caught her. Puck refused Sabrina's assistance and jumped on his own, his wings no longer visible.

"He's headed for the forest," Sabrina shouted and the three children sprinted across the field. Wendell was not a fast runner, but he had a big head start. He had already disappeared into the forest by the time the children reached the tree line.

"We lost him," Sabrina groaned.

"No, he left a trail," Puck said, pointing at deep, muddy footprints. The group raced on, following the trail.

"He's confused," the boy said as they followed the footprints up a hill. "He goes in one direction and then turns back and runs the other way. It's slowing him down. We'll find him soon."

Puck was right. It wasn't long before they found the chubby boy, cornered against a steep rocky wall. When Wendell saw them, he whimpered like a dog and looked frantically for an escape.

"It's not what you think," he said, wiping his nose with his handkerchief.

"Then why are you running?" Sabrina asked.

"I was trying to help," he cried. "I'm trying to stop them."

"Who's them?" Daphne asked.

Suddenly, the frightened boy pulled out a small harmonica and raised it to his lips.

"Don't make me use this!" he shouted.

"C'mon, tubby," Puck said. "We know you're the killer. We'll take you back and call the cops. It'll all be over in no time. Don't worry, I hear the electric chair only hurts for a second."

Wendell blew a long, sour note into his harmonica and the whole forest erupted with chatter and scurrying. The noise grew louder and louder and Sabrina thought that at any moment some horrible monster or giant was going to charge out of the brush. But the noise stopped suddenly, and a furry little bunny hopped out from behind a tree. It was the cutest brown rabbit she had ever seen and it bounded over to them and stopped at their feet. It looked up at the children with its soft, warm eyes and made a little twittering noise.

"A bunny!" Daphne cried, as she knelt down to pet it. "I love him!"

The rabbit snapped at her finger and let out a horrible, angry hiss.

"An evil bunny," the little girl said, yanking her finger away.

"So that's what your harmonica does?" Puck laughed. "Sends a rabbit to kill us?"

Wendell didn't say anything. He didn't have to. His silence was filled by the sound of hundreds of rabbits pouring into the clearing as if they had heard Puck's taunt. They jostled one another for room, then turned and faced Wendell as if he was some kind of general. It was obvious the boy was controlling them.

"Guys, I forgot to tell you the other clue I discovered," Sabrina said nervously. "Wendell is an Everafter. He's the Pied Piper's son and apparently the magic runs in the family."

"Now you listen to me," Puck said, as his wings sprouted from his back and flapped vigorously, until he was floating above the ground. "You're a killer and from what I've been told, that's against the law these days. Now, we can do this the easy way or we can do it the hard way."

"Puck, shut up," Sabrina demanded, but the Trickster just kept on talking and Wendell's face grew more and more desperate. Each furry little rodent twitched with eagerness, waiting for the boy to give a command.

"If you think a bunch of hairy little garden thieves are going to stop me, you are sadly mistaken," Puck continued. "So, call off your fur balls or I'm going to skin the lot of them and make me the biggest winter coat you've ever seen!"

Wendell lifted his harmonica to his mouth and another sour note rang through the air. The rabbits instantly turned and faced the kids. Their soft brown eyes were now red with anger.

"Get them," Wendell shouted and, like a furry army, the first wave of rabbits lunged at the children.

7

That's the best you can do, fat boy?" Puck shouted, spinning on his heels and transforming into a massive thirteen-foot brown bear. He roared so viciously that Sabrina felt it in her toes, but it did nothing to stop the rabbits. They dove onto Puck in waves, knocking his mammoth body to the ground and covering him from head to toe.

"Puck!" the girls shouted, terrified that he'd been killed. And for a brief moment it seemed as if their fears were true. But the boy soared out of the bunny pile, giant wings flapping, and into the sky. He dipped back down, snatched each girl by the hand, and began an awkward effort to fly out of the forest.

"Next time, why doesn't one of you tell me to shut up?" Puck cried.

Daphne and Sabrina looked at each other incredulously.

"I am so going to have nightmares about this," Daphne whined.

Puck sailed through the forest, barely managing to avoid the giant cedars and fir trees that seemed to appear out of nowhere. He ducked between branches and flapped fiercely to raise the girls over the brush and pricker bushes on the forest floor. One desperate effort to dodge a huge Chinese maple tree forced him to dive close to the ground, where one of the rabbits leaped up and sank its teeth into Sabrina's pant leg. She shook it off and it disappeared into the furry sea below.

"Head for the river," Sabrina cried. "They can't follow us over the water."

Puck frowned at her. "I know what I'm doing," he growled.

"If you knew what you were doing, we wouldn't have two million zombie bunnies chasing us!" she shouted.

"Guys," Daphne said, trying to get their attention, but her sister was too angry to listen.

"How was I supposed to know that kid was mentally unhinged?" Puck said.

"I don't know," Sabrina snapped. "Maybe when we found him running from a dead body?"

"Guys!" Daphne shouted.

"What!" Puck and Sabrina snapped.

"LOOK OUT!"

Sabrina looked up to see a fifteen-foot-high fence in front of them. Puck made a desperate swerve and narrowly missed smashing into it, but the near collision didn't slow down the argument.

"I don't know why I'm involved in this, anyway!" he cried. "I'm one of the bad guys!"

"The only bad thing about you is your breath!" Sabrina shouted. "All we ever hear about is Puck the villain! What kind of villain has creamed corn all over his shirt?"

The boy snarled, made a dramatic turn to the left, and looked Sabrina dead in the eye.

"You want to see how bad I can be?" he growled. "I'll show you what I'm capable of!"

He soared into the backyard of someone's home, a stocky senior citizen who was puttering around his yard. As the trio flew past him they heard the man shout, "Agnes! The rabbits have been digging up the yard, again. I swear, the next one I see is going to wish it hadn't been born!"

Puck howled with laughter as he led the bunnies right through the poor man's yard. By the time the old fellow saw them coming, it was too late. Sabrina caught a glimpse of his shocked face as the first wave of rabbits knocked him to the ground. "Agnes!" he cried. They hopped over him as if he wasn't even there.

"That was mean!" Daphne shouted at Puck.

Flapping vigorously, the boy flew across the street just as an old woman's car came to a stop at the intersection. She was a tiny old lady who could barely see over the dashboard. She must have been legally blind, too, because she waited patiently, unblinking, for Puck and the two girls to fly across the road, followed by a couple thousand rabbits. When her way was clear, she drove off as if nothing unusual had happened at all.

"People are going to see us! You've got to get us off the street," Sabrina insisted.

"Oh, you want me to get us off the street? Fine, your wish is my command," Puck yelled. He flew straight toward a house where a tall man had just opened his front door. As the man bent over to pick up his newspaper, Puck flew inside.

"No! Don't," Daphne cried as Puck sailed through the living room, into the dining room, and flapped awkwardly over the table. Below them, two small children were setting the table, oblivious to the scene above their heads. They were hungrily eyeing a glistening golden ham in the center of a dinner feast. Puck dipped lower and Daphne accidentally kicked the ham and a bowl of mashed potatoes onto the floor. The family's two hyperactive English springer spaniels then raced into the room and tore into the fallen food.

"Chelsea! Maxine! No!" the mother shouted, running in from

the kitchen and desperately trying to drag the remains of the ham from their greedy mouths. "Bad dogs!" She didn't look up, but the children did.

"So sorry," Daphne shouted to the open-mouthed children as Puck flew into the kitchen. They found the back door. Sabrina opened it and they zipped outside. The rabbits had noticed their detour and now tumbled through the house, knocking over furniture and sending lamps crashing to the floor. They blasted out of windows and knocked the back door off its hinges and still managed to gain ground.

Sabrina looked up at Puck and saw the proud grin on his face.

"That wasn't funny," she snapped.

"Yes it was," he said.

"They're still coming," Daphne cried. "We have to go somewhere they can't go."

"We're on our way," Puck crowed. Soon they were out of the neighborhoods and flying back over acres of overgrown woods. In no time, the Hudson River stretched out before them.

"If we fly out over the river, they won't be able to follow," Sabrina said.

"Oh, we're going over the river all right, but not to save you from the rabbits," Puck cried. "We're going over because you questioned my villainy."

Sabrina looked up into his face. "You wouldn't dare!"

"That's another thing you shouldn't question!"

He flapped his wings hard and soon the three were soaring over the rocky cliffs, high above the Hudson. Sabrina watched as the rabbits raced to the cliff's edge and then abruptly stopped.

"Anyone ready for a swim?" Puck asked.

"Don't do it!" Sabrina demanded.

"Next time you talk to me, maybe you'll do well to remember that I am royalty."

But before Puck could dump them into the icy water, his body buckled as if he had flown into a brick wall. Sabrina lost her grip on him and dropped like a stone, landing hard in the freezing river below. She sank deep into the river then swam frantically to reach the surface in time to see Daphne splash down beside her.

"Daphne!" she screamed as her sister sank below the surface. Sabrina dived into the water and, after several moments of frantic searching, her already numb fingers found something soft and fluffy. It was Daphne! Sabrina wrapped her arms around her sister and pulled her to the surface.

The little girl gasped for air and started choking as a mouthful of water spilled from her lips.

"Where's Puck?" she asked, between painful coughs.

Sabrina scanned the waves nearby, but there was no sign of the boy.

"Puck!" she shouted. There was no response.

Sabrina turned her sister toward the shore. "Can you make it?" she asked.

Daphne nodded. Sabrina let her go and the little girl doggy-paddled toward land. Luckily, their father had taught them both how to swim at the YMCA near their apartment and Daphne had taken to it like a fish. She'd be fine.

"Puck!" Sabrina shouted again. She took a deep breath and dived back into the cold water, knowing she didn't have a lot of time. The water was so icy she was losing feeling in her feet. She moved back and forth, searching in the dark waters with her hands, but finding nothing. Finally, her lungs ached for oxygen, and she was forced to return to the surface.

Gasping for breath, she noticed something odd floating in the distance. When she looked closer she knew what it was—giant, glittery wings. She swam as hard as she could and found Puck facedown in the water. She turned him over. His face was blue. She wrapped her arm around his cold body and swam to shore as best she could. There, Daphne helped her drag the motionless boy onto dry ground.

"Please don't be dead, Puck!" the little girl cried.

"Stand back," Sabrina said. She tilted the boy's head and looked in his mouth for obstructions. She had taken life-saving lessons in school but had only tried CPR once on a rubber dummy—never on a real, live person! Worse, she remembered her teacher had given her a C-minus for the course.

She took a deep breath and placed her mouth on Puck's, blowing all the air she could down his windpipe. Nothing happened. She did it again. She remembered to press on his sternum to force air in and out of his lungs. She counted off fifteen compressions and then returned to blowing into his mouth.

Suddenly, his eyes opened and he shoved Sabrina away.

"I'm contaminated!" he cried, wiping his mouth.

"Puck, you're alive!" Daphne shouted and hugged the boy.

"Of course I'm alive," the boy said, crawling to his feet. His wings disappeared into his back. "I happen to be immortal."

"We thought . . . you were . . . I tried," Sabrina stammered.

"You thought you'd give me a kiss while I was vulnerable," Puck said indignantly. "I guess I'm going to have to stop taking baths if you can't keep your hands to yourself."

Sabrina was so angry she was sure steam was coming out of her ears.

"What happened to you?" Daphne asked.

"I forgot how close the old witch's barrier was. I slammed into it pretty hard." Puck laughed.

"You think this is funny?" Sabrina snapped. "We could have died out there."

"Children?" a soft voice called out from behind them. They spun around and found Ms. White standing on the banks of the river. "We need to get you out of this cold."

• • •

"Well, I knew something was strange. I'd never had a student ask me for a detention before," the pretty teacher said, winking at Daphne, who sat in the front seat of the car with her. Puck and Sabrina huddled in the backseat under a blanket.

"Knowing your father as I did, I figured the two of you were up to something, so I thought I'd better come down to the detention room and find out what was going on. When I got there, the Queen of Hearts was trying to fight off the monster with a chair," she continued.

The children were stunned.

"Monster!" they said in unison.

"Was it a giant spider or a frog-girl?" Sabrina asked.

"Neither!" Snow White replied. "This was more like a wolf or a Bigfoot. I think it ate Charlie. It was going after the queen next, but lucky for her, I arrived. I managed to distract it, but I knew I couldn't fight it by myself."

"What did you do?" said Daphne.

"Nothing. I didn't have to. Wendell saved us," the teacher continued. "He blew into his harmonica and it seemed to stop the monster, at least for a second, but then it jumped out the window and ran off. Wendell was chasing after it when you saw him. I suppose if he were older he could have stopped the thing all together. His dad has been known to halt elephants in their tracks."

"So Wendell can control things with his harmonica," Sabrina said, her voice full of suspicion. "Just like his father, the Pied Piper. How do you know he was trying to save you? Maybe he was trying to help that thing escape."

"Oh, no!" Snow White argued. "That sweet little boy had nothing to do with this."

"Ms. White, when we confronted him, he sent an army of rabbits after us," Sabrina said. "Besides, he's an Everafter."

"What's that supposed to mean?" the teacher said.

"It means he has secrets," Sabrina said. "All of you walk around here, hiding behind your magic and when something bad happens, you just make it disappear. *Poof*, and the problem is gone!"

"Sabrina, shut up!" Daphne cried.

"I'm not hiding, young lady," Ms. White replied coolly, as she pulled her car into Granny's driveway. "Everafters are not all alike."

Before Sabrina could argue, Granny Relda and Elvis came running out to meet them.

"*Lieblings*, where have you been?" their grandmother said, rushing down the driveway as the children climbed out of the car. Elvis was so excited to see Daphne, he accidentally knocked her down with a series of excited kisses.

"In the river," the little girl said. "It was fun but very cold."

"In the river?" Granny Relda asked. "Why were you in the river?"

"The rabbits chased us there," Daphne replied matter-of-factly.

The old woman threw her hands into the air. "What are you talking about?"

"They've had quite an afternoon, Relda," Ms. White said as she got out of her car. "They could use some warm clothes and some soup."

"Thank you for bringing them home, Snow," the old woman said, taking the teacher's hand.

"My pleasure," Snow White said. She turned and went back to her car, but then, suddenly, she turned and eyed Sabrina. "I hope you'll think about what I said. You can't judge the many by the actions of the few."

Granny raised a curious eyebrow at Sabrina as the teacher drove away.

"*Lieblings*, we have to get you into the bath," the old woman said. "Daphne, you go first, and make that water good and warm."

Daphne nodded and rushed into the house, with Elvis at her heels.

"I think I'll go up to my room," Puck said, spinning around and heading for the stairs.

"Absolutely not!" Granny Relda commanded. "You're next in the bathtub."

The boy's face tightened as if he had just bitten into a lemon. "I've already had all the baths I'm ever going to take. We're not going to make this a habit. I have a reputation. I'm a master villain. What will people say if they hear an old lady is forcing me into the bathtub every ten minutes?" he demanded. "I'll be the laughingstock of every tree gnome, pixie, hobgoblin, and brownie from here to Wonderland."

"Well, everyone is just going to have to think a little less of you then, Mr. Master Villain," Granny said. "Now, rush upstairs and change out of those clothes and don't put on that ratty green sweatshirt and jeans. Put on something clean!"

Puck pouted, but Granny Relda didn't budge. After several moments of staring her down, he spun around and stomped into the house.

"You, too," the old woman said to Sabrina. "Run upstairs and put on a bathrobe and some warm socks and come back down. I could use your help with the soup."

The old "I need your help" routine, the girl thought as she plodded up the steps to change out of her dripping clothes. Nine times out of ten, when an adult asked a child for help with something, it meant they were planning a lecture. But Sabrina thought it best just to change and get it over with. Once she was out of her clothes and into a warm robe, she headed back downstairs, passing the bathroom door, where she could hear Daphne begging Elvis to get into the tub with her. A tremendous splash told Sabrina that the little girl had gotten her wish.

When she passed Puck's room, she heard a horrible smashing sound inside. Apparently, the idea of another bath was not sitting well with the Trickster King. She wondered what his garden paradise would look like after the fairy prince got through with his temper tantrum.

"Sabrina? Is that you, *liebling*?" Granny called from the kitchen.

The girl followed the voice and found the old woman had already put a pot of broth on the stove and was chopping carrots and celery into little pieces on a cutting board.

"What are we making?" Sabrina asked sarcastically. "Kangaroo-tail soup? Cream of fungus?"

"Chicken noodle," Granny replied. "Why don't you have a seat on that stool? I think it's time you and I had a talk."

Sabrina rolled her eyes, but sat down.

"You've got a lot of anger in you, child," said Granny Relda.

Sure she was angry! Who wouldn't be? She was tired of the secrets and the lies. Tired of the things hidden underneath, tired of the surprises that popped up every single day. No one in this town was what they seemed. One of them had her parents. Was she supposed to walk around making friends and passing out cookies?

"I get angry, too," her grandmother continued. "My son and daughter-in-law are out there somewhere and I can't find them. Every night, after you girls are asleep, I ask Mirror to let me take a look at them. In a way, it makes me happy that they are still there, sleeping so peacefully, not even knowing all the trouble that we're going through to find them.

"And I crawl back in bed and I want to scream," Granny said, tossing the chopped celery into the big silver pot. "I hate feeling helpless and I blame myself for not being able to find them. After all, there's more magic and books in this house than in ten thousand fairy tales combined, and yet I'm no closer to bringing them home today than I was six months ago.

"Sometimes I look around this town and wonder if the person responsible for all of our heartache is sitting next to me in the coffee shop," she continued. "Or maybe it's the lady behind me in line at the supermarket or the woman who styles my hair at the beauty parlor. Maybe it's the nice man at the filling station who pumps gas into the car. Maybe it's the paperboy or the mailman or that girl who sells cookies for the scouts."

Sabrina's heart began to rise. Granny Relda felt exactly the way she did. Why hadn't she told them her true feelings about the town? It would have kept Sabrina from feeling so guilty and confused about the place.

"You're looking at the wrong people," she said, feeling encouraged by the old woman's revelation. "You should be looking at the Everafters."

"*Liebling*, Everafters are people." Granny said, setting down her knife. "They have families and homes and dreams."

"And murderous plots, kidnapping schemes, and plans to destroy the town."

"You don't really believe they are all bad, do you? What about Snow White and the sheriff?"

"They're Everafters. We just haven't discovered what they're really up to yet."

"*Sabrina!*" Granny Relda shouted. "No grandchild of mine is going to be a bigot! Hatred can grow, child, into something terrible and beyond your control!"

"You're defending the Everafters? They took my parents away and you are defending them?" Sabrina cried. She jumped off the stool.

"Yes, I'm going to defend them and anyone else who people choose to discriminate against."

"How can you do it?" Sabrina screamed, on the verge of tears.

"Because that is what I choose to do," the old woman said. "Yes, there are bad people among the Everafters but there are bad people among us all. You can't blame them all for the actions of one. I know it is difficult when you don't know who is responsible, but the guilt cannot be everyone's."

Sabrina felt as if she were being suffocated. The kitchen suddenly seemed so small, as though there wasn't room for the both of them anymore.

"You can look at it any way you want," she said, taking a step backward. "But if they aren't all in on it, then they sure aren't stepping up to help. And every time you smile at one of them or shake one of their hands you are just making it that much easier for them to stab you in the back."

"Sabrina," Granny said. "You have to get a hold of your anger. If you cannot learn to control your hatred, your hatred will control you."

"I'll get a hold of my anger when my mom and dad are safe at home," the girl cried.

Sabrina spun around and rushed out of the room, up the stairs, and into her bedroom. She slammed the door and ran to her bed. Burying her head under the pillows, she broke into violent sobs. In two weeks it would be Christmas, the second Christmas since one of them—one of the Everafters—had kidnapped her parents. Why didn't anyone care about bringing them home? Why was she the only one who saw what was really going on in Ferryport Landing?

• • •

Sabrina awoke to a knocking on her bedroom door. She looked

over at the clock on the nightstand and realized it was already seven o'clock at night. She had been asleep for more than three hours. Still in her robe and socks, she crawled out of the bed and crossed the room to open the door. Mr. Canis was waiting on the other side.

"The family awaits you in the car," he said.

"I don't feel like going anywhere," she responded. The thought of seeing Granny Relda and Daphne right now made her sick to her stomach.

"Child, this is not an invitation," Mr. Canis said. "There is work to be done. Get dressed now and meet us at the car."

"Where are we going?"

Mr. Canis took a deep breath before he answered. "The answer to that question will not change the fact that you are going there. We are waiting in the car."

"I'll be down in a minute," Sabrina said. She closed the door and got dressed, but the fresh clothes didn't do anything to hide the horrible odor coming off of her. She had slept through bath-time, and now she smelled like a slimy, bottom-feeding fish.

She hurried through the empty house, put on her coat and hat, and opened the front door. Granny was waiting outside with her key ring in hand.

"Feeling better?" she asked.

Sabrina nodded. Thankfully, the old woman wasn't going to keep harping on their conversation.

"Good, a nap can do wonders for a person. Hurry along. Everyone is in the car."

Daphne, Elvis, and Puck were in the backseat looking warm and well fed. The little girl and the dog both stared out the window when Sabrina got inside. Apparently, her little sister was back to giving Sabrina the silent treatment, and this time Elvis was joining her. Puck, on the other hand, looked at her and laughed.

"You are in so much trouble." He chuckled, sounding impressed.

"Where are we going?" she asked.

"The sheriff needs our help," Granny replied.

They cruised through the country roads, heading toward the elementary school. Mr. Canis pulled into the parking lot. Sheriff Hamstead's car was parked nearby. When everyone piled out, the old man once again climbed onto the top of the car and sat in his meditative posture. Elvis whined when he realized he was being left behind again.

"Buddy, you can come in with us, but there's a criminal stealing blankets out of the backseats of cars," Daphne warned. "He might snatch yours while we're inside."

The big dog bit down hard on the edge of his blanket and eyed the windows suspiciously as the family went into the school.

They rushed to the principal's office, where they found the sheriff sitting in a chair taking notes while Mr. Hamelin paced back and forth.

"Relda, what are you doing here?" the principal asked.

"The sheriff asked us to come by," she explained.

"The Grimms are pretty good at finding people," Hamstead said awkwardly. It was obvious to Sabrina he was trying to be discreet about the family being deputized.

"We're happy to help," Granny Relda said.

"No offense, Relda, but my kid is freezing out in the cold somewhere. I don't need an old woman and two kids, I need the police department," Hamelin said.

"I've got the best tracking dog in the world in the car," Granny said. "I'd take Elvis over a hundred police officers any day. We'll find your boy."

The principal sat down in his chair and rolled it over to the icy window. "It's so cold out there," he whispered.

"My girls were chasing Wendell this afternoon," Granny said.

"I heard all about it," the man responded, without turning away from the window.

"Then you know he's involved with the deaths."

Hamelin spun around in his seat angrily and pointed his finger at the old woman. "He didn't do it," he shouted.

"I know that, Piper. In fact, I think he's been trying to stop what's going on in this school."

"He's so curious. One afternoon we watched an old black-and-white detective movie on TV together and he was hooked. Now, *everything's* a mystery. I should have known he'd get himself in trouble."

"He also seems to have picked up his father's flair for music. I hear he's using a harmonica to control animals."

"Relda, he's a good kid," Hamelin said.

Suddenly, there was a knock at the door and Mr. Sheepshank entered.

"Oh, hello, everyone. So sorry to interrupt," he said, pointing to the wristwatch on his freckled arm. "Mr. Hamelin, it's time."

"Counselor, my son is missing!" the principal shouted angrily. Sabrina turned to look at the rosy-cheeked man, who smiled nervously.

"Of course. We can talk later," he said. He closed the door and was gone.

Daphne took her silver star out of her pocket and pinned it to her chest so that everyone could see her badge. "Mr. Hamelin, we don't want you to worry. We'll find your son and bring him back to you."

Granny Relda smiled at the little girl.

"Why are you so eager to help me?" Hamelin asked.

"That's our job," Daphne said. "To protect and serve." The little girl reached down, yanked on her belt, and pulled her pants up. Sabrina almost burst out laughing, but quickly stopped herself when Sheriff Hamstead's angry face told her he recognized the little girl's impression.

"I know you've had a history with my family, Piper, but I like to think we're never too far along to start over," Granny said, extending her hand. Hamelin stared at it for a moment, then shook it firmly.

"All we need is his locker number."

The principal punched a key on his desktop computer and the screen lit up. He typed in a few strokes and smiled.

"He's number three-two-three. That's right around the corner, near the boiler room door," he said. "What should I do? Can I go with you?"

"Wait here," the sheriff said as he stood up from his chair. "We'll call you as soon as we know anything."

Hamstead and the family walked out of the office and down the hall until they found 323, right where the principal had told them it would be.

"Do you have some kind of magic that opens locks?" Sabrina asked, as she eyed the combination lock on the door.

Granny opened her handbag and pulled out a hammer.

"I wouldn't call it magic, exactly," she said, handing the hammer to Puck. The boy grinned and raised the hammer high over his head. He brought it down hard on the lock and it snapped in two.

"Can I do another?" he asked, but the old woman snatched the hammer out of his hand and placed it back into her handbag. Then she tossed the broken pieces of the lock to the floor and opened the locker. Inside was a winter coat Wendell had left behind. Granny pulled it out and tucked it under her arm.

"I really appreciate this," the sheriff said.

"Don't think twice about it," the old woman said.

Back in the parking lot, the Grimms and Puck found Mr. Canis still meditating on the roof of the jalopy.

"We're heading into the forest," Granny said, opening the back door and letting Elvis out. "Why don't you stay here in case Wendell wanders back to the school."

"Are you sure you won't be needing me?" the old man said.

"We've got this one handled," Granny Relda said.

"Can I ask you a question, Mr. Canis?" Daphne asked.

"Of course, little one."

"What do you think about when you're sitting on top of the car?"

Mr. Canis thought for a moment, then looked up at the moon, now high over the nearby forest. "I concentrate on all the people I hurt when I was unable to control myself."

"And that helps you stay calm?" Sabrina asked.

"No child, it helps remind me of my guilt," he replied.

Sabrina didn't know a lot of fairy-tale stories. Her dad used to say fairy tales were pointless. When other kids were reading about the Little Mermaid and Beauty and the Beast, her father was discussing the news with his daughters or reading them the Sunday comics using different voices for the characters. Sabrina and Daphne had done their fairy-tale reading on the sly or at school. Still, everyone knew the story of Little Red Riding Hood, and as Sabrina looked at Mr. Canis, a terrible realization ran through her. This man sitting on the car roof, who slept across the hall from them at night, had killed an old woman once upon a time. Only it wasn't a story, it had really happened. He'd tried to eat a child, too. How could Granny let him live in the house? No wonder her dad had forbidden even a copy of *Mother Goose* from entering their home. He was trying to protect them from the truth.

Granny was busy holding Wendell's coat under Elvis's nose. The giant dog took a deep lung full and was soon trotting across the school lawn, sniffing madly in the grass.

"Looks like he's got the scent, *lieblings*," Granny said. "Let's go find our Wendell."

8

lvis's big feet crunched on the hard ground. The night had grown bitterly cold and every once in a while Sabrina spotted a snowflake floating toward the ground. She was freezing, even in her heavy coat. If Wendell was still alive out in the woods without his, it would be a miracle.

Elvis sniffed the air. Once the big dog caught a scent, he never lost it. When he reached the edge of the trees, he stopped and barked impatiently at the family. It was obvious they were slowing him down.

"Oh, I wish I could bottle his energy," Granny Relda said, taking Sabrina's arm in order to help herself across the school's icy lawn. "I'd be a rich old lady."

When they finally reached Elvis, he led them into the woods. He sniffed wildly, rushing back and forth along a path, following the scent, but managing to stick close to the family, as if he knew the old woman would have a difficult time keeping up with his pace.

Sabrina heard a branch snap in the distance and saw the dog's keen ears perk up. She expected him to run off howling in the direction of the sound, but instead he continued to follow his invisible path.

It seemed as if they had been searching for hours and Sabrina's toes were getting numb. Puck complained and suggested that they give up several times, insisting that Wendell's rabbit army had probably turned on him and were now feasting on his chubby body. Sabrina was also ready to give up, when they came to a small clearing and a sight so incredible even Granny Relda gasped.

On the ground at their feet was a mound of fur nearly four feet high and six feet wide. At first, Sabrina thought it might be a small bear, but as they got closer they realized it wasn't a single animal, but a group of many. In fact, it was a pile of rabbits huddling together in the cold. Elvis growled at the pile, but if the little forest animals noticed, they chose to ignore him.

"I told you!" Puck cried. "His woodland army mutinied! I hope he was delicious, little rodents!"

The old woman stepped close to the pile and leaned down. "Wendell!"

The mound stirred for a moment but then became totally still.

"Wendell! Your father is worried sick about you," Granny Relda scolded. "Now come out of there this instant."

"No!" a voice shouted from the depths of the rabbits. "You're going to take me to jail. I won't go."

"No one is taking you to jail, Wendell," Granny said. "All we want to do is take you home."

The mound stirred and shivered. A brief note from the boy's harmonica was heard and suddenly the rabbits rushed off in different directions.

"Run, you dirty little carrot-munchers," Puck shouted after them. "But know today that your kind has made an enemy of the Trickster King!"

When they were all gone, Wendell lay at the family's feet. Granny stepped forward, helped the boy up, and got him into his coat.

"I didn't do it," he insisted.

"Then why did you run?" Sabrina asked.

"And send rabbits to eat us! I'm a seven-year-old girl," Daphne said. "Do you know how important bunny rabbits are to me?"

"I didn't think you'd believe me. I knew how it looked, but I was trying to stop them," the boy pleaded. "If I had gotten in trouble, it would have ruined all my work so far."

He shoved his hand into his coat pocket and pulled out a business card. He handed it to Granny. The old woman read it, looked impressed, and nodded at him.

Sabrina took the card and read it closely. It said, WENDELL EMORY HAMELIN, PRIVATE INVESTIGATOR. At the bottom of the card was a magnifying glass with a huge eye inside it.

"So, you're a detective," Granny Relda said with a smile.

Daphne snatched the card and studied it. "I want a business card, too."

"Something terrible is happening inside the school," Wendell said. "I'm trying to find whoever's responsible and stop them."

"We know. Why don't you tell us everything on the way back to the school," the old woman said. "Your father is there waiting for you."

The group trudged back through the forest and Wendell told them all he had learned.

"I was leaving the school yesterday, when I looked back and saw something happening in Mr. Grumpner's room," he said, stopping to blow his nose into his handkerchief. "Sorry, I've got really bad allergies."

"It's OK, go on," Granny Relda replied.

"Like I was saying, Grumpner fell backward over some desks and at first I thought he might be sick, but then a monster attacked him. I was kind of far away, so I couldn't really see, but it looked like a giant spider. It grabbed Grumpner and started covering him in its sticky web. Well, I remembered from science class that birds are a spider's natural predator."

"What's a *predator*?" Daphne asked.

"It's like a hunter," Sabrina replied.

"So, I got out a harmonica I'd bought and blew into it as hard as I could," the boy continued. "I didn't even know if it would work. Dad told me to never do it. He said musical instruments were off limits on account of his past. Please don't tell him I bought the harmonica. He'll get real mad."

Granny took his hand. "Don't worry, Wendell."

He relaxed and continued. "So, I just thought of birds and before I knew it the sky was full of them. They were looking at me like I was their leader or something, and it took me a while to realize they were looking for instructions, so I pointed at the window and said 'Save Mr. Grumpner'."

"How come you remember Mr. Grumpner?" Sabrina asked. "The rest of our class doesn't."

"My dad had a protection spell put on our house. Whenever they dust the town, we aren't affected.

"So, anyway, the birds went straight for the window and smashed it. They flew in and attacked the monster. Unfortunately, it was too late. Even from out in the yard, I could see the spider had already eaten him."

"That explains the feathers," Daphne said.

"And what about the janitor?" Sabrina asked, still not sure she believed the strange boy's story.

"Ms. Spangler gave me a detention for refusing to play dodgeball," Wendell said. "I mean, we know how to play the game. Let's move on, already. So, when I walked in, there was this ugly, hairy thing fighting with Mrs. Heart and Ms. White. At first I thought it was a bear, but it moved way too fast and it had these weird yellow eyes. Mrs. Heart was pretty useless against it. She hid behind a desk and screamed while Ms. White fought the thing. I got my harmonica out, wondering if I could control it, too, and at first it seemed to work, but it ran to the window, opened it, and leaped outside. When you guys saw me, I wasn't running away, I was trying to catch it."

"You're quite brave, Wendell," Granny Relda said.

"My line of work isn't for the faint of heart," he declared, wiping his nose on his handkerchief.

"We've also had a run-in with an unusual creature," the old woman said.

"I know this is going to sound crazy, but I don't think these creatures are monsters. I think they're the children of Everafters."

"That's an excellent deduction," said Granny Relda. "You've got the makings of a great detective."

The boy smiled. "The only thing I wasn't sure about was why the attacks were taking place in the first place. That is, until I found the tunnels."

"Tunnels!" Sabrina and Daphne cried.

"Yes, someone is digging under the school. They start in the boiler room and go on for a long time. I'm sure it's all connected—the tunnels, the giant spider, hairy things. I just don't know how."

"Perhaps we should team up," Granny Relda said. "Combining our efforts might solve the case sooner."

"Sorry, lady, I work alone," Wendell said as they reached the front door of the school. "Detective work is dangerous business. I don't want any dames getting in the way."

Sabrina rolled her eyes. *Someone's been watching too many detective movies, all right,* she thought.

"I understand," Granny said, trying her best to sound disappointed, just as Mr. Hamelin came running down the hallway. He swooped his boy up in his arms and hugged him.

"Do you know how worried your mother and I have been?" his father said, half lecturing and half laughing.

"I'm sorry, Dad," the boy said. "But there's a caper afoot, and I'm in the thick of it."

"Thank you, Relda," Mr. Hamelin said, reaching over and kissing the old woman on the cheek. "Thank you all."

Daphne tugged on her pants and stepped forward, mimicking the sheriff's funny little bow-legged walk. "Just doing my job, citizen," she said.

"You're welcome," Sabrina added.

"I've heard stories that you have a harmonica, young man," the principal said, reaching his hand out to the boy.

Wendell frowned. "But I need it," he argued. "It helps with my detective work."

"You're about to retire," his father said, sternly. "Until these monsters are caught, your days as a detective are over."

Wendell reached into his pocket and pulled out his shiny harmonica. He reluctantly handed it to his father and grimaced when Hamelin stuffed it into his pants pocket.

"Mr. Hamelin, before we go, I was wondering something," Sabrina said. "Are there any more children here at the school like Wendell?"

"What do you mean?" the principal asked.

"You know, children of Everafters?"

"He's the only one I know of."

"Anyone else on the staff?"

"Only Ms. White, myself, and now Mrs. Heart," Hamelin said. "About ten years ago Ms. Muffet, the Beast, and the Frog Prince were all on staff, but they went in on a lottery ticket and won millions of dollars and quit. I was happy for them but it was a real shame. Good teachers are hard to find."

"Anyone else?"

"I, uh, I'm not sure," Hamelin said. "They don't really come with tags. I suppose there might be a couple, but I wouldn't know."

"Of course," Granny Relda said. She looked at Sabrina and the girl saw a sparkle in her eye, the kind her grandmother got when she found an important clue. "Is there a phone I could use?"

The principal gestured toward his door. "There's one in the secretary's office."

"Thank you," Granny said, slipping out the door. "Children, I'll be right back."

The group stared at one another in awkward silence.

At last Puck spoke. "So, Piper, how many rats were there?" he asked, referring to the man's famous adventure.

"Thousands," the principal replied.

"That's gross," Daphne groaned.

Granny returned to the room and smiled. "Well, we have to be going, now," she said, turning to Wendell. "Try to stay out of trouble."

"Trouble would be wise to stay out of my way," the boy said, sounding like a movie detective.

As the family walked back down the hall, they passed the boiler room.

"We should check the tunnels now while no one is here," Sabrina suggested, walking over to the boiler room door and trying the knob. It was locked.

"No, if people are being killed to protect what's in them, I suggest we take the hint for now," Granny Relda replied. "At least until we find out who these murderers are. In the meantime, I think I know the parents of our killers. Let's have a chat with them."

• • •

A skinny Christmas tree sat at the entrance to the police station. It was hung with a few strands of tinsel and had a garland wrapped sloppily around it. A couple of boxes of shiny bulbs sat underneath it, waiting to be strung on the tree's limbs. As they passed the display, Sabrina finally realized how overworked the sheriff was. He didn't even have time to finish his holiday decorations.

Sheriff Hamstead was at the front desk, surrounded by six of the most unusual people Sabrina had ever seen. She recognized two of them immediately. Beauty and the Beast weren't a couple she would soon forget. The dazzlingly gorgeous Beauty was a complete contrast to her husband, the fur-covered, fang-faced Beast. As for the others in the room, there was a pretty blond woman in a tiara and satiny blue gown standing next to a tall, strong man with enormous green eyes and an odd scaly skin disorder. The Frog Prince, Sabrina realized. Next to them was a chubby woman covered in jewels, Little Miss Muffet, holding hands, or in this case, holding the leg, of an enormous black spider nearly the size of Elvis. All six of them were complaining and shouting at the sheriff.

"What's the meaning of this, Hamstead?" the Beast growled.

"We had dinner reservations at Old King Cole's," Beauty cried. "Do you know how long it takes to get a table at Christmastime? We called in September!"

The Frog Prince's bride was as angry as anyone. "Drag me out of my home in the middle of the night," she huffed. "We're royalty!"

"It's beyond rude," the scaly Frog Prince complained.

The spider clicked angrily with its gigantic pincers.

"Settle down, everyone," the sheriff shouted, as he stood up. "Relda Grimm will explain everything."

"What? Since when does Relda Grimm run the police force?" Little Miss Muffet demanded. Her spider companion clicked and hissed in protest.

"The mayor has asked my family to help with the investigation of the two murders at Ferryport Landing Elementary," Granny replied.

Little Miss Muffet stepped forward. "What's that got to do with us?" she asked.

"Miss Muffet, it has everything to do with you," the old woman replied. "And your children."

The crowd gasped and averted their eyes.

"Relda Grimm, you've lost your mind," the Beast declared. "None of us have children."

"That's what I thought," Granny Relda said. "Until my granddaughter asked a question that I should have asked myself. 'Who else worked at Ferryport Landing Elementary?' I had nearly forgotten that you, the Frog Prince, and Little Miss Muffet were all teachers there before the three of you won the lottery."

Sabrina beamed with pride. Granny may have disapproved of Sabrina's suspicions about the Everafters, but it was those same suspicions that were helping solve the mystery.

"We won the lottery more than ten years ago," Miss Muffet said. "And I go by Mrs. Arachnid now."

"So we worked at the school. What does that have to do with the murder?" the Frog Prince asked.

"It's your retirement that interests me. Let me explain. Witnesses say there have been attacks by two so-called monsters on school grounds," Granny said, crossing the room and stopping in front of the Frog Prince and Princess. "And my family and I were victims of a third attack during our investigation. This one involved a half-girl, half-frog creature. Luckily, no one was hurt."

The couple lowered their eyes and Granny moved on to Muffet, aka Mrs. Arachnid, and her spider. "Unfortunately, I can't say the same for Mr. Grumpner. He was killed by what we suspect was a giant spider."

The spider clicked angrily, but his wife was still. Granny moved on to Beauty and the Beast.

"Charlie, the school janitor, also met an untimely demise by a creature described as a hairy, man-eating beast with yellow eyes," Granny said.

"You can't prove those are our children," Beauty cried.

"You're right, but there is one thing that we can prove," Sheriff Hamstead interjected. "None of you ever won the lottery."

Everyone gasped, even Puck.

"I called the state lottery commission," the sheriff continued. "They have records of every lottery winner in the last one hundred years. None of you are on their lists."

"Where did you get the money?" Granny asked.

"Are you suggesting we sold our children?" the Beast growled.

"I think you know I am," Granny Relda answered.

"And so am I," Hamstead added. He reached into his pocket and took out a pair of handcuffs. "I also think you are going to be arrested unless someone starts talking."

"We were nearly broke when we found out I was pregnant," the Frog Princess said. "All of our money was gone; we were worried we'd lose our house. If you go broke in Ferryport Landing, you stay that way. There's no one to bail you out. You can't move to another town. We would have been beggars in the street."

Beauty broke down in tears, as well. "We were in the same predicament, barely making ends meet on Beast's teacher's salary. It was no way to raise a child. He told us he could help.

"One night, he brought over a spinning wheel and started spinning gold. By morning, we had enough to last us a dozen lifetimes. We sold it to a precious metals merchant from New York City. We were rich overnight."

"Who did this?" said Granny Relda.

"Rumpelstiltskin," the Frog Princess cried. The Frog Prince took her hand and begged her to be silent, but the tears and truth were already pouring out of her. "We had to come up with an explanation for the money, so we invented the lottery story," she said.

"You sold your children?" Sabrina cried. She had never heard a more horrible story in her entire life. "How could you!"

"He manipulated us," Mrs. Arachnid sobbed. "I know you don't understand, but when we gave him the babies it was like we weren't in control of ourselves. We were so desperate, so full of despair. It was like he crawled into our brains and rewired them so we really believed it was the best thing we could do."

"No, I don't understand," Sabrina shouted. "You filthy Everafters are nothing but animals! You would hand your children over to a monster so you could cover yourselves in jewels and furs!"

Mrs. Arachnid looked down at her sparkling necklace and started to cry.

"Sabrina," Granny said. "That's enough."

"I agree," Daphne said. "Take a chill pill."

Sabrina ignored them. "No wonder Wilhelm trapped you in this town. All of you belong in a cage!"

"*Sabrina Grimm, you will hold your tongue this instant!*" Granny Relda ordered.

"You got yelled at," Puck taunted.

"*Puck, that goes for you as well!*"

Sabrina was stunned. The old woman had never raised her voice to her. The girl's face was hot with embarrassment.

"If we showed you photos of all the children at the school, do you think you could pick out which ones might be yours in their human disguise?" the sheriff asked, picking up the Ferryport Landing Elementary School yearbook that was sitting on his desk.

"I don't think so, Ernest," Beauty said, trying to control her sobbing. "We haven't seen them since they were a day old. We didn't even get to name them."

"Well, we will do the best we can to reunite you with them," Granny Relda said.

"You would do that for us?" the Beast asked.

"Of course," Daphne said proudly. "We are Grimms and this is what we do."

"Do you need anything from me?" Hamstead said.

Granny shook her head and flashed Sabrina an angry look.

"Actually, can I have a police hat?" Daphne asked the sheriff. Hamstead smiled and nodded at the girl.

"You are so punk rock!" she cried.

• • •

Once the family was outside, Sabrina wasn't sure which was colder—the bitter winter air or Granny's attitude toward her. She also knew that Daphne was going to give her the silent treatment again. But it didn't matter to her anymore.

"I'm not sorry for what I said," she declared.

"Oh, we're well aware of that," Granny Relda said as they approached the car. Mr. Canis was waiting on the roof.

"I heard yelling," he said, crawling down to help the old woman into the front seat.

"I bet you're going to hear a lot more," Puck said, sounding hopeful.

"Everything is fine," the old woman said. "It is late and I think we all need a good night of rest."

"Good idea," Daphne said. "We can search the tunnels tomorrow."

"No, I don't think so," Granny said as they got settled into the car. "Things have escalated to a point where I don't feel comfortable having the three of you help out. A few Everafter children are one thing, but Rumpelstiltskin is another entirely.

He may be behind these murders, and he's one of the most deranged and mysterious fairy-tale creatures that ever came to Ferryport Landing. I can't put you into harm's way when I have no idea what to expect."

"This isn't about danger," Sabrina said, shaking with anger and hurt. "We've been in plenty of dangerous situations since we moved to this town. This is about me, isn't it?"

Granny Relda turned in her seat and eyed the girl. "In the past, I thought you two girls were smart enough to handle yourselves. I thought you might possibly be the cleverest Grimms in the history of the family, but right now, I don't trust your judgment, Sabrina. You're not who I thought you were, child. I'm sorry, but this case is closed for the sisters Grimm."

• • •

Everyone was furious with her, so Sabrina had crept upstairs to her room, rather than hear another lecture. As she lay in bed, looking up at the model airplanes her father had hung from the ceiling, she thought there might be an upside to being the black sheep of the family. While everyone was busy solving mysteries, she could spend more time searching for her parents. Just two days ago, she would have thought this was a perfect chance, but now, with Granny acting so blind to the truth about the town's residents, she worried the old woman would be their next victim. If that happened, the girls would get sent back to the orphanage and any chance of finding their mom and dad would be gone.

Daphne entered the room, dressed in her pajamas, and sat down on the edge of the bed.

"Well, we now know what Granny's like when she's mad," she said. "She's downstairs cleaning the house. She's been dusting for the last hour. If you get her any madder, she's going to clean out the closets."

"I didn't mean to make her angry," Sabrina said.

"You've got to get over this thing you have about Everafters," Daphne said.

Sabrina groaned. If Daphne was going to lecture her, she'd be happy to go back to receiving the silent treatment.

"No, what I've got to do is convince everyone to stop being so naïve," Sabrina said. "But let's just say I'm wrong about everything. Punishing us for my attitude isn't going to help solve the case. Granny can't do it all, and she's not going to get any help from Charming and the sheriff. We could be searching the tunnels. Who knows how far they've dug, or even what they're digging for? Maybe there's some kind of monster under the town. I know that sounds nuts, but we used to think the same thing about giants not so long ago. What if the bad guys are doing something really bad down there while Granny is running around trying to find out which of the kids at school are monsters?"

"So what do we do?"

"We do what we're supposed to do," Sabrina said. "We're Grimms and something is wrong in this town. It's our job to find out what it is."

• • •

Once she was confident her grandmother and Mr. Canis were asleep, Sabrina shook her sister awake and the two of them crawled out of bed. They crept out of their room and down the hall to Puck's bedroom.

"Don't step on the plate," Sabrina reminded her sister as she opened the door. Inside the boy's magical forest room, the sun had set, replaced by a sea of stars, each blinking brightly just for Puck. The boxing kangaroo was asleep in his ring and the roller coaster had been turned off. All was still, except for the cascading waterfall splashing into the lagoon.

The girls crept along the path around the lagoon and then into some heavy brush. Eventually, they came to a trampoline on which Puck was sound asleep. The Trickster King was wearing a pair of baby blue footie pajamas that had little smiling stars and moons on them. Held close to his face was a soft pink stuffed unicorn with a rainbow sewn on its side. If only Sabrina had brought a camera, she could have also recorded his thumb in his mouth.

"Time to wake up the sleepy monkey," Sabrina cooed in baby talk, doing her best not to roar with laughter.

Daphne giggled but held her hand over her mouth.

"Wakie-wakie, eggs and bac-ie," Sabrina continued.

Puck stirred in his sleep but didn't wake. A big stream of drool escaped his mouth and ran down the front of his pajamas.

"Does someone have the sleepy-sleepies?" Daphne said mimicking her sister's baby talk.

"Time to come back from dreamland, precious," the older girl said, shaking the boy roughly. Puck sprang from his sleep, with wings extended from his back. He waved his big pink unicorn like a deadly sword and slashed at the children.

"Nice jammies," Daphne snickered.

"I especially like Mr. Unicorn," Sabrina laughed.

"His name is Kraven the Deceiver," Puck corrected, before realizing what he was holding and who was with him. He tossed the stuffed animal aside and fluttered down to the ground.

"We've got a plan for tomorrow and you're going to help us," Sabrina said.

"Forget it," the boy answered. "Tomorrow I'm telling the old lady to find another bodyguard for her stinky offspring. It's beneath me!"

"But this plan requires a lot of a mischief," Sabrina said.

Puck's eyes lit up. "I'm listening," he said.

"We're going to get into the boiler room tomorrow to search the tunnels."

"The old lady will be furious."

"I know, but I'm willing to take the heat if it saves someone's life."

"Fine, what's the plan?"

Sabrina reached into her pocket and took out her set of keys.

"Where'd you get those?" Daphne asked.

"I've been swiping them off Granny's key ring one by one and making copies at the hardware store."

Puck's eyes lit up and he looked at Sabrina as if he had never seen her before in his life. "You stole those keys and made copies?"

She dropped her eyes. "Yeah," she said, thinking she felt disapproval.

"That's wonderful," the boy said, eyeing the girl like a child watching a fireworks display. He was in complete awe of her. He grabbed both the girls by the wrist and dragged them through his "room." "Let's put them to use, then!"

Once they were in Mirror's room, the three children stepped

through the reflection and came out into the Hall of Wonders. Mirror was standing in front of his own full-length mirror, sucking in his plump belly and making muscle poses like a body builder.

"Doesn't anyone in this house sleep anymore?" he asked.

"We need some help," Sabrina said.

The little man rolled his eyes and let out his belly. "Very well, what's the scoop?"

"We need something that will help us get into the boiler room at school," Daphne said. "The door is locked, so we need something that will turn us invisible or let us walk through walls."

"Children, this isn't Wal-Mart," Mirror replied. "I don't have everything, but there is something that might help. Follow me."

As they followed Mirror down the long hallway, Sabrina read the golden plaques on each of the doors, a favorite habit developed on previous visits: LEPRECHAUN GOLD; FLOOR PLANS FOR GINGERBREAD HOUSES; TALKING FISH; GHOSTS OF CHRISTMAS PAST, PRESENT, AND FUTURE; TIK-TOK MEN; CALIBAN—the doors went on and on. What was Mirror going to offer them?

Soon, he stopped at a door with a plaque that read THE PANTRY. He held out his hand and Sabrina gave him her key ring. He searched through her collection and found the one that unlocked the door. Everyone stepped inside where, much to the girls' chagrin, there stood an old, run-down refrigerator.

"I've never heard of the magic refrigerator," Daphne said. "Is that a Grimm story or someone else?"

"There's no such thing as a magic refrigerator," Mirror said as he opened the door. "It's what's inside that's important."

He opened the fridge, bent down, and rummaged around inside. He pulled out a bag of rotten carrots. "I really have to toss these out," he mumbled. He opened a carton of milk and took a sniff, his face crinkling up in disgust as he closed the carton and put it back in the refrigerator. Finally, he took out a package of juice boxes and handed them to the kids.

"Drink me," Daphne read.

"This is from *Alice's Adventures in Wonderland*," Sabrina said, happily. "This will make us shrink?"

"To about the size of an ant," Mirror said. "At that size you could just walk under the door and get into any room you want. But you'll need these, too." He reached in and pulled out several individually wrapped snack cakes. They looked just like the kind Sabrina used to buy at the deli near their Manhattan apartment, but the label said, EAT ME!

"These will make you big, but don't eat too many, they're not exactly Atkins friendly," Mirror warned. "Tweedle-Dee and Tweedle-Dum sold these for a week at their convenience store before your grandmother confiscated their stock. The town was filled with giant children. It took us a week to sort it out."

"We'll need four of each, I think," Sabrina said.

"But there's only three of us," Daphne argued.

"I have a feeling the great detective Wendell Hamelin is going to change his mind about being a loner," her sister replied.

• • •

The next day at school, the trio walked down the crowded hallway toward the boiler room. Sabrina scrutinized every kid along the way. Any one of them could be a giant spider or a frog-girl, but besides being exhausted, they all looked just like every other kid Sabrina had ever seen. At least her suspicions about Wendell proved correct. He was waiting for them by the doorway with a handkerchief and a runny nose.

"I've been doing some thinking and I believe that joining forces might be a great idea, but under a couple of conditions," he said, rushing to join the group.

"What conditions?" Sabrina said.

"I handle all the dangerous work," the chubby boy said, puffing up his chest like a tough guy.

The children looked at one another and fought off a laugh.

"Fine," Sabrina said. "I think we should have a look in the tunnels right away."

"I agree, but there's a problem," Wendell said, wiping his nose again. "They changed the locks on the boiler room door."

Sabrina reached into her backpack and tossed the boy an Eat Me cake and a Drink Me juice box.

"What are these?" he asked.

"The key to the new lock."

"You want to do it now?" Daphne cried. "Ms. White will notice I'm gone and come looking for me."

"We'll worry about that later," said her sister. "Lunchtime is too busy and the bad guys will probably be watching after school. We'll wait until the bell rings for class and once the hall is empty, we'll get started."

Soon enough, the bell rang, and the kids filed into their classes. Sabrina, Daphne, Puck, and Wendell milled around, trying to appear as if they were on their way to class without actually going anywhere.

Once they were alone in the hall, the children took out their Drink Me boxes and inserted the handy straws attached to the sides.

"How much do we drink?" Daphne asked, sniffing at the box.

"I don't know," Sabrina said. "I guess until it starts working."

Puck took a long slurp and when he was finished he opened his mouth and belched. "It's fruity," he exclaimed. Suddenly, to a sound like that of a squeaky balloon losing its air, his body shrank to half its size. Even his clothes, the Eat Me cake, and the juice box got tiny.

"Drink more," Daphne insisted. "You aren't small enough to get under the door."

"And hurry up," Sabrina said, scanning the hallway. The last thing she wanted was a teacher or student to see this craziness.

Puck took another sip and shrank even further. Soon, he was no taller than a quarter standing on its end. Sabrina bent down and examined the tiny boy.

"You have no idea how tempted I am to squish you," she said.

"And you have no idea how big your nose hairs are," he squeaked. Sabrina covered her face with her hand.

"Our turn," Daphne said. The three other children took big sips out of their boxes and in no time they were all shrinking, too. The liquid did taste fruity, like pineapples and cherry pie at the same time. A cool tingle ran down Sabrina's throat, into her belly, and then into her legs and arms. The sensation wasn't unlike having a good stretch after a wonderful night's sleep. When she finished the box, she was the same size as Puck.

"Let's get in there before we wind up on the bottom of someone's shoe," said the tiny Wendell. He marched over to the door and looked back. "I'll go first, in case there's something waiting for us on the other side."

He yanked out his hanky, blew hard on it, then shoved it back into his pocket. Then he walked underneath the door without even having to bend over. Daphne took Sabrina's hand and together they followed Wendell, with Puck bringing up the rear.

"I should be doing the dangerous stuff," he grumbled.

Once the group was on the other side, the children had a chance to look around. A bucket full of mops sat in the corner, boxes of trash bags and rolls of toilet paper filled a nearby shelf, and an ancient coal furnace rested in the center of the room. Not far off, a brand-new electric furnace clicked and popped as it pushed warm air throughout the vents of the school. But what was bewildering was how gigantic everything was. The mops looked as tall as the Empire State Building in midtown New York City and Sabrina suspected if one of the rolls of toilet paper were to fall off the shelf and on to them, they'd be crushed to death.

"Look at that table," Daphne cried, pointing at a nearby desk. "It's huge."

Sabrina nodded in agreement.

"Look at that chair," Daphne said. "It's huge!"

Sabrina agreed.

"Look at that button!" Daphne said, running over to a monstrous white button that had fallen off of someone's shirt. She tried to lift it, but it was too heavy for her in her shrunken state. "It's huge!"

"We need to find you another word," Sabrina muttered.

"Hey! I'm seven! I don't know a lot of words," the little girl said.

"All right, piggy," Puck said to Wendell. "Where's the entrance to the tunnel?"

"We need to eat the cakes and get big," the boy detective said. "The lever that opens the entrance is in the old furnace."

The children reached in their pockets for their Eat Me cakes when suddenly, the boiler room door opened.

"Someone's coming!" Sabrina shouted. The door closed and a man walked over to the coal furnace. He opened a small trapdoor on its side and reached in. Sabrina guessed he had pushed the lever because a hum filled the room, and the coal furnace began to slide across the floor. That's when Sabrina noticed it was Principal Hamelin.

The principal waited patiently, and when the coal furnace had slid away, he descended a flight of stairs hidden underneath the machine.

The children rushed to the center of the room.

"That was your dad," Sabrina said to Wendell.

"What is he doing?" he said.

"We have to follow him," Daphne insisted.

"We can't! If we eat the cakes and get big, he's sure to spot us, but at this size we'll never make it down those steps," her sister argued.

"No worries, girls. I have a brilliant plan," Puck said, proudly. He spun around on his heels and transformed into an elephant, albeit a tiny elephant. He let out a mighty roar and charged off into the far corner of the room.

"Puck, we don't have time for your stupidity," Sabrina shouted after him, but the boy-elephant did not respond. Soon, she could hear the scraping of metal on the floor. When elephant Puck returned he was pushing a dustpan with his massive head, all the way to the edge of the steps. When the pan was on the edge of the top step, the elephant morphed back into the boy.

"Get in," he said, beaming with pride.

Sabrina looked at the dustpan hanging precariously over the edge. "No way," she said. "We'll kill ourselves in that thing."

Daphne was already climbing inside and had found a spot in the corner to sit down. "We survived Granny's driving," she said. "We'll survive this, too."

"You'll be fine," Puck assured Sabrina. "You'll probably need someone to feed you for the rest of your life, but you'll make it. Stop being a baby and get in."

Sabrina looked at Wendell. He shrugged and the two of them climbed into the dustpan.

"You all need to stay in the back of this thing," Puck explained. "Oh, and one more thing . . ."

"What?" Sabrina cried. She didn't like the tone of his voice.

"Buckle up, kiddies," Puck shouted as he walked to the front of the pan and leaped into the air. His body came down hard on the end of the pan and the back tilted high in the air, sending the whole thing rocketing down the steps before Sabrina could even scream. Each step it cleared just made the dustpan increase its speed, until finally they crashed at the bottom of the stairs.

After Sabrina checked everyone for broken bones, she punched Puck in the arm.

"Hey, I got us here, didn't I?" he complained as he rubbed his sore shoulder.

The children climbed out of the dustpan, calmed themselves, and headed down a long, cavernous hall carved out of stone. Along the rocky path were pickaxes and dusty shovels, old buckets and miles and miles of rope.

What are they up to down here? Sabrina wondered, as everyone marched through the tunnel. The journey wouldn't have taken long if they were their usual size, but the length of a normal step now required a dozen.

"This is as far as I went before," Wendell said when they reached a place where the tunnels branched off into two directions. "Which way should we go?"

Sabrina heard voices arguing in the tunnel to the left.

"There's someone else down here besides your father," she said. "Let's go find out who."

The children followed the tunnel to the left, turned a corner, and crept as close as they could to the two men arguing in the dark. Sabrina couldn't make out the other person's face, but Hamelin was one of them for sure. The principal was wringing his hands.

"I'm telling you again. This has gone too far. No one was supposed to die," Hamelin said.

"Piper, you worry too much," a creaky voice said. To Sabrina, it sounded like the voice of a man who had been alive a thousand years without drinking a single sip of water. "Tonight we're going to reach our goal. We would already be there if it weren't for last night."

"My son was missing!" Hamelin cried. "What was I supposed to do?"

"Of all people, I understand," the voice crackled. "After all, I'm a father, too. The difference is that my children understand how important this is, while your child just gets in the way and puts this all at risk."

"Don't threaten me," the principal growled. "My boy isn't going to ruin our plans."

"Then we understand each other," the voice said. "Tonight we'll push forward, if you can find the time."

Hamelin's voice was so angry it was shaking. "Don't question my dedication. This was my idea after all."

"I'm glad to see you still remember that."

Hamelin spun around and rushed back up the tunnel, narrowly missing stepping on his own son, who just managed to leap out of the way.

"Are you OK?" Daphne asked, taking Wendell's hand in her own.

"I can't believe it," the boy said.

"We should go farther into the tunnel," Sabrina suggested. "We need to know where they are digging to." Everyone agreed, but just then something crawled out from around a corner and stopped the group in their tracks. An enormous brown mouse as big as a semi truck lumbered toward them. The rodent's pink nose and whiskers flicked and twitched as it sniffed at the children. Sabrina knew that at their current size they'd make a great snack for the hungry mouse.

"Eat the cakes," Sabrina advised, eyeing the mouse.

The children unwrapped their cakes and were just about to eat them when the mouse barreled forward and knocked Sabrina down. Daphne screamed and Puck leaped forward and dragged Sabrina to her feet. Unfortunately, she had dropped her cake right in front of the beast. The mouse spotted it, sniffed it, and with a quick flick of its tongue, ate it.

"That was a bad thing, wasn't it?" Sabrina said, sheepishly.

"Oh, man," Puck said, quickly shoving his own little chocolate cake into his mouth. "This is going to be awesome."

Daphne and Wendell were already munching their cakes, too, when Puck offered Sabrina his pinky.

"Hang on Sabrina," Puck said, flashing his devilish grin. "This is about to get interesting."

Sabrina grabbed his pinky finger and held it tightly just as the first changes affected the mouse's body. It sounded as if someone were blowing up a balloon. A ripple rolled across the mouse's skin and its eyes widened as its body inflated by a thousand times, yet its little legs and head stayed the exact same size, causing its massive body to plop to the ground. This was followed by a loud, squeaky rubber sound as the rodent's feet, legs, and head expanded in size. The children dashed down the tunnel to avoid the quickly expanding mouse.

Puck, meanwhile, was growing in the same awkward manner. His legs got big first, pushing him to his normal height and sending Sabrina soaring high into the air. When his upper body and hands finally followed, his pinky got thicker. Sabrina held on with all her might. Luckily, Puck was paying attention. He quickly swung her into his shirt pocket, where she clung to the top, just as Puck's head inflated.

Meanwhile, Daphne's head and feet were the first to inflate and the not-so-little girl hobbled around like a pumpkin that had suddenly sprouted shoes and was making an escape from the patch.

"I don't like this at all," she groaned. No sooner had she complained than her legs sprouted up like over-eager cornstalks, followed by her upper body, and lastly her neck. Wendell experienced the same kind of disturbing growth.

"It's all good," the runny-nosed detective announced, checking for all ten fingers. But what he didn't see was that it wasn't "all good." The mouse was also getting bigger and bigger until it was nearly as wide as the tunnel, and worse, it seemed very, very angry.

Puck grabbed Daphne and Daphne grabbed Wendell and they all rushed down the tunnel and up the stairs. When they got to the top, Daphne and Wendell raced across the room to the door, unlocked it, and hurried into the hall. Puck followed close behind, giggling like an idiot.

"Do you laugh every time we're in trouble?" Sabrina shouted.

The boy looked down into his pocket. "What are you squeaking about?"

When he was safely in the hall, Puck slammed the door shut and the children leaned against the walls on either side to catch their breath.

"I don't think we have to worry about him anymore," Puck said.

Just then, the door flew off its hinges, slammed against the opposite wall, and fell heavily to the floor. The giant mouse lumbered into the hallway and roared angrily. It was as big as a stuffed buffalo Sabrina had seen at the Natural History Museum. It let out a deafening squeak and licked its gigantic front teeth. To make matters worse, the dismissal bell rang and every classroom door opened. The hallway was immediately flooded with a sea of noisy children, eager to get to their next class. The mouse stomped hard, creating a chasm in the shiny floor, and all conversation ended abruptly.

"Well, piglet, you wanted to do the dangerous stuff," Puck laughed, as he turned to a stunned Wendell. "Be my guest!"

9

K, everyone, there's no need to panic. We're professionals and we know how to handle things like this," Daphne assured the crowd of stunned students. She flashed her shiny badge to the crowd. A teacher fainted to the ground as the mouse let out an ear-shattering squeal and stomped its giant paws on the floor.

"Stay calm," the little girl said. "It's as afraid of you as you are of it."

All at once, every kid at Ferryport Landing Elementary freaked out. They screamed and ran toward every available exit. Some raced into classrooms, barricaded the doors with desks, and climbed out windows.

Puck peered into his pocket and smiled at Sabrina.

"Hang on, I've got a plan," he said, flashing her a grin. He spun around on his heels and transformed into an orange and white alley cat. Sabrina found herself clinging to the cat's ear as it charged toward the giant mouse. Once he got up close, Puck the cat hissed aggressively, but the mouse only stared down at him. Suddenly, what Sabrina could only describe as a smile crept across the mouse's face. It leaned its head down to the cat, opened its mouth, and roared angrily. Puck's short tabby hair was blown back as if he were standing in a heavy wind and Sabrina nearly flew off his ear. The cat backed away and transformed into a boy again.

"It was worth a try," Daphne shouted.

"Don't worry," Puck said, with Sabrina back inside his shirt pocket. "I've got a million more ideas where that one came from." The boy spun around to face the mouse and his wings popped out of his back. Flapping strongly, he soared over the mouse, spun around, and landed on its back.

"*Yee-haw!*" he cried, jabbing the heels of his feet into the mouse's side. The mouse squealed in pain, lifted itself on two legs, and kicked wildly, causing Puck to bounce around like a rodeo cowboy and Sabrina to be tossed around mercilessly inside the boy's pocket.

The giant mouse slammed into walls, broke down doors, and put serious dents into a row of lockers. It shattered a trophy case, sending glass, brass track medals, and bowling prizes skittering down the hallway. It crashed into a banner announcing the library's bake sale and ripped it off the wall.

Of course, Puck laughed at every effort the mouse made to buck him off. Sabrina suspected he'd ride the beast all day if it didn't get tired first.

"Puck, cut it out!" she shouted, clutching the top of the pocket, but she knew the boy couldn't hear her over the commotion he was making.

Daphne rushed across the hallway, avoiding the mouse's wicked flapping tail. She reached into her pocket and pulled out her half-full Drink Me juice box and aimed it at the mouse's mouth.

"Daphne, you're a genius!" Sabrina cried.

Daphne reached back like a big-league pitcher, waited for the mouse to open its gaping mouth, and tossed the juice box as hard as she could. Unfortunately, instead of slipping down the mouse's throat, the box bounced off one of the rodent's gnarly yellow teeth and fell to the ground. The mouse stomped down on the box, spraying the contents all over the hallway.

"Uh, what's plan B?" Wendell shouted, just as the mouse headed for the exit door. Unfortunately, Daphne was right in its path.

"Daphne, run!" Sabrina yelled, but there was no way the little girl could move that quickly. Luckily, Wendell raced across the hall and pushed Daphne to safety just as the enormous rodent lumbered past them like an out-of-control train. It slammed into the exit doors, knocking them off their hinges, and stomped outside.

Puck howled and laughed the whole way, until a low-hanging tree with a thick limb knocked him off the mouse. He fell hard on his back, sending his Drink Me box flying and launching Sabrina out of his pocket and onto the lawn several yards away. By the time Sabrina got her bearings, the mouse was already on top of the boy, doing what it could to sink its sharp teeth into him as Puck fought it off.

"Got any more of that juice?" he shouted, as Daphne and Wendell raced to his side. Puck snatched Wendell's Drink Me box with a free hand and squeezed its contents into the mouse's mouth until the box was crumpled and empty. Almost immediately, a ripple ran across the mouse's skin. The rodent shrank rapidly until it was once again a little brown mouse, sitting on the boy's chest.

Puck looked down at it and laughed. Then he ran his finger over the mouse's coat. "Good try," he told the rodent. "You almost had me."

Daphne helped Puck to his feet.

"Where's Sabrina?" she asked.

"Don't worry, marshmallow, she's right here in my pocket," Puck said as he looked inside. "Uh-oh."

"What's uh-oh?" Daphne cried.

"She's not in there," Puck said.

The little girl's eyes got as big as saucers.

"Don't anyone move," Wendell said. "She probably fell out here on the lawn and we could step on her."

"Sabrina!" Daphne shouted.

"I'm here!" Sabrina yelled, waving her hands and jumping up and down, but none of the children could see or hear her.

"What if we've already stepped on her?" her sister cried, as tears streamed down her face.

"Let's check," Wendell said. He slowly lifted each of his shoes. "She's not on mine."

Puck slowly looked under his sneakers. "All clear!"

Daphne checked one foot and then the next. A big smile came to her face.

"See, we haven't stepped on her," Wendell said.

"I think we better get the old lady," Puck said as his wings sprouted. "Best that I fly us out of here so we don't squish her."

In a few moments he had snatched the other children off the ground and they were all flying away.

"Don't you dare leave me out here!" Sabrina screamed, but they were already gone.

She looked around. The school was only steps away for a normal-sized person, but for her it seemed like half a mile. Staying put was probably the best idea, but the air was freezing even with her coat on, so she shoved her hands into her pockets and marched toward the entrance to the school.

When she finally reached the school's main doors, she found them in a heap—knocked off their hinges by the giant mouse—which left the hallway open to the bitter winter wind outside. Her walk had chilled her to the bone, and finding somewhere safe and warm to rest was now her main priority. She remembered that the heat in Mr. Sheepshank's office was always on full blast. If she was going to get warm, that was the place to go, so she ran down the hall, dodging a giant mound of discarded bubble gum, and made her way to the main office door. She'd hoped it would be a safe place to hide until Puck could return with her grandmother, but as soon as she crawled underneath the door she knew she had even bigger problems to deal with.

"There's another roach!" the secretary with the big glasses

cried. She reached into a drawer and pulled out an aerosol spray can, shook it vigorously, and got up from her desk. One glance at the can told Sabrina all she needed to know about what was going to happen next. It didn't take a rocket scientist to know what ROACH-BE-DEAD meant.

She ran along the rug frantically, racing under the secretary's desk just as the gigantic woman rounded the other side. This was unbelievable. A giant mouse had just been rampaging through the school and these goofy secretaries were worried about roaches? When Sabrina came into the light, the other secretary was there, chomping on a sandwich. She mumbled loudly and pointed at tiny Sabrina, causing the first secretary to come back around. The girl dashed under the desk again, but this time the secretary got down on her knees, pointed the spray can at her, and pushed the nozzle. Sabrina was sure she would soon be covered in a horrible poison and die, but luckily the nozzle was pointed upward and the chemical death landed all over the desk.

"This one's fast." The first secretary scowled.

"Don't send it running over here," the second secretary cried. "Those things give me the heebie-jeebies."

The first secretary raced around the desk just as Sabrina darted behind a file cabinet.

"Where did it go?" she groaned.

The second secretary had gone back to enjoying her sandwich and mumbled an "I don't know" to her coworker.

"I know where the filthy thing went," the first secretary cried. Suddenly, Sabrina's safe hiding place began to rock back and forth. The file cabinet moved several inches before it stopped. "It's heavy."

"I'm not a cockroach!" she shouted, but she knew the woman couldn't hear her. A stream of the poison came showering in from one side of the cabinet. Sabrina darted out of the way, but the secretary seemed to anticipate her escape route and was waiting for her on the other side. The girl looked up to find the nozzle of the can pointing right at her.

"Now I've got you," the woman cried.

But she never got her chance to spray the poison. Sabrina heard the office door open, and Mr. Sheepshank say, "Hello, ladies. The commotion is all over."

"What was it?" the secretary with the roach spray asked.

"Oh, just a big dog some kid let in," he replied. "Scared everybody half to death. Most of the kids have already left for home. Principal Hamelin just told me to let you two go, as well."

"Early dismissal for the grown-ups? I love it!" The roach-obsessed secretary cheered. She quickly forgot about Sabrina and crawled to her feet.

"I'm going home myself," the guidance counselor said.

Sabrina couldn't see what was going on, but she could hear the women packing their things and leaving. Sheepshank followed them out and closed the door.

After several minutes, Sabrina realized that the entire school was empty. All she could do now was wait, so she walked over to the desk of one of the secretaries and lay down under her big chair. The room was warm and comfy and before she knew it, she had fallen asleep.

• • •

Sabrina woke up inside Elvis's nose. Granny and Mr. Canis had used the big dog's excellent sniffer to track the tiny girl down, and when Elvis found her asleep under the chair, he accidentally inhaled her. With her head now covered in dog boogers and mucus, she kicked for freedom, but this only caused the dog to snort deeply, and Sabrina rocketed into his nasal cavity, slid down his throat, and was coughed out onto the floor.

When Sabrina got to her feet, Granny Relda was already standing next to her, holding two Eat Me cakes in her hand. She was as tiny as her granddaughter, but the anger on her face was as big as the moon. Her round face and button nose were so red with frustration Sabrina wondered if smoke might blow out of her ears.

"Granny, you won't believe what I found out," Sabrina said, hoping her news would change the old woman's mood.

"I agree, Sabrina," Granny Relda snapped. "I doubt I'll be believing anything you say for a very long time."

She handed the girl an Eat Me cake and quickly unwrapped her own. She took a big bite and began to grow. Sabrina ate her cake and felt her body sprout up, as well. Unfortunately, Elvis's boogers grew at the same rate and when she reached her normal size, even the Great Dane looked disgusted at the goo that covered her from head to toe.

Daphne, who was standing nearby, ran to hug her sister but halted when she saw the disgusting mess that covered Sabrina. "I'm sorry. I love you but you are way, way too gross," the little girl said.

"We got into the boiler room," Sabrina said, still hoping to impress her grandmother.

"She knows," Puck said sheepishly. He and Wendell leaned against the wall, looking guilty. Why wasn't everyone excited? They had found an important clue to the mystery.

"I also know you did it by breaking almost every one of my rules," Granny lectured. "Mirror says you have a set of keys for nearly three dozen of the rooms in the Hall of Wonders."

"I've been making copies," Sabrina said, lowering her eyes to the ground.

"How sneaky of you," Granny said. "I suppose you are proud of yourself?"

Sabrina knew it was not the right time to brag.

"You told us that this was our job," she argued. "Daphne and I didn't come banging on your door hoping that we'd get chased by giants and evil rabbits. Now that we're actually trying to take on this destiny of ours, you want us to stop."

"Sneaking around behind my back, defying my requests to stay out of this case, stealing and copying my keys, testing out magic and potions in the middle of the night, and dragging your sister into danger," said Granny. "Add that to your attitude about Everafters and I just don't see you as much of a help right now."

Sabrina's eyes welled with tears, but she refused to cry. She bit her lip hard and squeezed her fists tight. The last thing she would do was show the old woman that her words had stung.

• • •

Dinnertime was a quiet affair. No one talked, no one made eye contact, and no one smiled. Even Puck, who could usually be counted on to fart during dinner, was oddly quiet. When everyone had eaten, Granny quietly washed the dishes while Puck, Sabrina, and Daphne stared at one another from across the table. Elvis eyed Sabrina from time to time, but didn't seem to want to go near her after she had been inside his nose.

Just then, there was a knock at the door. Granny Relda stopped washing the dishes and rushed to open it. Snow White was standing outside in the cold. The old woman quickly invited her inside.

"Thank you so much for coming, Snow," she said as she took off her apron and folded it.

"I'm happy to help! Any chance to spend some time with my favorite student," the teacher said.

"That's me!" Daphne cried as she rushed to the door.

"Mr. Canis will be coming with me, and the sheriff is on his way now," Granny said. "The children have eaten, but feel free to raid the refrigerator. Hopefully, we won't be gone too long."

Just then, a car-horn blast came from outside.

"That's Hamstead," Mr. Canis said as he opened the closet and took out his and Granny Relda's coats.

"What's going on?" Sabrina asked.

"We're going to go and put a stop to what's going on under the school," Granny Relda replied. "While we're gone, Ms. White will be looking after you."

"You got us a baby-sitter?" Sabrina cried indignantly. "I'm too old for a baby-sitter."

"*You're* too old?" Puck said to her. "I'm over four thousand years old. This is an outrage!"

"I might have thought the same thing this morning," Granny replied as she put on her coat.

"*We* should go," Sabrina steamed. "We've seen the tunnels. We know how to get down into them."

There was another knock at the door. When Mr. Canis opened it, Wendell Hamelin stepped inside.

"Oh, we've got a guide," Granny replied.

"The sheriff says we better get going," the boy said, wiping his runny nose on his handkerchief. He looked more sad than excited about this latest detective assignment.

"Honey, you don't have to do this," Granny said. "This is your father we're going to arrest."

"Maybe I can convince him to stop before anyone else gets hurt," Wendell said. "He's my dad. I have to try."

Granny Relda, Mr. Canis, and Wendell, looking apologetically at the other three children, said their good-byes and were soon gone, leaving Sabrina standing by the door with a stunned expression.

"Well now," Snow White said uncomfortably, reaching into her handbag and pulling out a board game. "Who wants to play Candy Land?"

• • •

Snow White did her best to keep the kids busy. She set up the board game, but Puck had no patience for it. When he landed on Molasses Swamp and lost a turn, he flew into a rage, flinging the board out the front door and into the yard. Later, after he had calmed down, Ms. White suggested they play charades. Once again, Puck was the spoiler, acting out the names of tree gnomes and pixies that had lived three hundred years ago and insisting they were as famous as any astronaut or president. Eventually, even Snow White gave up and let the children do what they really wanted to do—research.

The girls searched the library for titles that might be of help. With half their family traipsing around in some dark tunnels, Sabrina and Daphne felt the least they could do was make sure that nothing had been overlooked. Sabrina eventually came across her great aunt Matilda's pamphlet entitled *Rumpelstiltskin's Secret Nature*. She could see it was going to be a dry read, so she fell into a chair and started on page one.

Rumpelstiltskin's story was a famous fairy tale; everyone had heard it, but Sabrina wasn't taking any chances with what she thought she knew. Dad's attitude about fairy tales had left the girls at a disadvantage, and she wanted to know the story inside and out. But even she was shocked to see how much information Matilda had collected about the little creature. It looked as if months of work had gone into the analysis of every single nuance of his personality, powers, and actions. Her ancestor even had theories on how Rumpelstiltskin spun wheat into gold, where he had come from, and why he tried to trick people out of their children.

Matilda's book also recounted at least two dozen versions of the original tale. The story Sabrina had always heard involved a woman who begged Rumpelstiltskin for his help. In exchange, she promised to give him her first-born child. When the baby finally arrived, the woman demanded a chance to keep it, so Rumpelstiltskin wagered that she would never be able to guess his real name. Of course, by the end of the story, she had figured it out and got to keep her kid, making the little man so angry he actually ripped himself in two. But Matilda said there was an alternate version of the ending that not many people knew. In the other ending, Rumpelstiltskin didn't rip himself in half—he actually blew up like a bomb, killing everyone within a mile.

One chapter, entitled "The Power of Rumpelstiltskin," contained theories on the source of the little man's powers. Matilda believed he was like a walking battery. He stored energy and converted it into destructive power. Unfortunately, the more of Matilda's theories Sabrina read, the more questions she had.

"It doesn't make any sense," Sabrina cried. "What do Rumpelstiltskin, the Pied Piper, the children of Everafters, and a bunch of tunnels under the school have in common?"

"The barrier," Puck replied.

"What?" Sabrina asked.

"The barrier runs very close to the school," Puck said. "We flew into it, don't you remember?"

"You're just telling me this now?" Sabrina cried.

"Seemed obvious to me," the Trickster replied.

"They're digging to the barrier," Snow White gasped. "Baba Yaga's spell is probably not as strong underground. But what would be the point? They'd still need a powerful magic explosion to get through it."

"I think they've got one," Sabrina said, holding up her great aunt's book. "Matilda thought Rumpelstiltskin was a walking nuclear bomb. He might be able to make a crack in it."

"Still, they have the river to worry about. The waters would drown them all," Snow White pointed out.

"Maybe not!" Daphne said, rushing to the bookshelf and snatching down one of the family's journals. She ran over to the table and put it down in front of Sabrina. It was their grandfather Basil's journal.

"Granny had this out one afternoon and forgot to put it

back," the little girl said. "I was flipping through it and found some maps Grandpa Basil drew of the town." She flipped it open and searched for a page. When she found it, she pointed for her sister to read.

Today I did a little amateur mapmaking of the elementary school construction site, claiming I was just interested in the building. Charming hates when he thinks I'm snooping, but I wanted to make sure no one got any ideas about digging the holes deeper or building a tunnel over to the river. The barrier is much weaker underground. Baba Yaga compensated though by extending it over the Hudson River. If anyone tried to tunnel through, they'd drown. The only chance they'd have would be to somehow dig through the bedrock under the river over to Bannerman's Island, but without an army of miners, they'd never get close. I feel pretty confident that it's impossible. —April, 1957

Sabrina flipped the page and found a hand-drawn map of the town and the surrounding areas. A circle enclosed the town and Grandpa Basil had written THE BARRIER on it as a label. She had to admit, the circle wasn't very big. Mount Taurus was inside it, as well as the edge of the Hudson River, but it wasn't a lot of room. She found the very spot where Puck had slammed into the barrier and dumped them all into the river. It was close to the school—as was a tiny island that sat right on the barrier. Sabrina had never noticed Bannerman's Island before, but there it was on her grandfather's map.

"Kids, let's just calm down," Snow White insisted. "Your grandfather was right. Without a crew of workers, it would take Rumpelstiltskin decades to tunnel to the barrier. Your grandmother and the sheriff will stop him and the piper tonight."

"See, that's where I'm confused," Sabrina said. "What does the Pied Piper have to offer in all this? If Rumpelstiltskin can blow a hole in the barrier, then what does he need with a guy whose claim to fame is leading a bunch of rats out of town?"

"Maybe he's using the rats to chew through the rocks," Puck said.

"That's stupid!" Sabrina snapped.

"You're stupid!" he shouted back.

"Maybe he's not using rats," Snow White said uncomfortably.

"What else could he use?" asked Sabrina.

"You don't know how the Pied Piper's story ended, do you?"

The girls shook their heads. Apparently, their father's no-fairy-tales rule was coming back to haunt them again.

"He drowned the rats and became a hero, right?" Daphne said.

"Well, he did drown the rats, but he didn't do it to be a hero. He did it for a paycheck. In his day, he used to travel from town to town, using his pipes to clean up messes. He drove the spiders out of Paris, the monkeys out of Bombay, and snakes out of Prague. But he did it for *money*. When he showed up in Hamelin, the townspeople were desperate. They were completely overrun with vermin."

"What's *vermin* mean?" Daphne asked.

"Rats and mice," Sabrina explained.

"Rats were everywhere," Ms. White continued. "They spread a lot of disease and people were getting sick. Everything the town had tried hadn't worked. So the piper agreed to handle their problem, and in no time he was leading the rats right into the ocean where they drowned. But that wasn't the end of the town's problems. When the piper came back, he wanted payment, but the town refused to pay. They had used him and he was furious."

"What happened?" Sabrina said, already sensing the story's unhappy ending.

"He gave them twenty-four hours to come up with the

money and when the time was up, they just laughed at him. So, he blew into his bagpipes and the town's children congregated around him. The piper marched out of town with the children following behind him, just as the rats had. Their families tried to stop them, but reports say the kids were in a trance and kept on following the music. The families never saw them again."

"So, of course it makes a lot of sense to hire him to be principal of an elementary school!" Sabrina said angrily.

"Rats or brats," Puck said, before Snow White could explain. "What's the difference?"

Suddenly, the truth dawned on Sabrina. "He's providing the workforce!" she cried.

"What are you talking about?" Daphne said.

"The piper has been using his magic to force the students to work at night. You've seen the kids in my classes. They're exhausted. It's because they've been working all night. We have to warn Granny!"

"We can't do that," Snow White said.

"But, Ms. White! We have to!" Daphne cried, rushing to the closet and returning with her deputy's hat tied to her head.

"The sheriff and Mr. Canis are with her," the teacher replied. "They'll figure this out before anyone gets hurt."

"What if they don't?" Puck asked. Sabrina was surprised. The boy usually acted as if he didn't care. "What if they don't find out? We saw those tunnels. They go on and on. If Rumpelstiltskin blows a hole in the barrier, those walls will collapse on everyone inside."

Now Sabrina was stunned. "I thought you were a villain. If you come along, you're going to have to be a hero."

"As long as I'm ruining someone's day I'm in," Puck said.

Snow White looked from child to child and then reached for her car keys.

"Get your coats on," she said. "But if I think it's too dangerous, we turn right around."

Soon they were rushing out the front door. They were in such a hurry, Snow White didn't see Mayor Charming coming up the path, and the two ran right into each other.

"Snow," Charming said, surprised.

"Billy," the teacher whispered.

They stood holding hands in the cold night air. Sabrina rolled her eyes.

"We're not going to go through this again, are we?" she cried. "We've got to get going."

"What's the rush?" Charming asked.

"Rumpelstiltskin and the Pied Piper have been tunneling under the school for months and are looking for the weak spot in Baba Yaga's barrier so they can try to crack a hole in it and escape, and Granny, the sheriff, Mr. Canis, and Wendell are there now trying to stop them, but they don't know that Rumpelstiltskin is like a living battery and he has the power to create the hole, but if he does he'll collapse the tunnel and everyone inside will die," Daphne said, breathing heavily.

Charming stood still with wide eyes. "What was that again?" he asked.

"We're going to save the day," Ms. White said.

"We'll take my car," the mayor declared, leading the group to his stretch limousine. Mr. Seven got out of the driver's seat, but Charming waved him off.

"Seven," he commanded. "We're in a hurry!"

The little man crawled back into his seat, closed the door, and started the engine. Once everyone was inside, he pulled into the road and sped off like a NASCAR driver, leaving a tire stain on the pavement behind him.

"Billy, what are you doing here?" Snow White said, as she strapped on her seat belt.

"I have something for the girls," the mayor explained as he reached into his pocket and took out a small box of matches.

Charming handed the box to Sabrina and smiled proudly. "We made a deal. Here's my end of the bargain."

"Uh, thanks," Sabrina said. "I'll save these for the next time I need to build a campfire."

"Child, those aren't ordinary matches!" Charming groaned. "They're the Little Match Girl's matches. I just handed you something people in this town would kill for."

Snow White gasped. "You told me they had been destroyed!"

"I was trying to protect you," Charming said. "If anyone knew these still existed, your life might have been in danger."

"Great, so you give them to us?" Sabrina groaned. "Doesn't everyone hate us enough?"

"Grimm, no one is going to know you have them, because you are going to use them right away," the mayor replied.

Sabrina peeked into the matchbox. Two small wooden matches lay inside. "What do they do?"

"I thought you two were supposed to be experts on fables and fairy tales. 'The Little Match Girl' is one of Hans Christian Andersen's most famous accounts."

"You've been in our house. There are like a million books in the bathroom alone. We don't know everything yet," Sabrina said.

"The Little Match Girl sold matches in the street for money," Snow White explained. "One day she came across a box of them and set out to make a little money to help feed her family. But it was horribly cold outside and she was forced to light one. The flame became a magical portal, leading to a room filled with food and a roaring fireplace. The girl realized she had just wished she were in such a place before striking the match. People have been looking for those matches for a hundred years. They'll take a person anywhere they want to go, Sabrina. All you have to do is wish."

"Like Dorothy's slippers?" Daphne asked. She and her sister had used them to pop up all over town, but they had lost one of them while running from a giant.

"These are more powerful than the slippers," Charming said. "They could take an Everafter to the other side of the barrier, or they could take you to your parents."

Sabrina stared down into the box and a tear rolled down her cheek. She didn't deserve such an amazing gift and she knew it. For weeks she had looked at every Everafter as a suspect in her parents' kidnapping. She had turned everyone against her and practically broken her grandmother's heart. And yet, here was the most obnoxious, untrustworthy of the bunch, handing her the key to finding her parents.

"Why would you do this for us?" Sabrina asked.

"We made a deal," Charming said, glancing at the pretty teacher.

"You could have used these to escape," said Snow White.

"There was something that kept me here," Charming said, staring into her eyes. The beautiful teacher leaned over and kissed the mayor. "Billy Charming, make me a promise."

"What kind of promise?" Charming asked, somewhat breathless.

"When all this is said and done," Snow White said, "Take me to dinner."

"As long as we can leave your seven chaperones at home," Charming said with a grin.

Mr. Seven grumbled in the front seat.

"Oh, it's so romantic," Daphne blubbered. "I think I'm going to cry!"

"I think I'm going to lose my lunch," Puck groaned.

Suddenly, the car came to a screeching halt.

"Seven, why have we stopped?" Charming demanded.

"The road is blocked, sir," the little man said, pointing out the window to where dozens of children were walking in the middle of the street. They were all wearing pajamas and had glassy looks in their eyes. "There are too many of them to maneuver around."

"The piper is controlling them," Sabrina said as they passed some of the kids.

Mr. Seven honked the horn, but it had no effect on the children.

"We'll have to walk from here," Sabrina said. They got out of the car, leaving Mr. Seven to guard it. Puck's wings sprang from his back and he lifted off the ground.

"What I wouldn't do for a carton of eggs," he said. "I'm going to go get some and play dive-bomber on these zombies."

Before he could fly away, Snow White grabbed his leg and yanked him back down to the ground. "We should stay together," she said. The boy looked extremely disappointed, but his wings disappeared nonetheless.

The group weaved in and out of the crowd until they were standing on the front lawn of the elementary school. As they approached the main entrance, Sabrina noticed that the front doors the giant mouse had plowed through were still lying on the ground. A steady stream of vacant-faced children were shuffling through the doorway, ushered in by a hulking girl with a pink ribbon in her hair. When Sabrina studied her closely, she realized that it was Natalie.

"Natalie, you need to get as far away from here as you can," she warned. "And try to get some of these kids to follow you. This place is going to get dangerous."

"Oh, it's going to get dangerous, all right," the big girl replied as her skin began to bubble and inflate. Hair shot from every pore and two long fangs sprang upward from her bottom jaw. Her eyes turned a milky yellow and a long hound-dog tongue crept out of her mouth and licked her lips. Claws sprouted from her fingertips as she lashed out at the group, knocking Puck, Charming, Daphne, and Sabrina to the ground with one great swipe. Snow White just managed to step aside, avoiding Natalie's attack.

"E-gad, I didn't think you could get any uglier," Puck said as he crawled back onto his feet.

"Snow, get behind me!" Charming shouted, as he leaped to his feet. "I'll handle this brute."

"Billy," the teacher cried. "This is the twenty-first century. Women don't need the white knight routine anymore. I can fight my own battles."

She planted her feet and raised her hands. When Natalie charged at her, the teacher sent a hard jab and a right hook into the beastie's face. The monster screamed angrily and lunged again, but this time, Snow White's foot came up and landed a hard blow to the monster's chest. Natalie tumbled to the ground, but sprang back to her feet, clawing and scratching at the pretty teacher. Ms. White blocked each blow with super-fast hands, until one of Natalie's punches actually connected and sent the teacher painfully to the ground. Instinctively, Charming and Puck stepped forward, ready to take over the fight, but Snow White flashed them an angry look.

"Gentlemen, please!" she said sternly. Charming and Puck threw up their hands in surrender and stepped aside. She sprang to her feet, planted them again, and then eyed the monster with a smile.

"Come and get it, ugly," she said. "School is in session."

Natalie roared and leaped at her. Snow White stopped the attack by jumping into the air, spinning around, and roundhousing the monster in the face. One of Natalie's fangs broke off in the middle and the monster fell to the ground, groaning in pain. The teacher stood over her with angry eyes and eager fists.

"If you were smart, you'd stay down," she said.

Sabrina and Daphne looked at each other in amazement.

"Snow, where did you learn to do all that?" Charming asked, obviously stunned by what he had just seen.

"I teach a self-defense class at the community center," Snow White replied. "We're called the *Bad Apples*. We meet every Saturday at four p.m."

"Sign me up," Daphne said.

"*Piper!*" Natalie shouted angrily as she crawled to her feet.

The principal stepped from out of the shadows. He was carrying a set of bagpipes and looked distraught.

"Do it!" the hairy girl raged.

"This has gone too far," Hamelin cried. "Let them save their grandmother and her friends. The barrier will still be broken and they won't pose a threat to you or your father again."

"Piper, I'll tell my daddy," Natalie threatened. "He's got your precious Wendell."

The principal raised his bagpipe's reed to his mouth and took a deep breath. "I'm sorry," he said to the group, and then he blew a long, sorrowful note into the air.

Everything went black.

10

"abrina! Wake up!" a voice shouted from far away. She tried very hard to pay attention to it but she was exhausted and dizzy. "Sabrina, you have to wake up now!"

She slowly opened her eyes. Mr. Hamelin was standing over her with a wild, desperate look on his face.

"What are you doing in my bedroom?" she grumbled.

"Sabrina, we're under the school!" Hamelin said, sounding frantic. "I know it's hard, but try to concentrate."

Sabrina looked around and saw she was standing in a huge tunnel, where children were rushing back and forth with wheelbarrows full of dirt and rubble. She looked down at herself and saw she was covered in soot and holding a shovel.

"Do you understand what has happened to you?" Hamelin asked.

"No," the girl replied. Her head felt heavy.

"I entranced you and your friends," the principal explained. "I had to. They have Wendell and they'll kill him if I don't do what they want."

"Where's my sister?" Sabrina demanded.

"They've got everyone—your sister, your grandmother, Canis, Charming, the sheriff, Snow, Puck, and my son—at the end of the tunnel. I managed to send you off into the mine to dig, and so far they haven't noticed."

"How long have I been down here?"

"Six hours."

"Six hours! They could all be dead."

"This is the soonest I could get to you," Hamelin said. "They've been watching me, but now that they've tunneled so close to the barrier, they don't seem to care that I ran off."

"Oh, I wouldn't say we don't care," a voice from behind them said.

Sabrina heard the sound of ripping flesh and Hamelin fell to the ground. The frog-girl was behind him, holding a bloody knife.

"You're coming with me," she hissed, grabbing Sabrina roughly by the arm.

Sabrina swung her shovel and hit the monster in the head so

hard the frog-girl fell to the ground and moaned. Sabrina rushed to help Hamelin.

"Wendell," Hamelin said, as blood pooled beneath him. "You have to find him and get him out of here."

"I'll come back for you," Sabrina said, and rushed into the nearest tunnel with her only weapon—the shovel—slung over her shoulder.

She scampered forward, stumbled over jagged rocks, and accidentally kicked over some abandoned tools. Dust lifted into the air and filled her lungs, choking her and making it that much harder to concentrate on where she was going. Each step was a challenge to her balance and, unfortunately, her path was a complicated, twisting, turning maze. Every few yards, she would spot a child she recognized from school. Each was glassy-eyed, staggering through the tunnels, hauling buckets of broken stones. None of them seemed to notice Sabrina pass them, even when she stopped and begged for directions. They were still under the piper's spell.

At last she spotted a faint light in the distance. As she came closer to it, the tunnel widened dramatically, revealing an enormous room carved out of the Ferryport Landing bedrock. She paused at the mouth of the room, doing her best to calm her breathing and listen for any movement. Hearing nothing, she lifted the heavy shovel off her shoulder and entered, swinging the weapon in the air in case anyone was about to ambush her. But she was alone. Only a few old buckets and a couple of tools littered the floor. There were no exits other than the way she had come. The tunnel was a dead end.

She raced back the other way, passing more of the zombie-faced, filth-covered kids. *I should head in the direction they're coming from,* Sabrina realized.

She darted down the tunnel, fighting the crowds of children. At one point, Natalie and the frog-girl came lumbering down the tunnel after her, but Sabrina stepped into the line of children, and being as filthy as they were, went unseen by the monsters. The tunnels went on and on. Some led to massive rooms, while others narrowed so that there was hardly room for two children to stand side by side, but eventually Sabrina found what appeared to be the end of the dig.

The room was high and wide and filled with boxes of dynamite and mining tools. A few flaming torches illuminated the room, but there were still deep shadows along the walls that Sabrina could not see into. Anyone could be hiding in one. She knew she was vulnerable.

"I've come for my family," she shouted into the cave. Her voice echoed off the stone walls and bounced around her ears.

Suddenly, something hit Sabrina squarely in the back. Unable to keep her footing, she tumbled over a sharp rock and fell hard onto her shoulder. Searing pain swam through her veins, followed by a dull, throbbing numbness. She tried to scamper to her feet, but her arm hung loosely at her side—it was broken. She cried out more in frustration than pain. But she grew quiet when she heard an odd clicking and hissing sound, followed by a disturbed laugh.

Using her good arm, she picked up the shovel that had slipped from her hand when she'd fallen and swung it around, doing her best to make it seem as if she had not been seriously injured. She walked in small circles, scanning the room for the source of the noise.

A long, spindly leg struck out from the shadows, narrowly missing her head. It slammed against the wall behind her, pulverizing stone into dust. Sabrina lifted the heavy shovel and swung wildly at the hairy leg, sinking its sharp edge deep into the monster's flesh. Shrieks of agony echoed through the cavern.

"I'm not going to be easy to kill," she threatened, hoping her voice sounded more confident to the monster than it did to her own ears.

"Kill you? This is a party!" the voice replied. One of the torches was snatched off the wall. It rose high into the air, shining its light on the ceiling. There, suspended in mounds of thick, horrible spiderweb, were her family and friends. "And you're the guest of honor."

Daphne, Granny Relda, Puck, Mr. Canis, Snow White, Sheriff Hamstead, and Mayor Charming hung above, with only their heads free of the sticky threads. Their mouths were covered as well, but Sabrina could hear Daphne's choked cries and Hamstead's angry groans and knew they were alive.

The spider monster slowly crawled out of the shadows and walked along the ceiling. It was gigantic and as Sabrina stared up at it, she realized that it wasn't simply a giant spider. The lower body was spider-like, but the upper body had the chest, head, and arms of a boy. Even with the two huge pincers that jutted from his mouth and clicked excitedly, she could tell it was Toby.

"Surprised?" Toby laughed.

"Not really," Sabrina admitted. "The bad guy is usually the ugly, giggling idiot."

"Then, I've got a surprise for you," a voice said from behind her. Sabrina spun around and found Natalie standing there. Sabrina noticed her front tooth was now missing. Then someone else stepped out of the shadows, someone who made Sabrina's heart ache—it was her only potential friend in the entire school—Bella. The blond girl put her arm around Natalie's shoulders and smirked.

"You're one of them, aren't you?" Sabrina said sadly. "Why did you pretend to be my friend?"

"Duh! She's evil," Toby said. He and the girls burst into laughter.

"You killed Mr. Grumpner," Sabrina gasped.

"Yes, I did," Toby said. "He was just too nosy and way too heavy with the homework."

"Don't forget Charlie," Bella said, patting Natalie on the back. "They just kept getting in the way of our father's plans."

Suddenly, the girl leaped into the air, higher than any human being could possibly leap. Even more startling, Bella's hands and feet stuck to the roof of the cave and her body started to change. Her skin looked as if it were filling with water. Dark spots rose to the surface on her hands and legs. Her eyes bugged out to disgusting proportions and migrated to the top of her head. Her shoes exploded off her feet, revealing long, green webbed toes. Within minutes, she had transformed into the frog-girl that had attacked the family and Principal Hamelin. Like a streak of lighting, a long, slippery tongue shot out of her mouth, latched onto Sabrina's shovel, and yanked it out of her hand.

When Sabrina turned, she saw Natalie had already made her transformation into the hairy animal she truly was.

"Rumpelstiltskin is insane," Sabrina said. "When he cracks a hole in the barrier, these tunnels will collapse and kill everyone in them. All the kids will die."

"Actually, the children are already outside, trying to figure out what has happened to them," a new voice said. Mr. Sheepshank emerged from the shadows.

"Mr. Sheepshank!" Sabrina cried. "You have to get out of here. They're going to blow this place sky high!"

"Duh, Sabrina," Toby the spider clicked. "You're even dumber than you seem in class."

"Hush, Toby," the counselor said. He turned to Sabrina. "They're not going to do anything of the sort. I'm going to do it."

"You're Rumpelstiltskin!" she gasped.

"Oh, I have many names," Sheepshank said. "But the one I like best is *Daddy*."

Sheepshank extended his arms and Natalie, Bella, and Toby rushed to stand by his side as the odd little man began to morph and bubble. But, unlike the others, Sheepshank didn't get bigger. In fact, he got a lot smaller. When his transformation was complete, he was hardly three feet high. His head, back, and arms were covered in kinky brown hair, but his face and pointed ears were pink like a pig's. He had a short, stubby tail, hoofed feet, and a couple of rows of sharp razor teeth.

"No fair," the little monster said sarcastically. "You guessed my name. Someone told you! Really child, I must agree with my son. You aren't as bright as your records suggest."

"Well, at least I'm not some sick pervert who steals children," Sabrina shouted, hoping to distract the little man and his freak show for a while longer.

"I don't steal children, Sabrina," the little creature said, as if he were genuinely insulted. "I care for them. These children have been treated with nothing but love and affection. I give them everything they ever wanted."

"Then what do you get out of it?" Sabrina asked.

"Why, I get their love, and their joy, and their sadness, and their frustration, and their hope, and most of all I get their anger," Rumpelstiltskin cackled. "I get their feelings, child, every last delicious morsel of them. You don't understand, do you? Let me spell it out for you. I feed on their emotions."

"That's where you get your power," Sabrina said, as Mr. Sheepshank's advice about feelings came flooding back to her. Of course he would encourage her to express her anger. He was eating it.

"You're starting to get it. That's the reason I have always loved

children. Their emotions are so raw and uncontrolled. When people get older, they've already found ways to control their feelings, but not children. Children are like emotional all-you-can-eat buffets. So, where's a guy with tastes like mine going to find work? Why, Ferryport Landing Elementary, of course! And trust me Sabrina, it has been a *truly* rewarding experience. For years, I sat back and feasted on the fights and humiliations you kids pile onto one another. The senseless bullying, the humiliation of being picked last for baseball, the endless teasing about someone's hair or clothes—when it comes to being mean, kids have cornered the market.

"Well, when the piper came to me with his plan to blow up the barrier from below, I was hesitant. After all, I had a pretty good thing going here at the school, and at night, well, I have these little rug rats to keep me fed."

The three Everafter children laughed at their "father's" teasing.

"But then I realized there's a great big world of anger, war, and pain for me to feast on out there. So, I signed on. It wasn't easy, though. Piper used his magic music, and every night the children of this school came to dig out the tunnels. At first, we tried to use all the kids, but the little ones are so weak, we had to make do with the fifth- and sixth-graders. Unfortunately, there was another unforeseen problem. The next morning, those same kids—the ones who supplied me with the most energy—were too sleepy to argue with one another. They went from a raging river of emotions to a dripping faucet overnight. The piper and I were just about to give up when you walked through the door."

"What do I have to do with it?" Sabrina asked, doing her best to buy time until she could come up with a plan.

"Sabrina, you're like the Niagara Falls of anger—it just keeps pouring over the edges. Every time you lost your temper, it was like a four-course meal with all the trimmings," Rumpelstiltskin said, as blue electricity crackled out of his fingertips.

"Once I tapped into it, I turned up the volume on you and could barely keep up with the energy," Rumpelstiltskin continued. "Truth be told, we probably didn't have to kill Grumpner or the janitor, but I could sense how outraged you would get. And it worked! Every little paranoia and prejudice was amplified by a million. Thanks to you, I finally have what it takes to blast a hole into the barrier. Once it's open, I'll be free and the Scarlet Hand will march across the world, destroying anyone who gets in their way."

"So, *you're* the Scarlet Hand," Sabrina said, even now feeling the anger rise within her. "You took my parents!"

"The Scarlet Hand isn't a person, child. It's a movement, an idea. It's bigger than all of us and I am just one spoke in a very big wheel."

"Where's my son?" a man shouted. Rumpelstiltskin shrieked and moved to safety behind Natalie's hulking body, just as Principal Hamelin raced into the cave. He looked exhausted, beaten, and on the edge of madness. His shirt was covered in his own blood and he limped painfully. In his hands were his bagpipes.

"Tell me where my boy is or I will play a song that will tear you apart," Hamelin raged as he charged at the little man. Rumpelstiltskin cowered in a corner.

"The boy got in the way," he cried, gnashing his teeth at his much taller partner. "I warned you about keeping him under control."

"Where is he?" Hamelin demanded.

Toby pointed one of his long, spindly legs at the ceiling. High on the cave wall, away from the others, was a mound of webbing from which no head poked and no movement came at all. Hamelin fell to his knees and buried his head in his hands.

"Bring him down, Toby," Rumpelstiltskin said.

"Awww, Dad, he was almost ready to eat," the spider kid whined.

"Do it," Rumpelstiltskin demanded.

Reluctantly, Toby scaled the wall, cut the web loose with his razor-sharp legs, and carried the boy gingerly to the ground. He set him down at Hamelin's feet and scurried back to his father.

"He was causing too many distractions," Rumpelstiltskin explained. "He was jeopardizing our plans."

Hamelin ignored the explanation as he tore the rest of the threads off his son. When the boy was finally free, Hamelin leaned down to listen for breathing.

"He's gone," Hamelin cried, as he set his boy down gently and climbed to his feet. He took his pipes and filled them with air. "And you are going to pay for it."

Before he could blow a single note, Bella leaped across the room, shot out her sticky tongue, and wrapped it around the bagpipes. She yanked the instrument out of the piper's hands and into her mouth, swallowing it whole.

"That's Daddy's little girl!" Rumpelstiltskin cheered.

Natalie rushed to a corner of the room and returned with a can. She dipped her hand inside it and when she pulled it out, it was covered in red paint. "Should I lay the mark on the kid's body?"

Hamelin shook with fury. "You and your Scarlet Hand, killing innocents. This wasn't part of our plan, troll! I just wanted out of this town."

"You've never had the backbone to do what has to be done, Piper," the little creature cried. "Someone had to make the hard decisions."

"Like killing my boy?" Hamelin said.

"I know your pain," Rumpelstiltskin said. "If I were to lose one of my children, I would be heartbroken, too. But I would still put them in harm's way for the greater good."

"These aren't your children!" Sabrina shouted. "You took advantage of their real parents. You played on their fears and made them feel hopeless. Their real parents want them back."

Toby looked confused. "Is that true, father?" the spider boy clicked. "You said they abandoned me in a park."

"They did, son," Rumpelstiltskin said.

"He's lying," Sabrina cried. "I've talked to your parents, Toby. They've been searching for you since the day they gave you to this sicko. He played with their emotions, made them believe you'd be better off with him. You weren't found in any park. Rumpelstiltskin manipulated your mom and dad and then paid them millions of dollars for you. He bought you, Toby, for the same reason he bought Natalie and Bella—so he could feed on you!"

"She's lying, children," Rumpelstiltskin said. "People are always lying about me! They want to take you away from me! It's not fair, children. Something has to be done to stop the people who hate me."

"We believe you, Father," Bella said, her face boiling with rage.

"Can we kill them now?" said Natalie as she looked at Sabrina with murderous eyes. Sabrina knew that Rumpelstiltskin could control the anger in others. Looking at the two girls, it was obvious to her that the little man had turned his power all the way up.

Rumpelstiltskin grinned. "How could Daddy resist his little Natalie? Go have your fun."

The monsters stalked Hamelin, backing him into a corner. Sabrina wanted to rush to his side, but Toby blocked her path. The Pied Piper was about to die and there was nothing anyone could do about it.

"Without your pipes you are nothing, Hamelin," Rumpelstiltskin said. "And now that the barrier has been reached, your usefulness has expired."

The piper reached into his pocket and pulled out something shiny. He looked down at it lovingly, then he raised it to his lips and blew into it. A low, sorrowful note came out of Wendell's harmonica and the ground began to shake violently.

"I don't need my pipes," Hamelin shouted at his former partner.

Suddenly, the floor cracked and a huge fissure opened. At first, nothing but steam belched out of it, but soon a flood of ants, worms, roaches, centipedes, and a million other creepy-crawling things flew out of the hole and attacked Rumpelstiltskin and his "children." The frog-girl leaped onto the ceiling, but was immediately overcome by a swarm of flying cockroaches. Losing her balance, she fell painfully to the ground.

Natalie was quickly overrun with centipedes that wiggled and raced along her body, biting her fiercely. The monster girl growled and whined, but soon fell to her knees, unable to fight.

Toby scurried around the cave, spraying webs at the sea of maggots that poured over him. He shrieked and cried as he rushed around the room, but the tide of insects was too much for him and he was engulfed.

Rumpelstiltskin didn't fare much better. Leaches covered the little man and he fell over in agony.

"Mr. Hamelin, please help me get to the roof," Sabrina said, grabbing her shovel. Hamelin blew into the harmonica again, and a rolling wave of spiders, worms, and roaches lifted Sabrina high off the ground to the ceiling above. Granny Relda was hanging closest, so Sabrina used her good arm to pull the cobwebs from the old woman's mouth and hands.

"Oh, *liebling*," Granny said. "This is one time I'm glad you didn't listen to my rules."

Sabrina smiled as she used her shovel to cut the sack of

threads from the wall. The wave of bugs expanded to hold the old woman up and when she was free she reached into her handbag and took out a pair of scissors. She put these into Sabrina's hand and then descended a flight of stairs the bugs created for her so she could easily step to the ground.

Sabrina rode the tide of creepy-crawlers to the next person, who happened to be Daphne. She yanked and pulled until the little girl was free, using the scissors to cut her off of the wall. Daphne was in tears, but she threw her arms around her older sister and hugged her tightly. The hug hurt Sabrina's arm, but she bit her lip and let her sister continue.

It was then that Sabrina noticed that Rumpelstiltskin was emitting a blue energy that swirled around him. A fireball blasted out of his chest, sending a huge explosion ripping through the caves, incinerating the entire insect army. The wave of bugs that supported Sabrina and Daphne turned to ash and the two girls tumbled to the ground, jarring Sabrina's broken arm and causing an agony that nearly knocked her unconscious. Through the haze of pain, she saw that the blast had destroyed some of the cave tunnel and sent tons of rock tumbling to the ground, blocking the only exit. Worse still, the blast had damaged the foundation of the cave and large chunks had begun to fall from the ceiling.

"Look what you have done!" Rumpelstiltskin shrieked. He

lunged at the principal and knocked him down. In the struggle, Hamelin's harmonica slipped from his hand and slid across the cave floor, and was crushed by a falling boulder.

While the two Everafters fought, Granny Relda said, "Girls, we have to find a way to get the others down."

"I have an idea," Daphne replied. She took Granny Relda's scissors and shoved them into her pocket, then rushed over to the unconscious frog-girl. She kneeled down and rubbed her hands all over the beast's super-sticky skin. Then she rubbed her sneakers until they were covered in the goo, as well. Then she rushed to the wall, pressed her hands against the stone, and slowly but effortlessly climbed the wall. Each step made a squishy sound.

"*Liebling*, do be careful," Granny Relda cried.

"That is so punk rock!" Sabrina shouted.

When the little girl got to where Puck was trapped, she used the scissors to cut through the spider's web. Soon Puck was free and as indignant as ever. He sprouted his wings and fluttered around the room.

"Someone is going to pay for this," he shouted.

Meanwhile, Daphne went to work on Snow White. As soon as the teacher was free, Puck carried her back down to the ground safely. Soon, he was doing the same for Mayor Charming and then Sheriff Hamstead. Daphne crawled along the ceiling to the last of their group, Mr. Canis, but before she could even cut away a strand, she slipped and fell. Puck caught her just before she hit the ground.

"I ran out of sticky stuff," Daphne said.

In the meantime, Hamelin had picked up the gnashing Rumpelstiltskin and thrown him violently against a wall. The little man slumped to the ground and lay very still. The piper rushed back to cradle his son. Snow White followed and crouched beside him.

"It's too late," Hamelin whimpered.

"No, it's not," the pretty teacher replied as she felt Wendell's wrist. "He's got a pulse." Snow White took the boy, laid him flat on his back, and tilted his head up. Then she took a deep breath and blew it down the boy's throat. Instantly, Wendell shuddered and coughed. He was alive!

"He had some of the cobwebs in his throat," the teacher said. "He couldn't get any air."

Hamelin stroked and kissed Wendell on the forehead.

"Dad," the boy said, "I think I solved the mystery."

Hamelin laughed and sobbed at the same time. "I know you did, son! You're a great detective!

"Thank you! Thank you for saving my son!" the principal cried. He reached over and gave Snow White a huge kiss on the mouth. Charming was standing nearby and raised his eyebrows as Snow White blushed. Then he scowled.

Rumpelstiltskin crawled to his feet. He looked at his fallen children and a tear rolled down his face.

"It's over," Sabrina said.

"Oh, it's far from over," Rumpelstiltskin said. "All I need to do is collect some more power, and there's someone in this room that could give me enough to blow this little town off the map."

Sabrina had never been afraid of anything the way she was of this little man. He knew her anger, he feasted on it, and she had provided him with enough raw energy to destroy them all. But she wasn't going to let him play with her head any longer.

"You can't do it," she said. "I'm not angry anymore."

"True," the little man replied. "I'll miss your rage. It was delicious. But I'm not talking about you, child. I'm talking about the Wolf."

Sabrina gazed up at the skinny old man still trapped in his web prison. Even from such a distance, she could see the fear in Mr. Canis's eyes. It was the first time she had ever seen the old man afraid of anything. It seemed to unsettle Charming, as well, because the prince stepped in front of Rumpelstiltskin with his fists clenched.

"We're trapped down here, troll," Charming said. "If you pull that stupid trick of yours on the Wolf, you'll let him out, and he'll kill us all."

"No, my friend, he will save us all," Rumpelstiltskin said. "The Wolf will bring the barrier down, freeing us from this prison! Freeing himself from his own prison, as well. Look at him—trapped inside Canis, parading around like he's human! He's just like us, except his barrier is his own body. It's disgusting! We're Everafters. We shouldn't be acting like humans, we should be ruling over them. The Wolf will be thrilled to help. His rage will open the barrier and the world will be ours for the taking!"

Sabrina watched Mr. Canis struggle, but the change was already coming on him. The webs ripped as the old man's body tripled in size. A hideous roar echoed over the crumbling walls and the Wolf was free. He fell to the ground, sending a shockwave through the floor as he landed on his feet. He looked around at the desperate group and licked his lips.

"Guess who's back!" he snarled as he struck Charming, throwing him against a wall. The Wolf sniffed the air. "What's for dinner? Something smells good!"

Puck's wings sprang from his back and he stepped in front of the Wolf.

"What's this? An appetizer?" the beast asked. "Relda, you sure do put on a fancy party."

"You know me, Wolf," Puck said bravely. "You take another step or try to harm anyone here and you will have to answer to me."

The beast studied the boy for a long moment and then a chuckle came up through his throat. "Trickster," he said, sniffing the boy. "Love will be the end of you."

Puck blushed. "I don't know what you're talking about."

The Wolf turned and eyed Sabrina. He chuckled and then turned his eyes back on the boy.

"All right, hero. I'm going to make you famous," the Wolf growled.

The boy spun around on his feet and immediately transformed into an elephant. He snatched the Wolf up in his long trunk and smashed him against the wall. The Wolf fell to the floor, stunned.

"Fantastic!" Rumpelstiltskin cried out. A glimmer of the blue energy began to swirl around him.

"Puck, stop!" Sabrina cried out, but Puck was still in the moment. He transformed back into his true form and drew his wooden sword. He jammed it into the beast's belly and the Wolf winced. Puck couldn't know he was actually helping Rumpelstiltskin build the Wolf's rage.

"Stay down, dog," the boy shouted, smacking the Wolf on the top of the head with his sword. "Or there'll be no table scraps for you."

The beast opened his big blue eyes and laughed. "You're a funny boy!" He sprang to his feet so quickly that Puck nearly fell backward. The boy's wings erupted from his back and he flew into the air, hovering at the top of the cave. The Wolf leaped high, grabbing at the boy with his claws, missing him by only inches.

Puck laughed and stung the beast's paws with his sword. If it hurt, the Wolf didn't seem to mind. His face was a combination of anger and amusement. It was horrifying to watch. Luckily, Puck seemed to be out of his reach, until the boy's wing clipped the ceiling and he fell to the ground. The beast lunged at the boy, grabbed him in his huge claws, and opened his jaws wide. His fangs glistened in the tunnel light.

Suddenly, Daphne was standing in front of him.

"Stop it right now!" she demanded.

The Wolf turned to look at the little girl with sadistic amusement. "Don't worry, child," the Wolf said. "You'll get your turn to fight for your life."

"Daphne!" Granny cried.

"Leave Puck alone," Daphne said. "And let me talk to Mr. Canis."

The Wolf snarled. "Child, Mr. Canis is not real. There is only me."

"I know that's a lie!" the little girl cried. If she was afraid, Sabrina couldn't see it. "Mr. Canis is real because I said he is. He's part of my family and I love him!"

Briefly, the Wolf's face changed. For a flickering moment, Sabrina saw his steel-blue eyes change to Mr. Canis's dull gray ones. The old man was inside, trying to control himself.

"Daphne," the Wolf said quietly, dropping Puck. Then a shudder ran through him and any trace of their family friend was buried again. His disorientation gave Puck another opportunity to attack. The boy climbed to his feet and picked up a large rock from the ground. He tossed it as hard as he could, beaming the beast in the head.

"Hey, Wolf, you ever hear of a game called dodgeball?" he said.

"Death is moments away for you and you want to discuss a child's game?" The Wolf laughed.

Puck threw the boulder and it hit the Wolf in the chest, knocking the air out of the big brute.

"I don't want to talk about it," he shouted, bending over for another boulder. "I want to play it!" With impossible speed, he tossed one heavy rock after another at the beast.

"Puck! *Stop*!" Sabrina shouted.

The boy looked over at her. His face was red with excitement, but his eyes were full of confusion.

"Uh, I'm trying to save your life, Grimm," the boy said.

"You're going to kill us all," Sabrina said. "You're making Rumpelstiltskin stronger."

The Wolf staggered to his feet. "No child, you've got it wrong. I'm going to kill you all."

"Take a look around you, rover," Snow White said, stepping between the Wolf and Sabrina. "Your little tantrum is helping to fuel your destruction."

The Wolf turned to face the beautiful teacher. She continued, "The angrier you get the stronger the real enemy becomes." She pointed at Rumpelstiltskin, who was encircled in his blue energy. He seemed to be enjoying each second of the fight. The Wolf turned to face the little creature and immediately the blue glow around him expanded.

"What are you up to, little man?" the beast growled.

"Fantastic," Rumpelstiltskin cried. "Your rage is unbelievable."

"He's powering himself with your anger and when he has enough he's going to blow up this cave and bury everyone in it, including you," Granny Relda chimed in.

"You're signing your own death warrant!" Hamelin added. He had managed to get Wendell to his feet, but the boy was dizzy and obviously needed a doctor.

"Keep going, people," Rumpelstiltskin shouted. "Direct his anger at me!"

"You *want* my rage?" the Wolf said.

"It's fantastic," the creature said.

The Wolf eyed Sabrina closely. He had an odd expression on his face, filled with disgust and disbelief, one that seemed to say, *Can you believe this guy?* If Sabrina hadn't been so terrified, she might have laughed, but she did recognize the opportunity. The Wolf's attention was no longer on eating everyone in the room. He wanted a fight.

Sabrina cocked an eyebrow at the Wolf and said, "Sick 'em, boy!"

The Wolf turned on Rumpelstiltskin and lunged forward, grabbing the little creature. As soon as they collided, both were enveloped in the blue energy.

Sabrina's arm hurt so much she tried to prop it up with her knee. It brushed against a lump in her pocket. The little matchbox! Her eyes lit up as she pulled it out. Inside were the two matches. She removed one, wished she were outside, and struck the match. In the flame, she could see the outside of the school. Everywhere, dirty students milled around in confusion, having just broken free from the piper's magic.

"Sabrina, where did you get those?" Granny Relda asked.

"Charming. We need to get everyone out of here!" Sabrina shouted over the fighting. She tossed the match on the floor and a giant flame appeared.

"Mr. Hamelin," Sabrina shouted, "get Wendell out of here!" Hamelin nodded, picked up his son, and stepped into the flame. Daphne and Granny rushed to Toby, and together they dragged the big spider by his legs through the portal. As they did, Sabrina heard the old woman ask Puck to help with the other Everafter children. He spun around on his heels and transformed into a gorilla, hoisted Bella and Natalie onto his back, then raced through the flames himself. Snow White and Sheriff Hamstead helped the mayor to his feet and together they raced to the portal.

"*I'm* supposed to rescue *you*," Charming said to Snow White.

"Maybe it's time we both started trying some new things," Snow White said as the three disappeared into the flames.

Granny came back through the portal and waited for Sabrina.

"We can't leave him down here," Sabrina cried, as she watched the Wolf and Rumpelstiltskin fighting.

"I believe Mr. Canis knows what he is doing," Granny Relda said.

"I won't go," Sabrina insisted, but Granny grabbed her sweater and dragged her through the portal. In a flash, they were standing outside in the cold, with a hundred elementary school students, who were staring at the gorilla carrying a big, hairy girl and a frog monster.

"This is going to take a lot of forgetful dust!" Daphne said, under her breath.

"Get away from the school!" Sabrina shouted to the children and they obeyed. They ran for the parking lot just as Sabrina heard a slow, horrible rumble from below. Everyone raced to the other side of the road, where some children were already congregated. When she reached them, Sabrina turned and watched the school. The horror unreeled like a car crash you couldn't stop watching. First, smoke billowed out of the school's windows, then a terrible explosion blew out the glass and knocked the doors off their hinges. The roof collapsed, a flame a hundred feet high shot out of the center, and then the ground around it sank and the school fell into it. Finally, a cloud of dust rose up, covering the site, and when it settled again, the school was gone. Only a huge hole remained as evidence that there had been anything there at all.

"Mr. Canis," Sabrina gasped. "He's gone. I killed him."

"Sabrina, don't," Granny pleaded.

"This is all my fault!" the girl said as she broke down in tears.

"No, child, you are not responsible for this." Granny tried to reassure her. Sabrina pulled away.

"It was my anger and my prejudice that did this," she cried.

"Child, Rumpelstiltskin manipulated you," her grandmother insisted.

"He only manipulated what was already inside of me."

"Oh, *liebling*."

Suddenly, Beauty and the Beast, the Frog Prince and his Princess, and Little Miss Muffet (aka Mrs. Arachnid) and the spider raced through the crowd of children.

"We heard there was trouble at the school," the Beast grunted. "Have you found our kids?"

Puck pointed at the three unconscious monsters lying on the ground. The parents cried out in unison and rushed to their children. The Beast picked up his grotesque, unconscious daughter, Natalie, and lifted her into the air. "She's beautiful, darling," he cried to his wife.

Sabrina watched the happiness in the parents' eyes. The Frog Prince and his wife kneeled down to their unconscious daughter, Bella, and slowly caressed her face. Even the spider cooed over his son, Toby. They loved their monstrous, murderous children. Sabrina looked into her box of matches. She reached in and took out the last of the Match Girl's matches. She could save it until her arm was well, then rescue her mom and dad, but it would take weeks. She couldn't be without them for another day. She needed them right now. She made a wish, then struck the match against the box's flinty surface. The flame came to life and shined in the cold night.

"Sabrina, no!" Granny Relda cried.

"Look at what I've become," the girl said sadly. "I need my mom and dad."

"Sabrina, you listen to me! I forbid it. It's too dangerous," Granny said, but Sabrina could already see her parents, safe and asleep on a bed, inside the flame. She tossed the match to the ground and the portal grew. Without even a glance at her grandmother or sister, she stepped through and found herself on the other side.

The room was dark. It was also warm, which made Sabrina a bit dizzy, stepping from such icy cold air into the heat. She shook off the dizziness and rushed to her parents, embracing them both the best she could.

"I'm going to take you home, now," she said, dragging her unconscious mother from the bed and onto the floor. She pulled as strongly as she could with her one good arm, edging closer and closer to the portal, where she could see Granny, Daphne, and Puck waiting with worried faces.

Suddenly, Daphne's face grimaced in terror and she started shouting, but Sabrina couldn't hear a word. Sound didn't cross the portal.

What is she trying to tell me?

And that's when the figure stepped out of the shadows. Sabrina knew she might someday have to confront her parents' kidnapper, but her imagination had not prepared her for the person she now saw in front of her. She was a child, probably Daphne's age, wearing a red cloak and a sadistic grin. Sabrina had never seen an expression like that on a little girl.

"Did you bring my puppy?" the child asked, sniffing the air.

"Who are you?" Sabrina asked.

"No, you didn't," the little girl said angrily. "But you've been around my puppy. Where is he?"

The little girl reached out and put her hand on Sabrina's shirt. When she removed it, a bloodred stain remained—a handprint.

"I can't play house without my grandma or my puppy," the girl said.

"I don't know what you're talking about," Sabrina said, trying to find the strength to get her mother through the portal.

"Yes, gibberish, that's what I speak," the little girl agreed. "Not a word makes sense. That's what they said. They said I had imagination."

"What do you want?"

"*I want to play house!*" The little girl's face grew very angry and she pointed a finger at Sabrina.

"I have a mommy and a daddy and a baby brother and a kitty. Do you want to pet the kitty?"

Just then, Sabrina heard an inhuman voice slurping and slavering behind her. It said, "Jabberwocky, Jabberwocky, Jabberwocky" over and over again. She turned to see what was making the noise and a shriek flew out of her throat. Hunching over her was something too impossible to exist—a combination of skin and scales and jagged teeth. Even in a town like Ferryport Landing, Sabrina had never seen something that brought so much horror.

"My, you are an ugly one," a voice said from across the room. The monster turned. Puck was standing next to the portal, hands on hips, like some kind of comic-book hero. "Come on, Grimm. I'm here to rescue you."

With a hiss, the portal burned out and closed behind him. Puck looked back and grimaced. "Uh-oh."

The little girl screamed with rage. *"I don't need a sister or another brother! I need a grandma and a puppy!"*

Suddenly, the monster swung its enormous arm at Sabrina, and then the room went black.

To be continued . . .

Acknowledgments

I'd like to thank my editor, Susan Van Metre at Amulet Books, whose guidance helped me find the book inside my idea; my agent, Alison Fargis at Stonesong Press, for taking a chance on me; Joseph Deasy, who was honest enough to tell me when my writing stunk; my love, Alison, for telling me when Joe was wrong; Jonathan Flom, for all his support over the years; Joe Harris, for being a good friend; my parents, Michael and Wilma, for filling our house with books even when the checking account was empty; and Daisy, who was patient when I was too busy writing to take her for a walk. Also thanks to the entire team at Amulet Books, most notably Andrea Colvin and Jason Wells. Lastly, thanks to Paul Fargis, Molly Choi, Maureen Falvey, Beth Fargis Lancaster, and Doug Lancaster.